KW-329-420

ACKNOWLEDGMENTS

Thanks to Oxford Narrative Group, Scribblers and to everyone on my MA course at Oxford Brookes for their wisdom and encouragement. Thanks to Teresa Chris, for all her support and to my book group at Wallingford Bookshop, with whom I have shared many happy, bookish evenings. Thanks most of all to my family, who never gave up on me.

The Anatomy of Magic

C. E. Spriggs

ISBN: 9781520489889

For Tim

CONTENTS

*'Do not weep, do not wax indignant.
Understand.'*

Baruch Spinoza

Chapter One

Treleddan

Bodmin Moor
February, 1863

From the outside, the narrow townhouse on Fish Row looked the same as all the others in the terrace. Its bricks were blackened by the smoke of a thousand coal fires, each pumping tarry breath up into the clouds, staining the snow and sliding beneath the fingernails and into the lungs of everybody who lived in Treleddan. Beyond the parish boundaries, the dirty air began to clear. It blew across Bodmin Moor and the snow, that year, lay rich and sparkling, three or four feet deep in places, sitting like cotton caps on top of the Cheesewring and the Hurlers. The Fowey river flowed fast and fat with melt water, bouncing skeletal twigs over the rocks, twirling in chaotic spirals into streams bright as glass.

Dusk was turning to night on Fish Row, the falling flakes only visible in gaslit haloes, like tiny moths drawn to light. Figures were gathering at the Blackthorn's front door. They wanted to speak to the dead.

The gas was turned down by a grey-gloved hand, shrinking the flame to the size of a finger. Cora sat at a polished table, encircled by empty chairs. Her blindfold stopped her sight, but she could sense the ladies, it was usually ladies, entering the room. She heard the dull clip of their purses and the rasp of stiff, black crepe in their armpits as they tugged at gloves, rearranged shawls and smoothed their hair.

Nobody spoke. With quiet pats, Cora heard them placing their hands flat, palms down, on the wood, their gaze undoubtedly lingering on the violin in the middle of the table. She pictured them stretching their fingertips until their thumbs touched, smallest fingers connecting with their neighbour's.

Desperation rose from the gathering, like incense, for a message from the spirit realm.

Victor Morningside lowered the raw gas flame even more, until the pricks of light, just visible through the weave of Cora's blindfold, blinked out. Her breathing slowed, becoming more laboured with each rise and fall. As she sighed, pushing the out-breath so hard it grated in her lungs, a scrape sounded from the violin, though all hands remained still.

A thrill of shock rippled through the ladies. In the velvet black, more disjointed scratches sounded, each time the same eerie note. Without a sound, Cora rose from her chair, careful not to disturb the fake, wax replicas of her hands, which still touched the fingers of the women sitting either side of her, sustaining their belief that she remained at the table. Silent, she took a slipper from her chair and gently pressed it onto the shoulder of one of the breathless sitters, making her gasp 'O! Miss Blackthorn! A spirit is here!'

In a soft, dreamy tone, Cora bent behind her chair, so they'd believe she hadn't moved, and said to the quivering woman, 'it is Florence, your twin, who departed this world much too soon. She is well. All is well.'

Changing her voice to that of a small child, Cora

spoke into a hidden tube that ran down inside her chair, under the floorboards, up the wall behind the flock paper and across the ceiling to an opening concealed within the plaster rose, so that this time her words seemed to come from above, as if the tragic ghost of Florence really was hovering above the awestruck company, stepping from shoulder to shoulder.

'Miss Blackthorn speaks the truth. I am well, I am with Ma and Pa and also with the Lord.'

'Be careful, Florence,' Cora said, speaking as herself again.

As Florence she replied. 'I shan't slip Miss Blackthorn, but if I should, then what tragedies can befall me now?'

A tearful sigh washed through the ladies, like a breeze through a wheat field.

Cora pressed the slipper onto each of the sitters' shoulders in turn. Some jutted bone, others were soft as dough. At her touch, each woman shuddered in excitement. The creaks of the violin grew shorter, more staccato, like urgent cries. Cora navigated the dark with grimly practiced steps, thanks to the hours spent in the coal-black blindfold, avoiding Aunt Selina's strap. She moved expertly, avoiding creaky floorboards as a cringing dog avoids its master.

The resin thread scratched across the violin string once again. Cora pictured it running down through the tiny holes in the instrument, the table, the floor and the kitchen ceiling. She imagined Killigrew balancing on the kitchen table below, stretching on tiptoe in stocking'd feet, gripping each end of the thread in worksore hands. Her red hair would be sweaty at the temples, Cora knew, her jaw thrust forward in concentration.

Cora replaced the secret slipper on her chair and sat down, barely able to feel it through thick layers of petticoat. 'Oh,' she sighed, 'must you fade now Florence? You are a mere shadow, a wisp.'

Taking his cue, Victor Morningside waited a moment, then re-lit the gas. Hissing jets encroached on the stillness, rousing the ladies, who blinked wonderingly at each other, as the room grew steadily brighter.

Victor tugged the blindfold off Cora's face and she managed not to wince as the knot snagged her hair, letting the black cloth fall across her lap like unspooled ribbon.

They turned to Cora, who had draped herself in her chair, feigning exhaustion, and pressed fat coins into Aunt Selina's lace-mitten'd grasp. Weakly, Cora lifted her head to acknowledge the thanks and praise for her incredible gift. She watched through her eyelashes as they filed reverently out, heads bowed, mouths turned down, as if they were leaving a funeral. Florence's elderly sister dabbed wetly at her eyes and Cora felt another tiny bite taken out of her.

Almost everyone had left the room, leaving only Cora, Victor Morningside and a lady wearing a veil so dark that even the shadows of her face were obscured. The veil twitched. A pair of purple-veined hands lifted the gauzy fabric, revealing flared nostrils flanked by two eyes popping in blustering rage. 'There!' the wizened face screeched, 'them 'ands! They ain't real!'

Cora followed the woman's accusing finger to the waxen hands in their false, drooping sleeves and moved to snatch them up, but she grasped only one, the other was wagging aloft in the old woman's victorious fist.

'Mrs Furze,' Victor's voice was smooth. His snake-smile revealed the gap between his front teeth, his green eyes so pale the pupils showed hard and black. 'Nellie...'

'Don't you Nellie me! Rogue! Charlatan!' she crowed.

Cora jumped up and the hidden slipper fell onto the rug.

'An' look!' Nellie gasped. 'She were a-sittin' on a shoe! There weren't no ghost!'

From the front door, the other ladies began to spill onto the cobbles, where a coach was clattering noisily past, lanterns swinging, iron-clad hooves on stone almost drowning out the commotion within. Almost, but not quite. While they were chattering excitedly about all that had occurred, some of them heard Mrs Furze's exclamations and they stopped, turned and moved back towards the doorstep. Aunt Selina reassured and denied and closed the door behind them, refusing to let the mask slip an inch.

'I'll get the law on you!' Nellie Furze was shouting, her cries sealed now, behind closed doors. 'Diddlin' innocent folk! You'll be splashed all over the Herald!'

Cora's throat constricted as she stared at the woman, mouth hanging open. She had absolutely no idea what to do. She was schooled in secrecy; in sleight of hand and silence. Nobody had ever challenged her before.

Victor Morningside glided swiftly between Mrs Furze and the doorway to the hall, where the grim, angular Aunt Selina reappeared.

Mrs Furze must have realised she was

outnumbered and outmanoeuvred. She attempted to push past Aunt Selina, who didn't budge. Victor loomed over her, gripping her scrawny arm and steering her, protesting loudly, across the room and out of the door that led to the servant's stair. The door slammed, emitting a burst of cold, damp air, swallowing them both.

Without warning, a white-lipped Aunt Selina advanced towards Cora and struck her, hard, across the face. Cora walked unsteadily away, licking a salty smear of blood from the corner of her mouth, ripping the gloves from her shaking hands and letting them fall. She walked through the smartly furnished hall, with its spiky plants and clutter of ornaments. Up the patterned stairs and onto the bare boards the visitors never saw. Up past the washing, steaming white and grey on strings, past the dangling birdcages with angry canaries protesting, Cora believed, at their entrapment. Though Aunt Selina always insisted they were singing.

From the floor below, she could hear Killigrew sobbing as Nancarrow, the housekeeper, admonished her. Cora had seen her reprimanded enough times to know exactly what she looked like when she cried. Her freckles turned a muddy colour whenever the pale skin between flushed red. It wasn't Killigrew's fault that Nellie Furze had spotted the trick but, as the maid-of-all-work and most junior member of the household, blame had a habit of filtering down towards her.

Nancarrow had changed so much. Cora couldn't imagine what had happened to turn the soft, twinkling woman into such a cold fish. She'd been like a mother to Cora, nursing her through whooping

6

cough and putting mustard poultices on her chest when she had a cold. Now she spoke with a chilly detachment that made Cora ache for the days when, confined by Aunt Selina to her room without food or water, Nancarrow used to sneak her a paper bag of sugar-plums, aniseed balls or almonds.

Cora rarely cried these days. And it wouldn't do Killigrew any good either. She'd have to harden her heart or lose her position. Maid-of-all-work in a house on Fish Row was hardly the childhood dream of any girl, but a small wage was better than none. The frightened face of Nellie Furze bloomed in Cora's mind. She told herself that Victor was only trying to scare the old woman, that he'd buy her silence, nothing more. But a darker part of her knew what he was capable of.

She pushed Nellie and Killigrew from her mind, not because she was heartless, but the opposite. Her heart was swollen, too full of sorrow already.

She opened the door to the attic stairs and the familiar click released something inside her, as though she was letting a heavy pack slip from her shoulders. She felt a little lighter, a little freer, with every step up the narrow flight. She rummaged in her pocket for her candle stub and matches, and the shadows were soon fleeing before her, up and away into the dark.

Very carefully, she stepped from rafter to rafter, towards the corner she'd made her own.

Wedged between boxes of taxidermy equipment and unwanted portraits, which gazed disapprovingly from another age through a film of grime, Cora had made a sort of fort. She couldn't have called it that, having never been to school or held a history book in her life. She'd only been taught to read so she could stitch samplers and feign automatic writing. Up here, the noise and the smells of the house were muffled. The only sound came from the water pipes. Occasionally they rattled or thumped but, that night, they sounded like the creaking timbers of an old ship, listing in a storm.

Shivering, she drew a mouldy smelling blanket across her knees. The only warmth came from the brick chimney that stood in a reddish column rising from the rafters in the floor to the roof. Draughts blew in between the tiles, carrying the occasional flake of snow, which melted as soon as it landed, leaving a tiny smudge of damp.

Cora tugged her precious notebook and pen from their hiding places, candlelight vaguely suggesting old hat boxes, bolts of fabric and hammocks of cobweb strung above her head.

Ain't nowhere safe, she wrote, tilting the book towards the candle in order to see it, then she hesitated. Gripping the pen hard, her breath formed tiny clouds.

She drew a black line through the letters, bisecting them, and tried again to cram the events of the evening into words. She thought of the look on Nellie Furze's face and the cold, silken tone of Victor's voice. The slam of the door.

The pen hovered, bewildered and unable to perform its task.

Her lip was swollen and tasted of copper. Cora pressed too hard and the nib split with such force it splayed out on the page like two tiny, broken legs. Frustration flowing thickly now, she threw her pen across the cramped little room, marking a satisfying, ink-spattered dent in a bundle of moth-eaten curtains. Instantly regretting it, she started hunting for her pen, but the shadows were dense and the candle just a stub, which threatened to sputter out at any moment.

She thrust both arms down into the clutter, dust making her cough as she tugged broken chairs apart, causing piles of mildewed boxes to collapse. At last she found it, coated in fluff and trailing grey web. She opened the stiff, dry pages to re-read what she'd written before, hoping it would be like taking a poker to smouldering logs, sparking the flames of new words.

> *First time she killt me, it were for the amusemnt of the companey. Aunt Selina left it much longr, that nite, to tell em I were still a-live. I'd put the talcum to my cheeks while the lights were out so once the gas were re-lit, I were arranged pon the rug, white as a gost. With her speshal gasp, Aunt Selina put her shawl over my face. I have to breethe as quiet as I can when she does that, an keep my chest still to stop the wool from risin an givin us away. Then, every time, Aunt Selina says 'it was, after all, her callin'.*
>
> *Right on cue, I has to stir, my breths all short and fast.*
>
> *'What appened?' I says. 'Where am I?' An she peels the shawl away, an in their shock, the sitters look like a buckit of water's been thrown in*

their faces. Might as well lift folk
upside down an shake un, empty their
pockets that way.

With a grim sense of deflation, Cora realised that it wasn't only Aunt Selina's villainy that had found its way into her memoir, but her own. She did feel proud sometimes, of how well she could trick them. She couldn't quite meet their eyes when they thanked her for the messages though, or told her how comforted they were to know that their loved ones were at peace. Sometimes the guilt bubbled right up to her lips and she wanted to make them put their money away, to tell them she had no idea where the dead were. For all she knew, they might be hurtling into a void, or clawing at their own front doors, or throwing themselves into the paths of the living, desperately hoping to be glimpsed.

For years, Cora had feared that one day, people would compare their sensational visits to the Blackthorns of Fish Row and realise that the same extraordinary events had come to pass on a suspicious number of occasions. Tales of the ghostly violin that played itself and the messages from the spirit world improved with every mouth that passed them on, ratcheting up the numbers that flocked to their door, but Cora's sudden, apparent death in an ectoplasm-induced fit couldn't be repeated many times without even the most credulous beginning to wonder if, perhaps, it was all an act. That was how she thought it would end, with a murmur, an uncomfortable buzz of gossip, not with Nellie Furze thrusting the shady family business into sharp relief.

She wondered how soon they'd have to leave, doubtless in the dead of night. Ill-gotten belongings crammed into a cart. They'd bump across the moor to another town to defraud another round of lonely, unhappy people. And, much worse, she'd have to leave Tom Currigan.

Tom promised he'd wait for her, whatever happened. When he'd first suggested that she stuff her notebook with secrets and take it to the police station, in order to expose the fraud once and for all, she'd been astonished. It had never occurred to her that there was a way out, a possibility of another life, where she could walk with pride and feel an honest heart beating beneath her ribs, instead of this shrivelled scrap of criminal meat that flapped in terror at every rap on the door, afraid the knocking fist might be gripping a pair of handcuffs.

If she sought help now, Tom had reasoned, then at worst she'd be treated as an accessory. She was still just about young enough, at fourteen, to have been coerced into this life of deceit. But they both knew, in the pauses between their words, that she might go to prison for fraud. It had been easy as the last days of summer had ripened to autumn, to speak of waiting and of writing letters should the worst happen. They'd grabbed hold of any opportunity to wander over the moor together, between jutting granite boulders and disinterested wild ponies, finding excuses for errands so that they might snatch a few hours before the sun set.

Winter had come and she hadn't managed to inform the parish constable about a thing. Tom never actually said that his patience was wearing thin, or that he wouldn't marry Cora while she earned her living the way she did. He never actually said it, but she was afraid it was true.

She yearned to share his life one day, to revel in the freedom he had and the easy, direct way he could answer anyone who asked how he spent his days. Tom was an apprentice wheelwright. He worked alongside his father in Giddock's yard, further down Fish Row. They might have guessed by the rich sawdust smell that surrounded him as warmth does a candle, or noticed how rough his hands were for his sixteen years, with brown callouses and faded scars from a slipped spoke shave or a plane.

Cora wanted to be able to meet people's eyes as he could, without shame. She yearned to throw off the veil Aunt Selina insisted she wore in the street, to preserve her pallor, and let the sun pink and freckle her cheeks. She wanted to work behind a counter, to sell something real, to smile at customers' children as she weighed out currants, flour and coffee, or served cakes in a pretty tea room. Even a position in one of the noisy, stinking factories would be better than this life of lies.

But what if she jumped and he didn't catch her?

Doubt kept creeping in, though she tried hard to shake it out. What if the betrayal of Aunt Selina who was, after all, the closest thing Cora had to a parent, made her feel guiltier than she thought it would? She didn't care about betraying Victor Morningside. Everything had got worse since he'd come along. Aunt Selina was greedy and cruel before, but since his arrival on Christmas Eve, when he'd sought shelter from a sudden snowstorm, she'd grown even colder, with no time at all for her niece outside her instruction in the murky family craft.

What if, Cora tortured herself by wondering, she was sent to prison only to find that Tom's interest waned and she received no letters from him? What if his grandmother, Eseld, who'd always welcomed her at the family cottage, abandoned her too? She'd have nothing at all then. She might face months or even years in a mildewed cell, with no visitors and nobody to greet her when, if, she emerged. The scandal would ensure that she'd never work as a medium again.

Cora was lost, deep in her sombre daydream, when the dusty air around her started vibrating, as though a steam-powered engine was rumbling through the street below, but without a sound.

Her organs were trembling, her blood buzzing beneath her skin. She feared she might be dangerously unwell.

The air congealed into a shimmering mass before her eyes. It had a horrible, globular quality, filling Cora with a dread so deep her breath stuck in her throat, her lungs felt glued together, her tongue stitched to the inside of her mouth. The shape contracted, pieces wobbling together like a reflection in a pool. A shard of lip, a ribbon of skin, scraggy threads of whitish hair were all refracting and jerking until they resembled a figure, the size of a child, with shrivelled, corpse-grey skin and dried lips baring sharp little teeth.

Cora's bones crackled to life. She leapt to her feet, the candle sputtering out as she staggered blindly towards the door. She half-ran, half-fell down the narrow, attic stair and pelted down the next to burst out, shocked and gasping like a newborn, into the freezing cold street.

She only had one place to go. Tom's cottage was a couple of miles from the sprawling edge of the town and she fled towards it. She had no bonnet or shawl and the icy air turned her hair to razors. She hadn't replaced her soft, indoor shoes with boots and every cobblestone dug painfully in. She bunched her skirts into her fists as snow fell thickly all around her. The fabric grew fatter and heavier with every melting flake, until her freezing hands shone and her hair was pasted to her face and throat.

To keep the memory of the ghastly apparition at bay, she pictured herself arriving at the cottage to find Tom and his grandmother, who'd give her a steaming mug of something medicinal and dry her hair and clothes by the fire. How would she describe what she'd seen? The thought of the phantom made her run even faster, smashing frozen puddles hiding slimy horse dung, which splattered up her legs. How could she explain that horrible vision, surely a judgement from God? Or was it from Hell? Her lungs burned, unused to exertion and laced too tight to inflate properly.

Sooty posters covering the walls jumped and merged and the few people abroad at such an hour cursed her as she pelted past, spattering them with icy filth. Drunks slowly blinked, their hats pulled low as they shuffled out of smoky pubs, the din of clattering pianos and roaring songs suddenly loud whenever the doors bumped open. Still Cora ran, out past the grocer's, the chandler's and the bakery. Out past the dye works and the foul-smelling tannery, the abattoir and the lamp-black factory, until the noises of the town fell away with the gas glow of the street lamps, until the air held only the faint, mineral scent of snow.

On the moor, the wind blew harder. All Cora could hear was the snowy crunch of her feet and her breaths, tearing through her lungs and turning to steam. The night was moonless. The rocks were black, the trees were black and the sky, a vast starless black.

Even the snow, without the gleam of lamp or moon, might as well have been coal. Starving wolves might have lurked just feet away for all she knew, sniffing the air and licking ice-spangled jaws.

She sank to her ankles with each step, her shoes leaking freezing water, numbing her toes. The uneven ground, so familiar in daylight, seemed determined to trip her. She had to fight her sodden, dung-muddied skirts and petticoats, cursing the fashion for yards of bulky wool.

The terrible apparition reared again in her mind and she shivered, cold and fear both vying to shake her bones the hardest. Stretching her hands out in front of her, as if she was still wearing the blindfold, she groped ahead, fingers grazing occasional branches and rough, lichen-covered stones. But nothing that told her where she was. She panicked. She should be able to see the softly lit cottage windows by now, or at least smell woodsmoke.

She turned and looked back, trying to find the smoggy glow of the town, to get her bearings, but it had vanished. Resolute, she pushed her exhausted legs onward, thick petticoats sticking to her stockings. She was terrified the fabric would freeze stiff, glueing the layers to her flesh in frozen folds, immobilising her forever like the pagan hurlers who were turned to stone mid-dance. She saw herself as an icy statue, hidden beneath a drift until the spring thaw, when she would bloat, purple and soft with rot. She pressed on, blind and alone, sweeping relentless flakes from her eyelashes, determined to get there alive.

In the distance, she heard the thump of snow-muffled hooves. The rattling squeak of leather and wood. Horn lanterns swung from the sides of the coach, casting a feeble glow, dull with grime and fuzzed by flurries of falling shadow. It was travelling too fast for her to catch the driver's attention. He was so wrapped up against the cold, he resembled nothing more than a hat, balanced on a pile of blankets.

She watched the coach lights shrink, trying to work out where she must be in relation to the track, but the kicked mess of snow was becoming smooth before her eyes. The cold was making her drowsy. In the dying light of the lanterns, she glimpsed a black feather alighting on the back of her hand. She moved to brush it away, but it jumped, moving awkwardly upward into the falling snow.

It wasn't a feather, she saw with a jolt, as it landed once more on her fingers, but an enormous butterfly. In February! The size of a saucer, it had wings like none she'd ever seen. They were black, with the liquid gloss of a raven, reflecting light that wasn't there in crooked angles, as though it had been screwed up and unfolded. The creature wasn't solid, but ragged with holes, like torn lace. She couldn't understand how it flew. It was rimed with frost and should have been beautiful, but it wasn't. Something about it was profoundly unsettling. Ripped, bent and filmed with ice, it went against nature. It should be dead.

Its wings were slowing. Opening and closing until they shut firmly and it toppled onto its side in her open palm. Cora lifted her hand to look at the misshapen creature more closely. Its tiny legs were stiff and still. Snowflakes settled on its satin wings, before it burst into life, fluttering up and away from her, silhouetted against the dying glow of the coach.

She followed it down into a hollow, so desperate to catch it she didn't notice the texture of the snow changing beneath her feet. It was loose and springy, and it cracked as she walked.

At first she feared she'd stumbled onto a frozen river and cursed herself for getting distracted in such dangerous weather. It cracked again, swallowing her up to the knees. But no icy water rushed in.

Instead, snow puffed up to mingle with the falling flakes. It got into her eyes, making them itch. Despite her terror, she sneezed, her whole body shuddering with the violence of it and the ground cracked again, louder this time, snaring her up to the waist in ropes of wild ivy.

Splintered wood stabbed her legs, her corset the only thing stopping it driving into her abdomen. Her heart froze. She knew where she was.

Nobody knew exactly how deep the abandoned mineshaft went.

She tried to breathe, to think, but she could only swear, loudly, instinctively, as though the words could conjure rescuing hands from the cruel wind.

Her mouth filled with a scream, immediately silenced as the ivy ripped and the earth swallowed her whole.

Her skirts bunched around her. The mineshaft was slick with ice and she flew like a bullet down the barrel of a gun.

Chapter Two

Underwood

Cora expected to die. If she could, she'd have wailed aloud at the short, violent unfairness of it, but the air was rushing too fast. She shot downwards at such a speed, it made her eyes water, through air that was no longer black, but blue.

She saw mist rising from something impossible beneath her.

She thought she must be dead already, as the green treetops of a forest reared into view. But she didn't feel remotely dead when she hit the branches. They caught and ripped her hair, mangling her skirts even more than the mineshaft had, and she tumbled for what felt like another mile through snapping twigs, before crashing into water that shot violently up all around her, the velocity carrying her deep into the belly of a pool, streaming dark bubbles.

She kicked, desperately propelling herself upward to shatter the surface with a gasp. She kept inhaling, feasting on sweet oxygen, filling her mouth and lungs and brain with it.

Grasping at roots, she hauled herself out onto the bank, struggling with the weight of her sodden dress, into a thick tangle of flowers and curling ferns. Trees stretched to dizzying heights above her, higher than the pillars of a cathedral.

At first, she was too shocked to do anything but lie on her back, blinking. Her mind buzzed, busy as a hive, trying to make sense of it. Her vision was fogged and she rubbed her eyes with her knuckles, the lids sore underneath as if she had sand in them.

She tried to think rationally. She had fallen far beneath the moor. So, logically, this must be a mine, or a cave, but it wasn't. It was a forest. Beyond the distant leaves was a preposterous, light-filled sky. It was warm too, the air oddly silken. There was a strong smell, one that was so out of place she didn't recognise it at first. Burnt syrup. It was the same sweet, charred odour that floated up from the kitchen when Cook chipped sugar and made comfits from nuts and caraway seeds.

The light didn't shift, as it did in the woodlands she knew. Every leaf was still.

She propped herself gingerly onto an elbow, expecting pain, but she moved easily, without so much as a twinge. She examined her hands. Her palms were scratched, vivid scarlet in this sudden brightness, but she felt no pain whatsoever. She touched her temple and her fingers came away thick with fresh red.

Even when she pressed her wounds, nothing hurt. She stood up, the air so warm her clothes were already beginning to dry, the blood turning sticky as sweat formed on her forehead and upper lip. Gazing around her, she felt incredibly small. The roots were thicker than a man's thigh and rippled over stones furred with moss.

There were no roads, no paths even, that she could see. Huge, green-clad boulders formed deep valleys, where other pools quietly shimmered. Rope bridges were strung high above her, so far up they resembled cobwebs. She blinked, thinking they must actually be cobwebs, catching the light, tricking her eye. Some were jerking slightly, from side to side, as though people were walking across. She peered, squinting in disbelief, at the trees and saw doors and wonky little windows with carved shutters, in the trunks. Walls of timbered brick were tucked precariously in the y-shaped embrace where the huge branches forked. And there really were tiny figures hurrying along the bridges, more of them every time she looked.

Cora shrank back, afraid. If she wasn't dead, then she was in the grip of a hallucination, brought on by shock. Perhaps she was actually lying in the snow, having slipped and knocked herself out, being slowly buried by settling flakes, drifts forming over her eyelashes...

'No, of course it isn't dead!' barked a shrill voice, somewhere to her left. 'It's standing up!'

Cora spun round to see who'd spoken. But she saw no-one.

'Up here!'

She snapped her head up. Wooden struts had been driven into a nearby trunk, forming a spiral of steps, on which a curious party perched. They were adults, but the size of children. Their skin shimmered gold and they were dressed in bright satin. They wore feathers and jewels pinned everywhere, particularly the one who'd spoken, who'd left barely an inch of her costume unadorned. Her wild pile of hair was studded with pearls and leaves of gilt. Brooches sparkled at her shoulders and waist, in the shapes of snowflakes and snakes. The effect should have been ridiculous, but it wasn't. It was dazzling. Intoxicating.

Cora felt herself smile.

As they rounded the trunk, they peered at her,

amber eyes full of glittering laughter. A giggle rattled in Cora's chest. She coughed and covered her mouth, vaguely noticing a spray of blood in her palm. Her teeth tasted of metal, but she couldn't stop smiling. She tried to remember where she'd been going. Where she'd come from. Somewhere cold, she thought. Not lovely and warm like this place.

'This is my home, isn't it?' she heard herself say, then she laughed again.

Of course it was her home. She was born here, among the quiet, motionless trees, beside this glinting pool.

'That's right,' the decorated lady grinned, revealing tiny, pointed teeth. 'Come on, everybody'll be so pleased to see you!'

As she moved towards them, Cora noticed more butterflies. They were glorious. Red, gold and blue, as though they'd been daubed by a painter. A memory stirred in the back of her mind, like a forgotten dream.

Something winged, black and torn.

Something cold, falling, white.

And a shimmering mass, a face forming from thin air. But as soon as she tried to grasp them, the memories fluttered out of reach.

From within a cloak the colour of mercury, the lady produced a gleaming apple. She offered it to Cora with a flash of something like greed. 'You must be peckish,' she said. 'You do remember me, don't you?'

'Of course', Cora nodded, biting gratefully into the apple, suddenly ravenous. It was red inside and it didn't crunch. There was none of the cool, fragrant juice she'd expected. Instead, the apple had the texture of marzipan and tasted as she imagined a lily might.

'Of course,' Cora repeated, letting the perfumed sweetness melt over her tongue. 'You're...' she hesitated. She knew her, so why couldn't she say her name?

'Lady Ursell of course!'

'That's it, I must have forgotten, when I...' She looked up. It had something to do with 'up'.

'When you what?' asked another person, curiously attired in gold and green.

Lady Ursell shot him a dark look and he immediately shut his mouth.

'I don't know,' Cora murmured, trying to swallow the powdery apple flesh, its scent filling her head. The shadow of a memory passed over her again, distant as a cloud over the sea. But even as she thought of such a thing, the image of a puffed, white giant floating above endless, foaming grey seemed very alien, dangerously so. Surely there was nothing like that in the world? There were only trees. Only moss and ferns. Apples and pools.

'Come,' Lady Ursell beckoned, 'come with us.'

Grateful, though she wasn't sure why, Cora followed them up the steps sticking out of the tree trunk. One of her ankles wasn't working properly. It didn't quite lift her foot. But it didn't hurt, so she wasn't worried. The steps were narrow, made for smaller bodies than her own, and the width of her gown was a problem, so she wrapped an arm around the muscular wood and hoped for the best.

She was very high, where the air was even warmer, humid with steam from her dress. She paused to unfasten the top few buttons and tugged the fabric away from her chest, allowing a little heat to escape. She must have wobbled, because one of the small people grabbed her, yanking her close.

For just a moment, she was frightened and suddenly aware of her exposed collarbone.

Lady Ursell was speaking harshly in a language Cora didn't understand. She dipped her hand into a small leather pouch and blew a handful of dust into Cora's eyes, making her blink. The itching only lasted for a second, before the sweet, burnt sugar smell grew stronger and the foggy peace returned, spreading a smile across Cora's face. She looked down at the apple and saw how black and shiny the pips were, at its core.

They reached a precarious looking bridge and, like an automaton, Cora walked across with her new companions. It was beautiful up there, but something nagged at Cora as it creaked and swayed. Something to do with her greater size and weight and the notion that she oughtn't fall. She couldn't imagine why. Surely she'd simply land beside that lovely pool again, and listen to the silence of the trees growing.

As they made their way across, she saw more of the forest, which went on forever in a thousand shades of green. She noticed other groups, dressed more modestly but still in bright colours, carrying baskets of berries on their backs, pausing to watch her. They were smiling, but there was a sadness in their eyes and their smiles looked rather odd, as though their mouths were simply being drawn up at the corners, by tiny hooks.

On the other side of the bridge, they reached a tree even bigger than all the others. A pair of intricately carved doors were opened wide, the darkness inside lit by what looked like candlelight, only pinker. Something told Cora she ought to be nervous, but she simply let her arms swing loosely by her sides, humming a tune she couldn't quite recall. A dim recollection bobbed just beneath the surface of her thoughts, of a pinched mouth telling her not to slouch, to stand tall and straight. But the others weren't standing like that. Lady Ursell's hands were planted on hips that curved naturally from a rather thick waist, as if she wasn't wearing stays. The idea made Cora chuckle.

The doorway was flanked by two guards, each holding a pike staff at an angle, so that they crossed. Their faces were the first sullen ones Cora had come across. Upon seeing her, their features jerked into joyless grins. Lady Ursell hurried up to them and they lifted their spears to let the group pass into the trunk. Stairs carved from the inside of the tree wound downward. The rosy light and scorched syrup smell grew stronger with every step.

Giddy music floated up. Cora would have tapped her foot, but it was becoming irritatingly floppy. Spongy, like a dead thing. Her shoe had fallen off, she didn't remember when. The air grew even warmer as the steps continued down and she wiped perspiration from her neck.

They reached another pair of doors, flanked by two more guards. This time, they opened inward, releasing a swell of bright colour and noise. Fiddles, drums and tin whistles were being played at frantic speed and dancers whirled in a hall so crammed with mirrors and melting candles, it was difficult to tell how many people there were, or where the walls and roof met. The mirrors were different sizes, with ornate gilt frames, hung with green velvet and fringed with silver tassels. They reflected the pairs and pairs of dancers, some in weird, distorted grotesques, others at strange angles. The mirrors crowding the ceiling held a hundred more couples, dancing upside-down. Candles of a sickly olive colour were arranged in silver holders on every surface, dribbles spreading around their base and puddling on the ballroom floor.

The dancers whirled in flurries of silk, velvet, satin and lace, both male and female piled with jewels and enormous hair arrangements that bobbed and jerked in time to the music. In the few gaps between the silver, spotted glass were alcoves containing golden busts, decorated with ivy, chestnuts and slices of dried orange, as though for Christmas.

All at once, the music clattered to a halt. The laughter ended abruptly and the dancers stilled.

They stared at the new arrivals with a mixture of contempt and jealousy. Their golden faces were powdered so white, it made their eyes appear bloodshot. Their eyebrows were drawn in thin, black, unnatural arches, their lips red as bitten cherries.

Puffed with triumph, Lady Ursell seized Cora's hand in a fierce grip, tugging her forwards into the glimmering room. The silent dancers parted, rictus grins appearing on their faces each time Cora met their eyes. Her foot had swollen into a small cushion, with two purplish blue toes poking through a hole in her stocking. It dragged uselessly, hindering her steps, but Lady Ursell wouldn't be slowed. Her eyes were fixed ahead, filled with a brittle light.

With alternate squelches, as water bubbled from

the stitching in Cora's shoe, and soggy pats, from her swollen foot, they moved forward, the crowd continuing to part, until they revealed the most beautiful person Cora had ever seen.

A queen, she couldn't have been anything else, with an exquisite crown that looked as if it had been spun from molten barley sugar, sat on a silver throne at a table piled with all of Cora's favourites. Sugar-plums, whole roast geese, ices, ripe oranges, crystallised flowers, rabbit pies, almonds, cherry tarts, slabs of quince marmalade and cinnamon sticks had been crammed into bowls of gold and gleaming silver, which reflected the emerald cloth in elegant curves. Cora's belly growled and she glanced down, embarrassed both by the noise and her dirty, bloodstained appearance.

Beside the queen was a much smaller table, black as onyx, where liquid seemed to have been spilled. In the centre was a tiny pile of ash, which a nearby lady swept off as soon as she saw Cora looking.

A flash of metal and a crunching sound alarmingly close to her ear made Cora jump, in a foggy sort of alarm. She raised her hand to her head. And the queen grinned, drawing back a pair of scissors, a handful of Cora's hair dangling from her fist.

'Don't tell me you've forgotten our little tradition?' the queen chuckled, as though nothing was amiss.

As she spoke, Cora thought she heard the mournful chime of a bell. The sound was so faint, it must have come from far away. Perhaps she'd imagined it.

Lady Ursell snatched up a bottle the colour of absinthe, flipping open the silver stopper, and held it out to the beautiful young queen, who folded the hair and quickly dropped it in, as though it was something disgusting she didn't want to hold at all. Inside the bottle, distorted by the glass, Cora thought she saw a bloody tooth. She ran her tongue around her mouth and found a soft, wet gap. She lifted a hand to her temple, where a patch of rough stubble told her how close the blades had come to her skin. Something about it was wrong. Something about the whole place was wrong. Her foot started to ache and the edges of things were shimmering.

Lady Ursell looked up sharply, muttering those strange words again. She lifted another handful of powder and blew it into Cora's eyes. Cora sneezed, laughed and wipe her mouth with her sleeve, smearing the fabric with a pretty red.

'Eat!' Lady Ursell smiled. Cora looked down at the empty bowl she offered and grinned in confusion.

Lady Ursell broke a piece off the bowl's rim, releasing the delicious smell of gingerbread. Amazed, Cora took the peculiar morsel and bit.

At once, the room became a swirling mass of colour. Velvet sleeves blurred into candlesticks, sliced goose into laughing faces. Everything rose up and away as she sank to the ground.

Chapter Three

Curiosities by Gaslight

When she regained consciousness, Cora had no idea where she was.

She was in darkness, though her eyes were definitely open.

She tried to move and her body screamed in pain, but not a sound escaped her lips. She was completely immobile, frozen stiff in such an unfamiliar pose, it took a while to work out where each of her limbs was fixed. She appeared to be sitting on a hard little slat, her hands gripping ropes, her legs sticking straight out in front of her.

Her foot was making itself known, the spongy, dead feeling had gone and in its place was a crushing sensation that threatened to make her black out. Determined to remain conscious, she tried again to move, but she couldn't even inflate her lungs. She couldn't move her eyes, or blink, or wet her lips with her tongue. She felt as dry and stiff as wood, as if she wasn't a living creature at all, but something carved.

Was it a nightmare? Surely the place that she had come from, that peculiar forest full of strange people, was the illusion? Or perhaps they were both phases of sleep, interrupted by nothing worse than a thunderstorm outside her bedroom window. Maybe she was tucked beneath her blankets and a bolt of lightning had woken her, not fully, but enough to bring her close to the surface, before tumbling her into another dream?

She recalled her time in the wood with a pang of

sadness. The leafy light, the trees reflected in the pools, the feast in the mirror-filled ballroom, made Cora ache with a strange sense of violence, as though something had been stolen from her. Something she had to get it back at any cost. The extraordinary peace had held an odd, numb quality. It reminded her of when she was little, when Aunt Selina used to drip laudanum into her milk.

It wasn't just the peace she missed, but the exquisite sense of belonging. They'd welcomed her, hadn't they? It'd felt more like home than the house on Fish Row ever had. It was a fantasy though, a deranged vision, surely, brought on by her fall into the mineshaft. If that had been real. Perhaps she was lying, stuck and broken, at the bottom. But if that were true, surely she could have moved her eyes? The memory of the trees and the mirrored ballroom were jumbling into nonsense as she tried to recall them. The trees bent low, sweeping the pools into ripples, their branches reflected as dancing couples. Her mind was muddled, she began to see that. And her head hurt, as though weights pressed hard upon it from every side. She had to find a way to move, to break whatever strange bonds were holding her and get home.

But where was she now?

She stared harder into the gloom, hoping the edges of things might reveal themselves, if she could only distinguish black from blacker.

She tried to force the muscles around her eyes to contract, to swivel her eyeballs left and right, but to no avail. She was frightened, but her fear held a grain of comfort in it, because at least it meant she felt like herself again. Her mind was crammed with strange images, but at least it was her own, no longer dimmed by that sweet, smoky fog.

A thought sprang alarmingly into being. What if she'd never left the forest? What if she was, right now, stowed deep in an underground dungeon, beneath that peculiar ballroom, chained or poisoned by something that prevented even her eyes from twitching?

Would it stop her heart?

Had it already?

Was this what death felt like?

Was she now in a coffin, cold as the mud above and below, dead, yet somehow conscious?

The darkness split. The crack filled with light. It was a door! The yellow glow spread as a figure cast a shadow across a rug. Cora recognised the fuzzy outline of Killigrew's hair, trying to escape her cotton cap. The maid lowered a coal scuttle, stifling a yawn.

Cora would have let out a great shudder of relief, had her bones and muscles not been fused into one immovable mass. Killigrew knelt to light the fire, setting her candle beside her, where its glow revealed hints of the bow at the back of her apron.

Cora tried to call out, but her mouth and throat were like rusted metal. Try as she might, she couldn't make a sound.

The huddle of coals started to smoke, flames licking the kindling as Killigrew used the bellows. Once it had fully caught, she closed the door behind her, leaving the room almost as dark as before.

At least Cora knew she was back in the house on Fish Row, but what she could see of the room remained unfamiliar. The flames from the paper and twigs had died down and, in the orange glow of the coals, there was a dim suggestion of smoke-stained tiles. Everything else remained black. She scrutinised the pattern on the tiles of scratchily drawn ships, which held a vague familiarity.

The door opened again, revealing Uncle Granville, who brought the haddock waft of kedgeree. The glow of the candle he carried illuminated his bushy whiskers, which ran from his smoke-yellowed moustache up to his temples, leaving only his chin pink and bald. His mop of wild, white hair was in in its usual disarray.

He put the candle down, lit a taper from it and turned his back. At the hissing of the jets, he became a silhouette, his hair glowing from behind as he touched the taper to the gas, his scalp gleaming beneath tufty, translucent strands.

Cora tried again to draw breath and force it upward through her throat, to suck and blow like the bellows Killigrew had used but, though her insides glowed hot with pain, she couldn't forge a single word.

Surely he'd see her in a moment, she reasoned, even if she couldn't alert him to her presence. Bit by bit, as the gaslight spread, her uncle's study stepped out of the dark. It was filled with glass cabinets stacked on top of each other, housing all sorts of curiosities. There were locally procured squirrels, a pheasant and an assortment of rabbits, each with dull fur surrounding unnaturally bright glass eyes.

There were more exotic things too, on which he must have spent a small fortune, most of which Cora couldn't have named if it wasn't for their labels. There was the skeleton of a toucan complete with enormous bill, a monkey with a savage expression and the preserved brush tip of an elephant's tail. From the ceiling hung a swooping bat, wings spread wide and, on the big, mahogany desk, a leathery baby alligator curled around peculiar, whitish eggs. Upon the shelves were jars filled with dull brown liquid, where indistinguishable organs and embryonic creatures floated. Each gruesome object revealed itself in greater detail as more jets began to burn.

Uncle Granville turned and patted his pockets, eventually finding his pipe and sticking it in his mouth. He was facing her, but not registering her at all.

He poked a lit match into the bowl of his pipe, raising and lowering his substantial eyebrows, and began to puff warm smoke into the air, clouding it with swirls of grey, before sitting down at his desk and picking up his tools to resume his work.

His latest project was a tiny lamb, stillborn, bought from a nearby farm, its wool compacted in tight little curls. Much of his work, the stuff he got paid for, was the 'resurrecting' of beloved pets, but his latest passion was for procuring freaks of nature. The lamb had four eyes and two mouths pointing away from each other, its head on the verge of becoming two. He'd already acquired a four-legged chick and a pair of conjoined kittens, folded together as they must have been in the womb, staring morosely through blue glass eyes for eternity.

A terrifying possibility struck Cora. Was she frozen in time like these poor creatures? Had her soul been somehow transported into the body of a shrew, or the owl that had been descending upon it for ten years or more, claws outstretched? If she could, she'd have screamed.

There was a round mirror, spotted with age, on the opposite wall. She'd forgotten it was there until the gaslight brought it to life. When she looked at its silvery surface, the shock was physical.

She couldn't find herself in it at all.

The mirror reflected an oil painting of Granville as a child, stiffly arranged along with his brother and sisters in a summer garden, closed on four sides by an old gilt frame.

There had never been a girl on a swing in the background before.

Dark brushstrokes of hair flew backwards from the horribly familiar face, giving an impression of movement and rushing air that Cora wished she could feel. The brutally shorn patch revealed more of one ear than she was used to seeing, reviving the memory of sharp, looming scissors.

The ropes cut into her hands, as though they bore every ounce of her weight and more. Try as she might, she couldn't relax her fingers, every sinew was drawn mercilessly tight, yet the figure in the painting smiled serenely, expressing nothing of the agony raging inside. She knew her dress had been torn and bloodstained after the fall into the forest, yet this girl wore white, buttoned boots and a gown from the old king's time, loosely flowing lawn with no sign of a crinoline. A pink sash was tied high, just below the bust, its ribbons streaming behind towards fuzzy streaks of cloud.

Completely oblivious to his niece's predicament, Uncle Granville continued his gruesome task, carefully easing the disproportionately large, doubled skull of the lamb down through its wrinkled folds of neck, without tearing the skin. At one point, he must have had an itch in his whiskers, because he scratched with a bloody fingernail, leaving a streak of brownish red.

Around his hunched figure, the room filled with the watery light of a winter dawn. Once the sun had risen high enough to see by, he put out the gaslights and the warmer colours of the study drained to greys and browns. He left when the room reached its brightest, presumably for lunch, then returned to his work, continuing for a few hours before he needed to resort to artificial light again. Even after he'd put the raw, skinless carcass down onto the newspaper, smudging the dense print with blood, and tenderly lifted the woolly skin away to wash it in arsenical soap, then returned to tidy his things and turn out the lights, Cora still couldn't accept the truth.

He closed the door behind him and the painting, along with everything but the glowing coals, vanished in a sea of black. She stared into it, her eyes hot and dry, wondering if, in the blind dark, her painted eyes were turning red.

Apart from a lonely owl, somewhere outside in the freezing night, the only sound was the deep, steady tock of the grandfather clock in the hall, beating like the heart Cora wished she could feel. Now and then, she heard a soft hiss, as the mechanism inside began to whir, and a deep, resonant chime would record each quarter hour. She could still smell the lingering smoke from Uncle Granville's pipe. How could she possibly smell, and see, and hear, if she was nothing more than a daub of paint? But how could she know she was a daub of paint? How could she think without a brain? It didn't stand up to the most basic grasp of biology.

The second day passed much like the first, with Uncle Granville hard at work on the lamb, tugging the skin over a wire frame and padding it with wads of cotton. And as the animals continued to stare through the glass, Cora wondered if they, too, lamented their peculiar fate.

This went on for so long, she lost count of the hours solemnly intoned by the clock chimes. She felt no hunger, no thirst or tiredness, just constant, excruciating pain. The notion that she might remain like this forever was too awful to consider. That way madness lay so, instead, she focused on getting through each quarter hour at a time, by concentrating on the contents of the cases in as much detail as her restricted vision would allow.

She observed that the faded fox had black whiskers, not red as she would have assumed, and that the feathers adorning the pheasant's neck shone bright as blue-green satin, a shy echo of the brilliant peacock feather beside it. She began to wonder if the violent expression contorting the monkey's features was one of fright, rather than rage, though she didn't like to look at it for too long, because it had begun to appear unnervingly human.

Every morning, before dawn, Killigrew came in to light the fire. Later, Uncle Granville would enter, bringing the breakfast smells of bacon, coffee and devilled kidneys with him, to mingle with the stale pipe smoke he'd breathed there the day before, for he wasn't one to open a window. After an hour or so, the sun would rise and Cora could trace its ancient, diurnal path by watching the nine squares of light from the window inch across the rug.

Killigrew came in regularly to dust and polish and

the sharp fragrance of linseed oil mingled with the damp, earthy smell of tealeaves. Occasionally, Uncle Granville swigged from a hip flask and the peat scent of whisky sweetened the bitter smoke.

One day, the routine was disrupted. It rained so heavily that the room grew dark as twilight and the gas was allowed to burn all day. Cora was thrilled as she watched shadowy drops chase each other across the faded carpet. Another time, she noticed that Killigrew had taken to lingering in the room after she'd lit the fire, walking around with a bleary, exhausted expression and poking through Uncle Granville's things.

Cora had never been fond of her uncle. Though she'd arrived at Fish Row as a baby, she didn't remember ever sitting upon his knee or holding his hand on the way to church. She'd never had a conversation with him that she could recall, apart from the occasional, stilted request for salt or anchovy paste at the table. Yet she felt defensive and annoyed with Killigrew. What right has a maid to be so nosy?

Thinking she was alone, Killigrew had taken to unscrewing the lids on specimen jars, recoiling in disgust at the smell of ammonia. She peered at the rows of small fossils and crystal-centred geodes, picking some of them up and turning them over. Cora observed Killigrew's reflected scrutiny as the maid gazed at the motionless creatures, trapped behind glass. She rooted through drawers too, revealing the scalpels and sharpened spoons Uncle Granville used to scrape flesh from hide, beside boxes of needles, thread and glue. He must have breakfasted early one morning, because Killigrew heard him coming and almost dropped her candle as she pushed the knives hurriedly back into place, taking care not to nick her fingers.

She was much quicker with her investigations after that, giving things more of a cursory glance than an examination. She even came up close to the painting once and scrutinised the scene, her face close enough for Cora to see her individual, sandy eyelashes and the open pores in her nose.

That night, just after the twelfth chime, the door opened.

Cora was startled.

For an awful moment she feared the looming silhouette was a two-headed creature, like the lamb, only far more frightening for being human and living. But it was two women, one behind the other. If she could, Cora would have sighed with relief. She didn't expect them to notice her.

Yet, as she watched, they moved deliberately towards the painting.

The candle they carried was small and cheap, the wick must've been thin, for the flame gave off only the tiniest glow. One of them lifted a shawl from her head, where snowflakes had caught, not yet melted, and revealed a familiarly haphazard grey bun.

Eseld! Cora realised with a start. The other figure was Killigrew, her red plait much longer and thicker than Cora imagined it'd be, dangling over her shoulder. They were moving closer, swelling Cora's heart with hope. In the flickering gloom, she could just make out a wooden apothecary jar in Eseld's hand.

'Just here,' Killigrew whispered.

It was so long since she'd heard a human voice,

Cora strained to reply, though she knew she couldn't. As the weathered planes of Eseld's face drew closer, her wrinkles were etched deeper by candle shadow.

'That you, my duck?' Eseld whispered, anxious not be overheard and arrested for trespass, 'now, I'm sure this 'ain't been much of a picnic. We been lookin' everywhere for you. Didn't know what form you'd be in, see?' she grasped the edges of the frame.

Cora lurched terrifyingly up and down. The room that had been still for so long was suddenly swinging around, revealing gloomy shapes of things she hadn't seen before and rendering the familiar alien, by strange angles.

Killigrew cleared a space on the desk and Eseld put the painting flat upon it, so that Cora had no choice but to stare up at a ceiling crammed with dangling, ghoulish creatures. She kept reminding herself that this was Eseld, whom she trusted, but she wished she could shut her eyes to block out all those claws, feathers and teeth.

Eseld produced a twisted lump of metal, hung on a cord around her neck. 'Don't you worry, Cora love,' she was saying, 'have you out in a jiffy.'

'She can't hear you, can she?' Killigrew was doubtful. She gazed down in pity, as though Cora was stiff and cold in a coffin, clutching lilies.

'I dunno.' Eseld whispered over her shoulder, 'I ain't never done this afore. Though if I was her, and this were a-happening to me, I'd want to hear a few kind words, wouldn't you?'

She tugged the strange pendant over her head, frazzling her wiry pile of hair even more, and turned the painting over. To Cora's relief, the fierce talons and teeth swung away, replaced by the dimly lit, close-up grain of wood. Very carefully, Eseld prised the back off the frame and lifted the painting away from the glass. As she turned it over, Cora felt a rush of dusty air, sour with smoke and camphor.

She tried to focus on the grim set of Eseld's face, as the old woman lifted the curious pendant. It grew huge, blocking out the room as Eseld pressed it onto the canvas, which hissed. She took it away and Cora felt peculiarly thin, dry and hot all at once, as the old paint came up in blisters. At first, the burning smell was so bitter, Cora would have gagged if she could, but it was soon replaced by a crushed-grass, rain-on-nettles scent, which was growing stronger and more lovely by the second.

Cora felt a scorching shiver, as if she'd hurried in from the snow and warmed her freezing hands too quickly, by the fire.

The stiffness in her limbs began to ease, as though she was slipping into a warm bath. The shapes and shadows of the room began to slide downward, elongating as Cora felt herself falling, melting, all the tension unspooling as she slithered. She reached the bottom edge of the frame but couldn't stop. Soon she was engulfed by the smell of sycamore and orange oil and realised she must have been caught in the apothecary jar.

The lid was screwed on with a loud scraping noise. Cora heard muffled whispers as Eseld and Killigrew set the room as it had been before, whispering all the while.

Killigrew was fearful, 'there ain't no hope is there? She's just a blob of wet paint!'

'Well, what did you think she'd be?'

'I dunno, I think... I thought she'd just sort of...

step out, and be herself, you know? All flesh and that. I mean she can't be alive in there, can she? Not really?'

'You leave that to me, Sarah.' Eseld's tone was reassuringly steady, 'I ain't given up on her yet.'

'Will you tell Tom?' Killigrew asked. 'That we've found her I mean?'

'What, get him out of bed and tell him the girl he's been searching the moor for has been turned into paint, but it's alright, we got her in an old jar? No, I'll see what I can do for her first, see how much of her's left.'

'God be with you,' Killigrew said quietly, and her footsteps faded away.

Cora heard the quiet, careful click as the study door was closed. She was out! With a thrill of glee she luxuriated in her strange new form, utterly free from pain. She still couldn't move herself, but she was aware of an exquisite slopping sensation, back and forth in tiny waves, and she pictured Eseld tiptoeing through the silent house and into the street.

She could hear the steady clump of boots on cobbles, then crunching snow, before the occasional snap of a stick underfoot told her they'd left the town and entered the wood.

The familiar creak of the cottage door made Cora ache to see the worn table for herself, the frying pan and the poker on their hooks by the hearth, the soft rag rug and the clumps of straw poking from cracks in the plaster, keeping out the draughts. Another door, sounding much stiffer and heavier, opened and closed. Then it felt as though they were descending and Cora lost her bearings.

There were no stairs at the Currigans' cottage, just

a ladder to the loft where the girls slept. Had she got it wrong then, Cora wondered, were they somewhere else?

The scraping sound came again, as the lid of the jar was unscrewed.

'Now,' Eseld peered in, her single eye enormous, gelatinous, as she said 'I'm just going to tip you out, ever so careful like, onto the bed. And we'll see what we can do.'

Cora slipped as easily as mercury from the jar into candlelit dark. She no longer felt like a ghost trapped between worlds, unheard and unseen. Even if she died now, if whatever essence of self she had left drifted away, she knew that someone had bothered to find her. Somebody cared.

She found herself in the middle of a wide, striped desert of cotton ticking. A bed, Eseld had said. Bits of fluff the size of cauliflowers scattered the woven landscape and she couldn't bear to look at the translucent bodies of dust mites, legs clamped in death. There was something huge, black and glossy beside her too and, as Eseld started tugging at it, a vast yellow beak dropped, half-open, into view. If she could, Cora would have recoiled.

It was a dead blackbird, bigger than an omnibus, being pulled apart by Eseld's enormous, chapped fingers. Blood was in the grain of her skin and around her nails.

Eseld tugged the bones from the blackbird's flesh, stretching strands of purplish vein and sinew. It was repellent. The yellow beak fell open in silent, belated protest. Eseld was murmuring strange words, strung together without a breath. With threads of black feather clinging to the gory mass, Cora saw it loom closer, filling with shadow, until it blocked her view and at last, at long, long last, surrounded by bizarre chanting and the mingled scents of feathers, blood and nettles, she passed out.

When she woke, it couldn't have been morning, for the shadows across the ceiling were cast by a warm candle glow, not the chilled hue of a wintry sun. There were no windows, she realised and the room felt too square and solid for an attic. Perhaps it was some sort of cellar, so it could have been any hour. Cora was exhausted, although the thickness in her head suggested her sleep had been deep.

She blinked, she had eyelids again! And lips, and a wet tongue that she could run over and between them! She tried to sit up but that was a bad idea. Her skin burned and itched. She moved to brush off a crystalline, scratchy layer of something that looked like snow.

'No, don't do that, you need the salt.' Eseld was sharp, but tender. 'How about a bit of broth?'

'Broth?' Cora wanted to say, but her throat was too dry to produce more than a pitiful croak.

Eseld was grinding something pungent in a pestle and mortar.

'What's happened to me?' Cora managed to rasp.

Eseld tensed.

She didn't answer straightaway and Cora waited, gazing up at her back.

'Not sure you're ready for all that, yet,' Eseld said, gently. Her hand loomed, huge. She was only holding a teaspoon, but the metal stretched Cora's lips uncomfortably wide. The broth was thick, with threads of salted meat. Some of it spilled as she ate and Eseld scooped the greenish dribbles up over

Cora's chin.

Cora noticed the twisted metal pendant around Eseld's neck. 'What's that?' she murmured. 'You used it before, I remember, to get me out of the painting.'

'This?' Eseld lifted the cord with two massive thumbs, so that the pendant swung in between. 'It's my glyph. Very useful.'

Cora opened her mouth to ask more, then shrieked 'I've no teeth!'

She ran her tongue along unfamiliar gums and drew it back, afraid. 'What's happened to me?' she lisped, panicking. Eseld gave her a long look, still carefully feeding her and wetting her own lips, as if she was about to speak, but didn't know how to begin.

'At least show me what I look like, please? Have you a looking glass? I had to stare at that painting for so long, I want to know I look like myself again.'

'Well, you don't, not really.'

Cora swallowed. 'Let me see?'

Reluctantly, Eseld fetched a small, cracked mirror and held it above Cora. 'Don't say I didn't warn you.'

Cora closed her eyes for a moment, then forced herself to face it, however bad it was.

It was bad. She looked like a baby born too soon to live, no, worse, like a just-hatched chick fallen from its nest. Her skin was peeling and reddish-pink beneath the salt, her eyes disproportionately large in a head not much bigger than an egg, where tufts of hair were growing, actually visibly growing, the exact colour of blackbird feathers. Her mouth was a pink hole, without even the buds of teeth and she spied a tiny, twitching tongue, unable to believe it was really hers.

'Now,' Eseld moved the mirror away, 'that's enough of that. Won't last long, this bit. No more'n a few days, I shouldn't wonder.' She hooked a pair of spectacles over her ears and peered closely at an ancient looking book, covered in odd symbols.

'Where are the nettles?' Cora asked, looking around.

'Hmm?' Eseld kept reading.

'Or was it grass? Something summery anyway. Green. Like a meadow. I smelled it when you were getting me out the painting, and again, when you were...' she trailed off, not sure how to describe Eseld's giant, bloody fingers tearing at the blackbird's innards.

Eseld put her finger on the page, to mark her place, and pushed her spectacles up onto her head. 'Ah, that's the smell of magic. Good, clean, natural magic. Nothing to worry about.'

Cora blinked. She knew she shouldn't be surprised. Magic was the only thing that could explain it. But it was a childish, silly word. Not one for the real world.

'I'll tell Tom you're safe. I 'spect you'll want to see him as soon as possible, or would you rather wait a bit, until you're more yourself?'

'Wait,' Cora managed, 'definitely wait.'

Chapter Four

Cellar

While Uncle Granville's study was dusted with death, the cellar beneath the Currigan's cottage teemed with life. Beneath a wooden table, an injured hedgehog was quietly recovering in a hay-filled basket. Suspended in a birdcage, a dove cooed softly with a splint around its wing and along the shelves that covered the walls were more books than Cora had ever seen. There were bottles filled with tinctures, oils and tonics to promote health and vitality and boxes of powders and pills for everything from baldness to disordered nerves.

Liquids bubbled in scorched glass bowls. There were pestles and mortars, knives and ladles and different sized spoons of wood and pewter. From the ceiling hung dried herbs, flowers and seed pods, among copper pans on hooks. The air held a mixture of the familiar and the strange. Cora detected the scents of herbs she knew and a greasy, pig-fat sort of aroma. There were metallic smells too and sulphurous ones and peculiar spicy ones she couldn't name.

From the bed, wrapped in a blanket, Cora watched Eseld potter, an open book in one hand, peering alternately through her spectacles and over them, to add a few drops here, a sprinkle of powder there, sometimes sending a liquid fizzing.

Cora watched, fascinated, despite her extraordinary predicament. She'd always assumed, judging by the dust-coloured clothes and the warm, tired smile, that Eseld Liddicoat was an ordinary, marvellous grandmother taking care of her family. Cora knew she helped women in childbirth and made remedies for the sick, but she'd always imagined her medicines to be humble, simple things plucked from the hedgerow. This cellar was like nothing she could have imagined.

Cora was growing, very slowly, but she was definitely growing. Every few hours, Eseld carefully lifted her into a set of scales, her mouth working silently as she concentrated. Then covered her again with the itchy blanket, which was made worse by the salt. Above her bed, Eseld tied a posy of rowan twigs, dried witch-hazel leaves, copper nails and a pair of open scissors, all bound with red thread. They dangled rather threateningly, although Eseld assured her it was all part of keeping her safe.

That night, Cora woke in the dark with the lingering sense of having cried out, and Eseld came down the worn stone steps with a candle, to soothe her.

As she drifted back to sleep, Cora heard the floorboards creak above her and the gentle chatter of the family. How she longed to join them! But not in this state. Tom couldn't possibly see her without being horrified. Disgusted even. And the little ones would doubtless be frightened out of their wits.

The next morning, Eseld informed Cora that she'd grown to the length of a woman's shinbone. By evening, she was the size of a three year old child and had managed to learn to walk again, feebly, on wasted legs. But she struggled to eat. After a few spoonfuls, however delicious the mashed potato or thyme dumplings were, she was revolted and couldn't muster much of an appetite at all.

For as long as Cora could remember, Aunt Selina had possessed a peculiar horror of both herself and her niece growing fat. Consequently, Cora had never received quite enough food in the house on Fish Row and developed sunken cheeks and prominent collar bones as a result. Aunt Selina wanted her to remain small and young-looking, in order to make her false gifts seem more remarkable, so she always instructed Cook to make particularly insubstantial versions of consommé, boiled arrowroot or sago soup. She eschewed the simple, filling dishes that Cora loved, like mutton, pasties, bread and root vegetables, as fit only for common folk, or pigs. Whenever she visited the cottage, Eseld had delighted Cora by piling her plate with buttered cabbage, meat puddings, stuffed onions and boiled beef. Things that, all of a sudden, turned Cora's stomach.

The Currigans weren't a wealthy family, there was usually enough to go around, but Cora couldn't understand how Eseld could afford all those books. She asked her about it one day and Escld replied that most of them didn't belong to her. Cora wanted to ask more, but Eseld had changed the subject.

As her strength returned, Cora grew frustrated at breathing the damp, cellar air, where even the fire couldn't drive the chill from her bones. She'd begged to be allowed out, despite the cold weather, to escape the curious smell of bubbling concoctions and see the sky.

The children were at school, and nobody saw Eseld or Cora in the scrap of garden behind the cottage. The sun was a smudge of bright white behind thick clouds, which showed no blue at all. On the path, the snow was compacted, trodden and muddy with footprints leading to and from the privy. Either side of the path, the drifts bore only pock marks, where rain had silently punctured it, muffled as it fell. A wonky little snowman stood among the winter cabbages with sticks for arms, a rag for a scarf, stones for his eyes and a twig for a mouth. One of his eye stones was bigger that the other, which gave him a startled look. Delicate ridges of white traced the outlines of the birches, oaks and wild cherry trees that surrounded the garden. Cora stood unsteadily, wrapped in her blanket, her feet in too-big clogs. She'd grown rapidly overnight and was roughly the height of a nine-year-old.

The air was so cold it scoured her skin. She tried to keep her shivering to a minimum, in case Eseld sent her back in, because it felt good. Raw but good. Rather than fearing it, she began to enjoy the sensation of her newly hatched teeth and curious, sprouting hair. They made her feel alive, like a cousin of the freshly emerged snowdrops. Her new black hair was covering a bit more scalp by then, so the gaps between the strands showed less pink and bald as she moved her shawl away, letting in air as cold as water.

'Oi!' Eseld frowned. 'Put it back.'

'Does it look that bad?' Cora murmured, touching her scalp and drawing the shawl back up. 'Worried I'll scare the badgers?'

'Don't be daft. Catch your death the way you carry on.'

Eseld was digging parsnips, which Cora half-expected to come out frozen stiff. 'Are they pricey?

Your cures?' She was only making conversation when an awful thought struck her. 'I hope I don't I owe you no money!'

Eseld sighed. 'The folk what really need my cures is the ones what ain't got money to pay for 'em.'

Cora sagged with relief. 'What about that Mrs Appleby? She comes all the time for that nerve tonic. She don't look short of a few bob.'

'Ah,' Eseld stopped digging a moment and leaned on her fork, wiping perspiration from her forehead, her breath a puff of mist. 'But it's her husband's money she's wearing, ain't it? Not hers. He won't knowingly pay for anything that ain't from a lace merchant or a dressmaker. Thinks all her trouble's between her ears and the cure can be stitched.'

They were quiet for a moment. The only sound was the croaking of the rooks, the wind shushing through the woods and the slicing sound of the frosted earth, as Eseld's boot shoved down hard on the fork, then ripped back to expose pale, muddy roots.

Cora bent to pull parsnips out of the stubborn ground, their texture rough against her new, pink fingertips, when a sudden dizziness sent her staggering backwards.

'Back to bed with you,' Eseld frowned, guiding Cora into the house and grabbing the trug full of parsnips with her free hand.

Protesting feebly, Cora let herself be taken down to the cellar again, which seemed even darker now she'd felt the cold sun on her skin. 'When will you explain what happened to me?' she asked.

'You're not...'

'I am strong enough!' Cora snapped, surprising

them both.

Eseld exhaled through her nose, planting her hands on her hips and leaving dirty smudges on her apron. She turned away and moved toward the steps.

And Cora thought that was it. The conversation was over. But Eseld had stopped. She was standing very still, one white-flecked boot on the lowest step. A few grey curls had escaped from her cap and cast shadows onto the nape of her neck.

She turned her head just enough for Cora to see the folds of skin at her jaw and a wisp of eyelash. Over her shoulder, her voice was heavy as lead. 'Alright, love. I'll get the parsnips in the stock pot and, if you're still awake when I come back down, then I'll tell you what's what. But it won't be easy. It ain't...' she sighed as she disappeared up through the hatch, '...straightforward. Any of it.'

Cora was determined to stay awake, but Eseld had banked up the fire and its gentle crackling and the cooing of the injured dove wrapped her in warm, dozy sounds. Instead of lying back down on the bed, she forced herself to remain upright, blinking, stretching her eyes wide and rotating her shoulders.

She decided to examine the books. Working her way through the narrow gap between the table and shelves, she read the titles on the tattered spines, whispering the sounds of the letters. Some weren't books at all, just bundles of thick, yellowing pages. Many of the words were unfamiliar and some were so faded that even the most clear-sighted person would fail to decipher them.

Some were simply titled with strings of peculiar shapes. They didn't look like letters at all. There were books devoted to the treatment of gout and piles and the ridding of worms and moths. There were scientific periodicals on the constellations of the heavens and ancient, battered works on alchemy and hedge magic. There were books for couples desperate for a child and pamphlets to make them behave better once they arrived. She opened a volume that bore a bloom of dusty mould on its blackish leather binding, to a page with a list of instructions to make

Lady Delafountaines Strengthining
Pills.

Take the Jaw bone of a Pyke,
dried and beeten to powder.
Take Venice turpentine of the
bignesse of a nutmeg, steep it all night
in white vinigar being prick'd full of
holes and drie it.
Make it in sugar pilles and take
three, nine mornings together.
Eat not for an hour, the pilles
must be as bigge as a hazle nut.

She pushed the book back into its space between its companions and let her fingers trail along a little more. She opened a smaller one, bound in brown paper, but the letters fidgeted disturbingly on the page, wriggling to the edge as though they were trying to escape and she shut it in fright.

Warily, she tugged a thin volume, which felt strangely cold to the touch. It was stuck. The books were crammed in but not enough to make it stick so fast. Fuelled by its stubbornness, because she was made of the same stuff, Cora decided it must come out and tugged hard, harder, harder still until it jerked, the top part of the spine coming down without the rest of the book. Thinking she'd broken it, she hastily tried to put it right. But she couldn't, because it wasn't a book at all.

It was a lever.

A door-like section of the bookshelves, not much wider than herself, swung away to reveal nothing but musty blackness, until the dim light found a pair of eyes in which to gleam.

At first, Cora didn't know the scream was coming from her own mouth.

When the eyes lifted, she recognised the terrifying wraith from the attic in the house on Fish Row.

She fell backwards into the table, knocking glass bowls and crucibles from their clamps and sending boiling liquids in steaming arcs.

The dove was flapping frantically, making the birdcage swing and jig.

Cora couldn't stop screaming.

The trapdoor at the top of the stairs was flung up and she heard Tom's voice 'Wenna!' he was shouting. 'Wenna are you alright? I'm coming!'

He'd thundered almost to the bottom when Cora turned, not knowing whether to hide, to ask who the hell Wenna was or to run into his arms.

They stared at each other, breathing hard.

Cora struggled out from behind the table, away from the ghastly dark and the phantom behind the books. Tom was gaping at her, confusion bringing his eyebrows together and apart.

She'd thought so much about this moment, planned it so carefully in her head, yet here they were, flung chaotically together.

She lifted a hand self-consciously to her temple, to the sparse black threads where her sugar-brown hair used to curl. He moved closer. She looked up. She wasn't much higher than his elbow. She'd been level with his jaw before. Her eyes were different too. The irises were unnaturally big and no longer blue but deep, violet grey.

'Cora?' His voice was almost a whisper, his hand moving towards her, hesitantly, as if about to recoil. 'You're not... I mean, is it you?'

She nodded, speechless, clogged with emotion, tears blurring her sight. Would he accept her, like this? Could he love her, like this?

In answer to her silent question he took her in his arms, as gently as he could, and she felt his resistance. Misery squeezed her heart until she realised that it wasn't disgust or fear that made him pull back, but concern that he'd let his acute relief take over and crush her.

She drew his sawdust smell deep into her lungs and felt his hand move up to cradle the back of her head, as gently as if she was made of glass. His gladness at having her back needed no speech, it was all in the raggedness of his breath. And that was how they stayed, both struck dumb.

'Ah.' Eseld's voice came from miles away.

Cora kept her eyes closed, buried deep in Tom's shirt.

After a moment, when they still hadn't responded, Eseld cleared her throat. 'What you doing home then?'

'That all you got to say, Mamm-wynn?' Tom's grip on Cora tightened, as he stared at his grandmother.

'How long's she been down here? You know I been sick with worry, turning the town over looking for her, losing my voice shouting in the woods and on the moor.' His last word cracked and Cora thrilled with pleasure and pain, something she hadn't felt in so long, it was exquisite.

'Have you?' she managed to say, her voice thick as she lifted her face to his, 'you been worrying about me?'

'Course I have, you duffer.' He bent to kiss the top of her head. 'What happened to you?' he stroked her strange, feathery hair and the warmth of his fingers made her shiver, 'where you been?'

'It's all a bit...' she mumbled, 'I mean, I can't hardly understand it myself.'

'Why don't I stick the kettle on and we can...' Eseld stopped, distracted by a quiet click as the gap in the bookshelves closed.

For just a moment, Cora's joy at seeing Tom again had eclipsed the fear of the spectre behind the books.

'There's summat in there!' She gripped fistfuls of Tom's shirt, ripping one hand away to point. 'Summat hideous, unnatural's what it is!'

The books looked undisturbed, quietly gathering dust.

To Cora's astonishment, instead of looking worried, or even curious, Tom just smiled.

'That's Wenna,' he said calmly, trying to pluck Cora's small, bony fists from his shirt buttons as he gestured towards the bookshelf. 'She's been staying here because... well,' his expression clouded, 'she ain't safe.'

He looked to Eseld to explain.

'You heard of priest holes?' Eseld asked.

Cora was too frightened to listen. She refused to let go of Tom even as he moved towards the books. She tried to use her diminutive, determined body to bar his way. 'What? No! Tom you don't understand, it ain't a person in there, it's some sort of, I dunno, some sort of demon! It's followed me here, I brought it over from the other side by accident, during a seance!'

Both Tom and Cora glanced imploringly at Eseld, who'd obviously wanted to explain things one at a time, to fold each fact like laundry, crisp from the line, but who wore the look of someone chasing washing whipped away by an unexpected gale.

'Right,' Eseld sighed, 'all right. First things first. Get out of the way you two.' She bustled past the struggling couple and yanked the metal book-lever down. The secret door swung open as before, but only a few inches.

This time, it was stopped by something.

Chapter Five

Worms

Eseld set a mug of tea on the hearth and lowered herself wearily beside the fire, which she prodded with a poker, sending a shower of sparks up around the cooking pot, briefly illuminating the creases of her face. She tugged a half-darned stocking from a basket and, as she spoke, threaded mossy green wool through the eye of a large needle.

Cora could hardly bear to look. The ghoul was curled on the bed, her bed, wrapped in a shawl, gazing forward with horrible, yellow eyes. It seemed much more substantial now. It no longer wavered in smoke-like pieces, juddering and parting like a reflection on water, as it had in the attic. Now it was a whole, solid shape, with head, torso, arms and legs like a human, but a disfigured, disproportionate one.

With a deep sigh and a look that told Cora to stop staring, Eseld began.

'You might have noticed, Cora love, that you ain't the only creature down here, in need of care.'

Cora blinked, 'I'm the only human though, ain't I?!' She shot the creature a dark, suspicious look.

'Now,' Eseld paused, mid-stitch. 'I'm afraid that ain't strictly true.'

'Giss on,' Tom frowned even as he grinned at his grandmother, as if to ask her, respectfully, not to tease.

'That thing ain't human!' Cora gasped. 'It's a-a demon!'

'I weren't referring to Wenna who, as you rightly

say, ain't human. She ain't a demon neither, but we'll get to that,' Eseld said, meeting Cora's gaze with a far steadier one of her own. 'There's no easy way to tell you this Cora love, and God knows we been shilly-shallying enough, but I'm afraid you ain't human neither, not any more.'

Eseld drew a breath. Nobody else did. The silence thickened.

'That blackbird, d'you remember?' Eseld said. 'What was beside you on the bed?'

Cora nodded, numb.

'Well, when we got you out the painting there weren't much of you left.' She cleared her throat. 'Nothing biological anyway. So I needed to, well, I needed blood. And bones and brain and heart and all the rest of it, to regrow you. That's why your hair's...' She gestured towards Cora's inky, threadbare crop, 'and I've a feeling it's why you're off your food an' all. Which reminds me, try this.'

She delved in her apron pocket and pulled out a small tin, with a chipped advert on it for Buchan's carbolic soap.

'What is it?' It felt too light to contain food. Cora started, gingerly, to pull off the lid. She didn't question Eseld's curious tale about the blackbird. It didn't make sense, but nothing did anymore.

Upon opening the tin, her face puckered in revulsion. 'Worms?!'

'Try one, go on.' Eseld nodded encouragingly. 'Think about it, your mind is your own, but your body,' She made a see-sawing gesture with her hand. 'I reckon that bird belly's yearning for something a little more fresh. Bit more wriggly.'

Tom shot his grandmother a sidelong glance, as

though she might be losing her marbles. 'Now, Mamm-wynn, this is- I mean, Cora don't want to eat no bulugens. She's been through the mill, is all.' He swallowed, a little green, as though he was the one being offered a tin of earthworms. 'Just needs time to build up her strength.'

Eseld raised her eyebrows and drew Tom's attention to the untouched plate of mutton and dumplings, a waxen layer of cold fat congealed on top of the gravy. 'Brought that down myself last night, steaming it was, the angel's theirselves could smell it and were a-begging for a taste. Left it out in case she got peckish, but no. Sort of thing the old Cora would have wolfed down, almost swallowing my hand! But you barely noticed it, did you my duck?' The light in her eyes was gentle, bright with intellect. 'Said the smell turned your stomach.'

Cora felt strange. The mutton looked like something in a tomb, amongst mouldering spears, intended for a forgotten king's afterlife. Whereas the worms were actually decidedly tempting, slithering over each other, pink and plump as they lifted and twitched their heads, or it could have been their tails. Their movements were mesmerising. She could smell them. It was a rich, flesh and earth smell. Even the lingering carbolic odour didn't put her off and before she could stop herself, her hand was in the tin and she was munching delicious, squishy worms, their texture like whelk, but muddier, without the salt tang of the sea.

When she looked up, Tom's mouth was pulled into a gagging shape.

By contrast, Eseld allowed herself a triumphant little smile as she continued darning.

'Do you have to keep on with that?' Tom demanded, his ears growing pink.

'I do, yes.' Eseld replied, taking a long drink from her steaming tin mug, as though nothing out of the ordinary had occurred. 'If I get this done while I'm a-sitting down, then I can get the fence mended and those branches chopped into logs afore it gets dark, then gut the pilchards and you've got a chance of supper tonight. Or would you prefer me to fry this stocking up to go with your spuds? It'd save me a bit of time.' She winked at Cora, who was sucking bits of worm from between her teeth.

Tom scowled, especially when Cora couldn't resist popping the last worm in her mouth and pushing a particularly twitchy end between her lips. She knew she should have been horrified at the very thought, but the hunger was just too acute. She felt much better having eaten, as though her blood was richer for it. Amazed, she found herself wondering whether beetles and slugs tasted this good.

'Right, so, that's that out of the way,' Eseld turned her work to weave the stitches in the other direction, creating a lattice of green over the grey.

'Let me do the other one,' said a high, clear voice with a crystal edge, the way only the wealthiest of the visitors to Fish Row spoke, the ones with the big, trembling feathers in their hats and scented, velvet capes.

Cora was stunned. It could only have been the horrible creature on her bed that had spoken, but she didn't believe it. Surely a demon couldn't talk, without a host to possess? It rose unsteadily and walked, a little stooped, over to Eseld, to pick up Meg's other stocking and Cora's fear settled into a quiet loathing. It carried the limp woollen garment back, clutched in a bony grey hand. It was female, she realised, both by the voice and the fact that the rags she wore resembled a tattered gown. With a quiet dignity, she sat back down and proceeded to darn, not with the quick, practised skill of Eseld's fingers, but with the hesitancy of one who has only recently learned.

'Thank you, dear.' Eseld beamed. 'Now,' she scratched her forehead. 'Everything's back to front. Cora, I'd rather have introduced you to Wenna as soon as you woke up, but things being what they are, I thought...' She cleared her throat and started again. 'I reckoned that if you understood how things can take a turn for, let's say, for the unexpected,' she gestured towards the empty worm tin, 'then you might be more able to accept our friend, and her er, difficult circumstances.'

Eseld gave Wenna an encouraging smile, briefly returned.

'She ain't like us and, round here, we don't often get folks what ain't related to us or somebody we know, do we? Unless they're with a travelling show o' course. So, I reckoned, once you'd realised that you were different now, too, you might be better able to manage the notion of others being, um, different as well.' She faltered to a stop.

'It's only temporary, though, ain't it?' Cora said. 'I mean, I won't be like this for long will I?'

Eseld was grave. She spoke carefully, as though to somebody just waking up. 'Cora. You had almost completely gone. The hex was so severe, I could only find dregs of you, of your spirit I mean, barely that, to bring back.' She sipped her tea, staring over the rim. 'Course, I'd no idea where you'd end up. All I could do was get you away from her and all her poison. I mean, I tried to aim for your house, but I didn't know what form you'd be in. So you took a while to find.'

Cora stared at her. It was Eseld, she realised, who'd stuck her in that awful painting!

'A hex?' she managed to say. 'Someone put a hex on me? Like a- witch?'

Eseld hesitated, before she replied. 'Witch is a tricksy word. Bit like bird, innit? There's all kinds. You wouldn't mistake a blue-tit for a buzzard now, would you? Or a dove for a vulture?'

Cora didn't know what a vulture was, but she got the point. She glanced up at the bunches of herbs, the potions and the books.

Eseld sipped her tea. 'The hex,' she paused again, her eyes growing dark, 'was a vile one. She didn't just want you dead, else she'd have wasted no time at all. She wanted you more than dead, as good as evaporated. Nothing left. Not even the memories of you in other people's heads. She can do that, you know.'

'Who can?' Cora was clammy and light-headed. She wanted to curl up and run away at once. 'Who are you talking about?'

'Morgelyn Glasse.' Tom was the one who said it, the name rolling over his breath in a heavy sigh, the 's' like the crashing hiss of a breaking wave. 'She took the Faery throne by force, murdering everyone what...' He glanced at Wenna, then added in a softer tone. 'Everyone what stood in her way and cursing the rest.'

'Hang on.' Cora swallowed. 'Fairies? Are you

mad? You're saying you believe in *fairies*?'

There was a muffled snort of laughter from Wenna.

'I don't see what's funny,' Cora snapped, her voice shaking slightly. She wanted to warn them about the ghoulish apparition in the attic. Could it have been a premonition? A warning from the spirit world not to trust this monster? She couldn't bring the words to her mouth. What if they thought she was mad? What if the creature grew violent? She gathered her courage together, knotting it in her chest. 'What I want to know is, what was it, *she*, doing in my attic, scaring me half to death?'

'It was an accident,' Wenna said, quietly. 'I'm sorry I frightened you. I was scrying,' she frowned as she pulled the darning wool too tight, making the hole wrinkle. 'I was speaking with Petrok, my old tutor, when someone burst in and smashed his blackstone. That sent my image flying off to...' she coughed and Eseld shot her a meaningful look. 'It interrupted the thread, so instead of Petrok and I seeing each other as projected images, I appeared before you instead. I'm terribly sorry it alarmed you.' Something in her eyes seemed genuine. Intelligent.

Cora tore her gaze away.

Black magic, she surmised, her blood running cold. The devil's work. This creature had come from the other side to punish her for her fraud and now she'd twisted Tom and Eseld's perception, so they saw only its wicked disguise. They saw someone who needed shelter, instead of the demon that was really there. But when she looked into the strange, yellow eyes of the creature, Cora saw only gentleness. A bible verse sprang into her mind.

"Be sober, be vigilant, because your adversary the devil, as a roaring lion, walketh about, seeking whom he may devour." **1 Peter 5:8**

'No, Cora,' the creature said. 'I'm no devil.'

'What about the attic?'

'I told you. I was simply using my blackstone to communicate. It's just like writing a letter. There's nothing sinister about it. Imagine the postmaster made a mistake and you received a letter in error, one that was meant for somebody else.'

Nobody had ever written to Cora. She was about to ask Wenna why she'd laughed but, before the words were out, Wenna parted her dry, curiously wizened lips to ask 'why did I laugh?'

Disturbed, Cora nodded.

'Because you ridiculed Tom for believing in faeries, while you were practically sitting next to one,' she chuckled again and Cora felt the tiny hairs prickle on the back of her neck.

'I should've introduced you properly.' Eseld snipped the wool. 'Cora Blackthorn, meet Wenna Skyburiow, Queen of Underwood.'

Cora stared, doubting everything now. If Eseld thought this haggard monster was a queen, she must be mad.

Wenna's smile began to fade.

Cora remembered the bizarre way she'd answered her questions, reading her mind like a mesmerist. Demon or not, she didn't like it. Quickly, she tried to think of something nice to say. To think. 'Your um, English is good.'

Wenna's smile turned to wax. 'I should think it

would be, seeing as I am English.'

Cora blinked.

'There are many Britons, besides the ones represented here,' Wenna added, rather coolly.

No-one spoke for a moment. After a long pause, Eseld asked 'do you remember going into Underwood, Cora love?'

Cora blinked, recalling the dreamy warmth of trees and pools. It couldn't have been a real country, surely? The truth wasn't plausible, yet other people knew about it. It even had a name. *Underwood.* 'Yes,' she said quietly. 'I remember.'

'And the huge tree you went into, the Great Oak. Do you remember much of that?'

'There was a ballroom and a feast. And dozens of mirrors. I wish I was back there.'

Wenna snorted.

'Don't say that,' Eseld snapped.

'But it's true.' Cora sighed, closing her eyes, 'it were paradise.' She paused, opening her eyes again, hazy memories drifting through her mind, changing shape. 'Although, there were something odd about it. Something that weren't quite right.' She frowned in recollection, 'I think my foot might've been broken, but it didn't hurt.' She glanced down at the baggy child's socks covering her new, raspberry-pink feet. 'How did you know I was there?'

'We watched you,' Eseld replied gently, 'with Wenna's blackstone. But it don't show everything.'

The others were quiet, until Wenna murmured 'was it full of flowers and ferns and butterflies? Was it warm? Did everybody smile at you?'

Cora nodded.

'That was a fake magic-lantern version you saw.

Morgelyn's doing. She gave you a dose of glamour to blur your senses.' She met Cora's eyes with a bitter gaze. 'She can only create illusions. Nothing real. Always remember that. She can only distort and destroy.'

'You're talking as if I was drugged!' Cora retorted. 'Nobody gave me anything.'

'Glamour is a drug.' Eseld said. 'It's as strong as opium or wormwood, but much worse on your innards.' She gestured towards Cora's torso. 'Did anything get in your eyes? Before you were called, I mean.'

Cora tried to remember. 'I don't think so.'

They were silent for a moment, until Cora ventured 'there was a butterfly. With tattered wings.' She glanced down at her hand. 'I remember, because it looked sort of dead, only moving. I followed it, because it was so strange. That's when I stumbled into the mineshaft. Like a tuss.'

Wenna said 'they've been making more of them. Thin places. Traps.'

'Making what?' Cora swallowed.

'Thin places. Sort of portals, where you can slip from one realm into another. Practitioners of poisoned magic can create them almost anywhere. Those of us who use pure, unadulterated magic need to find naturally occurring ones. That must be what they did with the mineshaft. Turned it into a thin place.'

'But why bother?' Cora said. 'Why wait until I was out on the moor? Why not get me at home? Anyone could have come in with our regulars, especially with a mourning veil on. Nobody checks what's... what's underneath.' She stole another glance at Wenna's bizarre features. Her eyes were just a little too far apart. Her nose a fraction too high. Her browbone a little prominent. Apart from the shrivelled, grey skin, each feature taken individually could probably pass for human but, as a whole, taken together, definitely wasn't.

Wenna turned away.

Eseld said 'they couldn't have got you at Fish Row. I put a few bits an' bobs around.' Cora glanced at the bundle of herbs, copper nails and open scissors above the bed. 'But you'd never been inside,' she breathed, ''til you got me out the painting.'

'I got a friend. Keeping an eye on things. She's been stitching buttons and salt in the hems of your curtains for years. Poking fresh elder twigs into the underside of your mattress, every time she turns it. Sprinkling dried cuckoo-pint roots and stitchwort petals into the pot-pourri. She even dropped foxglove seeds under the boards when the floor was taken up, when they were a-fixing that burst water pipe. The whole house is reinforced with natural binders. No poisoned magic can be done in there.'

It took Cora a moment before she whispered 'Killigrew?'

'Course. Didn't you never wonder why she stayed?'

'I didn't think she had anywhere else to go.'

'Patience of a saint, that girl. Morgelyn sent the butterfly too, or at least, the illusion of it, to entice you to exactly the right spot. In the mirrored ballroom, did you see anything smooth and black? Maybe with blood or summat burned on it? And was there a smell? A sort of bitter treacly smell?'

Cora tried to remember. She had seen a smooth

black table. With spilled liquid on it and a small pile of ash.

Wenna grimaced. 'Morgelyn's attempt at a blackstone. She doesn't have a real one. She uses it to go seeing and to create her illusions. What you saw was the remains of the butterfly whose image she sent up into the moor.'

Eseld spoke softly. 'She used it to watch you, Cora love. She will have dropped bits of butterfly into her moving picture of you, running through the snow. She used it to call you.' She said this calmly but, all the while, she and Wenna were having another, private conversation with their eyes.

Cora's features grew slack. It was too much to take in. 'I weren't called,' she mumbled. 'I just fell.'

'You didn't,' Eseld added, as if Cora's head wasn't already too full of new information to think straight. 'You didn't fall beyond the first bit of the mineshaft. She just made it feel that way, so it would make sense to you.'

If Cora hadn't been so bewildered, she'd have laughed at the idea of any of this making sense.

'There's a reason Morgelyn called you-' Eseld began.

Cora interrupted 'I fell.'

'You were called,' Eseld and Wenna said, in unison, catching each other's eye with a rueful smile. 'Else you couldn't have got down into Underwood at all,' Eseld continued. 'I know it seemed like you just slipped,' she added, more gently, 'but you can't get into Underwood without magic.'

'But I did,' Cora insisted. She didn't know why she was being defensive. She was just so sick of pretence, exhausted by the lies at the house on Fish Row. She was fed up of this nonsense about an underland too. All she wanted now was truth, however hard it was to believe. 'I fell down a mineshaft and must've, I don't know, bumped my head. Had a funny dream.'

'Even the deepest mineshafts have a bottom.' Wenna said.

'An' if that were true', Eseld added, 'you'd still be down there. With broken legs, probably a broken neck. But you ain't. She brought you out of our world mid-tumble. Nobody can get into Underwood without magic. Just the way it is.'

'But why would Morgelyn, is that her name? Why would she call me down there? She don't even know I exist.'

Eseld and Wenna exchanged glances. Tom shifted uncomfortably. She found his hand and he gently squeezed it.

Although she dreaded the answer, Cora was determined to know. 'How does this Morgelyn woman know me? Why would she bother about me?'

Eseld silenced her with a lifted hand. 'That's for another time,' she said gently, planting her hands on her knees to push herself upright. 'Oh, two more things,' she said, swallowing the last of her tea and picking a bit of brown leaf off her tongue. 'Then you must get some rest.' She fixed Cora with her bright blue eyes. 'Did you eat anything, while you were there?'

Cora frowned, trying to remember. 'I bit something. An apple maybe? Or it might have been marzipan. And I ate a bit of a bowl I think. Sounds odd I know. Maybe I'm remembering it wrong. There was all this food, but they offered me an empty bowl. Tasted lovely, mind. Like gingerbread.'

'Think yourself lucky,' Eseld was grim. She set the finished stocking down in her basket, peering through her spectacles at a glass jar, where split seed pods and bits of beetle were infusing in a yellowish liquid.

Cora stared at her. 'Lucky?'

'If I hadn't regrown your stomach, you'd have had an unpleasant few days worth of enemas and emetics and whatnot to get it all out.'

Cora flushed, embarrassed at the mention of such things in front of Tom and annoyed at the implication that her last few days had been remotely lucky.

But it was Tom who asked 'why? Get what out?'

'Glamour. When it's put in your eyes, it wears off. But if you eat the stuff, well, it gets in your bones, you ain't never really right again.' Eseld moved towards the stairs. 'Right, I need to get on and you,' she pointed at Tom, 'ought to get back to work. What are you doing home anyway?'

Giving Cora one last, lingering kiss on the forehead, which made her flush pink, Tom unwillingly followed his grandmother up and out of the cellar, explaining something about a tool he'd needed.

Cora and Wenna remained in the cellar, awkward silence filling the gap that Tom and Eseld had left.

Wenna continued with her darning, the clumsy, childish stitches making her a bit less frightening.

Hastily, Cora crushed the thought. She touched her brow, which had become damp, and pulled her memories apart, as though rummaging through the clutter in the attic again, trying to recall some of the words that Wenna had used before. She glimpsed a name and grabbed it. 'Peter! What were you trying to tell your friend, Peter?'

'Petrok.' Wenna smiled, obviously caring for him a great deal. 'Before the uprising, he was chief adviser to my parents, as well as the dean of the university.'

'University?' Cora spluttered, unable to help herself. 'But you all live in trees!'

Wenna paused, her needle stiff in mid-air, and Cora noticed how straight her eyebrows were, before she said 'universities needn't be enclosed in stone or brick. Scholars have been graduating from Underwood since long before they built the colleges of Oxford. When the Danes came to slaughter monks for trinkets, many came below to seek refuge with us. The Danes were too terrified to follow, once we showed them what we could do.' Her eyes flashed and, for the first time, Wenna looked every inch a queen. 'Not that the starlanders remember any of that now,' she added, with a slight flare of her nostrils.

'Who are the starlanders?' Cora asked, keeping her voice even. She didn't dare ask what a Dane was.

'You, humanity. For anybody down in Underwood, you live up above our sky, you see, where the stars are?' She pointed upward with a wizened grey finger. With a jolt, Cora noticed she had no nails.

Cora nodded, glad to latch on to something logical, if anything about the last few days could be called that. 'Why do you call it Underwood then?' she asked. 'Surely for you, before you discovered Cornwall was up here, it was just sky?'

Wenna smiled. 'That's a very intelligent question.'

Cora found herself smiling too, heartened.

'Long ago,' Wenna said softly, 'humans and faeries shared the kingdoms of Britain, along with many other folk. I won't pretend they lived in peace, not all the time, but they managed well enough. There were many kinds of human back then. And many kinds of faery. All living up here together, in the Starlands, before war and famine drove us below. Some say the two aren't the separate species they seem, but distant, hominid cousins, the relatives in between having died out. There are those who believe that Underwood was the name given to our country by a refugee from the Starlands, because everybody winced when he tried to pronounce *Eardlufu*, the name my ancestors gave it when they created it, so he started calling it Underwood, which stuck. His name was Merlin. Have you heard of him? I'd be surprised if you haven't.'

Cora thought hard, she had a vague recollection of a story about an old wizard called Merlin and a boy king. Arnold, or was it Arthur? She didn't want to appear ignorant so she nodded, about to reply, then remembered Wenna could read her thoughts anyway, and the words dried on her tongue.

'He's existed in stories and songs for hundreds of years as a magician, mathematician, astronomer and poet,' Wenna said. 'It's impossible for him to have done all the things he's famous for. Like many great people, tales of his life have been padded by the minds, quills and mouths they've passed through over the centuries. Something we know for certain is that Merlin, a human, and Queen Mab, a faery, were lovers. They fled to Underwood together, once Arthur had passed a law in Cornwall making it illegal for humans and faeries to marry.'

Cora nodded, trying to digest Wenna's words and trying even harder not to stare at any particular part of her. She found everything about her physical appearance both repulsive and fascinating. She'd always imagined fairies to be beautiful, with translucent wings, small enough to alight on her hand.

'Some of us were beautiful,' Wenna's features hardened, 'once. Like humans, we were a mixture of everything between beauty and ugliness. We didn't look like...' She let her head hang for a moment, swallowing hard. When she lifted her yellow eyes, Cora saw a flinty sadness there that refused to give in to tears, 'like this,' she finished, flicking her fingers briefly towards her face.

'But that's not what matters.' She moved closer, fixing Cora with a gaze so intense, it stopped her breath. 'The curse killed us. We're dead, but still moving. Feeling. We no longer breathe or eat or age or sleep. That butterfly, before she burned it in order to use its image, was physically dead, but in its heart it was alive, like everything in Underwood. When Morgelyn first sent it, you saw it as it really was, because you hadn't yet been blinded by the glamour. You see me, now, as I am. But if your eyes were filled with glamour again, you'd see me quite differently.

I can see your memories, Cora, and your thoughts. For me, they float visibly around your head. Lady Ursell appeared to be beautiful didn't she? But that's not what she actually looks like at all. Her skin is like mine. Wenna pinched the grey flesh of her arm between a nailless finger and thumb. It stayed puckered, stiff as clay, before she smoothed it again.

Wenna paused, looking as though she'd sipped something bitter. 'Lady Ursell has the coldest eyes I've ever seen, always did, even before the curse. The costly fabrics and jewels are real enough though. Being a traitor has its rewards.'

'But how can you be dead?' Cora felt dizzy. 'It's impossible! You couldn't speak without breath!'

Wenna nodded. 'I know. But if you apply logic, you couldn't have been regrown from a blackbird corpse either, could you? Magic is the most troublesome of the sciences. You'll find it has little room for logic. We faeries have magic in our veins, even though the blood is gone. But Morgelyn had to learn all she knows.'

'Like Eseld?'

Wenna nodded. 'Morgelyn's magic is different though. Jealousy and greed are what fire her. Wicked intent poisons her magic, that's why it's no longer pure. While good magic smells of life, of greenness and renewal, poisoned magic reeks of decay. Sulphur and bad eggs. She sweetens it artificially to cover the stench, but nothing new or real can ever come of it.' Wenna grew quieter, Meg's messily darned stocking crumpled in her lap.

'She was trying to murder the resistance but, instead, Morgelyn accidentally half-killed everything in Underwood, putting the curse of living death on all that breathed, including herself. It was like a gas explosion in a factory that fouls the air for miles around. She couldn't control it and every living creature was affected. She spread a rumour that my parents,' she swallowed, 'and I were to blame and many were quick to believe it. But a handful remained loyal. Most of them have disappeared. We don't fully die unless we are destroyed by fire, like the butterfly, or dismembered.'

Sickened, Cora couldn't stop herself blurting 'is that how...'

'How she killed my parents, yes.' Wenna was brisk, her pain obvious. 'Fire and knives. To make sure they couldn't ever come back.'

Both fell silent and for a while the only sound was the crack and spit of the logs.

For a wild moment, Cora hoped it was all a hoax. She wanted to find the trick, the cheat, the thing they didn't want her to look behind. But that was precisely how she'd found Wenna. Here, the hidden things weren't mundane, spell-breaking violin threads, wax hands or speaking tubes. Here, the hidden things were the extraordinary, the virtually unbelievable.

Everything on Fish Row was fake. Her aunt didn't love her, she just used her. Cora had no idea what Uncle Granville thought of her. She doubted whether he'd registered her disappearance at all. Here, in this strange cellar, surrounded by even stranger stories, Cora felt part of something real for the first time in her life.

'Are there any left, of the other folk I mean?' She hardly believed what she was asking. 'The ones you said shared Britain with humans and faeries?'

Wenna smiled and, not for the first time, Cora was struck by how very much older she seemed, compared to herself. 'Yes, Cora. There are others. And yes,' her grin broadened, 'I am very old.'

Cora returned the smile, though she couldn't quite make it reach her eyes. 'What did you mean,' she coughed and started again, trying to toughen up her small, bewildered voice, 'what did you mean when you said that Morgelyn isn't like a faery? I thought she was, well, one of you?'

Wenna shook her head. 'No, she isn't. She's is from a deeper place, nearer the centre of the earth. A hot, dark country where nothing rests. As far as we know she's the only one of her kind left. She's taken many kingdoms, besides Underwood, for her own. She's planning to do the same to Cornwall and after that, who knows? The rest of Britain? Maybe the rest of the world.'

Chapter Six

An Unexpected Visitor

By the next morning, Cora was almost back to her normal size. Her strange, blue-black hair reached her shoulders in neat points, looking more like feathers than ever, though when she peered at the individual strands, they seemed human enough. She'd tried to wind it into a coil at the nape of her neck, but pieces tended to slither out, regardless of how many pins she used. Her skin was peeling less, and the raw pinkness had calmed to a more natural hue. Her eyes were still a peculiar shade of violet-grey, the irises so large they left only tiny triangles of white at the corners and she had no eyelashes at all.

The Currigan family sat at the scrubbed pine table in the middle of the kitchen, eating breakfast. Tom had left much earlier, to be at the wheelwright's yard before dawn and Cora was disappointed to have missed him. She'd expected Wenna to be the object of the children's interest, but they were apparently quite used to her. It was her own self-conscious nibbling of worms and slugs from a chipped china bowl that drew their wide-eyed gaze.

'Are they cold or warm when you bite?' Curnow asked, his mouth copying Cora's as it closed to chew.

'Does them worms wriggle about in your tummy?' Gwen asked, her voice low and husky because she had a cold. 'Can you feel them squiggling?'

'Eat up your porridge,' Eseld said, pouring more tea. 'Stop pestering Miss Blackthorn. And don't wipe your nose on your sleeve, Gwen! Or what's the point o' giving you a hanky?'

As she stood up, pain prickled between Cora's shoulder blades, down her arms and through her fingers. It wasn't sore enough to make her gasp, but an odd, pin-like scratching, deep in her bones. Not wanting to make a fuss, she carried the pan and porridge bowls to the tiny scullery and plonked them in the sink, while Wenna helped Gwen dress for school and Meg chased Curnow with a comb.

It was wash day and Cora was glad to find she had enough strength to be of some use. Selina never let her do anything that might redden or dry out her hands, in case they no longer matched their wax counterparts. Her lack of experience was obvious. She struggled to carry the tub from the copper, sloshing hot water into the snow and making it steam, then she added the whole packet of laundry blue, instead of a single cube, to the final rinse.

Wenna hadn't had much practice either and Cora wondered whether Eseld would have got on better without them but, eventually, the three of them managed to scrub out most of the stains and get the steaming clothes through the mangle.

The sun was bright but there was no warmth in it. Cora's fingers were almost numb by the time they'd finished pegging the wet shifts, drawers and petticoats on the line and draping the sheets and bigger nightgowns over the spiky, leafless hedge.

Wenna wore a large shawl of Eseld's pulled forward over her head, to hide her face from any passer-by out gathering firewood. Cora, on the other hand, looked so much more normal now, she was able to wrap hers snugly around her shoulders and feel the winter breeze stir her peculiar hair.

The next morning, they spread a blanket over the table and warmed the irons. As they moved them across the weave, the sweet smell of beeswax rose from the hot metal as it pressed the peaks and crinkles smooth. But the burden that had been weighing upon Eseld and Wenna now bore down hard upon Cora too. She wanted to ask about Underwood and the resistance, but the unnerving notion that Morgelyn knew who she was made her questions catch in her throat.

'That one isn't hot,' Cora pointed out to Wenna, who was using a folded cloth to pick up an iron.

'I know,' she replied, setting it before the fire to warm up, 'but it'd burn me just the same.'

A vague memory stirred in the back of Cora's mind, 'I've heard that before,' she murmured.

Wenna gazed directly at her. 'Have you? Do you remember where?'

Eseld was focused on her task, but Cora sensed her ears pricking.

'Oh, some old folk tale I expect. I heard that faeries can't touch iron, that it drains their, your, strength.'

'It doesn't drain our strength, just burns our skin. Think, Cora. Who would have told you a tale like that?'

Cora shifted uncomfortably. 'I don't know,' she shrugged.

It really seemed to matter to Wenna, so Cora thought harder, delving into her memories. 'I don't know,' she said again. She'd never read the few, dusty books on the shelves at Fish Row and neither Aunt Selina nor Uncle Granville believed in the telling of stories. Nancarrow then? Before she changed so cruelly? No. She'd told tales certainly, when Cora was little, but they were ground firmly in human adventure. Smugglers and highwaymen, princesses and locked towers. There was the occasional mention of a fairy, but only as a wicked old hag or a shapeshifter leading men astray.

A scuffling sound came from the wall. Then came a shower of soot from the chimney that doused the flames and brought a black, lumpy creature thumping onto the hearth in a cloud of coal dust, making Cora cough. She stared in alarm as it stretched, extending a wing to peck delicately beneath, then flapped up towards Eseld. Beneath the soot, Cora glimpsed a warm, orange tint to its breast feathers. A robin! But surely they were smaller than that?

'Birds always look bigger indoors,' Wenna mused.

Cora wished she'd stop answering her thoughts like that, then realised Wenna could hear her and tried abruptly to empty her mind.

Wenna grinned.

The grubby little bird hopped into Eseld's hand. It opened its sharp little beak to whistle, cocking its head from side to side. Cora watched, fascinated, sensing a peculiar kinship with the bird. Her own head came to one side too, listening. Though she couldn't understand the twittering peeps, it sounded like language. To her astonishment, Eseld was nodding, evidently understanding every chirrup.

Gravely, Eseld turned to Wenna. 'Message from Hendra,' Eseld said, her nostrils flaring slightly. 'It'll be tonight.'

Just as Cora opened her mouth to ask what would be tonight, something made her stop. A hot, stinging energy that she'd never felt before crackled through her body.

The robin sensed it too. He shook himself into flight, scattering soot across a white chemise and disappearing back up the chimney.

'What is it?' Wenna asked, staring at Cora.

'I dunno...' Cora stammered, her nerves on fire. 'Danger!'

At that, there was a loud rap on the front door. Then came a series of bangs, which shook the hinges, as though whoever was knocking was using the side of their fist.

Eseld lifted the hatch. Wenna scuttled down to the cellar.

The door opened it to reveal Aunt Selina, sharp arms bent, hands on hips. The shadowed angles of her eyes and cheekbones chilled Cora's blood.

'Ha! So it's true!' Aunt Selina didn't wait to be invited, but marched right into the cottage. Cora's fear shrank the room, fading its colours. She felt sick. The dream was over. Her refuge was as flimsy as a soap bubble.

'Your hair looks awful,' Aunt Selina lifted a handful, her hands smelling of violet oil. 'A disguise was it? Cheap harlot's dye? What is it, walnut juice? Serves you right if it falls out of your stupid head. Come on.' She snatched Cora's hand, her leather-gloved grip cold as bone.

Cora struggled, but it was no use.

Aunt Selina towered over her.

Fear made her weak. She glanced wildly around, desperate for Eseld's voice to cut through it all, for her warm arms to fold around her, just as they had when she'd lifted her to be weighed.

But Eseld was nowhere to be seen. Stumbling, dragged almost horizontal, Cora caught sight of her straightening up from behind the table, a piece of green chalk in her hand and a strange gleam in her eyes.

It was then that Eseld started to mutter.

The words were similar to those Cora remembered her using when the bloody, feathered mass lay beside her on the mattress.

Aunt Selina's nostrils flared in contempt, the skin showing white, her words flying like sparks. 'How quaint. You actually believe your little hedge rituals can...'

She stopped, the broken sentence hanging in her mouth. There was a scraping sound. Leather soles on wood.

Her feet were sliding, shifting, the rag rug was gathering into stiff ripples as her boots pushed against it. More angry than afraid, Aunt Selina tried to twist and kick, her skirt swinging violently on its hoops, but she only slid faster towards a green chalk circle that Eseld had drawn upon the boards.

The cottage floor remained flat but, as if she was on the deck of a storm-tossed ship, the green circle drew Aunt Selina towards it with a power that was terrifying to watch. The anger in her face unspooled into horror and a scream escaped from her throat, before Eseld lifted just the tips of her fingers. Cora froze, astonished at the sudden silence that fell, swift and shocking as an axe blade.

Aunt Selina was no longer skidding. She stood upright in the green circle, striking the invisible walls of her prison with her feet and hands. The ring of chalk was the same circumference as her skirt, the brown, patterned fabric crushed into creases around the hem. She was still screaming, but without any sound.

Her gloved hands were pressed curiously flat in mid-air, as though against glass, and her eyes boiled with fear, veins standing out in the folds of flesh beneath them.

Eseld lowered her hands, emitting a sigh of exhausted satisfaction.

Selina's bonnet had tumbled off and hung at a broken angle on its ribbon, jolting with every furious kick as her horror gave way to rage. Eseld watched, patient as a parent waiting for a child's tantrum to burn itself out.

When she didn't stop, Eseld picked up the chemise that the robin had scattered with soot and gave it a good shake, trying to get the worst of it off. Tutting, she got a clothes brush and had a go with that, all the while ignoring Aunt Selina's silent rant.

Cora stared, dumb with astonishment, unable to take her eyes off her aunt. Her blood was fizzing and her arm burned where her aunt had gripped it. With enormous effort, she turned away but, whenever she blinked, the furious face remained, like an after-image of the sun.

She tried to see her as a woman. An angry, bitter woman and nothing more. She turned back and forced herself to focus on Aunt Selina's small, wet mouth and the slightly protruding front teeth that lifted her upper lip, but every time she let herself look into those eyes, a hundred beatings flooded back and she ached.

Not one to stand idle, Eseld resumed her work and soon the only sounds in the cottage were the crack and spit of the fire, the shake of cotton folds and the hush of sliding iron.

Cora did her best to follow Eseld's example, feeling as though she was acting a part in a play, and she lifted a tray cloth to fold it, her fingers trembling slightly. Eseld caught her eye and winked, her face clouded by steam from the damp fabric, which dried in smooth stripes in the iron's wake.

As they worked, Cora concentrated on the scents of beeswax and lavender water to avoid looking at her aunt. The hatch lifted and Wenna came up from the cellar, a tattered veil covering her face.

Aunt Selina paused for barely a second to register her, but was soon protesting violently again, kicking and punching the air as if was glass and might shatter.

With a weary sigh, Eseld went over to her. She pulled the chalk out of her apron pocket and rubbed it over her palm, turning her skin a pale green, then moved it in a jerky, back-and-forth motion, as though rubbing a clean patch on a dirty window. Cora half-expected to hear a faint squeak of glass, but caught only a string of peculiar words.

Aunt Selina's voice ripped through the cottage, cracking the air like cannon fire. 'You're a devil Eseld Liddicoat! A low, damned dirty devil! You're going straight to hell, you are! You're as damned as Jan Tregeagle!' Eseld moved her hand again, this time in the opposite direction, cutting Aunt Selina off. She slammed the air in mute fury.

'Right,' Eseld sighed through her nose, her mouth pressed into a thin line. 'Not ready to listen yet then.'

A smile was creeping across Wenna's face, just visible through the gauzy fabric.

'What?'

'If you could see what she's thinking!' Wenna grinned, wincing.

Eseld was grim. 'Just as well I can't.'

'What are we going to do with her?' Cora asked. Something inside her was unravelling. She'd never been able to observe Aunt Selina's rage with this kind of distance before. From a place of safety. It was as though her aunt had shrunk, the monster rendered human.

Eventually, Aunt Selina stopped kicking and thumping and sank miserably inside the circle, her dress puffing up around her like a giant soufflé. She lifted a shaking hand and its shadow hid her eyes. Only then could Cora observe the blotchy forehead, where anguish bunched the skin.

Eseld knelt beside Aunt Selina, reached into her pocket and coloured her palm again with the chalk. This time, instead of screamed insults, the cottage was filled with the startling sound of sobbing. Aunt Selina's shoulders heaved with each shuddering breath.

Cora had never seen her aunt cry. She was astounded that this uncanny trick could reduce her to tears. Wenna's face snapped up, eerily fuzzed by the veil. She came close to Cora's face, her back to Aunt Selina so that she couldn't read her lips, so close that, if she'd had breath, Cora would have felt it heat her skin.

'It isn't the circle that's making her cry.' Wenna whispered, answering her thoughts. 'Remember Cora, I can see what she's thinking. Selina's afraid, but that's not all that's troubling her.'

'Afraid? Of Eseld?'

'Yes, of course. And she's afraid of magic too. She

had no idea Eseld's magic was real. She didn't know *any* magic was real. But there's more. Your aunt has been abandoned by her lover. I saw her thinking of someone. A tall, thin man with a black moustache. He loves another.'

Deep down, where Cora never allowed herself to think, she knew. 'Victor,' Cora whispered.

'Victor Morningside,' Wenna grimaced. 'The image was blurred and he was moving away so fast, I had to make sure.'

Cora's eyes widened. 'You know him?'

Wenna nodded, placing a gloved finger on her lips. As she pressed the flimsy fabric against her skin, her face became more visible. Through it, Cora saw her features harden as she whispered 'yes, I know him. He calls himself the head of the secret guard. But he's nothing more than a common assassin. A kidnapper. He's the one who betrayed my parents.'

Chapter Seven

Skin

Eseld checked the clock on the mantelpiece. 'The little ones'll be home soon', she murmured. Aunt Selina had wiped away her tears and simply glared, puffy-eyed, at Cora. Whenever Eseld gave her the chance to speak, she refused to say anything other than things like 'I'll get the law on you, Eseld Liddicoat. See if I don't.'

'What're we going to do with her?' Eseld jerked a thumb over her shoulder.

Wenna looked up. 'We have to hide her.'

Just as Cora was about to ask how you hide a fully grown woman in a tiny cottage against her will, she blanched, imagining shoving Aunt Selina, like Victor had shoved old Nellie Furze, into that cramped little space in the cellar behind the books.

'No Cora, nothing so drastic,' Wenna shook her head. Then she lifted her veil, revealing her face. Aunt Selina's bunched features shot apart in a silent shriek.

They put the folded linen away in various chests and cupboards, dropping muslin bags filled with dried sage, lavender and rosemary on top, to keep the moths out. Aunt Selina gestured frantically all the while, jabbing her finger at Wenna. They ignored her.

Once they'd finished, Wenna cut the top off a raw egg and stirred it with a rowan twig to break up the yolk. She used the twig to dab the gooey mixture onto the green chalk circle, while Eseld divided a scraggy bunch of rue and cowbane into two. Each of them held a handful of the stalks, flecked with papery yellow and white flowers, to the fire, until the leaves glowed. They started murmuring the strange words again, and the air held traces of the curious, crushed nettle smell of natural magic. Cora watched through the veil of smoke that rose from the herbs to coil in unnatural patterns, twisting around Aunt Selina's body, as she began to vanish, bit by bit, before Cora's eyes, like a pencil drawing being obliterated with a piece of India rubber.

Aunt Selina didn't seem upset, nor even frightened. She didn't seem aware of the smoke or what was happening at all. She remained sitting, frowning, arms tightly folded as the last traces of her disappeared.

'It won't harm her,' Wenna said. 'She's merely hidden from view while we decide what to do with her. Meg will be home soon, we'll explain and she'll look after the children while we're with the guild. The meeting must come first.'

'Meeting? What meeting?'

'You'll see soon enough,' Eseld replied distractedly.

Despite everything, Cora didn't like to leave her aunt in her strange, invisible cell.

She reminded herself of the scars, the shame and the misery she'd endured for as long as she could remember and she gazed at the whitewashed stones of the cottage wall, knowing her aunt was there, though her eyes insisted she wasn't. It made her queasy and she turned away.

'Won't Meg find it all very strange?' Cora asked, trying not to look at the pale ring of chalk, with its sticky coating of egg, as Eseld came away from the window, calling out that she'd spotted the children coming through the trees in the fading light.

'No,' Eseld tried to smile, but her eyes were just a little too bright. 'It'd take more than this to upset poor Meg. I'll have a word before we go.'

Cora wanted to ask what she meant about Meg, but Wenna quieted her with a small shake of her head.

At the lifting of the latch, three chilly children were ushered inside to warm up by the fire, their cracked boots leaving wet, muddy prints on the tiles. Eseld hung their dripping hats and coats on nails on the wall.

After a meal of creamy parsnip soup, beef tea and bread for the family and raw scraps of bacon for Cora, Eseld kissed Meg on top of her head.

'Tom and Piran will meet us there, straight from work,' she said, ruffling the little one's hair. Gwen barely noticed, busy as she was with wrapping her rag doll in a scrap of blanket.

At his grandmother's kiss, a small frown appeared between Curnow's brows, and he smoothed his hair back into place, static causing the finer strands to lift.

The meeting of the Spindleberry Guild was nothing like Cora had imagined. When they'd first mentioned it, she'd pictured dusty, wood-panelled walls, forms filled out in triplicate and pompous middle-aged men in straining waistcoats, fiddling with shiny fob watches. She assumed they'd be walking towards the clustered chimneys of the town, where rooftops thick with snow gleamed blue beneath the moon, which was only half-visible, like a silver coin pushed into a penny-slot machine. The hidden half was just like Aunt Selina, she thought. There, but not there.

Instead, Eseld and Wenna took her along a path that wound deeper into the woods, where the snow was patchy between roots and rotting leaves.

'Is it far?' Cora asked, nervously. She wore Meg's woollen cape, which was still damp, and wished she was curled up by the fire. The lantern swung slightly, with the rhythm of Eseld's steps, casting a shifting orb of light over the muddy path, alighting now and then on cracked, dry bark. A stiff breeze blew through the branches, making them creak and shiver and, in the gathering gloom, Cora saw trees that had fallen during the storms around Michaelmas, still stuck at strange angles, as though stunned and leaning on each other for support.

She hadn't ventured outside the cottage garden since they'd brought her there, in the apothecary jar. It felt like a lifetime ago and in a way, she supposed it was. Her feet hurt, her toes were squashed and sore in borrowed boots, which had been too big the day before. The sound of the wind mingled with tumbling water, which grew louder as the path took them downhill to run alongside a stream that rushed over glossy stones covered in fronds of green weed that dragged in the current like mermaids hair.

Cora had never been so deep into the woods.

The branches met above the water and the path was precariously narrow, with the stream rushing noisily on one side and waist-high brambles clogged with dead, brown ferns on the other. Only a little snow had made its way down through the tightly knotted trees and the curled leaf drifts from autumn lay undisturbed, quietly disintegrating. Cora felt dozens of eyes following their progress, though she saw none. The undergrowth twitched. Rooks croaked in warning. The skeletal trees rocked their branches, as if urging them on. She thought of foxes and badgers curled under the earth, rank breath forming tiny clouds, sharp teeth edged in fur. Threads of root poking into their burrows.

She tried hard not to think about the peculiar land below the moor, the strange grins that had appeared so unnaturally on the faces there or the horrible crunch as the beautiful queen cut her hair. She tried even harder not to think about what Wenna had said about Victor Morningside. She'd always know he was a villain, but it never crossed her mind that he wasn't human. Or was he? Did Wenna actually say he wasn't? He looked human enough.

The more she tried not to think about it, the more difficult it became.

She shivered, dark twigs trembling around her as though it was fear, not wind, that made them shake. She felt thin and frayed, threadbare as fabric that's been washed and worn too many times. She longed for that sweet, fuzzy softness she'd felt by the pool down in Underwood, despite Wenna and Eseld's warnings about glamour and its dangers. Surely it was worth it occasionally, just to soften the edges of reality, when it was too much to bear?

Wenna turned around and Cora almost bumped into her, barely keeping her balance. 'What is it?' she whispered.

Wenna rested her hands on Cora's elbows. She sounded reassuring, but her expression was stony. 'I don't want you longing for glamour, Cora. It's poison. It's addictive and it destroys people.'

'I'm not longing for it.' Cora retorted, her cheeks warming despite the chilly gusts.

Wenna turned her head a little, keeping her gaze on Cora, so that her yellow irises slid into the corners.

'All right,' Cora hung her head. 'I miss it. So what? I don't have any, and if it were offered me I wouldn't take it. Is it so bad to find all this just...' she waved her hand, 'a bit much?'

Wenna hesitated before she replied, and Cora remembered how much more Wenna had suffered. How much she'd lost. Cora's heart soaked up guilt like water, until it grew heavy and sank.

'No, Cora. There's nothing wrong with that. But we must face this with our eyes open. There's no point fighting in the dark.' Wenna turned to follow Eseld who'd stopped, a few feet ahead.

The lantern seemed to grow brighter, as the dusky blue air turned black. Now and then, wherever the trees were less dense, Cora glimpsed a few stars. They crossed a tiny footbridge and Cora felt like a moth, hovering as near to the lantern as she could, watching the bobbing pieces of its reflection in the stream.

Fresh snow began to fall as the trees became thinner, the muddy gaps between the roots filled with white, joining the speckled patches together until they became a solid layer. By the time they emerged from the forest, twilight had turned to night and the moor spread wide and wild. Distant peaks jutted towards the stars, uncluttered by mines, church spires or chimneys. It was beautiful, but terrifying too. It was a place much older than Treleddan. It made Cora think of the wild country outside the gates of Eden, where Adam and Eve were cast out. She shivered, the wind fierce since they'd left the shelter of the trees. The frozen earth was uneven beneath the snow and Cora stumbled more than once, sinking up to her ankles in hidden dips and old rabbit holes.

Wenna and Eseld plodded stoically ahead, one fist clamped to the ties of their capes, which flapped and let in the wintry gusts, and the other on the backs of their bonnets, lest they fly away. Cora copied them, forcing her limbs through wind as cold and solid as water. She couldn't help noticing that while she and Eseld breathed small white clouds, the air around Wenna's parted lips remained clear.

Wenna shot her a weary look and Cora felt not only ashamed, but angry too. She didn't ask for all this. She was fed up with having frozen fingers and sore feet and being unable to keep her thoughts private. She was afraid of Morgelyn watching her too and the more she thought about it the worse it was. She felt like an ant trying to escape a giant thumb intent on crushing it. What if Morgelyn found a way of penetrating Eseld's protective charms and she was sucked back down into the belly of the earth? What if Underwood wasn't far enough and Morgelyn took her deeper, all the way down into that hot, dark place where Wenna said nothing could rest? She'd never been further than Saltash, let alone out of Cornwall or across the sea, and now they said there'd been a whole foreign country under her feet all her life.

Wenna moved towards her.

Cora flinched. 'I'm sorry, I know it's not a foreign country. I know it's part of England, you're English, I'm sorry it's just all so new,' her voice wavered with more than cold.

Wenna didn't look annoyed, only tender, and she linked her arm through Cora's, the way Cora had sometimes seen other girls do. Girls with friends.

At first, Cora's arm was stiff and awkward. It didn't know how to respond. She mumbled something about Wenna losing her bonnet, but Wenna just tied a firm double knot under her chin and squeezed closer.

With sodden hems and a biting wind, nobody wanted to stay still for long and they pushed on.

'There it is,' Eseld swung the lamp ahead, as if it could light more than a few feet.

Cora peered, but the dim outline of the hills seemed just as far as they had before. There was nothing but snowy ground, boulders and what looked like a tiny, derelict cowshed from an earlier century.

To Cora's surprise, it was towards this humble, roofless dwelling that they seemed to be heading. It was so dilapidated, parts of the wall were just heaps of rubble. The space where the door used to hang was a jagged hole, holding nothing but tough, snowy weeds and black shadow. It stood in the centre of a ring of standing stones. Cora had seen similar circles dotted all over the moor, but she'd never seen one surrounding any kind of building. It seemed strange. Disrespectful somehow, though she wasn't sure why. It wasn't as if it was a churchyard. She remembered Nancarrow telling her that stones like the Cheesewring were all that remained of the giants who'd lived long ago, before people, who used to compete to launch the biggest rocks into the air. She'd never given them much thought, until then.

She had a peculiar feeling about the place, one that held nothing of the reckless, thundering jollity of a giant's game. The stones felt ancient. Solemn. As though they were guarding something.

The footprints from the edge of the forest began to blur and grow smooth with falling flakes. Soon they would vanish, as if no-one had trodden there at all.

Wenna stopped and turned to Cora again.

Eseld looked concerned. 'What is it?'

'We should have told her.' Wenna was anxious, her voice clear and deep. She didn't need to shout as loud as the others, to be heard over the wind. 'The guild might assume she knows.'

'Knows what?' Cora grimaced. She wanted to protest, to say she'd heard enough strange tales, but she didn't. Instead, she gathered her courage together and communicated directly with Wenna, through her thoughts. 'It's all right,' she said silently. 'I can hear more.'

Wenna's face opened into a wide grin, her tired yellow eyes suddenly dancing.

To Cora's astonishment, she grabbed her in a breath-crushing hug.

Eseld was confused. 'What just happened?' she asked.

'She did it!' Wenna shouted. 'She spoke to me!' She touched two fingers to her forehead and Eseld seemed to understand, though Cora was still at a loss.

'But you're always reading my thoughts,' Cora stammered.

'That's completely different.' Wenna shook her head, still brimming with joy. 'It's as different as, as your heart beating and you playing a drum! You see?'

'Um.' Cora felt stupid.

'Humans can't do it. They can't choose which thoughts to reveal and which to keep hidden.'

Cora shifted uncomfortably. She wished they would stop saying she wasn't human. 'You mean the bird thing? I have noticed...' she swallowed '...differences.' She wanted to tell them how she could sense the tiniest movements in hedges and subtle changes in temperature, and how unnerving it was, but Wenna was too excited to listen.

'No,' Wenna shook her head, 'the bird traits are just your body. This was always part of you, before you were born. Part of the real you.'

'The real- I don't...' Cora shook her head, pulling her cape more tightly around her shoulders. 'Can we go in there, just to get out of the wind a bit?'

Wenna was staring so intently into Cora's eyes, it made her skin prickle.

She tried again. 'Just to hear each other better? I mean, it isn't much, but at least we'd be out of the wind.'

But Wenna wasn't listening. 'Now you've felt it. It makes it so much easier for you to understand.'

'Felt what?'

Wenna touched her fingers to her forehead again, 'the threads.'

'I don't know what you're talking about.' Cora shouted over a sudden gust.

Eseld put an arm around her. 'Cora, my duck, you need to hear this. And Wenna's the one what ought to-'

'Hear what?!' Cora demanded. 'And why now?'

'Soon after Merlin and Mab were wed, they...'

'Please, Wenna, can't we talk about them another

time?'

'They had a child.'

'Hundreds of years ago. What's that got to do with me?'

'Their child wasn't safe, Cora. It's incredibly rare for a baby with parents of different species to survive. So rare, in fact, that their child is the only one in the world.'

Cora blinked. 'Is? Surely you mean was?'

'I mean what I say. The child of Merlin and Mab lives still. Fearing for her safety, they sealed her in a deep sleep and sent her as far away as they could. No land in Britain was safe, not in their time. So they cast a powerful spell, which sent her into the future. Which is now...'

'The present,' Cora whispered, but Wenna could hear her regardless of the cold air rushing past their lips. 'How-' Cora's voice was a croak. She coughed and tried again, 'how old is she?'

Wenna touched Cora's cheek, her voice thick with emotion. 'I'd say she was about fourteen.'

Cora felt very light, as though she might float away. 'And where does she live, this girl?'

'Until recently,' Eseld breathed, 'she lived on Fish Row. But she's got herself a new family now.' The wind died down and snowflakes whirled gently, like blossom petals.

Cora felt sweat bud, sticky, down her spine. 'But if I'm, then I'm half... half...'

'Faery,' Wenna put in.

Cora swallowed. The earth seemed to tilt, then right itself, leaving her giddy. Eventually she said 'that.'

'The hex Morgelyn put on you was a nasty one,'

Eseld flinched at the memory. 'If you'd been pure human, there's no way you'd have survived. Nor the regrowing either. '

'Then again,' Wenna shrugged, 'if you'd been pure human, Morgelyn wouldn't have bothered. She knows you're a threat. Not because your blood is mixed, which is what makes you strong, but because of who your parents were. Merlin and Mab were the most powerful sorcerers that ever walked the earth. Morgelyn was jealous of their strength and used the most poisonous magic there is, to make herself strong, even cheating death. She wanted to kill you as a baby, and she'd have succeeded if they hadn't got you as far away as possible. It broke their hearts, but they knew you'd never be safe as long as you remained with them.'

Cora gaped at them. It was too much to take in, too big to argue about.

'What happened to them?' she managed eventually. 'Did Morgelyn...'

'Kill them?' Wenna thought for a while. 'Nobody knows for certain. Some say they built the first rainbow, a bridge into the sky, to run across it into another world that we can't see. Others insist they hid themselves between words inside an enchanted songbook or became ageless water spirits. Some believe they simply got a few goats and lived out their days in quiet comfort, in a cabin on a mountainside in Bohemia.'

Despite the cold, Cora let her legs crumple and she sank down into thick, cold wetness, drawing her knees up to her chin and wrapping her arms tightly around herself.

'So Aunt Sel-, I mean, Selina,' Cora swallowed,

that would take a bit of getting used to. 'She lied, all these years, when she said I was her dead sister's child. Why? And how did she get hold of me in the first place?'

'She never had a sister,' Wenna said gently. 'Did you ever see a grave?'

'She told me my mother'd drowned herself,' Cora said quietly, 'out of shame. Being unwed. So she were buried at night in the very corner of the churchyard. No prayers. No stone. She said I were pulled out the river by a boatman, just a few days old. They thought I were dead too, at first, so they dropped me in a sack. Then they heard me crying.'

'Well,' Eseld blew her nose, whether from emotion or cold, Cora wasn't sure. 'She could have thought of something nicer'n that. Must've given you nightmares.'

Cora nodded. There wasn't a language to describe them.

'Selina got you from an orphanage' Wenna was gentle. 'Merlin and Mab looked into the future and found out where an orphanage would one day be built, so they went there. It was just heath then. They wrapped you up and performed the spell, tears running down their cheeks as you faded away. They made sure you'd appear during summer, just before dawn on the front steps, so you wouldn't get cold and you'd be found as quickly as possible.'

'Why didn't they send me to a family?' Cora asked, her voice oddly flat, as if someone else was using it, working her jaw with puppet strings. 'Instead of some horrible old orphanage?'

'Babies can't just appear out of thin air in family homes,' Eseld pointed out. 'Think of the scandal.

They wouldn't be safe and neither would any girls accused o' birthing them.'

Cora shrugged gloomily. 'Well, suppose it don't matter much now.' Though her eyes prickled, she suddenly laughed and shook her head. It was all so ridiculous. She wanted to feel some sort of tenderness for Mab and Merlin, but didn't know how.

'How do you know all this, Wenna?'

Wenna and Eseld exchanged glances. 'Your tale, and those of your parents, have been part of our folklore ever since the days of Arthur, Merlin and Mab. If I'm honest, I always thought you were a myth.'

Cora felt numb. Detached from it all. 'So, meeting me was like me meeting Cinderella?'

'Exactly,' Wenna nodded, smiling.

'But how do you know it's me? That I'm her, I mean? I'm sure plenty of babbies were dumped on those steps that year.' She swallowed, shivering. 'I could've come from anywhere.'

'There are two reasons I know,' Wenna was firm. 'Blackstones pick up magic, right? You are half faery, so you are part of a magical race, whether you like it or not. You might never have been aware of it, but you've caused things to happen around you, as all baby faeries do. This was why Selina chose you to adopt. In those days, she still believed in the gift of second sight. She was always greedy, but she wasn't always a charlatan. She thought you had the gift and she wanted to benefit from it. But, as you got older, she didn't know how to nurture your ability, so it seemed to fade. She became cynical and taught you the ways of manipulation and deceit instead. And you lost the things a faery family would have helped you develop.'

For a fraction of a second, Cora wondered how different her life would have been, had she been raised by faeries. But the closest she could imagine to such a possibility was a door, firmly closed.

'The other reason I know you're their child is your mark.'

'What mark?'

Wenna undid the row of buttons at Cora's wrist and pushed up her sleeve. 'There,' she said. 'Haven't you ever wondered about that?'

Cora looked down at her arm, goose pimples contracting the skin to make the tiny hairs lift. 'That's just a birthmark.'

'It's not a birthmark, Cora. It's a tattoo. One that can withstand anything. Burning, scarring, even regrowing from the bones of a bird.'

Cora stared at the pinkish mark on the inside of her elbow, just above a fork between thin, blue veins. 'Who on earth would tattoo their baby?'

'I know, it does sound a bit..'

'Barbaric?'

Wenna nodded uncomfortably. 'It's given you protection though, all these years. You survived cholera, didn't you? And scarlet fever. They poured all their love and hope for your future into this little mark. See? It's two M's twisted together, one for Merlin, one for Mab.'

Eseld glanced worriedly at Cora, who was staring at her arm as flakes fell and melted into watery beads that shone on her pale flesh. 'Roll down your sleeve. It's bitter, we should get inside.'

'Inside?' Cora couldn't prevent another laugh

bubbling up. 'Inside what, where? What's the point of coming all this way, to meet people in that derelict old cow shed? It doesn't even have a roof!'

'Come on, you duffer,' Eseld took Cora's hands and hauled her to her feet, brushing the snow off her skirt. 'Now, see this 'ere carving?' She held the lantern low, so that the flakes fluttering around it gleamed gold. On one of the old stones, Cora could just make out a carved symbol. A circle with a horizontal line through its middle.

'What is it?' She tried to focus on the dull little image, to steer her mind through the strange, turbulent waters, where it bobbed like a paper boat caught in a current.

'It's the mark of the Spindleberry Guild,' Eseld explained, pride lifting her face. 'The circle represents Britain and this line,' she pointed, 'there, is the ground.' She kicked the snowy earth with her heel, for emphasis, getting more animated as she went on. 'So, this semi-circular bit on top is Cornwall, Galway, Perthshire, Snowdonia, you know, all the counties above, the homes of the human Britons. And down here,' she pointed with her finger at the lower semi-circle, her skin showing through the threadbare, darned bits of her glove, 'is everything below. So that includes Underwood, below Cornwall and Devon, which reaches all the way to the border of Broadpuddle, the home of the spriggans. Broadpuddle's roughly beneath Somerset. It stretches all the way up to Leicestershire and out to Suffolk, under London, Oxford, all that. Then there's Redhill, which goes under the mountains of Cumbria, where the redcaps and bluecaps have been fighting for centuries.'

Cora's eyes widened as Eseld went on, warming to her subject and barely pausing for breath, 'the Tylwyth Teg live under Wales, in a realm called Gwyllion, and the Tuatha Dé Dannan live under the west of Ireland, County Cork up to Mayo. In the east, Antrim down to Wexford, in a land called Tír-nan-n-og, live the Murúghach. Sìdhe, the home of the Aos Sìdhe, stretches from the Firth of Forth all the way along the coast to Aberdeen and above that, the most northern territory of the British folk of below, live the Selkie, in Fáilte, under Caithness. I've a map somewhere, back at the cottage.'

'How many kingdoms are there, underneath?' Cora breathed.

'Altogether?' Eseld lifted her wispy eyebrows. 'I dunno, no more 'n I know all of the counties above. Did you mean under Britain or the whole world?'

'Under Britain,' Cora stammered. It hadn't occurred to her that there would be countries beneath anywhere else, though in some ways that was more believable. She'd heard that Abroad was a peculiar place.

'Course there are,' Wenna nodded, 'there are the Jinn beneath Arabia, Chin-chin Kobakama under Japan, Gandharvas under India...'

Cora felt sick.

'All a bit much,' Eseld gave her a firm pat on the upper arm, resting her hand there as she went on. 'Our motto, what we say to find out if someone's in the guild or not, is "above" and if they answer "and below," we know they're in the guild. That's what we want to get back to, you know? To the way it were. Folks above and below knowing about each other, getting along. God knows we need each other more than ever, now Morgelyn's back.'

Cora was cold and wet. Her arms itched under her woollen dress and pain prickled down her spine. She was impatient to get home, wherever home was. She wanted to be fascinated. Excited. She knew she ought to be. All those explorers who'd sickened and died in jungles with funny names would have given their eye teeth to be in her position. She tried to push her bad mood back, but it was like trying to shoo away the darkness, without a candle.

Eseld pull out her glyph and pressed it onto the symbol. Cora recognised the fragrance of crushed grass. And she felt a little calmer, a little safer.

Nothing happened at first, but something in the air changed. The wind dropped and everything grew still, as though nature itself was drawing a breath.

Chapter Eight

The Spindleberry Guild

When the glyph touched the symbol, the stone began to smoulder and turn black. Smoke coiled upward, blue in the lantern light. The symbol grew hotter. Deep red, yellow, then white. Cora knew little about geology, but she'd heard of mountains on distant islands whose peaks exploded, their stone cores so hot they liquefied, running red as blood. She drew back in fright, but the carved symbol remained solid. White heat radiated from the glyph out across the stones, thin as bindweed stems, coiling and criss-crossing, the colour of lightning.

The lantern was dim in comparison as the threads of light spread and tangled over the ruin, growing so bright they lit up the snow and the standing stones, shaming the stars into hiding. Cora squinted, watching even though it burned her eyes as the curious, glowing tendrils swallowed the humble cowshed in a seething mass of blinding white, which twisted hungrily out into black air, clutching onto it and coiling in every direction. Cora backed away, dwarfed by the writhing light that had grown to two, four, eight times the size of the cowshed. She wanted to run. It had morphed from a thrilling, luminous curiosity to a monstrous edifice and panic crushed her chest but, just as she was staggering backwards, the light began to dim, the green smell was less acute and the coiling, interlocking stems of light began to blur, melting into one another and turning into Cornish granite.

In place of the overgrown cowshed stood a huge, round building, the likes of which Cora had never seen. She'd heard that the great cities of London and Bristol held bridges, banks and museums bigger than the entire High Street in Treleddan, and she imagined they must look something like this in scale and grandeur, only this building held a rugged, ancient quality. As if it had been there as long as the cliffs, the sky, even the moor itself.

'Not quite,' Wenna was much closer than Cora realised. 'It was built a little less than three thousand years ago, same as these stones, which are here to protect it. It isn't weathered though, as they are, because it's usually hidden from sight, and from wind and rain.'

'Come on,' Eseld shooed them inside, where the walls encircled a roaring fire. Its heat felt good on Cora's damp, shivery skin. She stretched her fingers towards it. Smoke billowed up from the flames, disappearing into the cavernous gloom of the roof. Seated on huge logs, draped with furs and skins, sat more than thirty people, roughly sketched in the shadows of orange firelight. A few of the faces were familiar. Cora was amazed to recognise Mr Penrose, the blacksmith, and Mrs Trethowan, who worked in the bakery. Their hands and clothes bore traces of black soot and white flour.

A figure in a greatcoat hurried over to kneel before Wenna. With a quick, practised gesture he touched his mouth, his throat then his chest.

Wenna put a finger under his chin and bid him rise. There was something odd about him, though it was too dark to see properly. Cora was distracted by the familiar gait of one of the figures on the far side

106

of the fire, where it was even darker. He strode over to her, into the light, to grab her round the waist.

'Innit wonderful, Cora?'

'Tom!' she beamed, hugging him back. Eseld waited a few moments, before clearing her throat and jerking her head towards the company. They moved apart.

Piran was watching them with dull, dark eyes, which closed briefly as he swigged from his battered hip flask.

'I forgot he'd be here,' Cora murmured, even as she dipped in respect. She'd never felt comfortable around Tom's father. He'd folded his grief for his wife deep inside, letting no air to the wound, so that it festered instead of healing. He didn't let any of his children talk about their mother, but Eseld encouraged it when he wasn't there. She said Rosenwyn, her daughter, would never have forgiven her if she'd let them forget the songs she used to sing as she brushed their hair, or the way her eyes and nose crinkled when she laughed, just like Tom's.

'You're freezing,' Tom rubbed Cora's hands with his own, 'rumped up like a winnard! Come and get warm.' He led her to sit beside him on one of the enormous logs, layered with thick, brown sheepskin.

'I can't believe all of you were inside here, all the time we were out there. It just looked like an old ruin. Only enough room for a few cows, but its bigger'n the town hall!'

'I've wanted to tell you about the guild for so long,' he said excitedly, tapping the ash from his pipe. Some landed on his trousers and he tried to brush it away, leaving a grey smear. She loved to watch his big, dry hands. They were the hands of a man, while his blonde-lashed eyes were still a boy's. He pressed soft, crumpled tobacco into the bowl and lit it, puffing until it glowed.

'Why didn't you?'

'You'd never have believed it and besides, Mamm-Wynn always said it weren't the right time.'

She felt a little odd. All this time, she'd shared her most private thoughts with him and imagined she knew everything there was to know, yet he'd been keeping secrets.

'Tom, can you do magic?'

He grinned, shaking his head. 'I tried. Mamm-wynn did her best to teach me, but', he held out his hands, 'turns out these ain't good for nothing but turning wood. I did...' He chuckled in recollection, 'I did once have a go at turning a frog into a toad. Sounds simple doesn't it? Baby stuff. Couldn't do it though. All I did was make him grow a big, fleshy tadpole tail and he hopped about something terrible, like it were a-chasing him!' He laughed aloud. 'Don't know if the poor little bugger were frightened or angry.'

Cora giggled. 'Bet his mates teased him rotten.'

'Mamm-wynn fixed him afore he went back to his pond. Couldn't leave him like that.'

They giggled again, not because the frog story was particularly funny, but because it was such a joy simply to be together, hands entwined, beside a fire.

Checking over his shoulder that Eseld wasn't looking, Tom held the pipe low, near his hip, and offered it to Cora, who ducked to smoke, blowing it quickly away as Eseld and Wenna came to sit beside them.

Wenna looked longingly at the pipe, Tom's

brown thumb over the stem. 'I had one once, from Fáilte,' she spoke as if she was sighing, but without breath. 'It was carved all over with leaves and the bowl was a perfect thistle. My father brought it back for me after visiting his cousin.'

Unsure what else to do, Cora reached her hand into Wenna's lap where her fingers lay, thin and interlaced, to grasp her hand.

She sensed Wenna's surprise, and her gladness too, but whether from human intuition or any newfound faery telepathy, Cora didn't know. It didn't really matter.

A hoarse voice scratched the air.

At first, Cora thought it was a bronchial cough, before she caught the words within it and squinted through the smoke-smudged gloom to see a short, broad woman wearing an extraordinary number of ragged shawls, standing on a wide tree stump. Its roots dug into the earthen floor like the twisted, heavy-knuckled fingers of a giant. One of the old woman's arms was raised, the other leaned heavily on a stick. Brows lowered, she called gruffly for quiet.

The mumbling chatter subsided as everyone turned towards the old woman, whose back was so bent it hunched her over, making her jut her chin in order to see.

'That's Hendra,' Tom whispered. 'Oldest and longest serving member of the guild.'

'Shh!' Mrs Trethowan hissed.

Tom fell silent, pressing his lips together and raising his eyebrows good-naturedly.

Hendra continued in a grave tone, relaying what Cora knew must be bad news, judging by the sombre faces of the guild members though, to her, the meaning of words remained fairly muddled.

'Morgelyn Glasse has marched her troops from Underwood into Broadpuddle.'

Up went cries of 'no!' And 'wicked creature!'

'She has no interest in copying the spriggans, of course,' Hendra continued, 'and very few have joined her army. She's burned the forests of Giddydown, where so many had taken refuge, and is now advancing towards the Redhill border.'

Hendra turned a little, to beckon with a clamped, arthritic hand.

A solemn young man rose to his feet, holding something under his arm that resembled a slab of dark marble, about the size of a book. Its edges were rough, it's surface glassy smooth.

As he moved from the shadows, closer to the fire, his face was illuminated and Cora gasped, she couldn't help it, despite the frowns it drew from the gathered faces.

He was small and slightly stooped, with grey skin and yellow eyes, a little larger than Wenna's. His brow was a little heavier than a human's, like hers, and his sparse threads of white hair were wound tightly into a small plait at the nape of his neck, tied with leather strings that hung limp against his greatcoat. She recognised him as the one who'd knelt before Wenna.

Tom leaned so close that his whisper made Cora shiver, his breath tickling deep inside her ear. 'That's Meriwether Beetleblue, Wenna's chief bodyguard.'

Cora nodded, as if the name meant anything to her.

Meriwether held the stone slab out towards the fire and Cora suddenly understood what it was. A blackstone, the scrying tool Wenna had told her about, which had made her appear in the attic. Morgelyn had made one to watch her, to call and trap her. Cora's skin prickled and she eyed it with mistrust.

The faery, for he couldn't have been anything else, moved his fingers in curious, flicking gestures a few inches from the surface of the blackstone, murmuring all the while in the same language Eseld and Wenna used for magic. Through the woodsmoke, Cora caught the faint scent of crushed grass.

Tom was leaning forward, chin on his fists, elbows on his knees, listening to every word.

Meriwether turned the blackstone around, holding it up for everyone to see. People huddled closer, craning their necks. Nothing could have prepared Cora for what she saw. She'd expected a flat image, like a magic lantern show or a reflection in a mirror, but it was more like a three dimensional pop-up book or a stage with miniature players. Tiny people, formed from coloured smoke, were running for their lives across the stone, faces smeared with blood and mud. Burning pines were scratchy ink spikes of silhouette. Flames billowed up from the scene. There was no sound but the crack and hiss of the embers in the middle of the chamber, their once comforting hearth-sound horribly appropriate. The terrified, weeping people weren't human, nor faery but, for once, Cora forgot to think about that. Their pain was raw, their eyes saying more than any language ever could.

'That's enough, I think,' Hendra blotted her eye with a handkerchief and blew her nose. And Cora remembered the seances at Fish Row, which felt like years ago now, where she had toyed with other people's grief, like a child pulling the wings off a fly. Shame weighed heavily on her then, a wordless ache. Wenna turned to her, eyes glimmering with tears for the spriggans.

'If she gets across the border of Redhill,' Hendra continued, 'she'll stir up the hatred between the redcaps and the bluecaps, no doubt. She'll use their bitter history to destroy them both. Frame some poor bugger from one side for the assassination of someone on the other, something like that, in the hope that they'll end centuries of squabbling and wipe each other out once and for all. They'll be too pigheaded to realise what's been happening under their noses. Many of the redcap government have already been copied and replaced. They've been introducing curfews and organising the smashing of blue-owned businesses and goodness knows what. Although much of this is rumour,' she darkened. 'Our eyes up there are blinking out.'

Hendra paused, and it took Cora a moment to understand. Spies. Their spies were disappearing.

'Further north, things are looking even worse', Hendra went on. 'Since it fell, Fáilte has become another of her strongholds. From there she can invade all the Faerie counties of Scotland. As you know, the Royal family of the Aos Sídhe have vanished. Doubtless their copies will appear soon, having changed all their policies, ready and willing to embrace Morgelyn as their Empress.'

Cora's mind was racing. Copied and replaced were familiar words, yet here they seemed to hold a dark significance she couldn't grasp.

With a bitter look, Hendra's eyes swept the room, alighting upon Cora with an accusatory glare. She lifted a hand to point. 'Has she been checked?!'

'Yes, yes,' Eseld was saying, 'she hasn't left our sight. We drew her out of a...'

But Hendra wasn't listening. She'd climbed down from the stump and was pushing through those who'd clustered around her, presumably to assist her. Though she was invisible to Cora for a few seconds, because of her hunched stature, it wasn't difficult to track her progress, because of the way people moved, or were pushed, out of Hendra's way.

Cora stood up, out of respect, but ended up looking down on the bent old woman, so she half-curtseyed, half-crouched, in a position that quickly became uncomfortable.

Hendra forced Cora back down onto the log. Her hands were hard as wood.

Cora was winded. But it got worse.

With a menacing gaze, Hendra pushed Cora's head to one side, yanking off her bonnet and roughly parting the hair on the back of her head.

'Ow! What are you doing?' Cora struck out instinctively, her fist connecting violently with Hendra's cheekbone. The ancient creature clattered over backwards, narrowly missing the fire.

Amid angry shouts, Hendra was hauled to her feet, her wiry hair a lopsided mess as she scrabbled with her stick to lean on it again, but she was smiling. 'It's all right! She isn't a ghast!' She reassured the crowd, as if it were they, not she, who'd insisted upon the inspection, and her being knocked over was a mere trifle.

Cora was panting, her initial defensiveness

waning, turning to guilt when she saw the old woman rub her jaw, wiggling it left and right and touching her lips to check for blood.

'I'm sorry, I didn't...' Cora stammered, 'I mean, I didn't know what you were doing.'

Tom bent to retrieve Cora's bonnet, brushing off the dirt and staring at it, as though he couldn't bear to look up and meet her eyes.

Nobody spoke. The room held its breath. Hendra let out a croaking, wheezy noise and Cora was alarmed, fearing a serious injury, until she realised it was a laugh.

'I like this one,' Hendra grinned, still rubbing her jaw, revealing stumpy, gappy teeth, teeth that had nothing to do with Cora.

'What was that all about?' Cora asked Tom, shakily, as Hendra made her way back to the stump. 'What's a ghast?'

'Didn't Wenna and Mamm-wynn explain?' He re-lit his pipe, avoiding her eyes.

'They tried, there's just so much. I don't think there's enough room in my head.'

'It must seem strange.' He met her gaze at last and tucked a stray, feathery lock behind her ear.

'Isn't it to you?' she asked. 'I mean, how long have you known about all this?'

'Long as I can remember. Ma used to tell us stories about Underwood and the Skyburiows. The spriggans and the redcaps and the bluecaps. When she died, Mamm-wynn decided it were time we knew,' he puffed on his pipe, 'that the stories were true.'

'And you didn't think to let me in on any of it, when we started courting?'

'Mamm-wynn said best not to. The less people knew, the safer they were. But that was before the curse. Now Morgelyn's loose...'

Cora wished he'd stop assuming she knew more than she did. 'What do you mean? Was she in prison?'

Tom nodded, 'at Chy-a-Enys, yes. The Keepers had her bound. In a witch bottle she couldn't get out of. Or so they thought.'

Cora decided to ask about the Keepers another time.

'Now she's got the army on her side,' Tom went on, 'so-'

Cora's eyes widened, picturing scarlet coats and thudding hooves, then she realised. 'You mean the faery army.'

Tom nodded, as if it was obvious. Hendra was close to the stump again, one small, battered boot resting on it, one on the ground. She was deep in conversation with Meriwether, but looked as though she might resume her speech at any moment.

'Tell me about the ghasts,' Cora avoided the pointed stares of the others, since she'd struck Hendra. Beneath the shame was a tiny nub of pride. At least none of them would try that again.

'That's what she's been doing,' Tom whispered. 'Morgelyn. That's how she's been taking over. The most devoted of her followers prove their commitment to her by undergoing the ghasting, which is-'

Hendra was climbing back up onto the stump, clearing her throat and holding up a hand for silence.

'Quick!' Cora hissed.

Tom whispered as fast as he could in her ear.

More people frowned. 'They take a tiny bit of someone, like a fingernail paring, and Morgelyn uses dark, poisoned magic to make one of her followers look exactly like the person whose nail it was, see? Then the ghast comes up above, walks around Treleddan, or anywhere else, passing themselves off as the one they replaced, cool as you like.'

Cora felt sick.

'They find out as much as they can about the people they'll replace first,' Tom hurried on, keen to finish so they could listen to Hendra. 'They watch them, spy on them, you know, practice their walk, ways of talking, all that, so as no-one'll guess. Then they're kidnapped and replaced. If anyone notices they've changed, then they just think they've changed. Like people do. Wouldn't occur to you to think anything else would it, if you didn't know?'

'Kidnapped?' Cora felt sweaty, suffocated. 'What happens to them after they been kidnapped?'

Tom hesitated. 'They become slaves. They're put to work down the mines.'

Cora couldn't speak. She thought of dear old Nancarrow, who'd come to Fish Row as a nurserymaid and been by her side all her life, until she'd changed, a few years before, growing cold and distant when once she'd been tender as a mother.

Cora forced herself to listen to Hendra while her mind spun sickeningly, round and round like a malfunctioning carousel, unable to stop.

'We believed Petrok was kidnapped and had drawn up plans for a rescue attempt, but we now...' Hendra coughed, keeping her voice steady, 'we now have reason to believe he's dead.'

Cora remembered what Wenna had told her

about the curse of the faeries. True death could only follow burning or dismemberment.

The guild shuddered. Men removed their hats, revealing grimy hair stuck flat to their heads. Some had a clean inch of skin, below the hairline, where the hat had caught the coal dust ingrained in the rest of their faces. Wenna had said Petrok was her friend, the one whose blackstone had been smashed. That must've been why they took him, Cora realised, because he was loyal to Wenna. She knew there was nothing she could do, but give Wenna's hand a wordless squeeze.

Wenna leaned close. 'He isn't dead,' she whispered, 'Petrok. I'd know.'

Cora nodded. Many times, she'd heard people say it couldn't be their child, their fiancée, their parent, lying cold and still under cart wheels, on a river bank or in the morgue. When they saw for themselves and had to believe, they'd insist that only their earthly life had ended, that their spirit was still intact, because anything else was too much to bear. That's when they'd go and see the Blackthorns on Fish Row.

With a jolt, Cora remembered that Wenna would see her thoughts, clear as the images on the blackstone, and she tried to empty her mind.

'It's alright,' Wenna patted her hand. 'It's alright to think that way but, among the faeries it's, well, different. Do you remember I told you about the threads?'

Cora nodded.

'They stretch between us, like spider silk. We communicate by their tremors. They cannot be broken, until one of us dies. You'll let yourself feel it, once you embrace who you are.'

Hendra was still speaking about mountain cities and the movements of Morgelyn's troops. The place names were unfamiliar, but Cora's heart ached as Meriwether solemnly held out his blackstone to reveal miniature, smoky tableaus of tragic scenes. Battles. Burning villages. Bodies.

All of a sudden, a smoky replica of a tiny Aunt Selina appeared, scowling, sitting with her elbows on her knees in the corner of the Currigan's cottage, her dress puffed up around her in its invisible prison. Meg was brushing a cross-looking Gwen's hair, which bobbed and shifted like the rest of the image. Curnow was presumably outside or crouched with his toy horse on a string, somewhere out of sight. It all held a silvery, ghostly quality that Cora found unnerving.

She turned to Wenna 'why are they showing us the cottage? And why is Aunt... I mean, Selina, so faded?'

'Because she's under a spell,' Wenna said, pointing. 'They're using the blackstone to see where magic is being done, to keep an eye on things. Although we can't always tell if it's pure or poisoned.'

Eseld raised a hand and told the guild that it was she who'd imprisoned Aunt Selina, then asked what they thought she should do with her.

'Send her home, can't you?' Hendra said.

'But what if she tells folk?' Eseld was unsure. 'About the chalk circle and that?' She hesitated, then added 'there's more. She's been consorting with Victor Morningside. Smitten, she is.'

A beat of silence was followed by a worried murmuring amongst the guild.

'She don't know it, but he'll have been using her

118

for something. Preying on the poor, mourning folks what go to Fish Row, seeing who he can pick off no doubt.' Eseld paused, sucking on her pipe for a moment.

'Would she tell that husband of hers?' Hendra asked. 'Or Victor himself?'

'If she told Granville, he'd never believe it' Eseld said, smoky puffs escaping with each syllable. 'Ain't got the imagination. He'd call a doctor most probably, get him to shut her up with a dose of choral hydrate. But she wouldn't have to tell Victor Morningside much for him to work it out and well, I doubt he'd recognise me but I'm not risking it unless I have to.'

Cora leaned close enough to Tom to whisper 'what does she mean? Why would he recognise her?'

Tom was more uncomfortable than she'd ever seen him. He seemed pale, even in the fire glow. 'Didn't she tell you? Ain't you seen her scars?'

Cora shook her head.

He took a deep breath. 'She were a slave down there. For eight months she were a slave in Morgelyn's mine. I don't want to think what would have happened if Wenna hadn't got her out. They didn't bother with a ghast. They knew we'd know. Just took her. All that time we didn't know if she were alive or dead.'

Cora stared past him at Eseld.

Hendra was speaking and Cora did her best to listen. 'Mrs Liddicoat, couldn't you put an addle in this Selina woman's mind? Make her think she were just out for a walk? Then she could go home, thinking nothing of it. No memory of you or the cottage at all. We can't have Victor Morningside nosing around the cottage, if word got back to Morgelyn that Wenna was there, well, none of you'd be safe.'

A muscle jumped in Eseld's jaw. 'It's not the sort of thing I like to do, Mrs Killigrew. Holding her at the cottage is bad enough, but meddling about with folk's memories...' she shuddered. 'It's dangerous, is what it is.'

Arguments on the morality of addles and forgetting spells rumbled back and forth between Hendra, Wenna, Eseld and Meriwether, with others chipping in too.

Cora understood little more than half of what was said.

Mr Penrose stood up to speak. 'Why not just put a bit of blackstone powder in her pocket?'

Eseld winced. 'Spying?'

'We're at war!' Hendra pointed out, gruffly. 'This is no time to worry about what's proper, just how to win!'

Eseld was dignified. 'I don't give a monkey's what's proper, Mrs Killigrew. But I won't dabble in no spying, nor poisoned magic, is all.'

Cora was startled. Killigrew?

'Sarah's Grandmother,' whispered Tom.

Then Piran spoke. Cora couldn't remember the last time she'd heard his voice. 'Morningside will know if we put blackstone on her,' he said. 'It's too dangerous. What if-'

'It's a risk we'll have to take,' Hendra interrupted, holding up her hand. 'We have to know what's happening in Treleddan. He's snatching more folk from there than any other town. We need to know why.'

'He's taking them from Treleddan 'cos is it's the only town with more'n a hundred folk in it.' Piran's tone, Cora noticed, contained none of the respect the others had shown Hendra. 'Who's he going to snatch from Five Lanes or Trewint without anybody twigging? Folks know each other inside out, places like that.'

'You got a better idea?' Hendra asked.

'I'll watch Fish Row myself.'

'How? You'll be spotted.'

'Giddock's yard is just along from the Blackthorn's house,' he answered, pulling out a pouch of tobacco. 'They won't notice nothing.'

The matter seemed to be settled, and Cora's gaze drifted back to the miniature, smoky image of the Currigan's cottage. It was like the ghost of a room in a doll's house, only instead of sitting stiff with straight arms at awkward angles, these figures were alive and moving. Curnow was coughing and Meg was patting his back, rubbing firmly up and down. When he'd got his breath back, she poured him some milk from the jug. Gwen was dancing with her doll, twirling round and round, holding its tiny hands as its head flopped back. Selina glared ahead, apparently no more aware of them than they were of her.

Hendra had changed the subject and was asking for volunteers. But Cora missed what for, because she'd been distracted by the tiny forms of Aunt Selina and the children. In dismay, she saw Tom's hand shoot up, along with Wenna's.

Eseld seemed torn. Meriwether Beetleblue was counting. Mr Penrose and Mrs Trethowan were looking unsure but, soon enough, their hands floated upward too. Piran's remained by his side.

'What are you volunteering for?' Cora whispered, not sure if she wanted to know.

'Meriwether and Wenna reckon Petrok's still alive,' Tom's eyes gleamed. 'The rescue's back on.'

Chapter Nine

Feathers

When they got back to the cottage, Tom stopped to stare as Eseld rubbed at the air concealing Selina. Cora hoped she'd be asleep but, instead, a stony face was revealed, its mouth buckled in a snarl.

Piran barely glanced at her before going to bed.

'Right,' Eseld was firm, but apprehensive. 'I'm going to let you speak and, what's more, you're going to listen.'

But, as soon as she could be heard, Selina's voice tore through the room, hoarse as if her throat was crammed with thorns. 'I'll get you for this! All of you! Think you can scare me with your cheap hocus-pocus?'

'Mrs Blackthorn, please!' Eseld tried to get a word in. 'You'll wake the children! We're just trying to warn you! Victor Morningside ain't what you think.'

But Selina's words thundered on, ripping through the cottage, unstoppable as a charging bull. 'I've worked it out! You can't fool me. There's a glass tube what's come down from the ceiling. I know all the scams. And you told those snot-nosed brats to ignore me, act as if I weren't here! You're trying to drive me mad, ain't you? Make me think I'm invisible! Cart me off to the asylum so Cora can get her filthy mitts on my house when my good-for-nothing husband pops his clogs? I know your game. I been sitting here all these days working it out.'

'Mrs Blackthorn, it's only been few hours-'

'Well, I got news for you. She ain't even my niece!

Bad blood, that's what. I got her from an orphanage. Hear that Cora? You ain't got no family. You're base, nobody wanted you!'

Eseld silenced her, making her invisible again with an angry rub.

Cora stared at the empty space, feeling like a wrung-out rag.

'That's not true, my love,' Wenna placed a thin arm around Cora, who shivered at its coldness. 'You remember what happened in the attic, when I appeared?'

'Won't forget that in a hurry,' Cora murmured, her voice compressed and small. She felt oddly detached, as though she was seeing everything from the wrong end of a telescope. 'Half frightened me to death.'

'If a signal between two blackstones is interrupted like that, the image diverts to the nearest relative of the sender.'

Cora was silent, digesting Wenna's words.

'Mab was born into an old, aristocratic Faery family. I'm a descendant of her first cousin, which makes me your cousin too, albeit a distant one. You and I are the last of that bloodline, so you do have family, Cora. Me. And, more important, you've the Currigans, who love you as if you were born here, in this cottage.'

Cora didn't know what to say. Deep inside her chest, something prickled, painful but exquisite.

Tom smiled. 'I'm glad you weren't born here,' his eyes twinkled softly, like they always did when he was trying to cheer her up. 'Else our courting would be, well, more'n just frowned upon.'

'Tom! Don't be coarse!' Eseld swatted him with a

tea cosy. 'Get off to bed, you daft bugger.'

During the night, it snowed again. The next morning, when they opened the curtains, the windows of the cottage were deep blue, scattered with stars.

Cora's footprints sank deep as she crunched down the garden path to the privy, her breath steaming, her fingernails mauve with cold. She was glad to get back inside the warmth of the cottage, to see Curnow, by candlelight, biting hungrily into bread sticky with honey, which coated his crumb-flecked cheeks. Gwen had finished hers and a few strands of her hair were stuck to the corners of her lips.

Meg struggled in with a slopping pail from the well and started wetting a cloth in the scullery. Cora took it from her. 'Here, let me,' she said. 'You do so much,' and she tenderly wiped Gwen's face with the damp bit of flannel, even as she squirmed to get away. Curnow screwed up his face in dread anticipation. Meg shrugged and yawned.

'That dolly needs a bath,' Cora commented.

Gwen looked down at the grubby rag doll crushed in the crook of her elbow. 'No, she doesn't and anyway, anyway, she likes honey.'

'Did you feed her some?'

Anxiety flashed across Gwen's face, 'I ain't allowed to.' Then she leaned close and whispered, 'but it's her favourite, so I give her just a teensy weensy bit. So she wouldn't be sad.'

'I won't tell,' Cora smiled. 'Shall we give her a bit of a wipe too? Can she be as brave as you d'you think?'

Gwen regarded her coolly, as if she hadn't decided yet, whether to trust the girl with strange hair who ate worms. Even if she could keep secrets about dolls who liked honey.

'What's your dolly's name?' Cora asked.

Gwen blinked. 'Dolly.'

Cora finished cleaning Gwen up, and Dolly too, glancing uneasily at the patch of room where she knew Selina to be, while Gwen scampered off.

Cora rolled her stiff shoulders. She hadn't slept well. Wenna didn't sleep at all. She simply curled up to read at night, by the fire in the cellar, while Cora lay on the little pallet bed, comforted by the candle glow and the gentle shush of occasionally turning pages. Cora had dreamed of being chased, of falling and trying and failing to catch things. She'd jerked awake a few times, unsure if she'd called out or just dreamed she had, to find Wenna holding a book in one hand, stroking her hair with the other.

Eseld had saved some windfalls from autumn in a drawer, carefully wrapped in brown paper, and Cora bit into the fragrant, wrinkled fruit for breakfast. She hadn't realised how difficult worms were to find, beneath all that snow, and she hadn't found any at all after half an hour's searching. She heard the whistling twitter of birds outside and recognised the calls of lapwings and stonechats. She wondered what they ate at this time of year and went outside to see.

She couldn't spot any birds at first, though their chatter filled the trees. She looked up and a few tiny, far away crosses of black sailed above, too intent on their own business to notice her. The prickly sensation in her spine and arms had disturbed her sleep and, despite the icy air, she pushed back the loose sleeve of her borrowed dress to examine a pimply rash, which had spread from her arms to her fingers and up over her shoulders.

She knew she shouldn't scratch it, she should show Eseld, who was bound to have some ointment or a poultice that would ease the itching. She picked at a particularly red, angry looking bump, which seemed to have a curled black splinter in it, the size and shape of a comma.

Trying to dig it out, Cora realised it was deeply embedded, coiled around itself, like an ingrown hair. Once she'd released it and tried to pull it out, it tugged in her skin, exactly like a hair, only blacker than any of the others.

Two arms were suddenly around her waist and she turned, yanking her sleeve down, to see Tom, grinning sleepily. She pressed her cheek into the warm fabric of his jacket.

'What's this?' He caught her hand and rubbed his thumb across the small, red stain on her sleeve.

'Nothing.' She tried to pull away. 'Must've cut myself doing those parsnips the other day. Knocked the scab off.'

'Be more careful,' he said tenderly, kissing her forehead before heading into the privy.

She waited until he shut the door, then she pushed her sleeve back up and picked at another bump, then another. Each released a smudge of blood and a tiny black curl. She knew what they were. She'd known straightaway, she just hadn't wanted to admit it. They were the beginning, the roots, of blackbird feathers.

She came back inside, and soon the men left for work. As the front door was closing, Eseld asked 'what is it?'

'I'm alright,' Cora lied, rubbing her eyes as though

it was tiredness that made them pink.

'Wenna said you had a bad night. Not surprised after yesterday.' She put a tin mug of tea down in front of Cora, who sipped politely, though she didn't really want it.

'What are we going to do about her?' Cora asked, jerking her head towards Selina. 'Sooner she's gone the better.'

Eseld nodded, looking as though she wanted to say something, but thought better of it.

'What?'

'I was thinking as maybe we should follow her, see what she says to folk.'

Cora was struck by a grim possibility. 'But what if she finds a policeman? Says we kidnapped her?'

'Hmm. Good point.'

'You got any ideas, my duck?' she asked Wenna who was coming up out of the cellar. 'About how we get Mrs Manners 'ere home without her getting us arrested?' She rubbed her face and stifled a yawn as she cut some bread.

Wenna smiled conspiratorially. 'I've been thinking about that. I say you take her into town, telling anyone who'll listen that you found her wandering in the woods, smelling of gin, spouting nonsense.'

'Ooh, that's wicked,' Cora grinned. 'Perfect.'

As soon as Eseld rubbed the air, making Selina visible, Cora braced herself for another onslaught.

But Selina wasn't there.

Cora sprang to her feet, terrified that she'd got out and was crawling up behind her with a knife.

'Hush, Cora, it's all right.' Wenna soothed her. 'She's just worn herself out and slid down. She's fast asleep, see?'

Eseld was removing the last of the obscuring spell, to reveal Selina's face, about the height of Eseld's thigh. The side of her forehead was pressed flat into a white, bloodless circle, her mouth hung open. Once Eseld had removed the silence, a ragged snore filled the cottage.

'How do you let her out?' Cora was nervous.

'Simple,' Eseld dipped a cloth, slightly sticky with honey, into the sink. 'You just wipe away the chalk.'

She knelt down and started scrubbing.

Selina tumbled out, sprawling loose as an octopus across the floorboards, crumpled and disoriented at first, until she gathered her anger. 'O! You fiend, vagabond! Let me go this instant!'

'You're free,' Eseld said calmly. 'You can go anywhere you want,' she turned away and added 'good riddance,' under her breath.

'What?' Selina scrambled to her feet, touching the air as if she couldn't believe it. Once she'd taken her first wary steps, she pointed at Cora. 'Fetch your own clothes, you look dreadful in that scruffy getup.'

'Ain't got 'em,' Cora replied, uneasy.

'Haven't, not ain't!' Selina snapped. 'Live in the sty long enough and you become a pig.'

'She ain't coming back with you, Mrs Blackthorn,' Eseld stated. 'She lives here now.'

'We'll see about that,' Selina advanced towards Cora, who shrank a little, however hard she tried to stand her ground.

Eseld stepped between them. She didn't say a word, issue any threats or cast any spells. She simply stood, feet planted apart, arms folded, bright blue eyes fixed on Selina, who faltered.

'I'll be back with a... a policeman,' Selina

stammered. 'You can't just kidnap my niece!'

'Oh, so she's your niece again now, is she?' Eseld's tone was flint-hard. 'Just remembered who butters your bread, have you?'

Something like shame, but more angry, flashed across Selina's face. It was the look of a fox interrupted killing chickens. Her only regret was being caught.

White-lipped, Selina stalked to the door, held open by Wenna. She glanced back at Cora, then at Eseld, whose nostrils flared in warning.

'Hold on a minute.' Eseld turned towards the sink and picked up the pail of icy water. Selina was on the path outside the front door now, squinting in the gloomy grey sunrise. Eseld marched out and threw the freezing water over Selina, drenching her from head to foot.

Selina gasped, unable to catch her breath, her mouth stretched wide as if she was drowning.

Cora felt a prick of sympathy. She thought suddenly of the mother she'd believed, all those years, to have drowned. She'd always pictured her last, unhappy breaths trailing above her, bubbles shuddering through her hair. She'd sunk so many times, down through Cora's dreams and, in her sleeping terror, Cora had tried desperately to save her; to grab her mother's dress as it turned to slime, her fingers shrinking to the weak, helpless ones of a baby.

Yet none of it had ever happened. It was a lie that had leaked poison all these years, corrupting everything it touched. Anger crackled, white hot, through Cora's veins. She owed this woman nothing.

Selina wiped her eyes, grabbing fistfuls of her

dress to shake water from it. Her teeth were chattering as she declared 'the first thing I'll do, Eseld Currigan, is tell a policeman *exactly* what you did and, and-'

'Come off it,' Eseld retorted, 'you wouldn't go near a copper, line of business you're in.'

Selina blinked.

Eseld took Selina's arm, as though she was elderly and needed help crossing the road. Selina froze, utterly startled.

'Had a long night, have you?' Eseld's tone was completely different. 'Lucky we found you when we did, this weather. You're soaked through.'

Selina was struck dumb, rage and disbelief fighting for control of her face. 'You-you crone! You bitter old *hag*!'

'Yes, yes. Now let's get you home and into bed eh? Oh, I nearly forgot.' she rummaged in her apron and found a small bottle of rubbing alcohol, which she splashed into Selina's face, coating her lips and chin with the strong smelling liquid and making her splutter as she batted it away. Cora could smell the fumes from where she stood.

'Now, Cora, love, are you coming?' Eseld asked. 'I think she could do with one of us on each side. Keep her steady.'

Selina was struggling to break Eseld's grip. Cora marvelled at Wenna's cleverness for, as she and Eseld walked into town, Selina looked for all the world like a bedraggled, ranting drunk, found sleeping in the snow, lucky to be rescued from an icy death.

Selina fell quiet as they walked, hiding her face as they passed a disinterested policeman, his dark cloak rimed with frost.

It was very strange to be returning to the house on Fish Row, in the gathering light. The mist was already thick and smelled of tar as they reached the front door, which was opened by a goggle-eyed Killigrew, who didn't know what to be astonished by first. She stared at Selina, then at Cora, then back at Selina again, then at Eseld, gaping all the while. 'Don't just stand there like an idiot, let me in!' Selina screeched, startling a butcher's boy and making his basket wobble.

Selina pushed past Killigrew, tearing off her soggy cloak and bonnet and thrusting them at her without a word.

'What is it, Sarah?' Eseld asked. 'You're looking wisht.' With a shaky finger, Killigrew pointed behind her, towards the stairs, where a girl stood.

She had tumbling curls the colour of brown sugar, exactly like Cora's used to be.

Cora stared. The girl had her face. Her eyes were still blue and framed with lashes. She was the height that Cora used to be, when Morgelyn had crunched those horrible scissors in the mirrored ballroom. It was like the fingernail paring Tom had told her about. The piece of her that Morgelyn had needed. It was far worse than the painted girl on the swing, because this one was slowly drawing its mouth into a smile.

Selina whirled around, her crinoline creaking as she whipped her gaze from Cora to the ghast and back again. Lost for words, she merely pointed, until Victor Morningside appeared, dark as a shadow behind Cora's ghast, making Eseld turn and hide her face.

Killigrew shielded them both by half-closing the door and blocking the gap with her body. 'Not today thank you, Mrs Higgins,' she called, 'we've all the buttons and thread we need.' Her voice remained steady as she disappeared, but panic stretched her eyes wide.

Chapter Ten

The Round Table

The pavement lurched. Eseld caught Cora as she staggered and, somehow, managed to get her back to the cottage.

As soon as they appeared, Wenna saw what was wrong and mixed some brandy with hot water. Cora sat, shaking, sipping the liquid and tasting nothing.

'It's happening,' Eseld's mouth was a thin, hard line. 'We have to move. I'll send word to Meriwether and the others. It's now or never.'

Cora wished she could stop shaking. She felt weak every time she pictured that girl, the one she used to be. It wasn't a happy life, but it was her own. She took a deep breath. She'd think about it later, another day, when her mind was less crowded.

She tried to focus on what was important. Which was finding Petrok. That was her life now; the guild, the makeshift family she had now, not the false one on Fish Row. But she didn't want to go back into that eerie world below the moor at all and the very idea of it made her heart wobble in her chest. She wanted to feel brave, to be fearless like Wenna. But the dread was thick as river sludge in her veins.

'I wasn't always brave,' Wenna covered Cora's hand with her own, hesitating before she said 'I was a spoilt little girl. A princess, with pets wearing golden collars. I could summon servants to bring cakes and jellies with a click of my fingers, any time of the day or night. I never thought about their need for rest. I'd stamp my foot if my chocolate was too hot or my ices too cold. I'd throw my dolls if I didn't like their dresses. Even as an adult I had no idea how cosseted I was, until everything collapsed.

My parents tried to shield me from the rebellion, to pretend nothing was wrong. It was only when Morgelyns's troops brought flaming catapults and bloody pikes right to the doors of the Great Oak that...' Her chin crumpled and she pursed her lips, visibly controlling her emotion as she went on. 'There are those who seek blood Cora, who beat their ideas into other people's heads and grow giddy on the power of it. They'll use any excuse, anything to get what they want. Bravery is simply saying no. Saying that this might be happening, even that it's inevitable, but not in my name.'

'How did you survive? How did you get away?'

'I was hidden by my closest guards, Meriwether Beetleblue, who you met at the meeting of the Guild, and Bronnan Mayflower. They understood the danger before I did. They got me out. Sometimes, in the dark hours, I wish I'd stayed and died beside my parents. To live feels like cowardice.'

Wenna looked uncomfortable and Cora didn't answer for a moment, she had the feeling that Wenna hadn't meant to say it out loud.

'Well, it ain't,' Cora was firm. 'A coward wouldn't be fighting back, would she? A coward would've joined Morgelyn.' She faltered to a stop. Her own troubles shrank, silly compared to Wenna's. She noticed that Eseld had disappeared, then heard her whistling, in the garden.

'What's she doing out there?'

Wenna smiled, though her eyes still glimmered. 'Calling an old friend. Ah, here they are.'

Eseld came back in with a robin perched upon her shoulder.

Cora was unnerved. She'd never recognised a particular bird before, but he was definitely the same one she'd last seen covered in soot. Her spine itched. He hopped onto Eseld's finger and listened intently as she whistled short staccato tunes, to which he replied in twittery bursts of his own.

As she watched, Cora understood a few of the sounds. She heard them as words. 'Chamber', 'hostage', 'trap'. She shut her mind to it. Refused to listen.

The robin flew out of the back door, opened only briefly by Eseld in order to keep the warmth in. 'He says Bronnan and Meriwether will meet us there. Yestin...'

Wenna's brow puckered in sympathy.

Eseld swallowed. 'Yestin isn't doing too well. But we'll find him, do what we can to persuade him.'

'Who's Yestin?' Cora asked.

Wenna glanced at Eseld, then back at Cora, 'Petrok's husband,' she said.

Cora blinked, confused. 'Sorry, for a minute I thought you said...'

'You heard right,' Wenna smiled, slightly wary.

Cora shook her head, deciding that the Faerie were a very strange race indeed, as she tugged her sleeve to cover the buds of black feather on her wrists.

Cora saw Wenna looking at her, slightly quizzically. Before she could say anything, Cora got up and pulled on a pair of gloves, asking Eseld, who was bustling around, packing things into bags, if she needed any help.

'I'm alright thanks, duck,' Eseld smiled, but it didn't reach her eyes. She stuffed bread, cheese and apples into a bag to sustain herself and Tom, then a tin of weevils she'd picked out of the flour bin, and a few handfuls of the grain they fed the chickens on into another. She packed various bottles and herbs into a battered satchel, along with two small books.

She gave Cora a bracelet to wear, made of red thread with copper nails woven into it, 'for protection.'

'Thank you,' Cora said, glancing down at it. She trusted Eseld and she trusted her magic, she was living proof that it worked after all. But the bracelet did look strange, like an amulet for the desperate than anything else. She hoped that wasn't what it was.

'Is that your blackstone?' Cora asked, gesturing to the smooth slab in Wenna's hands.

Wenna nodded. 'It's old and rather scratched but yes, it's mine. We can use it to see which entrance will be the safest.'

'Oh. I thought we'd just sort of, I don't know... disappear here, reappear there.' Cora felt a bit foolish.

Wenna frowned, 'don't know anyone who can do that. Not safely anyway. We'll meet Meriwether and Bronnan at the Round Table. And we'll get there on good old Shanks's pony.'

Tom came home looking glum.

'What's up with you?' Eseld asked, frowning.

Tom shrugged. 'Nothing that can be helped.'

But Wenna had already seen it. 'Oh no, Tom. Not your apprenticeship?'

'So,' Eseld frowned, 'old Vinegar Breeches wouldn't give you a bit of time off?'

He shrugged again and hung his coat on a nail.

'What about your father?' Eseld said. 'Didn't he say anything?'

'He's on a final warning as it is, since they found him asleep in that cart, stinking of gin.'

There he hesitated, his back to them all. 'Petrok gave up more'n a job. He gave up everything for...'

'For me,' Wenna was grim.

'I was going to say,' Tom said steadily, turning round, 'that he gave up everything for what's right. He could have joined Morgelyns's side couldn't he? He could have continued living at the palace and gathered all sorts of cronies around himself, but he didn't. He did what was right, not what was easy.'

Tom swallowed the mug of tea Eseld handed him and, with his mouth full of bread, gave Cora a rueful smile.

She returned it, but it felt as fake as it looked. How would he live without a trade? She told herself they'd think about it when they returned. If they returned.

When they went out through the woods, they took a path Cora hadn't followed before. Thick snow lay on the wide fir branches and in ragged patches on the ground.

A group of people in winter coats and snow-flecked capes with baggy hoods were talking in low voices and blowing smoke from pipes and cheroots, huddled around a fork in the path. Some had rope coiled diagonally across their bodies, others held hammers and pick axes. All carried bags. In the twilight, Cora could just make out the features of Mr Penrose and Mrs Trethowan.

They followed a twisting route down into a

hollow, crammed with naked silver birches, towards a sparkling waterfall.

'Are you sure it's safe?' Cora shouted over the tumbling water. The path had become even narrower and she gripped Tom's arm for balance as they inched along.

'Don't worry!' Wenna called back. 'I've been coming this way for centuries. We won't go all the way along.'

Cora couldn't think of an answer to that, so she followed the others carefully, afraid her feet would slip on the wet rock, as the ledge went right behind the sheet of rushing water. To her surprise, she saw Eseld and Wenna squeeze through a fissure ahead. She glanced at Tom, whose wet skin shimmered, his eyes bright with adventure. She noticed a faint mark in the rock, cloudy through the spray, and she was sure it was the same as the one carved on the cowshed in the stone circle. Once she was through the fissure, the roaring water became quieter. She followed Tom through a narrow space, which opened out into a cave.

'This way,' Wenna called over her shoulder, her voice echoing loudly. The winter sunlight, which filtered through the water falling behind them to ripple across the rock ahead, became dimmer the further in they went and it became hard to see, then the last traces of light ahead disappeared and she was staring into nothing but blackness.

Cora wiped her eyes and face, trying not to shiver. She could hear a steady, distant dripping, but the last of the daylight was behind them and too faint to give any idea of the size of the cave. The blackness was so dense, it could have stretched far above and ahead, or ended at the brush of a fingertip. Cora had heard that caves could be the size of cathedrals or narrow to a crack that could crush a body if it tried to squeeze through, but she tried to not to think about it.

Eseld was rubbing her hands together and blowing on them. She watched them for a moment. Nothing happened, so she rubbed them together again, more vigorously this time, and blew a bit harder until a flame, not much bigger than a candle but with a wider base, sprouted from her palm. 'That's better,' she grinned. 'My hands was a bit damp, is all.'

Despite all she knew, Cora was mesmerised by the soft triangle of amber light, which jumped and bent as Eseld moved. 'How did you-?'

'Hmm? Oh this, it's a funny one this. There's folk what spend years trying to conjure it, using books and charms and whatnot. But what they don't understand is that it's a much older magic, from long before writing and book learning. Before words even. Some say it's from the time of our earliest ancestors, the ones what weren't faery or human, nor spriggan nor any of 'em, those what came before. You got to think about what really matters. About why you need the flame. You got to sort of feel it deep inside. Stiffen your sinews and summon up your blood. Like that king, in that play.'

Cora had never seen a play. She wasn't allowed to the music hall for what Aunt Selina called 'base entertainments'. She was surprised that Eseld had been, but didn't say so.

Guided by the glow, they moved carefully over the uneven rock. The flame spread over a lumpy wall, the circle of light revealing nothing but stone, glistening with water. Cora couldn't see very well, but Wenna appeared to be doing something a little further along. It was as if she was writing large, sweeping letters on the rock with her fingers, without paint or chalk. Cora watched, thinking she'd see some marks or a picture appear soon, if she stared hard enough, but all that happened was that Wenna drew her index finger back and then stabbed with it, deep into the stone, hard enough to break her bones.

Cora's eyes grew round with disbelief, as the apparently solid rock yielded to the pressure. It was soft and pliant as dough, and Wenna kept pushing until her arm disappeared up to the elbow, and the suddenly spongy rock began to tear.

Cora was astonished to see the once-solid wall peeling back, creating a door-sized space for them to pass through.

On the other side, the cave was just as cold, just as dark, and the dripping sounded louder. Cora hated it. It felt like a doomed place. The air tasted of death, despair and nothingness. The ground sloped downward and she stumbled, clutching Tom's arm. Her feet were suddenly much colder.

'Got to paddle a bit now,' Eseld called, and Tom put his hand over Cora's, steadying her. 'Don't worry it ain't deep,' Eseld added. 'Just imagine you're at the seaside.'

'I ain't never been,' Cora gasped as the cold, black water inched up her shins and over her knees. 'And if it's like this, I ain't never going.'

The glow in Eseld's hand shimmered on the surface of the water. They had to lift their bags high, to keep them dry.

'Not much further!' Wenna called over her shoulder.

At first, Cora thought she was imagining it but, no, there was definitely a light ahead, which pooled in a wavering path across the water ahead of them, spilling down a carved flight of steps leading to an opening in the cave wall.

As they moved towards it, Cora could hear voices. One male and one female.

Wenna climbed the steps and shook the water from her cape, scattering glittering droplets.

Eseld was next, and Cora heard her grunt with effort as she climbed, even though Tom helped her. Cora understood why when it was her turn. The first, underwater steps were much higher and more difficult to negotiate than the visible ones.

'Makes it harder to sneak in,' Eseld explained, turning to give Cora a hand.

'Why would anybody do that?' Cora asked.

'This is where Arthur conducted his most secret meetings,' Wenna explained as they went inside.

'He didn't want no spies earwigging,' Eseld put in.

Candles glued to the floor with their own dribbly wax flickered here and there. As she glanced around, Cora made out two figures, who dropped to their knees. Both made the same gesture Cora saw Meriwether perform at the meeting.

Wenna bid them rise. Cora recognised Meriwether Beetleblue from the guild meeting. The other faery must be the female, she concluded, though she'd never have guessed. She looked more like a warrior than Meriwether did and her skin was different, a darker, brownish grey, like the faded leather of an old book. Her hair was tightly bound in three wispy plaits, woven with twisted threads. She had several metal rings in each ear and eyes were a burnished amber, instead of buttery yellow like the others. They narrowed at Cora, who tried to stop staring.

'Why do they do that?' Cora asked Eseld, hoping her voice was low enough for them not to hear, and that they were too busy to watch her thoughts.

'What, this?' Eseld touched her mouth, neck and chest as they had done. 'Well, what'd you do if the Queen, Queen Victoria I mean, was here?'

Cora's stomach lurched unpleasantly at the thought. 'I don't know, um, curtesy I s'pose. Or salute or something? Not sure what you're supposed to do.'

'It's like that. It's a respect thing.'

'It's more than that,' the female faery snapped. 'It's the sign of her majesty's personal bodyguard. We touch our mouths to demonstrate that we will keep Queen Wenna's secrets, our throats to demonstrate our readiness to die for her and our hearts to show our loyalty is deep.'

Eseld looked a little flustered. 'Well, alright then. Didn't say I knew everything.'

The faery gave both Eseld and Cora a cool, appraising look, which flickered over the other humans as they came in, shivering and wet. Her gaze lingered on Tom.

'You've already met Meriwether,' Eseld flung her arm towards him, then squatted to get something out of the bags. 'And that's Bronnan Mayflower. Bronnan, this is Cora Blackthorn. There, introductions over,' she added, 'best get on.'

143

Meriwether crouched too. 'I've already started. Had some trouble with Petrok's thread though. Morgelyn must've done something to his blackstone.'

Wenna gave them a meaningful look and they reacted as though she'd spoken aloud.

Bronnan's head snapped up, nostrils flaring in anger.

'She *smashed* it?' Meriwether was incredulous.

'Couldn't he get another one?' Cora asked, looking from one stricken face to another. 'Are they very expensive?'

Bronnan shot her a condescending look. 'What's she on about?'

'It's not something you can replace,' Wenna said. 'Blackstones are given to toddlers on their twentieth birthday. They absorb memories as a faery grows up, so that their thread becomes strong. It's much harder to detect a thread when someone doesn't have their blackstone.'

Meriwether placed his blackstone on the rocky floor of the cave. Wenna put hers close beside it. There was another one there too, presumably Bronnan's.

'So, what do we do?' Cora asked everyone and no-one. 'We don't have blackstones.'

'You don't need one for this.' Meriwether replied. 'It's awfully clever. It's a particular kind of circular system that Merlin developed, based on his observations of whirlpools, in order to combine different strains of magic, so that faeries and humans could join forces at thin places like this, in order to travel from one place to another. Arthur told Merlin to destroy it after they went their separate ways. But of course, he didn't. He formed the Spindleberry

Guild instead, to guard his secrets, so that the knowledge couldn't be lost.'

Cora nodded, more to be polite than anything else. She couldn't have replied even if she had understood. No-one except Wenna had mentioned her father before. There'd been no need. The word hadn't had any meaning. She'd always known that she must have had one, but nobody had ever confirmed it. Now the word 'father' referred to someone who'd died hundreds of years ago. She fought to swallow the lump in her throat. She didn't realise she could miss something she'd never had.

At Wenna's instruction, they joined hands to make a ring.

'Where's the table?' Cora asked, as she clasped their cold, grey hands and tried not to think about corpses.

'It isn't exactly a table, not in the literal sense.' Meriwether smiled, deliberately lifting his eyebrows and Cora got the feeling he was trying to look less anxious than he felt. 'The circular system creates a layer of atoms whose particles... Do you know about protons and neutrons?'

Cora shook her head.

'Well, inside an atom are positively charged protons and electrically neutral particles, called neutrons. These particles are nearly identical to each other, except in electric charge. By reversing...'

'For goodness sake, Meriwether,' Bronnan said through her teeth, 'she hasn't got a clue what you're talking about!'

'Oh, perhaps another time then?' he smiled warmly at Cora, not seeming offended at all.

It was Wenna who started the chanting first. She

spoke in the old language, which felt more familiar and comforting every time Cora heard it, particularly after Meriwether's well-intentioned gibberish. The guild responded, as grave as if they were delivering a eulogy. The words were the same each time and, soon, Cora felt able to join in, hesitant at first, until Eseld nodded encouragingly. '*Wit behefp síp Eardlufu*' Wenna said, and they responded '*Eardlufu, Eardlufu*'.

As they spoke, wisps of fog started rising from the surface of the blackstones, joining together and swirling gently, so that the smoky tendrils stretched and separated as cream does, when trickled into coffee. As she watched, Cora was astonished to see glimpses of dark green between the rags of swirling mist. Something solid, like treetops, seemed to be rising, growing bigger and clearer by the second, or was she fading and growing smaller?

The voices sounded further away, and it became harder for Cora to keep repeating '*Eardlufu, Eardlufu.*' It wasn't like falling down the mineshaft at all, when the wind had rushed so hard it'd made her eyes water. This was more like fainting, a gradual dissolving of consciousness, as though she was becoming part of the mist.

Something was pressing hard and flat against her back. She opened her eyes wide, but the blackness was the same as when they were closed. Panicking, Cora feared she'd gone blind, until a match flared and she smelled tobacco. The dim light suggested a low, curved roof, not the rough rock of a cave but a suggestion of narrow bricks. She was lying flat on her back in the bottom of a dank tunnel.

Eseld was puffing on a pipe. Its glow illuminated

the creases of her face, as she leaned closer. 'She's a-waking up,' she said. 'Lets get on.'

Meriwether was surprisingly strong as he helped Cora to her feet. 'All right?' he asked, his gaze bright and friendly.

She nodded, brushing dirt from her dress.

'What happened?' Tom was murmuring. His was sitting up, one hand on his head.

Eseld patted his shoulder and helped him up. 'Feels funny the first time, I know. You'll be all right in a minute.'

'We're actually here!' he breathed, grinning and gazing around, though it was too dark to see much. 'We're in Faerie!'

Cora nodded, trying to feel excited, instead of afraid. After a moment, she asked 'when are we going to Underwood?'

'That's where we are,' Wenna's voice came from the gloom.

'Is she a bit... you know?' Cora could just make out the contours of Bronnan's face, and the finger she used to tap her temple.

'No, I bloody well ain't!' Cora tapped her own temple savagely.

'She's never been down here before,' Wenna said gently.

'I *have* been down here, remember? I know I was dosed with that glamour stuff but it still counts.'

'I didn't mean you'd never been to Underwood, Cora.' Wenna took Eseld's match and put it to a candle in a tiny lantern on a hook in the wall. The glow revealed a brick tunnel, thickly furred with cobweb, green lichen and whitish frills of mould. Other tunnels ran off it, until it curved out of sight in both directions. 'I meant down here, in the sewers.'

'Sewers?!' Cora wrinkled her nose in disgust. But there was no stench, no rats or rivulets of sewage; nothing to be disgusted about. If this really was a sewer, then it hadn't been used for a long time.

Wenna was watching her, patiently. Waiting, Cora realised, for her to think about the fact that faeries no longer ate or drank. To join the dots.

Bronnan hitched up her bag. 'Lets go.'

They followed the tunnel, occasionally crunching through old, dried sludge that Cora didn't want to think about, and clumps of dead leaves that must have slithered down drains.

'How do we know where to go?' Cora asked. 'Is he being held at the Great Oak?'

'Why would he be there?' Bronnan was scornful.

'She's still learning about all of this,' Wenna cut in.

'Well, she'd better learn quickly. And use a bit of common sense.' Bronnan bit the top off a dried root, spat it out, then stuck it between her teeth and chewed as they walked, occasionally spitting bits over her shoulder.

Cora didn't ask what it was.

But it was too late, Bronnan had already heard her thinking about it. 'Just because we can't eat doesn't mean we can't chew and spit.'

Cora nodded dumbly, resolving to have as little to do with Bronnan as possible.

The tunnel went on for a long time. Eseld smoked her pipe as they walked and, although she found the smell bitter, the familiar haze of it comforted Cora, even as her whole scalp prickled with fear.

She had no idea what they were walking into. The

world she'd seen was a lie, she knew that. But what had the glamour been covering up?

'Here we are,' Wenna stopped. She pulled the small, pointed stone from her pocket, the one she'd used in the cave, and began running her hands carefully over the curved wall, striking it with the stone, sometimes quickly dragging it, making sparks.

In the dimness, Cora could just make out the circular sign of the guild in one of the bricks.

The others came to a halt around her, murmuring '*weælldore*' in response to Wenna's words. Cora watched as the bricks began to wobble, grating against each other as they fidgeted and faded, revealing a small wooden door.

Cora marvelled, touching the wood as if it might burn her, though it looked completely ordinary, scuffed and dusty like any door.

'It was always there,' Wenna knocked, but there was no reply. 'I just removed the spell that was hiding it.'

'Does somebody really live down here?'

'I did, for a while. This is Yestin and Petrok's house. They built it when their home was burned.'

'Because they're...'

'My supporters, yes.' Wenna knocked again, a bit louder this time.

'I knew it,' Bronnan muttered. 'Might as well go straight to the Crooked Chimney.'

'But he promised.' Wenna's voice was painfully soft.

Eseld and Meriwether exchanged glances.

Bronnan bit her root. There wasn't much left. 'Doubt he's in a state to promise anything these days.'

Wenna pushed a small key into the lock, a grim

set to her features. 'He might not have heard.'

They pushed the door inward and a damp, mouldy odour wafted out. Wenna went in first, with her lantern, and she used it to light a bigger one that hung from the ceiling, revealing a shabby little room. It was bitterly cold and Cora shivered. 'Shall we get a fire going?' she suggested, glancing around in vain for a hearth.

'There isn't one,' Wenna said, pulling a threadbare blanket that smelled of mildew off a wooden settle. 'Nowhere for a chimney to go without arising suspicion,' she explained. 'And if you don't need food anymore then, well...'

Cora thanked her for the blanket and tried to ignore the smell as she wrapped it around herself.

'Yestin!' Wenna tugged a thick, patched curtain away from a doorway and wedged it on a hook at the side, before disappearing into another room.

'Come out Yestin, you old bag 'o bones!' Eseld called, following her.

It was dirty and untidy, but that wasn't what chilled Cora. It was the lifelessness that she found so unsettling. The lack of a fireplace was strange enough, but there was no evidence of cooking or sleeping because there was no need, which made the place very bleak. The only comfort, apart from the sparse furniture with its musty blankets, was to be found on the shelves that ran along the walls, where books were crammed, piled on top of each other, ranging from those not much bigger than matchboxes to enormous bible-sized tomes, along with bundles of paper and worn periodicals. Thank God, she thought, for words.

Wenna reappeared, looking grim. 'He isn't here.'

'We know that.' Bronnan rolled her eyes as she pulled out another root. In the enclosed space, its faintly liquorice smell mingled with the mouldy one and made Cora queasy.

Meriwether glared at Bronnan and the air seemed to thicken. 'Have some respect,' he muttered.

Bronnan shrugged and bit her root.

'Could Yestin have gone for a walk?' Cora ventured.

'A walk?' Bronnan snorted, 'with regime thugs crawling everywhere and posters stuck up all over the place with his face on?!' She glared at Cora, who shrank. 'What are you even doing here?'

'She is here at my request,' Wenna answered calmly.

'I'll wait outside,' Bronnan lifted her hands in irritation and disappeared through the front door.

'She doesn't mean it,' Wenna said heavily. 'She's just angry.'

Wenna turned to Eseld, addressing her, Tom, Cora, Mr Penrose and Mrs Trethowan. 'You cornalls need to sleep,' Wenna said. 'We'll wake you when it's time to go.'

'We're all right,' Tom protested. 'We want to get to Petrok!'

'I admire your courage, Tom,' she grinned. 'But you're human and it's dark. You need sleep.'

Early the next day, the humans ate some pasties that Mrs Trethowan had brought and Cora made do with a handful of weevils and chicken grain from Eseld's bag. As she swallowed the last one, she happened to glance up at Meriwether and saw the same envy she felt, in his eyes, as he watched Tom lick flecks of greasy pastry from his fingers.

When they left the strange little rooms in the sewer, it was just as dark as it had been the night before. Wenna cast the concealing spell again, shuffling the bricks back into place and rejoining the strands of web and patches of mould, so that it looked the same as the rest of the tunnel, apart from the tiny mark of the Spindleberry Guild, which she caked again, with grime, so that nobody would see it unless they looked very closely.

They came to a ladder that took them up a wide, vertical pipe to a manhole cover. Meriwether pushed and it lifted, allowing a shaft of grey light to filter down through the gap at an angle. Meriwether made sure everyone stayed quiet for what felt like a long time. The rungs were pressing uncomfortably into Cora's feet by the time he decided it was safe to emerge.

They struggled up through the hole and found themselves on a wide, earthen road that curved away between enormous trees. Under the influence of the glamour, the trees had towered over her, smooth as cathedral pillars, emerald brilliance filtering through their leaves but now they were a higgeldy-piggeldy mass of leafless branches. Many had grown down into the ground and emerged again, the roots so huge it was hard to distinguish them from the lowest boughs. Lumpen walls bulged between the natural curves and forks; a mixture of plaster, timber and brick, as though they were frequently patched up. Cora spotted the little doors, window shutters and staircases that wound up from one bough to another, but there was none of the tranquillity of before.

Most of the housetrees had been blasted, their walls ripped apart to expose circular rooms inside the trunk and sloping halls within the branches, where pictures still hung and broken shelves spilled their contents. Most of the homes had been burned too and the charred remains of rocking chairs, clocks and smashed crockery was heartbreaking. There were thin ropes of seed pods and dried flowers looped over bedposts and around smaller twigs, like necklaces. Without needing to be told, Cora knew they marked the places where faeries had died.

Wenna was glancing around, her eyes keen and narrow, creasing the skin of her temples. 'We have to move.' She strode away and they hurried after her, through the chilly air. A fine drizzle began to fall and Cora glanced up, confused, expecting to glimpse the rocky roof of a cave in the jagged gaps between the branches. Instead she saw flat, grey sky.

She regretted it the minute she said it, but all that came out of her mouth was 'where's the sunshine gone?'

Bronnan's face was like granite. 'That's the thing she notices. It's winter, Cora.'

'She was englamoured when she was here,' Wenna stated.

'But it isn't snowing,' Cora went on, unable to stop herself. 'It's snowing up on the moor.'

'We are a few miles closer to the centre of the earth here,' Wenna explained starting to move off, 'so it's always a few degrees warmer.'

Meriwether said 'we should go on ahead, your majesty, Bronnan and I. You should stay here with the cornalls, just in case there are any...'

'We go together.' Wenna was firm.

They followed Wenna, who led them along the road at a jog. Cora hadn't seen her do it, but Wenna had pulled the hood of her cape up over her bonnet, pulling it low to conceal her face. A dagger had found its way into her hand.

'There's an old story,' Tom squinted up at the trees and the rain coated his face, making it shine, 'Mamm-wynn told it me when I were a little-un, what says that Merlin missed the sky above Cornwall. Down here, it were just rock, like in a cave, so he tweaked it, and he made the hours lighter and darker and the different seasons come and go, like they do at home. He made a sun and a moon too. They're not the real thing, but not bad. He was a great wizard but, you know, still just a man. Else he wouldn't have run off with Mab and got himself in Arthur's bad books in the first place, would he?' He nudged Cora, trying to cheer her up, to lift the leaden sadness coming off the trees like smoke.

Cora managed a small smile, but she let it drop as soon as he turned away. She didn't like the sound of anybody, let alone her father, coming down and changing things. She wondered what Wenna thought about it.

The forest was chilly and a charcoal smell soured the fog. There wasn't a breath of wind. The air was peculiarly still, as though it had never moved, so that part of her first experience of Underwood, Cora surmised, was real. Everything else was completely different. It felt dead. Ruined. Gone were the bright flowers and curled ferns. The glittering pools had vanished and in their place were flat, muddy puddles reflecting nothing but bare sky and skeletal branches. The only signs of life were clouds of midges hovering above the mud. Cora was briefly tempted to eat them, as she watched them dart between leafless shadows slanting through thick, grey air and across the path, like outstretched fingers.

Eerie silence exaggerated their footsteps and it wasn't until the shadow of a bird slipped across the dirt that Cora realised something else was missing. This was a dense, ancient forest but there was no birdsong, not even the faintest twitter. The shadow of another bird, smaller and swifter this time, darted ahead, over the path and across the drifts of brown, sodden leaves that formed the forest floor. Cora glanced up, but the air was empty.

Meriwether followed her gaze. 'They're gone,' he said, answering her thoughts with a sad shrug. 'The birds. When Morgelyn unleashed the curse they hid themselves and their song. They'll become visible again when we break it. When it's over.'

'How?'

'Birds have magic all of their own,' he smiled. 'They go places none of us can, even while their shadows stay behind.'

Cora was intrigued, glancing up again, where threads of mist hung between the housetrees. 'No, sorry,' she clarified, 'I meant how will you break the curse?'

'The Merlinshard of course. You do know, don't you? About the Merlinshard?'

Cora shook her head, trying to be patient. She was getting fed up with people expressing surprise at how little she knew.

'Meriwether!' Bronnan turned on her heel, coming nose to nose with him. 'You can't be talking about the Merlinshard with just anybody.' She scowled at Cora, finishing her angry speech without words.

Then it happened. Cora saw fleeting, uncanny shapes twist and dance around Bronnan's head.

She stumbled backwards, afraid. The shapes made no sense at first, until she made out a crude, unflattering miniature of herself, with sausage limbs and a pinched, ugly face.

Wenna smiled, the heaviness in her eyes disappearing for a moment. She grabbed Cora's hands. 'I knew it! Coming here is making the magic rise within you, like sap in spring!' She pointed at Bronnan. 'Those are her thoughts! You're seeing them!'

Bronnan's nostrils flared and Cora remembered seeing an expression like that before, when anybody passed the only African servant in town.

'How could *she* read me?' Bronnan sneered. 'She's nothing but a scrawny cornall! I don't know why you let them get involved. Greedy, short-sighted mammals. They're a race of children. Dead by eighty. They're born, then snap,' she clicked her fingers, 'they die.'

'Hold your tongue,' Meriwether put himself between Cora and Bronnan.

Now Cora glimpsed thoughts swirling around his head. With a jolt of shame, she saw herself there, clouting Hendra. But it was nothing compared to what the tiny figure of Bronnan was doing. Blood-smeared swords whirling in each hand, she was running towards a scattering crowd.

Meriwether frowned, his thoughts vanishing as though he'd drawn a curtain.

Cora realised it wasn't polite to stare.

'If her majesty wants to join forces with the cornalls,' Meriwether said, 'then our duty is to-'

'They've been snatching cornalls too, so they're involved whether we like it or not!' Wenna was firm. 'And making ghasts of them, just as they've been doing down here.' She sliced the air with her palm, to emphasise her point. 'And don't call them that. They call themselves humans, not starlanders or cornalls.'

After an awkward silence, she added 'we need to keep moving, find Yestin. We don't know who's watching.'

Cora glanced around, anxious. Tom fell into step beside her. 'I don't know anything about no Merlinshard either,' he said.

Bronnan was looking at Tom, her face unreadable, her thoughts closed off.

Cora put her arm through Tom's, doing her best to return Bronnan's cold gaze.

'There's a book,' Wenna said, speaking to Cora, though her eyes darted up and around and behind. 'Back at the house, it'll tell you all about the Merlinshard. About lots of things. All you really need to know is that we need it and Morgelyn's got it, in the crown she stole from my father. It was a gift from Merlin to our ancestors. The most powerful thing he ever created. And the most dangerous.'

Cora flushed, keeping her voice down. 'I mightn't be able to read it. I only know my basic letters.'

'Which are the basic ones?' Bronnan's eyes narrowed in amusement.

Cora wished she hadn't spoken. 'Oh, just enough for spirit writing, you know.'

'Spirit what?'

'Writing.' Cora swallowed, colouring. 'Messages from the other side. Only they weren't, you know. It were just me.'

Bronnan's eyebrows lifted and she shook her head. 'Don't you cornall's have any science? Don't you have schools?'

Wenna shot Bronnan a warning look.

'We have 'em.' Cora looked down at her boots, appearing and disappearing beneath her hem as she walked. 'Only not everybody can go.'

'She can read and write better'n me,' Tom cut in. 'Maybe it's you what needs a book, Bronnan,' he added, winking at Cora. 'Teach you about above.'

Bronnan shrugged, as if she didn't care, but Cora caught the stung look as she turned away.

'What's the book called?' Cora asked Wenna. 'Did he-, did my father have anything to do with it?'

'What would your *father* have to do with anything?' Bronnan spluttered. 'Who is he, some slack-jawed farmer?'

'Didn't you know? Weren't you listening before?' Wenna cut in, 'it's her. Cora's the daughter of Merlin and Mab.'

For just a second, Bronnan's frown fractured, opening up into an expression of fierce amazement, but she masked it immediately. 'What, the one from the stories? Forgive me, your majesty, but you don't believe they're true?'

'I do.' Wenna walked a little faster. The others hurried to keep up. 'I know they are. And I can prove it.' She looked at Cora, who sensed that she was going to ask her to reveal the tattoo. Silently, she asked her not to. Wenna nodded, a twinkle of excitement at Cora's new abilities returning to her eye. 'But not now,' she finished, making Bronnan scowl more than ever.

Cora squeezed closer to Tom, her back prickling

painfully. She tried to pull her sleeve down to cover the gap between the cuff and her glove. Either her dress had shrunk or her arms were growing longer and the pale skin, flecked with black, hairlike feathers, obstinately showed.

It grew darker as the trees became more crowded. Soon they were following each other through a tangled tunnel, where branches had woven themselves together overhead, vaulted at the top like a cloister and letting in only the thinnest shafts of light. Beneath their feet was a path of roots, twisted over and under each other, thick with dead moss.

As the path curved to the left, the trees above broke apart and Cora glimpsed a flight of steps. They were wide and grand and led up to an arch-shaped door bleached to the colour of old bone, surrounded by intricate carving and set six feet up in a massive trunk. Dead ivy hung in twisted, witch-hair hanks across windows full of shadow, embedded in the bark. The remains of shattered glass stuck out, jagged in the frames. Further up, timbered walls held windows still partly glassed beneath a lattice of lead. Spiral staircases, their banisters beautifully carved with flowers and huge insects connected bough to bough, room to room. The tree was so enormous that, even without leaves, it was impossible to gauge its true size. It looked as though it might brush the clouds.

'The university,' Tom breathed. 'It's just like you described it, Mamm-wynn, only...'

'Only ruined' Wenna said. 'Dead.'

Wenna produced a bunch of keys from her bag and drove one into the lock.

Cora expected the door to stick, warped with

disuse, but it opened immediately, emitting a loud creak and air that smelled of dust and burned paper.

'Is this where Petrok was, when they took his blackstone?' Cora asked.

Wenna nodded. 'It was, it *is*, his life.'

Cora gazed up and around her. The walls were lined with slightly uneven shelves from the floor to the beamed ceiling. A portrait was hung at an angle, its face scratched to oblivion, the canvas hanging in tatters. There were other dark rectangles, where more pictures must have been. Empty sconces, here and there, were thickly coated with dribbled wax. Leaves had blown in through the broken windows and rain must have too, for in places the boards were swollen with damp. Stairways and halls led in different directions, including downward, to subterranean rooms, reached by corridors inside the largest roots. Little carved signs with pointing hands, some with their words viciously scratched out, said things like '*Mathematics and Metaphysics*', '*Herbcraft*', '*Dissection*' and '*Talismanic Engineering*'. Others directed students to the '*Alchemical Laboratories*' and the '*Chamber of Bewitching Arts*', which had a faded note underneath that read '*Danger of Befuddlement. Amulets MUST be worn at all times.*'

'This way,' Wenna strode purposefully ahead and up a narrow flight of steps carved into the trunk wall. She took them two at a time, the dagger glinting in her hand.

The steps became wider and shallower. Soon they were treading on threadbare maroon carpet, sloping gently upward, with a faded pattern only visible at the edges. Patches were mushy with rain. The corridor led them along the inside of a huge bough, with shelves running each side. Through the broken windows, Cora glimpsed more branches, slicing glimpses of sky into tiny triangles.

'What are all the shelves for?' Cora asked. 'I can't see any ornaments or-'

'Down there.' Bronnan pointed out through one of the windows. Cora moved closer.

She peered out of a window not much bigger than her head, careful not to let her face touch the sharp edges of broken glass. Having never been so high up in a tree, without the numbing effect of glamour, it made her giddy to look down, but she hid it from Bronnan as best she could.

Bronnan was pointing to the remains of an enormous bonfire on the forest floor, the trees around it scorched black as the earth. Grey spines with stumps of pages amongst the ash told Cora the awful truth.

'The books?' Cora's voice was almost a whisper. Such a loss took her breath away.

Wenna said 'do you see why they took as many as they could down to the sewer house? And to the guild?'

'And to the cellar,' Cora breathed, 'at the cottage.'

Wenna nodded. 'Hendra took as many as she could too, and Mr Penrose and all the rest. We got as many to safety as we possibly could, once we thought we knew what she planned to do. If only we'd got more people out.' Her voice caught, but she steadied herself. 'We didn't realise. We didn't guess.'

Meriwether gazed at her, concerned, but Wenna shrugged, swallowing hard as she indicated with her dagger that they should keep going.

The corridor continued to slope upwards, then divided into two, divided again, then again. Sometimes they came across a flight of steps, where the branches sloped more steeply. Each corridor was a little narrower than the one before, until the humans had to duck to go through a door which stood open.

'He didn't have time to put the spell back.' Wenna froze for a moment, as though gathering her courage. And Cora realised that this door must normally be hidden, like the one in the sewer.

A little plaque on the door read *Petrok Noon, Ma. Mag. Tech.*

Wenna stepped inside and stared around, bereft.

The walls were full of empty shelves and a branch, about the thickness of a person, spanned the room from the bottom left to the top right corner, with nails driven into it, on which were hung a leather bag, turned inside out, its contents on the floor, a hat and various brass instruments. One of the two winged armchairs was overturned. A pipe was smashed and there were piles of torn paper littering the desk and rug. A small, embroidered slipper lay by the hearth.

Swallowing her misery, Wenna started picking things up and trying to put the room in order. But one of the chair legs was broken and it wouldn't stand.

'Forgive me, your majesty, but why are we here?' Bronnan asked. 'What can this place tell us that we don't already know?'

Wenna glanced at each of them in turn, as if trying to make a decision. 'I'm looking for message. If he could, he'd have left something for us to find, before...'

'You're not serious?!' Meriwether's usual politeness seemed to have deserted him as he stared, dumbstruck, at Wenna.

She met his gaze.

Bronnan was deep in thought.

'What?' Eseld asked. 'What is it?'

Cora waited for Wenna to explain to the other humans, but she'd seen it too, a shimmering thought, floating beside Wenna's head. It was a curious thing of dusky blue, with a smooth surface and rough, jagged edges, like a piece of mirror reflecting twilight.

'*He* had it?' Bronnan spluttered. 'You trusted it to *him*?!'

Wenna answered her with a regal stare. 'As dean of the university and chief advisor to the royal family I believed him to be the-'

'His mind is, his... brilliance isn't in dispute. But as a guardian of such a treasure I, well I-'

'You expected me to choose you? So that if you were captured along with me, the hopes of our people would be captured too?'

Bronnan closed her mouth, but seemed unconvinced.

'You have protected me ever since my father gave you this.' Wenna touched a tiny 's' on Bronnan's temple, which Cora had never noticed. It was blue, not pinkish brown like her own mark. 'But this was his burden,' she said. 'He chose it.'

'He wouldn't have left it here,' Meriwether said. 'And she'll expect us to come. We're lucky we weren't ambushed.'

'You are here to protect me,' Wenna snapped. 'Not to offer counsel.'

Meriwether pressed his lips into a thin line, but bowed in apology. 'My lady. I forgot myself.'

'No,' she rubbed her forehead, 'no, you didn't deserve that,' she looked more unhappy than Cora had ever seen her. 'You're right. Of course you are. He couldn't have left us a message. If he can contact us, he will. Until then, we must keep searching.'

Nobody spoke as they left the little room.

They left the university and followed a path that led to an even bleaker place. It wasn't ruined, but something about it made Cora gather her cape close about her.

They approached a housetree that hadn't been blasted or burned, but looked very old indeed. A stout door, studded with metal, was flanked by roots so thick they were taller than Tom, pasted all over with peeling advertisements. Above the door swung a peeling sign with a wonky black chimney painted upon it, on the point of collapse. She could just make out the real chimney between the highest branches. It looked virtually impossible, leaning as far as it did. An enormous beam was stuck up at an angle to prop up a window-studded bough, which looked ready to crash to the ground, bringing half the tree down with it. Like the other dwellings, it was partly made of lumpy brick or timbered plaster, but this one was terribly distended. It bulged and sagged, the walls like a waistcoat after too many courses, with buttons ready to burst.

Chapter Eleven

The Crooked Chimney

As they pushed the door inward, it was gripped from the other side by a big, grubby hand. A thickset faery, taller than most, with a bald head, fixed them with a nasty stare, barring their way.

'Farthing,' he growled.

'We're looking for Yestin.' Meriwether was polite, though he kept his hood low, hiding his face. 'Is he here?'

'Farthing each.'

'Yestin Kneebone. Used to come here all the time.'

'Farthing.'

'We don't want to come in, we just want to know if he's here.'

'He's here.'

'Can you tell him it's his friends? We want to speak to him.'

The snarl broadened into a grin, revealing brown stumps for teeth. 'Penny each.'

Bronnan shifted menacingly towards him, but with the lightest touch from Wenna on her sleeve, she stopped.

Each of them dug around for a coin.

The bald faery peered at each penny in turn and moved back, letting them into the dank, musty room, which took up most of the base of the hollow trunk. The walls were bare wood, black with soot. Cora had vaguely heard of things called opium dens. She imagined they looked something like this.

Faeries lounged on upturned barrels. Some lay on the ground, eyes half-closed. A few were humming or chuckling softly to themselves, one was marvelling at his own fingers. There were high backed settles along one wall, facing each other over stained tables, where faeries slumped, some with their heads in their hands or embedded in folded arms. Someone in a tattered John Bull hat with white tufts of hair escaping round his ears was tipping a tankard that dribbled liquid all down his arm.

'Yestin!' Wenna gasped, hurrying over to him just as he snatched up what looked like a pewter salt shaker.

'Yestin, please, don't!'

Undeterred, coughing liquid he couldn't swallow, he tipped the sparkling powder into his eyes before she could stop him and blinked several times, mouth wide, eyes red and watering, and something inside him visibly unspooled, loosening his limbs and his smile.

'Your majesty?' He blinked, frowning at Wenna as though he required spectacles.

A few of the other patrons glanced around, not seeing.

'Want some?' His speech was strange, the consonants oddly accentuated, the syllables slow and drawn out. 'It's a new blend.'

He held it up. 'Junehock and... and garnet and um,' he looked at it. Then he put it down, as if he'd not been talking about it at all. 'Have you seen these?' He picked up the tankard, which was leaking. It smelled strongly of cheap gin. 'Look at that craftsmanship.' He traced the patches of rust with a dirt-crusted finger. 'It's amazing isn't it? See the patterns? So intricate. Amazing what they can do over... over there.'

'Over where?' Wenna asked patiently.

'Hmm?' He sipped the gin, trying again to swallow, though it made him retch and Cora feared he'd choke, as he coughed and sprayed it over the table.

He fixed Wenna with a bleary gaze. 'Oh yes,' he nodded emphatically, 'I imagine so.'

He looked at Bronnan. 'Bronnan! I love your hair, such a dazzling purple and all the moths! So clever!'

'Come on,' Bronnan jerked her head. People were beginning to stare, although most of them were too absorbed in their own glamour-spun reverie to care. Cora saw Bronnan's hand slip onto the hilt of the dagger hanging from her belt. Sweat dampened Yestin's face and throat, clumping the tufts of visible hair around his ears. Cora remembered the warmth she'd felt when she'd been englamoured herself. Had she really unbuttoned her dress to tug her corset out, to let the air in? She hoped not, flushing pink at the thought. Could everything in that paradise really have been an illusion? Even with the evidence laid before her, it was difficult to believe.

Meriwether took Yestin's arm.

'We don't have to go, it's early!' Yestin picked up the shaker again and Meriwether smacked it out of his hand. Sparkling powder spilled across the table and horror spread over Yestin's face.

'What have you done?!' he screamed, his dreaminess evaporating, teeth baring in a snarl. 'I'll kill you! Villain! Murderer!' His bloodshot eyes were suddenly wild, watering dangerously as he went for

Meriwether's throat.

Cora's heart twisted with sympathy as they grappled, Meriwether dragging him away from the spilled mess as Yestin tried to fight him, his movements too weak and clumsy to have much effect. And as they pushed through the pub to the entrance another faery slithered behind them and scooped up the shaker, licking his fingers and stabbing them over the grimy wood. He rubbed the glamour into his eyes, then ran his hands over the table again in case he'd missed a grain, this time beaming and pressing the heel of his other hand to his forehead, the shaker now safely in his pocket.

'No!' Yestin screeched again, bashing relentlessly against Meriwether until, between them he, Mr Penrose and Tom dragged him to the door. 'But that's mine! He can't have it! She can't have him!'

He was hitting out at all angles and tears stood in Wenna's eyes, even as she helped them haul him outside, where it was raining hard.

'We're going to get him back,' Wenna said, emotion snagging her words even as his flailing fist struck her across the nose, making her stagger.

Immediately, Bronnan pulled a cloth out of her bag and pressed it over Yestin's face. A strange, sulphuric smell permeated the watery air.

'But that won't work,' Cora protested, 'not if he doesn't breathe!'

'It isn't chloroform,' Bronnan replied, 'this stuff goes right through the skin.'

Wenna was disapproving, though she didn't stop Bronann. She rubbed her injured nose with a wary look at Yestin.

Bronnan stoppered the bottle. 'Unless we shut

him up, the army'll be here.'

Sure enough, Yestin's movements became slower and even more confused, until he slumped, unconscious, into Meriwether's arms, his hat tumbling off. With a heavy sigh, Tom bent and slung him over his neck, arms over one shoulder, legs over the other, like a shepherd with a sheep.

Cora was shocked. She picked up Yestin's hat and brushed off the bits of leaf, unable to keep her eyes off Bronnan.

'Don't worry,' Meriwether said. 'It's not what I'd have done,' he shot a glance at Bronnan, 'but he'll be alright. He'll have a headache from hell, but he'll be alright. We'll get him home, then when he's awake we'll find out what he knows about Petrok.'

They set off through the wood. Over the pattering rain, Cora thought she heard drumming. She put it down to the strange, windless acoustics, then caught the high, scratching notes of a fiddle. She looked questioningly at Wenna, who'd heard it too.

'What's that?' Tom asked. It got louder and they stopped to listen.

'I thought she banned music,' Eseld whispered.

'She did.' Meriwether was grave.

They started walking again and, because the manhole cover lay in the same direction as the music, the sounds grew louder, becoming more cohesive as the path sloped down between the ruined housetrees.

Before they rounded a bend, Cora glimpsed coloured flags with a vaguely familiar face embroidered on them, wearing a silver crown. The face was female, with thick, moon-white hair and straight eyebrows. She glanced sideways at Wenna.

The similarity was uncanny, except the silky fabric face on the flag wasn't withered or sunken. And its skin was sunset gold, not grey.

'Of course it's her,' Bronnan snapped.

A crowd of thirty or forty faeries had gathered. Some banged drums hung from cords around their necks, while others scraped at instruments like violins, but with smaller bodies and longer necks. The jiggling bows were shorter and more arched, like those used for arrows.

They were singing too, not particularly well, but with fervour. Even from a distance, Cora glimpsed sweat on their brows.

'Down here,' Wenna pointed. They crammed themselves into a hollow behind a fallen tree, sheltered by branches, to watch the crowd through cracks in the log. Tom managed to slip Yestin from his shoulders and Cora caught his head, to lay it gently in the rotting leaves, beside his hat.

'Why are they performing?' Cora asked, 'if it's banned?'

'They're not performing,' Bronnan's eyes darted about, scanning the scene. 'They're protesting.' Through her teeth she added. 'Idiots.'

'They're not idiots,' Wenna's brow creased. 'They're brave.'

'They're risking their lives,' Meriwether was grim.

'Exactly' Bronnan and Wenna said together, then frowned at each other.

Bronnan broke eye contact first, bowing her head.

A screech came from somewhere and Wenna's eyes bulged.

'What kind of instrument is that?' Cora asked, rising on her knees and peering through the branches, until Bronnan yanked her down.

'That's not an instrument,' Meriwether was pale, squinting to scan the sky. 'That's a pterydon.'

Cora was about to ask what an pterydon was, when her question was answered by an enormous, swooping shadow that chilled her blood and flipped up the terrified faces of the protesters.

Some fled, but most stood their ground and a few even tried to carry on singing, their voices thin and reedy in the misty air. One who stood closest to them suddenly lifted off the ground, her feet kicking wildly, scattering leaf mould.

Cora's heart was in her mouth. She must have imagined it. Whatever those long, scaly feet she'd glimpsed belonged to, with black talons digging deep into the shoulders of the protester, it couldn't have been what she feared.

But her heart knew the truth and it beat the word through her blood; thumped it in her ears. The word was in the air, in every beat of the vast, winged shadows cutting through the fog.

Dra-gon. Dra-gon. Dra-gon.

The drops of mist grew bigger, heavy enough to fall and patter quietly, as though nothing was amiss, when a sudden flash turned everything, for less than a second, blinding white. Another flash and a housetree exploded, showering sparks.

A protester ran screaming, streaming smoke, straight towards them, bringing a horrible smell of burning meat. His eyes were huge as he twisted to fight the fire. Cora and Tom rose to help him, even though it was too late, until Bronnan snatched them back down. The faery was still running towards them, tripping and staggering, until enormous wings beat close overhead, their dark wind fanning the smoke and rolling it back, rattling the branches overhead and making the huddled band press themselves deep into the forest floor, where even the dampest leaves dried in the heat and started to curl and blacken. Just as the burning faery reached the log, a pair of huge yellow feet with black talons dug into his shoulders, snatching him into the air.

Cora screamed. Bronnan groped at her mouth to stop the noise, which was swallowed by the roar of a falling branch. Eerie, keening cries of the pterydons pierced the forest as they swooped, gripping the struggling faeries with ease.

That was when Cora realised they weren't as wild as she'd imagined. They wore saddles just behind their sleek, twisting necks, carrying armoured faery soldiers with painted faces and fat daggers strapped to their thighs.

In one hand, the soldiers gripped leather reins. In the other, each held a long, barbed spear with a mechanical attachment, which sent bolts of lightning among the protesters, splintering what was left of the housetrees and sending shrapnel in all directions. Some of the protesters lay dead already, their clothes charred shreds around red lightning-scars in the shape of branches.

Between flashes, Cora stole a horrified glance up at the flying monsters. They weren't dragons as she'd imagined. Their heads were long and reptilian, with iridescent, blood coloured scales. They were bald as crocodiles, except for quivering crest like a peacock's. Their bodies and huge wings were covered in bird-like plumage, with a prehensile tail the length of their body, ending in a diamond fan of red-orange feathers.

A squeaking rumble sounded, followed by a procession of wooden cages on wheels, drawn by straining wild boar. To her horror, the pterydons began dropping the faeries inside with sickening thumps, until they formed a writhing heap, crushing each other in their desperation to escape.

Some faeries were snatched and whisked high above the treetops. So high, the pterydons shrank to the size of winged lizards, flapping in silhouette, before they dropped their prey. The screams of the falling grew louder, then abruptly stopped.

Wenna's upper lip drew back, baring her teeth as she rose, every sinew taught, dagger already drawn, before Eseld tugged her back down.

'That's just what she wants innit?' she hissed, struggling to keep hold. 'To flush you out, so she can lop off your head and stick it in that mirror room of hers!'

Cora felt sick as she realised what Eseld meant. The decorated busts she'd admired, blinded with glamour in the mirrored ballroom, were actually severed heads.

Meriwether grabbed the straining Wenna too. 'Don't give in! We're hopelessly outnumbered. Save it for a day when we've got a chance!'

But Tom couldn't bear it. He rushed out into the chaos, scarlet with fury, eyes reflecting the blaze of a branch, whose flame turned to smoke in the rain as it pelted down. He seized it to wave and stab at the swooping monsters. A pterydon snatched the branch away as easily as a twig, tossing it aside. Another dived down to catch hold of Tom, who kicked and fought as it flapped harder.

Cora was giddy. Everything around Tom grew blurry and muffled, while he was absolutely clear, more vivid than he'd ever been. The only person in the wood. She burst up from behind the log and threw herself at Tom's legs, the added weight startling the pterydon into letting go, sending them both tumbling to the ground in a mess of limbs.

The pterydon hurtled off course, crashing through the branches of a ruined housetree, bringing half of the scorched walls down with it, its huge wings awkward and clumsy as it tried to take off in the restricted space, blood pouring from its long, muscular neck.

The soldier slipped to the ground as the pterydon staggered, whining like an injured dog, one of its wings obviously broken. With a grimace, he threw his spear straight into its eye. A final screech stretched its jaws wide, before it thudded into the ground, its head falling last, sending up a flurry of charred leaves.

Cora glimpsed Meriwether inside a cage, a ragged hole in his cheek. He was slashing desperately with his dagger at the knotted rope holding the criss-crossed bars together, but it was old and grimy and feet ground his fingers, as people scrambled ineffectually to escape, whenever a soldier pulled on the rope to open the hatch to receive a fresh catch.

She saw Eseld crouching in the ruin of a housetree, frantically mixing herbs into a paste and waving her glyph to make it spark blue. But whatever magic she was trying to perform must have fizzled out because, when Cora lifted her eyes back to her squatting figure, she'd vanished.

All Cora could see, beside the dying blue embers,

was a slender hare that kicked its back legs and darted out of the housetree, away into the shadows of the forest.

It took her a moment to realise what she'd seen. Cora didn't know which shocked her more, the transformation or the abandonment.

A pterydon swooped terrifyingly close and snatched up Bronnan's plaits in its claws, dragging her into the air and flapping towards the cage. Furious, she punched, bit and kicked all the way, even whipping out her dagger to stab the shadows and saw at her hair. Her fight came to nothing and she was dropped into the cage with the rest.

Cora didn't know where to run. Tom was hurling blackened sticks at the pterydons, trying to make them release their grip and drop the faeries before they got to the cages. Cora followed suit, the branches hot in her hands as she heaved them, trailing smoke, stinging her eyes, but they all missed. She wished she was as strong as Tom, who worked with wood all day and knew it like he knew his own limbs.

A scream, suddenly halted, made Cora look up.

Mrs Trethowan was tangled in the branches of the nearest housetree. Her bonnet was lost and her hair, half-loosed from its pins, covered her face in bedraggled hanks. Blood stained her cape and dress around a broken, reddened branch, which stuck out from under her collarbone. Her boots dangled with the horrible stillness of the hanged.

A faery child in a grubby orange tunic was banging on his drum, little eyebrows drawn into a fierce 'v'. He'd opened his mouth to sing, but fear must have stoppered his words, for he managed only a scratching, discordant noise. A pterydon wheeled and turned, diving with deadly accuracy. The soldier in his saddle lowered his spear, while the child stared upward, eyes full of hate and water.

Cora couldn't bear it. She flung herself towards the little boy, trying to grab him in time.

But time itself deserted them. Her hands were maddeningly slow. They gripped empty air, missing his feet by inches as he swung up out of reach, his drumstick falling softly.

Bile rose in Cora's throat as a fork of lightning pierced the air, blasting the earth black just inches from her feet. Smoke stained the mist as she whirled around, coughing, shielding her face from the heat, trying to make sense of the falling and the fallen. Trying to shut out Mrs Trethowan's snagged, broken body and the little drumstick lying like a scar in the leaf mould. She beat the air helplessly, as if she could push the smoke away, dodging left and right, not knowing where to run, until a yellow foot clamped hard, black talons piercing the tender flesh below her shoulder and burning deep.

It hurt too much to cry out.

Pain strangled the sound, as her entire body dangled from the wound. The ground was snatched from beneath her feet. Housetrees swung past at impossible angles and smoke-filled air rushed hot against her skin.

She landed painfully amid the flesh and bone and hair of all the others in the cage. A wheezing intake of breath and a coughing fit told her that a human was in there too. It was Mr Penrose, the blacksmith. His eyes were red in blackened folds of skin and she scrambled instinctively through the mass of panicking bodies toward him, because his face was the only one she knew.

With a violent jerk, the cage wagons were dragged, bumping over the muddy ruts and splashing through puddles.

'Tom!' she screamed, over and over again until her smoke-sore throat wouldn't do it anymore. Then she heard a voice, small at first, but growing stronger. It was the little drummer boy whose feet she'd tried to catch, singing the song they'd all been singing before the pterydons came. Some of the others joined in, their voices weak and shaky. She recognised the tune as the same as the 'recruited collier', though it was disrupted with the lurches of the cart.

And we'll laugh beneath blue skies again
and we'll drink deep and slumber.
We'll build all that's been lost again,
our children will grow older.

The ale will flow the birds return,
and she will go back under,
And we'll laugh beneath blue skies again,
when she has gone back under.

Cora marvelled at the child's bravery. He even knocked the drum rhythm on the wooden stakes of the cage with his knuckles. She shivered, the sweat cooling as the blood dried and became sticky, the pain in her shoulder burning as if the talons were still inside. The cart halted and squelching footsteps heralded the approach of the driver.

'Stop yer noise!' he spat. 'Want me to send a spinner in there?'

Cora didn't know what a spinner was, but by the looks on the faces of the faeries, who all started frantically shaking their heads, she didn't want to find out.

'If you send a spinner in,' the little boy piped up, 'then you'll have no slaves will you? For the mines. Then you won't get paid.'

Everybody turned to gaze at him.

'I doubt you even have a spinner,' the boy continued, with a boldness Cora found astonishing. 'They're only for the elite soldiers. You're just a driver. Probably too weak or simple to handle a pterydon or join the proper guard. That's why you drive the carts. Anyone can do that.'

'Why you little!' The squat, round-bellied faery was about to open the hatch but he stopped, letting the leather rope drop. 'Oh, very clever. Nice try. You won't fool me that easily.'

The cart squeaked and shifted as he scrambled back up into the driving seat to slap the reins, making the boars snort, and Cora heard him add 'Mr Morningside'll hear about this, an' you'll be sorry. Bloody little...' The rest was lost in the shudders of the cage as the wheels heaved back into action.

'It was a good idea,' Cora said, trying to encourage the boy, who stared gloomily out into the darkening forest, where the rain had stopped and left the broken twigs dripping. 'Getting him to open the hatch, so we could escape.'

'I was going to pull him in,' he grinned, darkly.

She hesitated before saying 'you're very brave.

How old are you?'

'In a way, I'm ten.'

It took her moment to understand what he meant. 'And how long have you been ten?'

He met her gaze with a steady one of his own, then flashed a smile and she glimpsed missing teeth. 'A while.'

'I'm Cora,' she ventured. 'Blackthorn.'

'Jago Lampbright.'

She managed to smile back, despite it all, bizarre as it was to be making introductions, squashed in a miserable heap, being carted off to hell. 'And this is Mr Penrose.' She would have gestured with her hand, if she'd had room to move it.

Mr Penrose didn't manage anything more than a bleak nod and Cora tried to emulate Jago. To be brave and blot out the horror. But the images of Mrs Trethowan's motionless feet and of Eseld scampering away as a hare remained printed in her mind. And the acute ache as she'd lost sight first of Wenna, then Tom and the others just got worse.

They rattled through shafts of smoky air, in and out of shadows, past more and more ruined housetrees. The forest was bigger than any she'd encountered in Cornwall. She missed the wideness of the moor. The huge trees of Underwood felt menacing, as if they were deliberately crowding around to crush her. She glanced up and saw the rope bridges, jerking from side to side, with figures crossing. They weren't as high as they'd seemed on her first, englamoured visit and some of the slats were broken or missing. The baskets on the faeries' backs were enormous, bending them double. An armoured faery, his face painted in different colours to those of the pterydon riders, was shouting at them to go faster. At the unmistakable sound of a whip, Cora snatched her gaze away.

She focused instead on the sloshing sounds of a river, which grew louder as they crossed a stone bridge, then fell away again. And the groans of the faeries on the bridges and the cracks of the whips died away too, leaving only the rumbling creak of the wheels and the steady drip as rain, again, began to fall.

Chapter Twelve

Mine

Twilight closed around the cart as it jerked through the forest, the trees spectral against a leaden sky. After hours of travelling the discomfort of being piled on top of each other was becoming tortuous. Yet nobody wanted to arrive.

But it was inevitable. The trees fell away and a huge crater opened up ahead of them, its sides a mass of ridges with sinewy, rag-clad figures working in rows along each ledge, striking the rock face with pick axes. Along the top of the crater were claw-like spikes, each one bigger than a scythe. Their razor edges glinted in the moonlight, curving in all directions.

They entered through a heavily guarded gate with watchtowers each side. The pterydons flew in overhead, swooping one after the other into a cave in the opposite wall. As well as the pterydon cave, there were other gaping holes in the sides of the crater, arch-shaped, like the sewer tunnel. Now and again, Cora caught glimpses of a strange, green-blue light, deep inside.

As they got closer, Cora saw faeries and humans toiling together in the bottom of the crater, up to their thighs in water, bending down and heaving dripping lumps over their shoulders into buckets on their backs, held by straps across their foreheads. Lanterns gleamed here and there, washing their wet skin with a yellow glow and reflecting off the oily surface, which rippled and shuddered as they moved.

The smell of the mine was a toxic mix of ammonia, unwashed bodies and a sour, chemical odour Cora recognised from the tannery in Treleddan. Vomit churned in her gut, threatening to rise, as the cart lurched to a halt and ropes were untied, spilling everyone onto the ground in an ungainly heap. Cora's breath was crushed from her chest by arms and legs. Before they were able to untangle and separate their limbs, the faery guards searched everyone for weapons, stripping them of all they found.

The wild boar glistened with sweat but, while misty breath surrounded the mouths of the humans, the air around the wet snouts of the beasts remained clear. One bore a bloodless, unhealed wound in the slicing shape of a whip's lash. The wrists of the new arrivals were snatched up and clamped in iron manacles. As each faery winced, Cora remembered Wenna using a cloth to lift the iron back at the cottage, because she said it'd burn her even when it was cold. Their skin blistered as the metal was clamped heartlessly in place by guards wearing protective gloves. She wished she could do something. Anything. She scanned the sky, where a few pterydons were circling, as if help might appear from there. A chain was passed through a ring on each manacle, so that when the first was tugged, everyone else was forced to follow.

They were led into a long wooden hut, without windows. The chain was fastened to a ring in the floor with a huge padlock. Their heads were shaved, one by one, by an enormous, yawning faery guard, who threatened to send in a spinner if anyone struggled. He had trouble with Cora's. The roots were thicker and more like quills than ever. She was too numb to do anything but let her head jerk with each scrape of the shears, until only rough, black stubble remained.

The night was spent shivering on bare wooden boards, still chained together, the last of the light draining around them. The hasty shaving had cut Mr Penrose's scalp and blood had dried in a brown smear above his ear. During the darkest hours, a few faeries had started to sob and mutter among themselves, but the thumping on the door and another bellowed threat to send a spinner in terrified them into silence.

Cora didn't sleep a wink. She spent the night hugging her knees and staring ahead, worrying about Tom, Eseld, Wenna and the others. Her head felt naked and she touched it only once, drawing her hand away in horror. She tried to lie down, but the wooden floor was hard and cold as stone.

It wasn't quite dawn when the humans among them were given bowls of thin gruel, before they were marched up to one of the ridges, still chained in a line at the wrists, and given pick axes to strike the rock. Height was the only thing that distinguished the two species, because everyone was bald, their skin coated with brownish grey dust. Weak and terrified as she was, it occurred to Cora that the pick-axes would make formidable weapons, if used against the guards. She glanced around, looking for potential weak points and remembered Tom saying that escape from the mines was extremely rare. He said Eseld had been rescued by Wenna. A bud of hope unfurled in her chest. If Wenna had managed to orchestrate a successful rescue once, might she again? But Cora wasn't going to wait for that. As soon as a chance came, she'd swing her pick axe right into the throat of a guard. With a jolt, looking down at her curiously elongated hands, she realised she was prepared to kill.

For hours, she copied the others, hacking orbs of rock from the cliff face, which they threw into sacks. She had no idea what they were. They varied in size from a duck's egg to a soup tureen and their surface, when released from the slightly softer rock, was pocked and rough like ancient bone.

It was twilight when everything changed.

Cora was coated with sweat. When she stopped working, her damp skin made her shiver. Her hands burned, blistered and red. Her wrists and ankles chafed in the manacles every time she moved and hunger gnawed at her innards with a savagery she'd never known. She knew she wouldn't last long in the mine. Many of the others were so emaciated, so worn down with misery and starvation that the light had completely gone from their eyes. They longed merely for the end. If she was to strike back, or to attempt to flee, she knew she'd have to do it quickly, before her spirit was too depleted.

She forced herself to forget about rescue. She refused to allow fears of what had happened to the others consume her. She let everything fall away so that her thoughts of escape would be the only thing on her mind. Her focus must be like a hunter's spear, poised, without distraction, always scanning the guards for weakness.

But it was the boy, Jago, who suddenly let fly with his pick-axe.

He swung it, just as Cora had planned to herself, towards a guard's throat, but his diminutive height made it glance off the breastplate instead, barely denting it.

The guard stiffened with outrage, his eyes glittering angrily through the slit of his helmet.

Silence spread from the two of them, like ripples surrounding a stone dropped in water, as everyone lowered their tools to stare.

The guard stood very still, fists clenched. Then he snatched up the wriggling boy, whose legs kicked, running in mid-air.

'Spinner!' the guard's guttural cry ripped the silence. The order was repeated by guards all along the ridge until a cannonball shot out of one of the tunnels, streaming smoke.

Only it wasn't a cannonball, Cora realised, as it curved round in an unnatural arc. The guard with the dented breastplate set Jago back on his struggling feet, holding his ear with his fist. He held up his other hand, revealing something metallic, strapped to his palm.

The smoking ball hung eerily above the crater.

Everybody stared, but only with their eyes. They tried desperately to turn their faces away.

The ball still hovered, making a low, humming noise. The gloomy light of evening revealed dents and marks in what looked like pewter. As Cora watched, thin tendrils snaked out of the metal surface. An awful murmur rumbled through the slaves and, though she still had no idea what it was, their dread thickened her own.

The ball began to revolve. The tendrils grew longer and people began pushing against each other in a hopeless attempt to get away. Some accidentally stumbled near the edge, their chains dragging others closer to the sheer, fatal drop. Strangers panicked, grabbing each other, as if it would do any good.

The thing revolved faster, its velocity straightening the whip thin tentacles, spinning them into a silvery blur.

The guard flicked his wrist, making the spinner lunge toward his glinting hand, which he held for a moment in front of Jago, then snatched away at the last moment.

The mass of whipping metal zoomed straight towards the boy and the guard stepped back, shoving Jago fully into the path of the spinner. Bloodless rags of flesh and orange cloth whirled through the air then sank, pale and wet, into a small heap.

Jago's bare feet were the only part of him that remained whole and recognisable, still chained at the ankle.

A plume of vomit erupted from Cora's innards, splattering down her ragged dress. She kept on heaving, bent double, even though there was nothing left inside her but horror, anger and bone-deep grief for the boy she'd hardly known.

The slaves stood silently, staring at Jago's remains, until whips were cracked. Cora wept as she swung her axe into the cliff face, flinching at the narrow, metal gaze of the guards. Tears shook her shoulders and dripped off her chin. Most of those around her wept too, the men trying to disguise their emotion with a glare.

A few glanced casually at the mess that was once a brave little boy as if he was a pile of gutted herring, before continuing on with their work; their hearts as hard as the rocks in the buckets. What's wrong with you? Cora wanted to scream at them. Haven't you any compassion?

They toiled late into the night, sweat trickling down Cora's spine as she worked, while her knuckles grew stiff with cold. Her mind was working hardest though, going over every possible idea for an escape like a blind man's fingers over the buttons of his coat, trying to make sense of it, to fit the pieces together.

Perhaps it was because she was exhausted. Perhaps because she was so distracted by thoughts of lock picking, spinner stealing and hopeless ideas for diversions. Whatever it was, something made a rock slip out of Cora's hands and miss the bucket. She bent to pick it up and realised it had cracked in half on impacting the stone ledge. Its insides were filled with sparkling crystal.

She picked up the two halves, one in each hand, her palms suddenly clammy as she realised that breakages probably meant punishment. She panicked, turning to the wall to hide them, when she remembered where she'd seen something like these before. They were geodes, like the ones in Granville's study, but the colours of the crystals inside were completely different. They were the rich blue-green of a peacock's feather, but even more iridescent. As she shielded it from view, she realised it wasn't reflecting light, like a normal crystal, but actually producing it, glowing with a light all of its own.

The geode wasn't much bigger than a chicken's egg and she stuffed the two halves down inside her corset, pushing them as close to her armpits as she could, where they'd be less visible. They grated painfully against her skin.

After several more hours of working in the dark she followed the line back to the cabin, where the chain was once again fed through the ring around hr ankle and locked to the floor. She stared around at the exhausted faces as the guard's lantern swung out of the door, leaving them in pitch darkness. Her heart sank, heavy with sympathy as she remembered that the faeries couldn't even escape into sleep. She expected to be staring into the dark for a while too, even as her eyelids were sinking, her eyes sore and scratchy with dried tears. Every muscle ached and her head throbbed with thirst.

She began to drift off, but every time she closed her eyes she saw Jago's face, eyes brimming as he sang and beat his little drum and she jerked violently awake, as if to stop herself falling.

'Cora!' said a voice she knew well. An impossible voice.

Sitting bolt upright, Cora was startled to see a ghostly figure, shimmering like a reflection in dark water.

In the silence, the figure spoke to her again, without moving her lips. 'Cora, it's me!'

'Wenna!' Cora exclaimed aloud, mouth falling open in amazement. And a nervous shifting of iron manacles rippled through the dark. The light from the dear image that had once horrified her in the attic washed the miserable faces of the slaves with a pale glow.

'Mr Penrose! Everybody! Look!' Cora frantically pointed, but everyone just frowned and blinked, not looking at her, or each other.

A ragged, grumbling noise came from Mr

Penrose and the manacle chafed against Cora's ankle as he turned over.

'Wake up!' she hissed crossly. 'Look!' And then it dawned on her. They couldn't see Wenna at all, they were moving their eyes like blind people might, as though listening, with nothing to draw their gaze.

Wenna's face was creased with urgency, 'Cora', she said again, 'they can't see me, nor hear me. You're the only one who-' she hesitated, glancing over her shoulder and the image shuddered, flickering on and off.

'Wenna?!'

'It's not saf... here anym...' Her voice was crackly, the words breaking into fragments. 'I have... move. Use... geode you bro... composite of... raw powerf... Meet... Fiddlers Riddle. Pendlest... Broa...uddle.'

Wenna disappeared and Cora lunged forward, grasping thin air. 'Don't go! I don't know what you mean!'

'I've heard about this sort o' fing,' someone whispered.

'Heard about what?' said another voice.

'Well, stands to reason,' said the first voice. 'If any place is going to send you mad, this is it innit? She ain't the first and she won't be the last.'

'I'm not mad,' Cora snapped, struggling to keep her voice to a whisper. She stared angrily at the dark, into which everyone had vanished.

'That was Wenna!'

'Wenna who?'

'Your Queen! My friend and,' she swallowed, 'my cousin. She was trying to tell us a way to get out of here! Didn't you see her?!'

'If you say so,' someone mumbled, and there was

an exhausted snuffle, which would have been a snigger, had everyone not been so miserable.

'You really didn't see *anything*?'

'If somebody sent you a blackstone message then we wouldn't would we? S'just for the receiver.'

'Mr Penrose, you believe me don't you? Mr Penrose?'

Snore.

'Mr Penrose!' Cora hissed.

'Hmmf?'

She nudged him. 'Tell them. Tell them about the guild and Wenna's plan to unite-' then she stopped. She didn't know these people. But they were enslaved, surely that meant they'd be on her side? She had to take the risk.

'I have a mark. A tattoo. On my arm. I'd show you all but... Obviously, it's too dark.'

She took a deep breath, trying to remember exactly what Wenna had said, before the memory slithered out of reach. Something about using the geode she'd broken. Something about raw composites, whatever they were, and a fiddle, in Pendlestow. She repeated what she could remember and her words floated away into the void.

She didn't know where, or if, they would land.

She waited, convinced they weren't listening, until a thin, nasal voice replied out of the blackness.

'If it *was* her majesty you saw, somehow managing to project her image to you without the aid of a blackstone...'

'Oh, she does have one, she-'

'I meant you don't have one. Of course she has one! As a human, you wouldn't understand, your magical technology is in its infancy. Anyway,' the disembodied voice went on, 'that's not the important thing, what she was trying to say was obviously...' he hesitated. 'Upon reflection, my dear, can you prove that you're on personal terms with her majesty?'

'I can't,' Cora said simply. 'Not in the dark.' She swallowed, trying to make her voice stronger than she felt. 'If I could, I'd show you a tattoo on my arm.'

'A tattoo? But you're female. Only sailors and circus folk have-'

'If you'd listen, I'll explain. It's two Ms entwined. The mark of Merlin and Mab. I don't know if you've heard of them, but Wenna said my parents became sort of legends. They sent me forward through time, to keep me safe...'

'You don't expect us to believe that?!' said a deep voice she hadn't heard before.

'I know. It's a ridiculous story,' Cora trailed off, recalling the ravings of an old woman who used to loiter around the gin shop in Treleddan, waiting for it to open. She'd tell passers by she was the Countess of Cornwall.

'We know the story!' The owner of the deep voice struggled to keep it down, squashing his words into a gruff whisper. 'But that's all it is. You people think the fey'll believe anything.'

'No,' Cora answered calmly. 'I don't.' Once, she'd have found his aggression alarming. She'd have lashed out or cowered. Now, all she had to do was picture Jago and think how easily he could have been Meg, little Gwen or even Curnow, for calm courage to flood her veins.

'The point is, I think Wenna was telling us about a way to escape. If you want to get out of here, you'll have to trust me. If it works, then it doesn't really matter if you believe me or not, you've nothing to lose.'

A cynical murmur went around the room. Cora took the broken halves of the geode out of her bodice. The glow of its jagged interior spilled across her fingers.

She used the halves like a candle to illuminate the faces that turned towards her, drawn by the light and the strange things she was saying.

She searched the bluish faces for the owner of the nasal voice, hoping he'd finish explaining Wenna's message. But he could have been any one of them.

Mr Penrose was still fast asleep and she nudged him again, startling him awake.

'What now?' he mumbled crossly.

'Wenna came to me,' Cora tried to suppress her rising irritation, 'she told me what we could do to get out, but the signal was corrupted and I don't know what she meant.'

Mr Penrose was quiet and Cora drew a breath, about to nudge him again. But he was shifting painfully upright.

'You sure it was her?' he whispered, exhaustion making his voice more gravelly than usual.

'Course it was! She came to me like that once before, in my attic, when Petrok Noon's blackstone was smashed.'

A shocked silence said she'd got their attention.

Whispers rumbled around the cabin. Cora couldn't tell who was speaking. The glow was too dim to reach more than a foot or so.

'Petrok Noon? The dean?'

'Nah, they wouldn't dare.'

'They kill kings and queens, there ain't nothing

they won't do.'

'Isn't he here?' Cora asked. 'Petrok? We came to rescue him.'

'Hah,' barked the deep voice. 'No-one gets rescued from here. Not possible.'

'They do.' Cora swallowed, her throat dry. 'Eseld was. Do you know her too? Eseld Liddicoat?'

A dismissive murmuring told her they did not.

'So what did Wenna say?' Mr Penrose asked, his face saggy with tiredness as he rubbed it, trying to wake up properly.

'Something about these,' she held up the broken halves of the geode. 'She said something about raw composites and the guards. Then something about a violin. In Pendlestow.' Cora ran out of words. Saying them aloud made them seem even more disjointed and nonsensical, like a half-remembered dream.

Mr Penrose was looking hard at the geode, but it was the nasal voice that spoke. 'The Riddler's Fiddle is a tavern in Pendlestow, which lies on the border between Underwood and Broadpuddle. The intriguing part is what she inferred regarding the geodes.'

A barking argument broke out among the guards outside and, for a second, they froze, silent, waiting for it to abate.

After a few moments, when one of the guards seemed to have stomped off, Cora let herself breathe again. She moved the geode halves to find the speaker in the gloom and almost dropped them in alarm.

One of his eyes was perfectly normal. Grey-lidded and yellowish green, but he must have suffered a dreadful injury to the other half of his face, so much of it was missing. Without the curse, it definitely would have killed him outright. Big stitches held the edges of skin together, but without bleeding or healing, it reminded her more of death than ever.

She tried to concentrate on what he was whispering. 'The geode contains arkanite, a vital component of glamour. On its own, it's utterly toxic.'

He grinned with the half of his mouth that worked.

Cora glanced around to see if anyone else understood.

With a sigh, he tried to simplify things. 'Glamour is a composite, you see. That's why her majesty mentioned the word.'

'I don't know what a composite is,' Cora stated.

He blinked. 'It denotes a mixture of ingredients. That's what the mine is for. We get the arkanite out of the ground ready to go to the next stage, down in the tunnels, where they process it by dipping it in acid and grinding it with an alloy of...' He blinked rapidly. 'But that's irrelevant. What I believe her majesty was saying was that in its *raw* state, arkanite works as a rather effective poison. And there's enough there,' he nodded at the broken geode, 'to kill a guard or knock the whole lot of them out for *hours.*'

Cora looked down in horror and the innocent looking crystals, their peacock hue suddenly noxious. Her skin prickled where they'd pressed it. Was she burnt? Or was it just the fear of poison leaking from the stones into her skin?

'But they wouldn't want us working with poison, surely?' she stammered.

'You think they *care* how long we last?'

'No. I just mean it seems a little- obvious, convenient even. Surely people must have tried to use it against the guards before?'

He gave her a despairing look, as though she were a little simple which, she was beginning to realise, compared to him, she was. 'It's not remotely toxic in its current state. You'd have to drip the right acid onto it, *obviously*.'

'Oh.' Cora's shoulders sagged with relief. Then tightened again. 'What acid? How do we get hold of any acid?'

His bleak look said it all. 'Well, it's not straightforward.'

Cora tried to keep positive. 'What acid?'

'Lacrimas lacerta noctis'

'Pardon?'

'Pterydon tears. Gathered at night.'

Cora's heart sank. He was a lunatic. She hastily hid her thoughts.

'Obviously, we won't have to harvest at source!' He seemed amused at her ignorance, but not unkindly. 'They use it in the processing section. In the tunnels. I don't know why I didn't think of it myself.'

Cora was silent as she digested this. He said it as if it was easy. It would certainly be easier to get the stuff from the tunnels than the pterydon themselves, but not much.

'Can't someone just use magic?' she said. 'Something to open the walls? Wenna did it, in a cave.'

'Firstly, Queen Wenna is a great sorcerer, taught by the best her parents could find. Secondly, there is a pall here. An invisible fog that prevents anyone from using magic, natural or poisoned.'

'But the guards, they use it!'

'Do they? I think not. They use technology. Science, that's all. The spinners are controlled by transmitters in their hands. They emit a signal from their minds, which controls their flight.'

Cora was sceptical. It sounded a lot more like magic than science to her. 'How do you know all this?' she asked.

'Me?' He seemed surprised. As though his knowledge was common. 'I'm- I was, a senior lecturer in chemistry and natural philosophy at the university.' He paused. 'I knew Petrok well, but no-one has seen him for a long time. Come on, why don't you come clean? You don't need to be the fabled child of Mab and Merlin for us to get on. What should I call you?' then he half-smiled again. 'Or is that a silly question, Elowen?'

It took a moment for Cora to answer. 'What did you call me?'

'Elowen of course, that's what Mab and Merlin called their daughter, in the story. You need to work on it a bit, if you're going to tell people you're her.'

'It's not, I don't tell people anything,' she swallowed hard, pushing the new, burning word right to the back of her mind to deal with later. 'Look.' She put down the geode halves and rolled up her sleeve, the wound in her shoulder making her wince. She held one close to her skin, to illuminate the tattoo.

He peered with his good eye at the interwoven letters. Other faeries craned forward too, until Cora felt like something in a zoo.

'Well,' he said eventually. 'I'll be jiggered.

Chapter Thirteen

Elowen

Hope, fragile and delicate, bloomed in the faces of the faeries around her, as they gathered as close as their chains would allow. When they lifted their gaze from the mark on her skin up to her face, they were looking at somebody extraordinary. A living myth.

'Hairy ain't she?' whispered one of the children. 'And her hands are funny, even for a cornall.' When she realised Cora had heard, she snapped her mouth shut, eyes wide.

'They're not hairs, they're... well, feathers. Sort of. And my hands... It's a long story.' There had been so many more important things to worry about, Cora hadn't noticed that her hands had grown even longer, or that the fine sprinkling of budding feathers had crept along her fingers.

Mr Penrose had finally woken up enough to think properly. 'We'll have to get their armour. Dress like one.' He gestured with a big calloused hand, 'I'll do it. Taking one of them down ain't a problem, it's when you're facing them all, with their pterydons and their filthy spinners... But just one, I can do.' Then he hesitated. 'But I won't be able to fit into it.' he shrugged his massive shoulders.

'I'll do that!' said the disfigured faery with the nasal voice. 'If you can get the armour, I'll put it on and pass unnoticed in the tunnels, where I shall steal the acid. Mr...'

'Eh? Oh, Tobias Penrose.'

'Professor Ruan Polperro.'

Awkwardly, manacles clanking, they shook hands.

'How on earth can we give it to the guards though?' Cora asked herself as much as the company.

Nobody spoke for a moment.

The answer flowered in her mind, like blood in water. 'Jago,' Cora whispered.

'Who?'

'The boy who died today' she said. 'The one they killed with the spinner.'

Silence.

'I fail to see your point,' said the professor.

'Let's just get the acid first,' Cora whispered, for the key was rattling in the lock of the door, though no light showed beneath it.

They were led, still linked together, out to a yard full of shadows, where they were unchained and rechained in different groups. Presumably to stop any plans hatching, Cora thought, glancing wildly at Mr Penrose and the professor, as they were led away onto different ridges and handed the hated pick axes.

Blisters from the day before burst and wept as Cora worked and splinters from the rough wooden handle were driven into the raw, newly exposed flesh. The deep wound in her shoulder stopped bleeding for a while, then oozed again through the rusty fabric in ragged red petals.

That night, weary and caked in grime, Cora was led to a different slave house. She decided to risk telling these strangers her plan too. The more of them involved, the better their chances. She tugged the geode halves out of her bodice and rolled up her bloodied sleeve to show them her tattoo.

A gasp, and a soft repetition of 'Elowen' and

'Elowen Ambrosius' followed, everybody crowding around to see.

'No,' she wanted to nip that in the bud. 'I'm her, the girl in the story, but the name I've grown up with is Cora.' She coughed and tasted dust. 'Blackthorn. I were adopted as a baby and only just found out recently that my aunt ain't my aunt. And my name ain't my name. Call me Cora. It's what I'm used to.' She pushed all thoughts of Selina to the back of her mind along with the strange new surname, cramming it up against her fears of what was happening to the others. It was getting very cluttered back there.

'Cora?' A thin, wobbly voice came from the gloom. 'Not really? I must be dreamin'

Cora's jaw clenched, the muscles around her temples taut as arrow strings. 'Nancarrow?' The word was dangerous in her mouth. Too much to hope for. If she'd heard right then the woman, the creature, who'd been living in the house on Fish Row had been pretending to be Dorothy Nancarrow while the real, dear one was suffering unimaginably.

A shuffling clank of metal meant people fidgeting out of the way, looking from Cora to an elderly, hunched figure who seemed to be made of rags and bones.

Cora held up the geode halves, blue light trembling in her hands as it revealed a sunken, scarred face, one she loved more than any other in the world. No longer framed by a cap or plaited loops of dark grey hair, the face was barely recognisable, the stubble on her scalp clogged with dirt.

'Nancarrow!' Cora fought her chains to get to her, as if she was drowning.

'My Cora!' Nancarrow breathed, tears carving ragged pink paths down her cheeks.

'Shh!' people were hissing, 'you'll bring the guards!' but Cora and Mrs Nancarrow weren't listening, they were too busy scrambling towards each other, getting as close as their chains would allow, without crushing everyone in between. Hard as they stretched, they couldn't reach to touch.

They yearned to hold each other; to trust their fingers when they couldn't believe their eyes. Instead they were forced to stare in wonder, taking in every new curve and line of the other's face.

'My Cora!' Nanacarrow breathed again.

Words failed them. Both weeping, they remained with their arms outstretched until they ached. Nancarrow had changed. It wasn't just her near starved cheekbones or her sunken eyes. All respectability and decorum had fallen away. Her once smart, polished boots were just rags of leather, held together by frayed laces. Her wrists were roped with scar tissue and she sat with her knees flopped out to the sides beneath her ragged dress. Her shoulders had always been set back, not bowed and shrunk. She'd aged decades in the few years she'd been in the mine.

It was painful to look, but Cora couldn't drag her eyes away.

'You look different,' Nancarrow said.

Cora wiped her cheeks, gritty against her blistered hands. Language virtually deserted her. 'Yes,' was all she managed. 'I do.'

'Older.'

'Yes, that too. How-?' Cora couldn't form the word kidnap. It wasn't a word for the real world. It was something from a history book or an adventure story.

Nancarrow lifted her gaze, her eyelids crêpey and hooded. 'Victor,' she said.

'She ain't a cornall in the story,' whispered someone, into the gloom.

'Shh.'

'Well, she ain't.'

'I can hear you,' Cora snapped. 'I'm only half cornall ain't I? And half faery. That's the point.'

'What?' Nancarrow frowned, looking from Cora to the barely visible faces of the faeries.

One of the faeries told the story of Elowen, Merlin and Mab, with more detail this time about their love affair and the rift it caused, within Camelot. Cora listened quietly, still barely able to believe it had anything to do with her, until Nancarrow astonished her by whispering 'I always knew you was special. No ordinary baby. You'd make things move when you clapped your hands.'

'What things?' Cora's voice shook. She knew this wasn't the time, they should be hatching plans to escape, but the moment was too precious to rush.

'I'd save your aunt's orange peel for you, 'cos you loved the smell and you'd make all the pith and bits hover in the air and sort of swirl 'em around your head.' She lifted a knobbly hand to make a circular gesture. 'Never seen anything like it. Course, I didn't tell no-one. *She* were always trying to make you do it with gloves and tambourines and whatnot, to diddle folk. But you couldn't do it after a while, not for her.' Mrs Nancarrow shook her head.

'They didn't come,' Cora realised. 'The guards, when we talked properly, instead of whispering.

Maybe they don't patrol outside all night, like we thought.'

'Probably playing dice and rubbing a spot of the old sparkle in their eyes,' muttered someone.

'That gives us hope, doesn't it?' Cora ventured.

'What do you mean, dear?' asked Nancarrow, sounding a little bewildered, as if hope was something she hadn't felt in so long, she'd forgotten what it was for.

'Hope. Of escape.' Cora stammered. Wasn't it obvious?

'Escape?! Pshaw,' muttered someone.

'Of course. Haven't you thought about it? Made plans? Surely it's better to die trying to get out of here, than just rot? After what happened to poor Jago-'

'Don't you mention him!' came a voice, sharp with pain.

'That was her brother's boy,' said a wheezy voice in the gloom, 'don't you say his name.'

Cora moved the geode to see who had spoken. A faery with a pouchy, dough-like face squinted in the sudden blue and looked away.

Cora was silent for a moment then, very gently, she tried again. 'I meant no disrespect. I just think we should try. In the cabin I was in before, we worked out a way to-'

'I don't want nothing to do with it!'

'Me neither' grunted the wheezy voice.

'It won't last,' another voice said. 'Someone'll finish her off, then we can all go home. Put this place behind us.'

'You mean Morgelyn?' Cora tried to keep calm. 'Who will? Who'll finish her off if everybody gives up?'

Silence fell, as thick and black as the darkness outside the fragile halo of the geode.

'I've heard,' somebody ventured, 'that the princess, the Queen I suppose should say, got out.'

This was met with a murmuring of voices. None of which sounded very positive.

'What do you mean,' Cora whispered cautiously, moving the geode to try to work out who was speaking, 'that she got out?'

'Well, from the Great Oak. When they killed the rest of the royal family. She's alive.'

'Rubbish,' sneered someone.

'Bunkum,' muttered another.

'She is! She's my friend and my cousin. She came to me last night, projected herself. You can only do that with a relative can't you?'

As Cora explained how she'd met Wenna the first time, Nancarrow gasped when she got to the part about the apparition in the attic. She almost fainted when Cora told her she'd ended up in the mirrored ballroom.

'You actually *saw* Morgelyn Glasse?' Nancarrow recoiled, crossing her wasted chest, as if Cora had come face to face with Satan himself.

Cora nodded. 'I were englamoured.'

Nanacarrow inhaled sharply.

'I didn't take it on purpose! She gave it to me. Tricked me.' She felt powerless as the moment slipped away.

'Enough talking,' murmured a voice. 'We need to rest.'

'We need to make a plan,' Cora persisted.

'Make it yourself,' was the surly reply, 'in yer own

head. Then, when you see there's no way out, maybe you'll stop filling everyone else's wi' nonsense.'

Hurt, Cora lapsed into silence. How quickly the novelty of her birth had worn off. But she'd found Nancarrow. Something she hadn't dared hope. She didn't want to take her eyes off her. Her eyelids were sore and scraped against her corneas every time she blinked and it burned to let them close, but she knew she must try to sleep. Her pierced shoulder hurt even more as she tried to lie down. Maybe the answer would come in a dream. Maybe Mr Penrose and the professor would go ahead with impersonating a guard and getting the acid. It didn't give them a way to get the arkanite into the other guards though. Or a way to get past those horrible, curved spikes.

Her brain kept going over the problem, exhausted as it was, and soon the ideas made no sense as they disintegrated into miserable sleep.

Chapter Fourteen

The Green Spinner

Before dawn, they were woken by guards kicking them in the ribs with metal-capped boots. As everyone was heaving themselves upright, Cora rubbed her eyes. Something was different. With a jolt, she realised that while her ankles were still clamped in iron, her elongated hands had slipped out of their manacles during the night.

It was a chink of light in this nightmarish place, but she'd wait, keep it secret, until she'd decided on the best time to use it and pushed her shaking fingers back in before anybody noticed. And as the chain was drawn free from the rings around her ankles she felt a little lighter.

Working on the ridge, she saw Mr Penrose lifting his pick axe with arms roped in muscle, bringing it down with a thump that loosed a dozen or more geodes from the softer stone in a small avalanche. Keeping her head down, so as not to attract attention, she watched those around her, all working, eyes down, massively outnumbering the guards. It was the fear of the spinners that shackled them, more than any iron.

She scanned the bent backs, desperate to glimpse Tom, Bronnan or Meriwether, but with rags coated in the same greyish brown dust and stubbled heads covered in grime, everybody looked similar, like grim automata, repeating the same hacking actions over and over again.

Cora glanced at the tunnels as subtly as she could,

between the swinging thuds of her pick axe. She watched the strange green light and curls of blue smoke and the geodes being hauled up to the caves in leather buckets on ropes, by slaves with sinewy limbs that looked thin enough to break.

She must have stopped working for a moment, because a stripe of pain shot diagonally across her back, sending her tumbling to her knees. Another searing sting landed and this time she saw the whip rise into the air to strike again. The pain was excruciating, as though flesh had been torn from bone and she shrank in horror, as the guard lifted it high, ready for another lash, but the next sound was different.

It was more of a crunch.

He staggered backwards and Cora glimpsed a large dent in his breastplate. A geode of the same size rolled away. She glanced wildly around. Someone must've thrown it. A spinner would be released. She would die. She'd be a bloody mess of ribboned flesh, she and whoever threw it.

But she wasn't going quietly. Frantically, she scrabbled in a bucket for geodes and threw them as hard as she could at the guard, who lifted his arms to shield himself, as others started picking up more geodes and broken rocks, throwing them even as the guards started roaring 'spinner! Spinner!'

The eerie whoosh of spinners filled the air and Cora felt her insides unravelling, though none of the monstrous weapons had touched her. Panicking, people rushed in different directions. With a rattle of chains, many were tugged from their ridge, crashing down onto those below, struggling to throw anything they could at the guards, who'd started hurling them back.

More and more slaves were caught by the spinners. No sooner had a guard held up his palm than a splatter of grey or red marked another death and Cora knew that this was their only chance and they were already losing.

She slipped her hands out of her manacles and ran full pelt, dodging past the screaming, rioting bodies and the hail of thudding geodes.

A guard was dangling on the edge, fingers scrabbling at the crumbling rock. Without a moment's hesitation, Cora squatted down and yanked the metallic spinner control off his hand, then stamped on his fingers, sending him hurtling into the crater.

Lifting up her hand, she panicked. She had no idea how to control it. She might do more harm than good. She looked hard at a spinner that was hovering, tentacles whirling, and she tried to access the part of her mind she'd used when she'd spoken directly to Wenna. The spinner lurched and wobbled at first, as though it was malfunctioning, then she commanded it to swoop towards a guard, who must have assumed it was heading for a slave, so he didn't react until the last minute, when it was too late. Cora felt nothing.

'Cora!'

She turned to see Bronnan hurling rocks with deadly accuracy, the muscles standing out in her neck as she sent guards crashing backwards with every throw.

'Take this!' Cora tugged the controller off her hand. 'Don't stop!'

'Where are you going?' Bronnan shouted angrily,

tugging the controller onto her fist.

'You'll see!' Cora yelled, trying to sound like she knew what she was doing.

'It's her!' she heard someone call out, over the din. 'It's Elowen Ambrosius!'

'Who?'

'She'd be taller'n that.'

'No it ain't, that's Cora Blackthorn, she's in on it! She's one o' Morgelyn's spies!'

Cora whipped around to see who'd spoken. A familiar, haggard face with bulging eyes was jabbing an accusatory finger at her.

'Mrs Furze?' Cora gasped, running past, 'I'm on your side. I'm trying to get us out-!'

'I know you Cora Blackthorn! I know your words is as rotten as your heart! That Victor Morningside, your auntie's fancy man, he's the villain what stuck me in here!'

There wasn't time to argue with her. Cora brushed Nellie Furze's words out of her mind, focusing instead on getting to the ropes where empty leather buckets sagged, geodes spilling around them, some marked with blood. Lifting her skirt to make a pouch, she grabbed as many as she could.

Everyone at the top was either dead or desperately hurling rocks at the guards.

'Pull me up!' Cora shouted, scrambling into the bucket. 'I know what to do!'

The slaves along the ridges were running out of missiles. Spinners were hurtling towards them even they were struggling to dig more out of the cliff side. Cora knew they couldn't last much longer. 'Now!' she shrieked.

With an angry, terrified look on his face, one of

the slaves started heaving her up in the bucket and Cora lurched violently from side to side, almost hit by a geode that whizzed past her head.

At the top she pushed past those still able to throw and bolted into the tunnel, her skirt bunched around the geodes.

'Hey! Don't go in there!' The cries behind her died away with the dust-filled daylight, as she ran headlong into blackness, no longer swirled with greenish blue. It was hot and slippery in the tunnel and a thumping, scratching sound like heavy machinery bounced off the walls around her head, growing louder the deeper she went inside the cliff.

She couldn't see a thing, so she slowed to tug the geode halves from her bodice to light the way, but lost her footing on the slippery rock and sent geodes crashing out of her skirt, bouncing all over the rocky tunnel. Some split in half, their light revealing walls slimy with condensation. And as she gathered them up and ran ahead around a bend, she saw why. The tunnel opened out into a cave with a vast cauldron in it, green steam coiling up from its middle.

Around the cauldron were more buckets, this time filled with blue, powdered crystals. A fearsome looking machine that must normally smash the geodes with a complex arrangement of lump hammers, stood dormant. Above the cauldron was a massive iron funnel, flared at the bottom. She couldn't tell how big it was, its blackness melted into the black of the void.

A tall, thin ladder was just visible, leaning against the cauldron's side and, as her eyes travelled up, Cora shrank in horror.

A faery guard was balancing on one of the highest

rungs, leaning over the edge to pour glittering blue shards from a bucket into the steaming contents. Whatever was inside began to hiss.

Cora snatched up a geode and threw it hard at the faery's helmet, where it ricocheted and spun off into the gloom.

'Ow!' said a familiar, nasal voice, straightening the helmet.

'Prof- professor?' Cora didn't dare believe it.

'What?' He lifted the visor of his helmet to peer down at her with his single eye. 'Oh, yes of course. Pass up another of those will you? They're *unbelievably* heavy.'

'Professor! Outside, it's all... It's carnage! They're slaughtering us!'

'Not for long, my dear. Pass it up.'

Cora heaved a bucket and started to climb the ladder, sparkling grains shifting to the edge and trickling out as she did so, sharp enough to cut.

'That's it. Quickly. Don't spill it!'

'I'm trying not to!'

She passed it up to him and he tipped the glittering shower into the cauldron. The hissing grew louder.

'One more,' he said.

Breathless, Cora scrabbled back down the ladder as fast she could, the muffled screams and cries outside the tunnel chilling her blood, then heaved another bucket back up, raw skin flecked with bloody scratches grinding against the leather handles.

After emptying the bucket, the professor hurried down the ladder as quickly as he could, hindered by the stiffness on his right side. He lifted off his helmet and turned his eye to Cora, 'I got this from another chamber, *lacrimas lacerta noctis*,' he grinned a sad, peculiar grin as he unwrapped a ragged bundle, moving towards the ladder, a brown glass bottle in his hand.

'I'll do it,' Cora said. 'It'll be quicker.'

His face fell a little, but he nodded and moved aside, giving her the bottle and producing a drawstring pouch of dark leather. 'You'll need to add this as well, it'll make the guards armour attract the arkanite gas. Don't forget to stir it thoroughly! Or it won't work. And put this stuff in first, the tears second.'

She put both the pouch and the bottle in her pocket and reached the top of the ladder, gasping at the mass of noxious liquid. The sulphurous smell was much worse up close, especially whenever one of the enormous bubbles burst. Trying to breathe through her mouth, she tugged at the strings of the pouch, letting the chalky grains fall from it, shaking it upside down until it was empty. She grabbed the huge, wooden paddle and stirred as well as she could without falling off the ladder.

Then she tugged the stopper from the bottle, pouring the contents into the fizzing green, making it bubble and convulse. A drip splashed onto the back of her hand. The bead looked as innocent as water but it smoked, eating into her flesh as she swiped at it, leaving a burning spot of red. She swore, trying to ignore the stinging, and stirred again.

'Careful!' The professor called, then 'come down! Now!'

There was a loud crack and a mushroom of green cloud shot up from the cauldron. Cora overbalanced and the ladder came away from the edge.

She screamed as she fell, landing painfully on her elbow. But there was no time to think about that. She kicked her skirts away as she got to her feet. The smoke was pouring up into the funnel and the professor was hurrying towards her, struggling to carry what looked like a cannonball.

Sickened, she recognised the spinner. She managed to heave the ladder upright and stand it against the side of the cauldron again, then scrambled back up using only one hand, to drop the spinner into the roiling, stinking liquid. It disappeared at first, sinking to the bottom. Then it bobbed and jerked on the surface as the bubbling liquid gathered pace, before shooting upward, carried into the funnel by the column of smoke.

'Now,' the professor staggered a little. 'We go.'

'Shouldn't we put in more than one?' She gestured to the heap of spinners she hadn't noticed before, crouching in the gloom.

'One'll be easier to control. It'll be enough, you'll see.' He produced a transmitter. 'Come on.'

Cora turned to the passage she'd come from, but he shook his head, 'no, this way!'

She followed him past the cauldron, where its black shadow flickered and jumped. They picked up broken geode halves and used their glow to navigate the greenish dark, until they found another tunnel. Cora glanced up at the rattling iron pipe running from the funnel, where the spinner was travelling over their heads into the maw of the passage. She glimpsed daylight ahead, coating slivers of rock as the professor strapped the controller to his hand, holding it up to guide the englamoured spinner above their heads. The mouth of the spinner pipe was directly above the opening of the tunnel in the cliff side, and the professor threw his hand forwards, sending the spinner out to hover, trailing green smoke while the others, some dripping with blood, trailed white.

He guided it towards a guard who'd seized a whip and started thrashing left and right into a mass of fleeing slaves. Another spinner zoomed towards them, flashing silver. The green spinner shot into the silver one, sending it reeling off course, away from the slaves, who stumbled over each other in disoriented terror.

It looped back, trailing green, then smashing down hard on the guard's helmet, shredding it instantly, leaving a mess of metal slivers and grey flesh in the dirt. The other guards were horrified, some even snatched off their helmets to look wildly around, to see who was controlling it. Despite the grey skin, white hair and war paint, some of them looked very young.

All of a sudden, one of the guards threw up his arm, stabbing an accusatory finger towards the tunnel where Cora and the professor crouched, and Cora managed to duck back into the tunnel just in time before a spinner thudded into the professor, ripping him to shreds.

She couldn't look, but turned her face to the wall, bile rising at the horrible noise.

She curled into a ball, eyes glued shut, hugging her knees and shaking all over. What now? The screaming outside rattled her bones. Her heart was hammering so hard in her ribs she could barely breathe. She'd started something terrible. So many would die and she still had no idea how to get past the spikes. It was pointless. Rash. They'd put the plan into action with no thought as to how it would end.

The drone of a spinner buzzed deep in her ears and she waited, trying to not be afraid; accept her fate and think of heaven.

The buzzing continued. The whipping of the tentacles got faster and faster. Sweat coated her face and the wind of the spinner cooled her scalp. It would be over soon. Any minute now and she'd be a pile of red ribbon. It wouldn't hurt. It'd be over too quickly to hurt.

She squeezed her eyes so tightly they ached. The buzzing, whipping noise was deafening, as though an angry wasp had crawled into each of her ears. It felt like it was coming from the inside of her own head, making her brain vibrate.

Then it stopped and the rushing wind stopped and the air was suddenly still.

There was a metallic thud and something hard bumped against her hip, its heat seeping through the weave of her dress.

She opened her eyes a crack. The spinner was suddenly inert, lying on the rock. A ball of horror, its withdrawn tentacles mere needle tips on its surface.

Numb, Cora stared at it. Then she got to her feet, unlocking wobbly joints she'd expected to lose forever, wiping a lip she thought would lie shredded in a heap. She refused to look at the mess that was once professor Polperro and forced her gaze out, instead, across the crater, where the sounds had changed.

It wasn't just screaming anymore or the crash of bodies struggling to get away, or chains dragging slaves off the edges of the ridges. There was a cries of victory too. Exultant shrieking. Cora scanned the scene to find the knot of slaves who were shouting, and she suddenly saw why. Other spinners had dropped from the sky, landing with harmless thumps as, one by one, guards shook their heads, staggering left and right and falling to their knees, then forward into the ground, the controllers limp in their hands.

The only spinner still active was the one trailing green smoke. Cora watched as its snaking fumes encircled each guard, darkening their brassy armour to a sickly olive before whipping them to shreds. Cora's eyes narrowed, trying to spot who was controlling it.

It was Bronnan, her fierce expression fully focused on guiding the spinner from one unconscious guard to the next. Each had been knocked out by a geode.

Cora felt clammy as the hatred drained from her heart, leaving only revulsion. Bronnan was murdering them in their sleep.

Cora stumbled away from the mouth of the tunnel and down the sloping ridge towards Bronnan, whose teeth were bared, her mouth opening a little every time she killed, each death sending a ragged cheer up from the surviving slaves.

'Bronnan!' Cora shouted. 'They're unconscious! Stop! We can go now, we need to find a way out!'

Either Bronnan was ignoring her or she couldn't hear, transfixed as she was upon her gruesome task. The glint in her eyes was horrible to behold.

Cora got close enough to swipe at the controller, startling Bronnan and sending the green spinner upward in jagged spirals.

'What are you doing?' Bronnan snapped, righting its course to send it into a guard without a helmet who lay, eyes closed, lips parted, his head dangling over the edge of a ridge. 'Get off!' Bronnan snapped, pushing Cora away without looking at her and destroying the unconscious guard.

Cora looked shakily around, she couldn't be the only one, surely? All the dust caked faces she saw were hungry for death, each pair of eyes following Bronnan's massacre of the guards with an eerie gleam.

No, not all of them. One face was disgusted. As sad as her own. Tom! Cora hurried towards him with energy she thought she'd lost.

She flew headlong into his arms, one of his hands moved up to cradle her scalp as she lifted her face, wet with tears.

His head looked different, angular and severe somehow, without his messy thatch. She'd never noticed that his ears stuck out a little. An old scar, usually hidden, showed white above his stubbled hairline and she traced it with her fingers. She wrapped her hands around the back of his neck. It was wet. Her fingers came away stained red.

'What happened?' she gasped, turning his head to see a gash.

'Geode,' he shrugged. 'It doesn't hurt. Could've been much worse.'

Not caring for decency or what Eseld would think, Cora stretched up on tiptoe, grabbed his cheeks and kissed him fully on the mouth, the heat of his lips almost obliterating the horror around them. Almost, but not quite.

She pulled away, lips bruised from pressing on

her teeth.

His cheeks went pink.

'Tom,' she said, as she tried to rip off her sleeve. It was much harder than she thought but eventually she managed it and tied the dirty fabric around his head to staunch the bleeding.

'We have to get out. Bronnan's gone mad. She's killing the guards even though they're unconscious-'

'Why are they out like that? What happened?'

'They, I mean we...' She stopped. There wasn't time to explain and besides, something about his soft, unfocused stare was unnerving. Hunger and exhaustion, she told herself.

'How will we get out?' people around them were panicking, 'there's no way through the spikes without the watchmen.'

'Watchmen?' Cora asked, turning to look up where the others were pointing, at the high tower beside the massive gate. At the top, two piles of ruined grey flesh, threaded with slivers of armour, were just visible.

The drawn bolt across the gate was the size of a roof beam.

'How do they get up there?' she wondered aloud. 'There's no ladder or anything.'

'Dropped, ain't they?' somebody said. 'By the dragonbirds.'

'Pterydons.'

'Whatever. Them vicious, flappy things. I seen 'em. Two go up on the back of one, and then one fella hops off onto the tower an' the other keeps going, off on a raid.'

Cora suddenly understood the significance of his words. 'Raids? They'll be back, won't they? They'll come back on the pterydons and see all this and-.'

She stared at the horrible scene. So much blood. So much death. If they didn't escape at that moment, then more guards would arrive to chain them up again and it would all have been for absolutely nothing. She forced her gaze back up, towards the tower. 'We have to climb it, get that bolt drawn.'

She ran towards it, followed by the others, many of whom were limping or supporting someone and struggling to keep up. Some were missing arms which, without bleeding, left pale skin to hang in rags around bone and grey muscle. She heard someone whisper something about her tattoo and Merlin's blood in her veins. 'That's Elowen,' said someone, 'you know, the real one, from the stories! She'll get us out!'

The faeries kept repeating the name that wasn't Cora's to each other, encouraging the most frightened to keep looking up and ahead and at her, not down at the mangled bodies. And soon they were all following her as she approached the tower, which rose in front of her, steep sided and utterly unclimbable.

Chapter Fifteen

Flight

Tom helped the tallest man climb onto Mr Penrose's shoulders, but he still couldn't reach the bolt.

The sound they all dreaded was barely audible at first, like a ladies' fan, but it became louder with every beat of wings, until the screaming drowned it out.

For a second, the faery guards on the pterydons were oblivious, sailing over the tower towards the centre of the crater, as if to alight as usual. But, on sighting the carnage, each one suddenly wheeled around and flapped towards the terrified huddle, raising their spears.

'Spinner!' shouted a guard, and everyone pressed against the cruel, immoveable gate.

But no spinner appeared, because there was nobody to answer the guard's command and release one from the cliff.

'Where's Bronnan?' Cora was frantic. 'Where's the green spinner?'

Then she saw her, crouching, rubbing an upright piece of wood on a flat one as if she was trying to start a fire, her hands a blur.

'What are you doing?!' Cora yelped. 'They're coming!'

'The glamour's worn off the spinner,' Bronnan said, shortly, 'and the flying smoke too, like all the others.'

'But why are you-?'

'They hate fire!' Bronnan snapped, as the shadows of the pterydons drew closer.

'Then do the magic hand fire thing!' Cora screeched. 'Like Eseld in the cave!'

'I can't.' Bronnan hissed, as if Cora was very stupid. 'You need blood.'

'Mr Penrose? Can you do it? Anybody?'

'I ain't got no magic,' Mr Penrose was grey with fear, as his own death flapped closer.

Cora's heart hammered in her chest as she tried to remember the strange words Eseld had used. And time began to stretch, slowing each second as she remembered. Eseld hadn't used words. She said she'd summoned up her blood and thought about why she was there and what really mattered. Staring hard at her trembling hands, knowing there was next to no hope, Cora tried to think about what really mattered. She'd got away from Selina and she'd never be her puppet again. But her hands remained cold, shaking and filling with nothing but the dark shadow of the pterydons.

Her blood rushed in her ears, she felt faint. She'd let them all die. If she couldn't do this, then everyone would die.

'Elowen?!' They were crying out. 'Do something!'

Anger at the name flooded her body 'I'm not Elowen!' she shouted, tears filling her eyes as the pterydon talons stretched down towards her. 'I'm Cora!' Her palms itched and both hands burst into flame, not like Eseld's soft little candle tip, but guttering torches, billowing smoke.

The pterydon veered away so violently it made the faery guard tumble off its back and the others flap straight up into the sky, almost losing their riders too.

Cora stared at her flaming fingers, completely unharmed inside the blaze.

'Quick,' Bronnan was at her side, 'the gate, the tower, burn all of it!'

Wordlessly, Cora bent towards the wood. It was old and coated with dirt, but there were splinters here and there, which caught, curling black and red.

Focusing hard on her task, refusing to question it, Cora forced herself to stay in the part of her brain where language didn't exist, where there was only blood and fire.

'Put her out for mercy's sake!' Nancarrow was hobbling towards Cora, her eyes wild as she shoved Bronnan, putting all the strength of her wasted body into it, barely moving the startled warrior, but sending herself tumbling to the ground.

More irritated than concerned, Bronnan dragged Nancarrow to her feet. 'What are you doing you mad old bat?'

'You set my Cora alight! It must o' been you! I seen you with all your tricks!' Nancarrow pushed and slapped Bronnan, whose nostrils flared.

Cora put herself between Bronnan and the frail old lady, shielding her. 'She's my nurse! She doesn't know what she's saying!'

In her distraction, the flames engulfing Cora's hands disappeared.

Once she'd helped Nancarrow down, she stared at her fingers in dismay and at the blackened stain on the gate, which wasn't burning. She scanned the sky for the tiny black crosses of the pterydon. They were still there, circling.

'Cora, look!' Tom was pointing at the gate. A

splinter must have been glowing still, because Mr Penrose was blowing hard, coaxing a red scar along the ashy grain, until a bright orange flame licked up towards the wooden bolt.

A cheer rose from the bedraggled group as the fire caught hold and Nancarrow hugged Cora tight, she and Bronnan regarding each other haughtily all the while, until they had to move backwards, away from the gathering heat, shielding their faces with their arms.

Soon enough, the flaming gate started to collapse. The bolt crashed to the ground, bringing half the burning tower with it and sending up a shower of sparks. Smoke belched upwards in a great cloud and they used their ragged clothes to cover their faces, as they charged into the burning mess, trying their best to get over and out before they, too, caught fire.

Freedom was all Cora could think about as she coughed, stumbling over the charred wood, her skin scorching as she helped Nancarrow over the smouldering timbers.

Tom carried a child on his back, whom he set down on the blessed dirt where she lay, spluttering and bewildered, before he charged back in.

Cora went over to the girl, who stared up at her in fear before taking her proffered hand. They got everyone away from the road and into the forest. The winter trees were wilder there, with no buildings in their branches or paths between their roots. Thick, ancient trunks with frilled shelves of black fungus cast them into ragged shadow and they had to scramble over enormous fallen logs, soft with rot. Thin saplings twanged and shuddered as they fought their way through a waist-high snare of black, leafless brambles.

'What's your name?' Cora asked the girl, hoping it would comfort her a bit. But as she looked into her frightened face, it felt foolish. Too little, too late.

After a moment the child spoke, but in a voice so faint it was lost in the rustling of the undergrowth.

'Sorry?' Cora tried to be gentle.

'It's Anneth,' the girl whispered. 'Mudroot.'

'Well, Anneth Mudroot, don't you worry. Everything's going to be all right.' The lie slipped out with alarming ease and Cora thought of the countless people that must have said the same thing over the centuries, in a thousand different languages, each firming up their voice to reassure a wet-eyed child. It made her feel less like a child herself and, in a strange sort of way, less afraid.

The child looked at her, sideways, and Cora remembered that as a faery, Anneth could see the fear beneath her honeyed words. And that, like Jago Lampbright, her childish form didn't need to hinder her age.

Cora tried to trust that Tom had made it out, that he hadn't succumbed to the fumes as he kept returning to help more people. She wanted to be proud of him, but fear for his safety crushed any of that. They had to keep moving.

'Down!' Bronnan hissed. Everyone obeyed, squashing themselves into wet, scratchy undergrowth. Instinctively, Cora grabbed Anneth, trying to protect her from the brambles, even as Nancarrow pushed them away from Cora's scalp.

Cora couldn't see or hear anything at first, except her own stifled, frightened breath.

Then she heard it. A steady flap, flap, flap, soft at

first, building to an unmistakeable rush of enormous wings, chilling them all to the marrow. They couldn't help turning to see.

The pterydon landed on the road, claws outstretched, huge wings gliding then thumping forward, before folding behind its back.

Cora watched through the web of bramble, her heart clattering discordantly in her chest.

Then she saw Tom.

The pterydon was enormous, standing taller than Tom and covering him in shadow. He held an unconscious man over his shoulders.

Before she could think, Cora was up and crashing through the undergrowth, pushing everything out of her mind but fire and thumping blood. She lifted her hands, rubbing them together as Eseld had done, but they were wet and she wiped them on her sooty dress before trying again.

The pterydon was even more terrifying up close. Its muscular legs were bigger than a man's and covered in sleek feathers. Its head was disproportionately long and reptilian, its eyes hard and shining black. It whipped round to face Cora as she crashed out of the forest, opening its jaws in a harsh, whining screech.

Cora flew headlong into Tom, unable to stop herself, making him stumble and almost drop the man.

Tom tried to put himself between Cora and the pterydon, but he was staggering with the weight and she refused to budge. In their panicked scuffle, neither realised that little Anneth Mudroot had followed Cora, and was now lifting her hand towards the pterydon's feathered wing.

Too stunned to do anything but stare, horror-struck, Cora saw Anneth open her mouth wide and emit a high-pitched screech.

'Get away from it!' Cora shouted, reaching to grab her.

But the pterydon was bending its neck towards the child, making a softer noise now, more like a cat's mewing than the shrieks it had fired at Cora.

It lowered its head even more, jaws opening to reveal curved, yellow teeth alarmingly close to the child's head.

'No!' Cora shrieked, lunging towards Anneth. But it was too late, the pterydon had snatched the fabric at the back of the child's frayed collar and swept her up into the air.

Instinctively, Cora rammed the pterydon with her shoulder, thumping and kicking at the warm feathers of its powerful chest, making the creature stagger back and open its massive wings.

'Stop it!' yelled the girl from somewhere high up.

'Yes, put her down!' Cora shouted at the dumb creature, even as her whole body was shaking in fear of it. Where was its faery rider? Where were all the other pterydons?

But, even as she raged, Cora noticed that the strange sounds Anneth made were not those of a frightened child. She moved backwards, to try to see better, and spotted the girl perched astride the fearsome beast as calmly as if she were sitting on a rocking horse.

As the pterydon squawked and mewed, Anneth was nodding gravely, mewing in response. At last, it dawned on Cora that she wasn't witnessing one animal threatening another at all, but two, communicating.

'How can you *speak* to it?' Cora protested. 'It's a dumb creature! And don't fall off, you'll break your neck!'

'No it ain't!' came Anneth's voice from above and Cora was suddenly reminded of Florence, the phantom of a ghost, whom she'd pretended to plead with so long ago, in another life.

'I'm from Rose Mountain, the curse didn't reach that far so they're not affected. We were visiting my cousins unfortunately,' she shrugged. 'Rose Mountain's where the pterydons come from, so we grew up speaking both languages. They can't speak ours as they haven't got the right sort of tongue.'

Cora was too astonished to speak. Eventually she managed 'what do you mean, it's where they come from. Did you farm them?'

Anneth frowned. 'They're not like pigs, they're like... well, us.'

Cora shifted her gaze from Anneth to the creature and saw, for the first time, intelligence glinting in its black, crocodile eyes. But it only made the thing more frightening.

She scrabbled for something to say. 'The right sort of what? Tongue?'

'Mm,' Anneth nodded, *smiling*. 'They've got a brush tip to help them drink nectar. From flowers.'

'Nectar?!' Cora feared for the child all over again. What if she was mad? 'What about all those teeth?' Cora stammered. 'They're not for flowers!'

Anneth laughed. She actually laughed! Sitting astride the most terrifying creature Cora had ever seen in her life. 'They eat other things too, silly! Wildcats mostly.'

Cora swallowed.

Tom knelt to let the man slide from his shoulders onto the road. Cora bent to catch his head, heavy and prickled with grey stubble. He was human, but he wasn't breathing.

'It's too late, Tom,' she said quietly.

'But I thought, if I could get him out we could, I don't know...' Tom stared down at the man, at his wasted limbs and sunken cheeks. 'I don't even know his name. You're sure he's dead?'

Cora nodded sadly, her eyes returning to Anneth and the pterydon, who seemed to be trying to get their attention.

'She says we need to go' Anneth was practical. 'She'll get us away, but we'll owe her.'

'*Her?*'

Anneth was nodding, seeming calmer than ever. 'Morgelyn's got their eggs.'

'You're sure he's dead?' Tom was murmuring.

'What? Yes. I'm sorry Tom.'

'We need to bury him.' He lifted his gaze to stare back through the mess of burnt wood into the mine. 'All of them.'

'No, look, Tom I think you're in shock.'

'We have to go!' Anneth repeated, more urgently this time, as the pterydon started scraping the ground, wings fidgeting as though she was anxious to take off.

'And the guards, too,' Tom mumbled. 'They were only following orders.'

'Now you're being ridiculous!' Cora snapped. She turned away from Tom and the dead man in his arms. 'Anneth, are you absolutely sure you can trust this... creature?'

'Her name's Ququraouk Sfhelluorch. At least, that's the closest I can get with our sounds.'

Cora regarded the creature, its eyes as hard and unreadable as ever. With a stab of shame, she remembered seeing Wenna for the first time and all the terrible assumptions she'd made. Determined not to repeat her mistake, she asked 'what does Quro-Quaqua-'

'Ququraouk.'

'What does she want us to do? To help her get her eggs?' It only hit her then, as she said it. 'Hang on, Morgelyn's stolen their eggs? Their babies? Is that how she-'

'That's how she gets them to work for her. After twenty raids, she gives one egg back to one mother or father. But nobody knows who it'll be, so they keep on, hoping the next time will be their turn. Any eggs they lay are immediately taken. If they resist, the guards smash the eggs on the rocks at the mine and threaten the pterydons with a spinner.'

Cora stared at the creature. That explained how they obtained a plentiful supply of tears. 'That's horrible,' she said quietly. 'Does it, sorry, does *she* know what I'm saying?'

Anneth nodded. 'Course. She just can't answer because-'

'Her tongue, yes.' Cora searched for heartbreak in the monster's features, but saw only dry reptilian skin, drawn tight over bone and tooth.

'I'll ask Bronnan and the others.'

Bronnan, along with everyone else, except the few who'd taken their chances and fled into the forest without looking back, agreed that while it didn't appeal, it was their only real chance. Flying on backs of the pterydons, they could cover a decent amount of ground and get to the Riddler's Fiddle in less than half the time.

'But we won't all fit on Quro-' Cora flushed, concentrating. 'Ququraouk.'

'No,' Anneth addressed the frightened, half-starved faces of the escaped slaves, who peered from the undergrowth. 'That's why the others are waiting nearby. They knew they'd have frightened us off if they'd all landed together.'

Despite everything, Cora's flesh prickled with alarm. She glanced wildly around, fearing a trap. But, as the other pterydons began to land, called by a screech from Ququraouk, which made everyone cover their ears, Cora forced herself to see beyond their frightening demeanour. For it was with care that they bent low to allow the trembling figures to clamber onto their backs. Cora didn't ask what had happened to their riders. This was evidently the chance the pterydons had been waiting for, to rebel.

Bronnan used a long stick to vault onto a rather startled pterydon, who flapped her wings in surprise at the sudden weight, almost tipping Bronnan off and making everyone even more nervous.

With two or three riders each, the fifteen pterydons took to the air, running and jumping and landing and jumping again before their wings found their full strength and flapped hard, forcing the air down and making their rider's heads jerk backwards in a slow rhythm, as though on horseback. Cora climbed up behind Tom and wrapped her arms tightly around his waist.

'They'll take us above the clouds!' Anneth called, 'so no-one'll see!' and as they soared higher, the air grew faster and much colder. Cora gripped the warm, feathered body with her legs. Her bracelet felt loose and she knotted it, to make it smaller so it wouldn't fall off.

Tom turned, his breath hot on her face as he asked 'where are we going?'

'To the Riddler's Fiddle,' she replied, 'to Wenna and Mamm-wynn, remember?' she tried to put his confusion down to their ordeal and ignore the smell of blood soaking though the sleeve.

By the time they reached the cloud layer, the misty air was so cold it was like rising through water. Cora feared that if she got any colder, she might grow too numb to hold on. Around her, the terrified huddles of faeries and humans flying on the backs of monsters lost their colours, fading to grey shapes with long, tapering wings.

In the ragged gaps between the clouds, Underwood spread in a dark tangle. The spikiness of the branches blurred, with distance, into something softer. She laid her head against Tom's back.

'How will they rise?' he mumbled. 'At the judgement day?'

'What? They'll... I don't know.' Cora grew flustered. 'The Lord will provide. That's his job isn't it?'

Tom wasn't convinced.

'Look, we'll come back when it's all over. Bury them properly and put up a, I don't know, a memorial.'

He didn't reply.

Exasperated, Cora tried again. 'Think of your Mamm-Wynn, Tom. And Gwen and Meg and little Curnow. And everyone else. We've got to get to

Wenna and stop Morgelyn, or she'll do to Broadpuddle what she's done to Underwood. Then she'll do it to Treleddan.'

Tom turned to stare at her, the whites of his eyes showing pale against his soot smeared skin. 'All right.' He blinked, the creases of his eyelids grimy and black. 'All right.'

She held on to him even more tightly, as the freezing wind streamed past, burying her face in his coat, inhaling his scent of sweat and wood shavings even as it was whipped away.

Chapter Sixteen

Broadpuddle

The sprawling forest began to thin, just as the sky was dimming. The shade of blue was just a little too Prussian to be natural and the clouds were eerie in the glow of the moon, reflected in pools that glimmered between the last, skeletal trees as Underwood became Broadpuddle.

Stars appeared. Just a few, here and there. Fog misted the mysterious place below, making it difficult to distinguish between water and land. As they descended, Cora couldn't see any sign of a town. No lights in the darkness. The wind remained cold, rushing against her face as they descended.

They alighted with a squelch and, as she struggled down from the pterydon's back, Cora's relief at being on land again turned to distaste. The pterydon's clawed feet had disappeared into the sodden ground and there was rotten smell in the air, like old water in a vase of dead flowers. Unable to do anything else, she dropped onto the soft, wet marsh, which instantly soaked her boots, water bubbling up through the cracked leather and into her frayed stockings. Tough stalks of grass poked up through the puddles and bulrushes reflected themselves in the deeper water in sharp, angular lines.

'I can see why it's called Broadpuddle,' Cora murmured, as Tom landed next to her. It was flat, treacherous expanse. Through the fog she could just make out ragged patches of reeds, but over most of it spread gleaming water, which could be hiding anything. 'I can't see any sign of a town though.'

Around them, the pterydons were spreading their wings and beginning to run, dripping as they took off, as the shivering band called out their thanks.

'Why are they leaving?' Cora asked everyone and no-one. 'There aren't any inns! How do we find the others?'

'They don't get on with the spriggans,' Anneth explained. 'They think it's best if we go the last bit of the way ourselves.'

Cora nodded, feeling small and apprehensive as the enormous creatures flapped into the sky. The rising silhouettes that had terrified her just hours ago seemed so free and alive, their departure making the gloomy landscape feel even more desolate than before.

'This way!' Bronnan threw her arm up to get everyone's attention, then thrust it forward. People started moving in the direction Bronnan had indicated, but Cora hesitated.

'Shouldn't we get lanterns? Candles at least? It's getting dark and we won't be able to see a thing soon.'

'Where from?' Bronnan asked coldly. 'Do you see a chandler's shop?'

'No, but...' Cora rummaged in her pockets for her candle stubs, then remembered she was wearing a borrowed dress.

She tried to conjure a flame in her palm instead, still astonished that she could do such a thing at all and keen to practice, but she wasn't angry enough. She was afraid, certainly, but it was a cold, bleak sort of fear. The fiery terror of the escape from the mine had been quite different.

'Stop that.' Bronnan glared. 'Last thing we need is

to attract attention. Just because a few pterydons helped us out, doesn't mean she hasn't got plenty more at her command.'

The remark would've wounded her once. But all Cora could think about was finding Wenna and Eseld. A small voice in the back of her mind pointed out that she was the one who'd received the message about the Riddler's Fiddle. What if she'd misunderstood, or professor Polperro had got it wrong?

'Over here!' Bronnan ordered. 'It's firmer. Some kind of wooden walkway.'

Cora followed the others as they moved towards Bronnan and a partially submerged row of planks. It was broken in places and slippery with moss, but much more solid beneath their feet than the soggy marsh. They followed it for what felt like a long time, surrounded by nothing but barely visible, unchanging bog. There was something different though, Cora noticed. She could hear insects and possibly a frog, somewhere far off. It was what had been missing in Underwood. Life. Encouraged, she found a small comfort in the croaks and the buzzing of tiny wings, until Bronnan, who'd elected herself leader, suddenly stopped, making those who'd huddled closer for warmth bump into each other.

'Crossroads,' Bronnan explained. Cora saw her crouch to read the scratches in the damp wood. Even at a distance, she could see they weren't letters she knew.

'This way!' Bronnan called and they were off again.

Cora was wondering about the people who needed such low signs, and about to ask Tom what he knew about the spriggans, when something slithered from the water with a plopping noise and wrapped itself around Cora's ankle.

Screaming, she kicked at it, trying to shake it off, but its grip only tightened, yanking her towards the edge.

'Help! Tom!'

She fell to her knees, kicking hard with her free leg and screamed to see something like a human head emerge from the marsh.

In the gloom, the snakish grip became a webbed hand, green-black as seaweed, which refused to loosen even as her frantic kicks broke its toadish skin.

Cora glimpsed Bronnan, who was holding a rock and narrowing her eyes. 'What are you waiting for?' Cora yelled. 'Kill it!'

Nancarrow started tugging Cora's arms, fearing she'd be sucked down to a muddy death. Tom lumbered towards her, thrusting both arms into the bog and grappling with the creature, but it must have been agile and slippery as it ducked and dodged like a boneless thing, evading his grasp. Mr Penrose snatched up a loose bit of board from the jetty and smacked it savagely onto the monster-like fingers around Cora's ankle, breaking it into splintery halves and at last, the slimy hand released her. She scrambled to her feet, collapsing into Nancarrow's frail arms.

Instead of disappearing, the monster slapped and slithered up onto the wooden walk, terrifying everyone. When it stood up, it became a very different beast altogether. Its arms, head and upper body were large and powerful but, once it's lower

body emerged, Cora was startled to see that its legs
and pot belly were small, making it look vastly out of
proportion. It wore a large bag, it's strap diagonal
across a surprisingly ordinary coat, waistcoat, cravat
and breeches, all of which were black or dark green,
each sodden and dripping.

Bronnan moved forwards, lifting the rock high
but, instead of using it as a weapon, she threw it into
the bog with a splash and grabbed the creature's
slimy arm in a sort of handshake. After breaking her
grip, Bronnan began to make rapid movements with
her hands, to which the creature responded with his
own.

Then it turned. Cora realised it had no mouth or
nose, just dark, unnaturally round eyes in the middle
of its face and a glistening fan of lizard-like skin
under its chin. Out of its bag it produced a globe of
dull, transparent material, which it put on its head
like a diving helmet. Then it dropped a length of
tube into the marsh and somehow filled the globe
with water, the quivering level rising up over its face.

All at once, the foggy gloom was filled with light.
Orange torches, lanterns, voices and a cacophonous
clattering noise like a hundred wooden sticks banging
together filled the air.

Cora panicked. Barely able to believe that the
creature who'd tried to drown her was now allowed
to construct its bizarre breathing apparatus and
converse with Bronnan, the noisy arrival of yet more
marsh-dwelling creatures filled her with dread, and
she was temporarily blinded by their torches. Every
time she blinked, nonsensical shapes and images
were imprinted in her vision. She could no longer
see the slimy creature properly, or Bronnan or Tom

or Nancarrow, but she held on tight to the latter two. Whatever happened next, she wasn't letting go of them.

'Halt! Who goes there?' came a squashed, scratchy sort of voice from behind the lights, as though the speaker was being throttled. And the wooden boards thrummed and shuddered with the weight of more approaching feet.

'Bronnan Mayflower! Imperial Guard. On her majesty's business.'

'Eh?' The group moved closer and a torch was thrust towards Bronnan, who didn't flinch as her face was suddenly illuminated.

'And Lord Gendal,' she added. The monster who'd grabbed Cora's ankle performed an elegant bow, the torchlight on his outstretched hands revealing shining scales, scattered like freckles.

There was a shuffling noise and Cora's eyes finally adjusted enough to see a band of small people, no higher than her hip, clad in leather helmets, with breastplates woven from rushes, holding lanterns on poles and long torches that gave the illusion of a much taller group.

They moved forward, the better to see, and Cora was amazed when they lifted their visors.

Before she stopped to think, Cora blurted 'but you're female!'

'We are the Night Watch of Pendlestow!' retorted one.

'Most of our men went to fight,' said another, 'we ain't seen 'em since.'

'Lord Gendal,' said the one who seemed to be in charge, moving her hands into a series of rapid shapes as she spoke both languages simultaneously, 'can you vouch for these...' she moved closer, casting light across the exhausted huddle '...people?'

Lord Gendal's hands flickered. Soon the fierce, wary expressions of the Night Watch gave way to those of sympathy, particularly as they moved their lanterns to reveal the haggard faces and scarred, shaven heads of the escaped slaves.

'Bronnan Mayflower, as I live and breathe,' said the woman who seemed to be in charge. 'I don't suppose you remember me?'

Bronnan's gaze narrowed, and Cora wasn't sure if she was trying to recall her name, or pretend to, out of politeness. No, not politeness. Pride.

'Goodwife... Winifred?'

'Nearly. Goodwife Jenifry! So you do remember?'

Bronnan nodded and attempted a smile that didn't convince Cora for a second. 'Of course.'

One of the women lifted a horn and blew a rich note. Like an extraordinary spell, dozens of lights appeared behind the group, out of the foggy dark, revealing wooden buildings perched upon a low, wide pier-like construction, supported by stilts. Their reflections glittered, gold and orange, in the water below.

'Pendlestow.' Tom grinned, giving Cora a squeeze. She looked up at him, at the dried dribbles of blood on his neck and ear.

'What about that thing?' She eyed Lord Gendal with suspicion, as he picked splinters out of his hand. She reminded herself of her initial revulsion of Wenna. Although Wenna hadn't tried to drown her.

Bronnan answered her thoughts in her brisk, impatient manner as they followed the crowd of small, bobbing helmets, as the path widened and sloped upwards towards an arched gate. 'He was alarmed at the sound of our feet and feared we might be Morgelyn's troops. That's why he grabbed your ankle.'

'Well,' Cora breathed through her nose, slightly mollified, 'he wouldn't have lasted long if we were, would he?'

Lord Gendal signed something to Bronnan.

She turned to Cora and said 'he says he only needed to last long enough to raise the alarm.'

Cora tried to see an expression through the dim water-filled globe, but the round eyes stared flatly back. If there was any emotion in them, then it was expressed in too foreign a way for Cora to understand.

'But why would he care? He isn't a spriggan.'

'They're neighbours, Cora. The marshrai live under the water, the spriggans live above it. It's not complicated.'

'Did you really remember her?' Cora asked.

'It's called diplomacy,' Bronnan replied, keeping her voice low. 'We've come here to ask for their help. It wouldn't do to anger them.'

The gate was flanked by blazing, smelly torches, which hissed and sparked as they passed underneath. It was very high, Cora noted, for such tiny people, as was the door to the wooden building they entered, which had a sign swinging above it, as though dwarves were living in a place abandoned by giants. Cora couldn't decipher the strange marks, but there was a peeling painting of a violin, so she hoped against hope that this was, at last, the Riddler's Fiddle.

They were hit by a wall of smoke, filled with the

smells of beer and roasting fish. Someone was playing the pipes and another was keeping time by scraping a stick back and forth on the ridged underside of a clog. As Cora scanned the faces gathered around a central hearth, she saw Wenna and Eseld, arms outstretched and her fears scattered like darkness before a flame.

Cora flew into their arms and the three held each other tightly. In the past, she'd heard people say they'd been to hell and back, but had never understood what they meant until now. The mine in the crater felt like a horrible dream. She wanted to bury her memories of it and never dig them up again. After tearful reunions and introductions, those who could eat were given barbecued fish skewered on sticks and moss coloured scones that smelled of mashed river weed and they ate hungrily. Some clutched their stomachs afterwards, having grown unaccustomed to feeling full.

Lord Gendal held a live eel, which twitched and flapped, curling this way and that even as he lifted the fan of green skin to reveal two rows of needle-thin teeth and sank them into its flesh. With a shudder, Cora looked away, though his supper appealed to her much more than the roasted fish the others were devouring.

She glanced back, unable to keep her eyes off him. Through the greenish murk of the water inside the globe, she saw gills in the sides of his head, opening and closing. A minnow darted past his face as he turned, offering Cora a leech from a bowlful of squirming black.

Hesitating at first, Cora couldn't help glancing down at her ankle, and at his hand, where the scratches looked sore. He still alarmed her, but she was impressed by his bravery.

'Bronnan?' She tried to get her attention. 'How do I say thank you?'

Bronnan blinked, possibly surprised. She made a movement with her hands that Cora copied, more slowly, and Lord Gendal appeared to nod inside his globe, the water sloshing slightly around his head.

Cora ate the leech, which would have been delicious, had she not been acutely aware of Tom's averted eyes. He was eating like a sleepwalker, his face devoid of expression, however much she tried to catch his eye.

'So, why was the town all dark?' Cora asked Eseld, who looked up from her meal. 'We'd have seen it from miles away if they'd shown their lights.'

'They're calling it a blackout,' Eseld replied, picking a translucent scale off her tongue. 'Cos of the raids. They want to stay hidden from the pterydons. Filthy beasts.'

'They're not though!' Cora shook her head. 'Morgelyn's taken their eggs, that's why they've been doing it.'

Eseld took another bite, chewing thoughtfully before she finally said, with a grimness that made Cora uncomfortable, 'no excuse.'

Cora didn't mention their offer of help in return for their flight from the mine. She stole a glance at Wenna, whose steady gaze told her she already knew.

Cora tried to focus on one thing at a time. 'What if the pterydons come in daylight?"

'Wouldn't dare. The spriggans are a deadly shot, give 'em a bow an' arrow. That's why they started snatching at night. So they shutter all the windows and whatnot, don't carry no lanterns. And only if they get the signal, they reveal the town.'

Cora tried to blot out the memory of being snatched. 'Why did you run away, when you turned into a hare?' She'd hoped to sound like a soldier discussing tactics. Instead, a rather feeble, plaintive voice emerged instead.

'Oh Cora, love. You don't think I'd have gone if there'd been any choice do you? Some of us had to get away to rescue them what didn't.'

'Only you didn't.' Cora swallowed, turning pink. 'Rescue us.' She hated this wretched, tearful child inside herself, the part that couldn't hold on to the joy of finding them again. Her gaze shifted from Eseld to Wenna.

'You know we'd have stayed if we thought we could do any good,' Wenna said gently, putting her cold hand on Cora's feathered one. 'You know it, you just need to believe it.'

As she ate, trying to understand what Wenna meant, Cora's eyes grew accustomed to the smoky dark. She could just make out the puzzling shapes of enormous swords and shields hanging on the walls. But they were far too big for a human to wield, or a marshrai, let alone a spriggan. Bronnan had said that the marshrai and the spriggans were neighbours. Perhaps they had other, bigger neighbours too. The thought made her scalp prickle.

Soon, they were taken to different houses and given places to sleep. The whole of Pendlestow had opened its doors to the sorry flood of refugees. No, not the whole, Cora noticed with dismay, as they walked through the creaking, wooden streets. Some of the houses were shuttered and silent. The only sign of life was the smoke from the central chimney. At first, she thought illness or worse might have made them separate themselves in this way, until she saw the signs on the doors, crudely painted, of what were possibly meant to be faeries but they might have been humans, slashed with crosses.

Cora was anxious not to be parted from Wenna, Eseld or Nancarrow again, particularly if there were those who wanted rid of them. She wanted to stay in the same house as Tom, but male and female guests were strictly separated.

Each home consisted of one long room with a central fire, like the one in the inn. They were given bowls of water to wash and, as she ran her fingers over skin filmed with dirt, Cora felt bumps all over her face, the kind that had appeared on her arms, before the feathers had erupted. She snatched her fingers away.

The sleeping mats were rolled out on the floorboards, each plank so long that, as Cora lay down, she sensed the movement of other people shifting at the other end of the house, which pressed and slightly lifted the boards beneath her, making them creak. She found it surprisingly comforting. Each mat was thickly woven from reeds and covered in blankets that weren't made of wool, but something smoother, like flax, and large enough for four or five women to share. Fortunately, it was warmer and more comfortable than it looked and, before long, while Wenna stayed sitting up, gazing deep into her blackstone at something Cora couldn't see, Cora, Eseld and Nancarrow fell fast asleep.

When Cora woke, her ankle hurt and for the first

bleary seconds she thought it was still chained to the floor of the slave house. Then she remembered she was free, with a mixture of gladness and grief. The others must have got up already, as she was the only one in the bed. Wenna sat cross-legged, a few feet away, still gazing into her blackstone.

'Eat up, you're as thin as a rake.' Nancarrow appeared just as Cora was pushing herself upright. She held a bowl of stew, with grassy herbs floating in it, close to Cora's face.

'What's in it?'

'Frog and otter, they said. And that's marsh samphire there. Not proper food I know, but needs must.'

'Ugh,' Cora failed to conceal her distaste, glancing ashamedly at the spriggan women, bundled in scarves, who were ladling steaming stew into bowls held by grateful human hands at the other end of the room. The other mats had been rolled up and put away, making Cora self-conscious at sleeping so long.

She didn't want to be rude, but the smell alone made her want to retch.

'Now, Cora,' Nancarrow used her firm-but-patient voice, reminding Cora of years of teeth-brushing, lice-combing and cod liver oil. She held the spoon up to Cora's lips.

'No, I can't,' Cora turned away, trying to explain, but as she opened her lips Nancarrow deftly pushed the spoon in.

Spluttering as she swallowed, Cora held up her hand. 'No, you don't understand. It makes me feel sick.'

'Nonsense.'

Wenna tried to intervene. 'Cora's been through a

lot, she isn't the same-'

'Ain't we all?' Nancarrow was brisk. 'Needs to build up her strength is what.'

'No!' Cora barked, dulling the chatter to an awkward silence. Everyone turned to stare. 'It's the same as *me* forcing *you* to eat live worms!'

Nancarrow's expression didn't flicker. 'Now, I don't know what ideas they've been putting in your head, but all this has got to stop.' She dug around in the stew with the spoon. 'Live worms, she says. Psh.'

A good night's sleep and some proper food was apparently all Nancarrow needed for her fragility to practically vanish overnight. 'You ain't yourself. This silliness about eating worms and leeches and goodness knows what is doing you no good at all.'

Wenna was quiet for a moment, then said gently, 'do you understand, Mrs Nancarrow, why Cora looks the way she does? She was inflicted with a powerful curse, and the only way to-'

'That's another thing,' Nancarrow frowned. 'All this talk o' curses and spells and whatnot. Rubbish! I heard a lot o' them blitherin' on about it last night. Poppycock!'

A slight frown hovered between Wenna's eyebrows. Very gently, she asked 'What do think's happened to Cora?'

'I dunno,' Nancarrow looked out of the glassless window at the low, cloudy sky reflected in the water. 'All I know is she ain't well. She ain't been looked after properly.'

The accusation hung in the air.

'Look at her, Dorothy.' Wenna's voice was so soft, it was barely audible, and those at the other end of the long hut politely resumed their quiet chatter.

'This isn't an illness' Wenna said. 'This is magic. Look at her hair. Her eyes. Her hands. She's changed, hasn't she?'

Only then, Cora realised how difficult it was for Nancarrow to look at her.

'It's not that bad is it?' Cora asked, attempting humour.

Nancarrow shook her head, but she still wouldn't lift her eyes. The spoon dripped.

Wenna was gazing meaningfully at Cora and, inside her mind, she heard Wenna say 'look, Cora. Look to her thoughts.'

Tired as she was, Cora narrowed her focus, staring hard at the air around Nancarrow's stubbly head. But all she could see were floating motes of dust, caught in the chilly light from the window.

Slowly, shapes appeared, filmy as smoke. She saw what Wenna saw and it stopped her breath. The images were muddled; misshapen. Nancarrow was haunted by memories of the slave house, but overlying each of the faery guards, when they removed their helmets, was the ghostly image of a human face, like any hawker or fisherman in Treleddan. The spriggans too, weren't as small, and their features hovered between human and not. Even Lord Gendal, his water-filled globe twisted into a sort of hat, had a human air. His flat, dark eyes were still strangely low in his face, but they rested above a ghostly mouth and nose.

Cora saw herself, too, her prickly black hair overlaid with brown curls, her oddly enlarged irises no longer violet but the blue they used to be. Even her fingers which, in reality, were abnormally long and virtually covered now with silky black feathers, had not, in Nancarrow's mind, changed at all.

'Where do you think you are, Dorothy?' Wenna asked, with a tenderness that brought a lump to Cora's throat.

Nancarrow shrugged, rubbing her forehead as though it ached. 'I dunno. Somewhere foreign. Far from home. Ireland? No, we didn't cross the sea. Scotland then? I know it ain't Wales 'cos I been there once, an' this ain't Wales.'

It struck Cora like a punch in the chest. Nancarrow had lost her marbles. Her kidnap and toil in the mine had all been too much. Her mind was trying to protect itself by filtering everything through a distorting lens, altering truths to make them bearable.

Cora wondered how old she was, for Nancarrow. She peered harder at the image of herself, as Nancarrow saw her. Her cheeks were plump and pink, her forehead rounder and her hair was curled in fat little ringlets tied with bows.

Nancarrow drove the spoon deep into the stew. 'Now, open wide. This'll do you good.'

And Cora did open wide and eat the stew, though it made her violently sick afterwards.

She managed to get outside and hurry away from the houses just in time to crouch at the edge of the wooden platform that held the town, her vomit narrowly missing a small, tethered boat.

The air was cold as it blew across her scalp and she wiped her chin, watching the bits float down beneath the surface and disappear. Then she stopped. The water had stilled and she glimpsed a shadowy reflection of a person she barely recognised. She turned her head to the side, to see her nose in profile. It was definitely bigger and more hooked. Like a beak. Long fingers trembling, she reached up and felt for the bumps she'd found the night before. To her dismay, they had spread overnight and now covered her cheeks and forehead, tipped with tiny points of feather. In the reflection, they looked like a man's stubble.

But she was alive, she told herself crossly, briskly wiping a tear away. She was alive.

And she wouldn't be if Eseld hadn't saved her the only way she could. She thought of the old Waterloo veteran who wheeled himself around the streets of Treleddan in a cart, selling stories and songs. He may have lost his legs, but for him the battle wasn't over. Survivors, Cora reminded herself, weren't always pretty.

A shout from one of the houses startled her and she almost toppled off the edge, regaining her balance just in time. Goodwife Jenifry was blowing her horn and arrows were poking out of cracks in the shuttered windows.

Chapter Seventeen

Beneath

The hastily gathered Night Watch looked far less impressive without the drama of torchlight. Some were still buckling straps and pulling on helmets as they fell into step, marching behind Goodwife Jenifry towards the town's gate. Lord Gendal was walking with them, looking stranger and even more unnerving, if that was possible, in daylight.

Terrified, Cora scanned the grey, cloud-mottled sky for pterydons, but she saw none. She stood up and looked out over the horizon, where a bedraggled group of figures, smudgy in the lingering fog, were struggling to wade through the marsh.

At one of the windows was a wooden telescope, elderly hands clamped to it. An ancient spriggan, one of the few males left, judging by the wispy beard, was peering through the end. 'Looks like more of 'em,' he grumbled. 'There'll be up to their armpits if they don't find the walkway soon.'

'Or worse,' said a thin, elderly lady's voice.

'Get a fish on the fire, Mildred.'

'There ain't none left. I'll find summat else.'

'Who goes there?' Goodwife Jenifry called out across the marsh.

The figures' heads snapped up, glancing around to find the source of the voice.

The Night Watch advanced towards them, Lord Gendal's orb of water bobbing above the other's heads, catching the light. Cora couldn't hear what they were saying as they faded into the mist. Soon they were as ghostly as the struggling figures. The fog grew heavier and turned to rain, wetting Cora's skin. Others gathered around her, craning to see. She could just make out Lord Gendal jumping off the wooden walk into the water. It must have been a trick of the light, but it seemed as though he changed, mid-air, from a human-like creature into something else, something long and limbless, which slipped into the water with barely a ripple.

Cora blinked, trying to focus, as one of the bedraggled refugees was pushed up out of the water and onto the wooden boards. Lord Gendal looked the same again as he sat, legs dangling, emptying his globe and refilling it with fresh water. The person he'd saved was on their hands and knees, wet clothes hanging in rags as they were patted and helped to their feet.

The Night Watch trudged back, a trail of bewildered humans and faeries in their wake. The rain was falling harder now and soon the rescuers were as sodden as the rescued, each figure becoming more defined as they approached.

Cora's breath caught in her throat as she recognised Meriwether and Yestin, who looked terrible. The wound in Meriwether's cheek was bloodless and grey, like something that had decayed in water. Through it, Cora glimpsed his teeth and the torn flesh of his gums. Yestin's eyes were dim and baggy, his skin collapsed in on itself as though he'd aged another ten years since she'd last seen him. She wondered if his gloomy aspect was due to the absence of Petrok or the absence of glamour.

Wenna was thrilled to see them. Goodwife Jenifry started ordering people to serve and cook. Cora helped to prepare the beds, which were much more crowded, that night, than the one before. Yestin spent the evening staring unhappily out of the window. Cora wanted to approach him, to say something encouraging or hopeful about Petrok. But she couldn't think of a single word.

The next morning brought a clear sky. The shining marsh stretched in every direction. Wenna announced that they were moving on.

'Where?' Cora asked.

'To the city of the marshrai. Lord Gendal has said he will act as ambassador for us.'

'Isn't he their leader?' Cora frowned. 'Won't they have to do what he says anyway?'

'What gave you that impression? Oh, the lord thing. In the city of the marshrai, lord just means mister, lady means mrs, although they don't have marriage, so it's just to differentiate male from female. As goodwife and goodsir are for the spriggans. Neither race has surnames, as we do. So the marshrai are all lord this or and lady that, except their grand vizior, Raegh. He'll be the one who decides.'

Cora nodded. 'So, how will we get there? We can't slither under the water like Lord Gendal did. Is it a long walk?'

Wenna met her gaze. 'It's a little more complicated than that I'm afraid. I'll address everybody together.'

Slightly hurt, Cora moved out of the way as Meriwether came to talk to Wenna. Soon enough, the whole town seemed to have assembled at the Riddler's Fiddle, which grew so full, many had to stand out in the street. Wenna put a finger to her throat, which somehow amplified her voice.

She called for the oldest and most infirm humans to put up their hands. Skeletal fingers, some still encrusted with dirt and blood, trembled here and there, above the crowd. Many were leaning on someone for support and struggled to raise their hands high enough. Wenna explained that she could transport them home, via a powerful spell, to Treleddan. The frailest faeries, Cora remembered, had no homes to return to.

An angry young man with dirty blond stubble over his head and chin said he wasn't going to stay in Pendlestow a minute longer.

'But you're strong enough to fight!' Meriwether protested, disgust twisting the corner of his mouth.

Wenna touched Meriwether's arm. 'Nobody has to fight. Not if they don't feel compelled to. But I must remind you that if Morgelyn isn't stopped, Treleddan will soon resemble Underwood. Cornwall will fall soon after and perhaps even the rest of England.'

'Rubbish!' sneered the man, 'we got the finest army in the world! We got an Empire covering most of it! This Morgelyn witch ain't going to touch us! She comes up to Cornwall and we'll send in the 32nd regiment.'

Wenna was very grave, casting her eyes across the gathered faces, some of whom were evidently mulling over the man's words.

'There is a very real threat to your Empire,' she said heavily.

'Your majesty,' Bronnan spoke quietly, moving her face away from the crowd to face Wenna, so that only those closest caught her words. 'Is it wise to-'

Wenna held up her hand.

Bronnan shut her mouth.

'Those who wish to return to Treleddan must understand what it is they are returning to. Morgelyn Glasse has perfected the copying process. Her early experiments resulted in horrible disfigurement, quickly followed by death. But they continue to volunteer, such is their blind devotion. She's now stabilised her ghasts so that they can live for weeks, probably months.'

She paused and the silence thickened. Everybody was listening. 'Last night, I received intelligence to suggest that Morgelyn was on the brink of creating ghasts that might live indefinitely. Once she's achieved this, she plans to turn herself into a ghast of Queen Victoria. She would therefore control the human British army and, as this gentlemen pointed out, most of the world.'

Gasps flew up from the crowd.

'Which means,' Wenna raised her voice even more, to cut through the rising panic, 'that Morgelyn intends to kidnap your queen, in order to replace her. My aim is to warn Victoria.'

There was another audible intake of breath amongst the humans and even Cora found herself a little shocked to hear her queen addressed by her first name.

'I'll warn her of Morgelyn's plan and enlist her help, along with the support of the human British army, just as we have secured the allegiance in battle, should it come to that, of the spriggans of Pendlestow.'

Goodwife Jenifry and the elderly, telescope man, nodded solemnly.

The blond man snorted 'them? What're they gonna do? Sure, they gave us food, if you can call it that, an' a bed when we needed it, but they ain't goin' be much use on a battlefield are they?'

'*What* did he say?' The old man glowered.

'Now, Goodsir Ned,' Goodwife Jenifry said, 'don't get het up,'

'Did you hear what that ungrateful bastard *said*?!'

'I know, but you mustn't-'

'How dare you!' The reedy tone of the old man's voice was getting deeper, louder, resonating unnaturally, as his face turned a furious red.

'Get in the water, Ned!' Goodwife Jenifry was shouting.

To Cora's confusion, she started tugging him towards the edge. 'Get him in! Don't let him smash any boats!'

Other spriggans and faeries were jostling to help push him away, for he seemed to be falling into some kind of trance. As they did so, Cora's eyes stretched wide in amazement.

The whiskery old man was growing. His crooked, puny body was bulging. His neck, once scrawny with folds of loose skin, was swelling into a thick, meaty roll.

He was pushed into the water, still spitting rage and fury and Cora began to understand why they'd done it, for his sudden weight had splintered the edge of the town's platform. He was taller than the houses now. A true giant. Cora felt her insides slither in horror as the shadow of his arm cast her into shade, swooping to snatch the blond man up by the scruff of his ragged jacket.

'I didn't mean nothin'!' the man pleaded, wild with

terror as he kicked in mid-air.

Cries of 'put him down!' and 'leave him be!' went up and Cora realised it was only the humans that were shouting now. The spriggans and faeries were watching with stricken faces, as though the man was already dead.

The eerie shade swept over the crowd again and again as the monstrous spriggan whirled the man like a rag doll around his head, cracking his bones with sickening snaps before letting go.

The blond man grew smaller and smaller as Cora watched, unable to breathe. By the time he landed, it was too far away to hear the splash.

The giant spriggan fumed through his massive nostrils, still glaring at the spot where the man had met his end, huge chest heaving, enormous eyes as cold as a shark's. After a few moments, he began to shrink again, shrivelling like a deflating balloon.

'He's going!' Goodwife Jenifry called out.

Those who'd scrambled into a boat stretched their arms to catch him as he collapsed, dragging him aboard.

Everyone stood silent, staring at the spriggans in horror.

'They can't all do that can they?' a human muttered.

'Any spriggan,' Wenna's voice cut across the murmuring, 'may undergo such a transformation when angered. Their gentle hospitality has saved us to fight another day, but please, do not underestimate them as warriors.'

The shields, Cora realised, and the huge swords and helmets, suddenly made sense. There was no race of giants living nearby. She'd been sleeping amongst them. She shivered, glancing warily at her hosts with newfound awe. And it occurred to her that their clothes must be enchanted to grow and shrink too, or the old man's would have been shredded.

'So,' Wenna regained her attention. 'I will transport all who wish to return to Cornwall now, then reveal my plan to warn Victoria to those who wish to remain.'

'Tell us the plan first,' with a jolt, Cora saw that it was Nancarrow who'd spoken. Suddenly clammy, she hoped her old nurse wouldn't anger a spriggan. The elderly man was still snoring gently, in the boat. All who regarded him did so with a nervous look. But Nancarrow seemed blithely unaware. Perhaps, Cora thought sadly, she had already blocked it out, or turned it into something she could cope with.

'I will do as I say,' Wenna was firm. She didn't expand, but it was obvious to Cora that anyone who took the information home with them was a potential risk. Morgelyn's spies were everywhere. It could easily find its way back to her.

'How are you going to warn the queen, then?' Nancarrow went on as if Wenna hadn't spoken. 'March into Balmoral? Or Windsor bloomin' Castle? You'd be locked up before you could say Tower of London.'

Cora was troubled, the bleakness of the situation washed over her like nausea. And not just because she feared Nancarrow might be flung across the marsh. Queen Victoria wouldn't take them remotely seriously; they wouldn't be able to get near her. Wenna and everyone else who wasn't human would find themselves in a circus sideshow or a jar of formaldehyde, donated to science. Any humans who protested would be strapped into straitjackets.

Bronnan was glaring at Nancarrow, but Wenna remained unruffled. 'I will explain precisely how we will be granted an audience with Victoria once those who wish to return have done so. Now,' she stepped down from the box on which she'd been standing but kept her finger to her throat, so that everyone could still hear. 'My dear friend, Eseld Liddicoat, has been brewing a mixture that will aid you in your journey. All those who wish to go home to Treleddan, step towards the gate. Everybody else, please move back.'

Cora started moving away with those who were staying, wanting to draw close to Tom, but there were too many people in between. He looked exhausted and kept blinking, as though he was trying to stay awake.

'Cora!' Eseld beckoned. 'We need you as well.'

Cora was startled. 'M-me? What for?'

Wenna fixed her with a 'not now' expression.

Cora hurried over.

Eseld was carrying a heavy pot, which she set down near the gate. Inside, Cora glimpsed a thick, blackish paste which smelled awful, like rotting vegetation and mould.

Eseld proceeded to roll up her sleeves and rub the foul gunk up her arms, over her elbows, then over her face and hair. She looked horrible and smelled worse.

Cora faltered, until Eseld smiled encouragingly, her teeth and eyes peculiarly white as she daubed on more of the muddy paste, indicating that Cora should do the same.

Nervous, but trusting, Cora copied Eseld, and Wenna, who was rubbing the stuff up her own arms too. They reached for each other and soon all three were holding hands, each smeared with the rancid stuff. Both Eseld and Wenna were speaking the strange language that they had before and gestured that Cora repeat it as well. It was difficult to get the pronunciation right but she persevered and soon, to the softly spoken repetition of *edhwierft, edhwierft, edhwierft,* the mixture on their arms, faces and heads started heating up. Smoke curled from its surface as it cracked, turning from black to grey as it dried and Cora inhaled the crushed nettle smell of natural magic.

The heat was uncomfortable, but not painful. Instead of drifting upwards, the smoke began to whirl in an unnatural spiral, within the triangle formed by their arms. Bronnan took Nancarrow by the hand and led her stiffly towards the three women, who crouched down, so that she could step over their arms into the smoke. Cora fought to keep the tears back as Nancarrow sank slowly down and disappeared.

One by one, all those who could not, or would not, fight, stepped into the smoke, sinking with oddly calm faces.

After it was over and they'd washed off the muddy concoction, Cora looked out over the marsh and wondered what they had returned to. Would they encounter ghasts of themselves? Nancarrow certainly would. The ghast wearing her face had convinced everyone. Even her. Cora felt suddenly guilty, even though Nancarrow had definitely wanted to go. Had she understood Wenna's warning? Had any of them really taken it in? What would happen to Nancarrow when she tried to return to the house on Fish Row?

Would she assume that the creature masquerading as Cora was her?

Wenna rested a hand on Cora's shoulder. 'It's alright. I haven't sent them straight back. Not exactly.'

'What do you mean?'

'It wasn't easy, but with Eseld's help, I managed to work out a way of holding them in an in-between state, somewhere they'll be safe until Treleddan is ready to receive them again.'

'But what if we fail? What if Treleddan falls to Morgelyn? What if we're all killed? Who'll bring them home then?'

'Should that happen, then they're probably better off where they are. They can't feel a thing there, Cora. They don't even know that time is passing.'

Cora wanted to protest. It was unthinkable that she'd helped send so many into some sort of netherworld limbo, and that they hadn't known or understood where they were going.

But it was too late to do anything about it now. And who was she, after all, to question a queen? Across the diminished crowd, Cora caught Bronnan looking at her. As soon as Cora met her gaze, Bronnan broke away.

The flapping of wings brought all conversations to a halt.

Everybody looked up.

'Inside!' shrieked Goodwife Jenifry. Children were snatched up, doors slammed and bolted and shutters closed, with arrows poking through the cracks.

Cora moved to run inside but, as she did, Wenna cried out 'follow me! Everyone who wants to get away, do it now! Morgelyn must be watching! She knows we're going to warn Victoria! That's why she's risking a daylight attack!'

Cries of Fire! went up as flaming arrows rained down, thudding into walls and rooftops. Everything in Pendlestow was made of wood or rushes and soon the whole town was ablaze. A pterydon crashed to the ground, along with its rider, both studded with spriggan arrows. Its eyes were red and rolling in its death throes. Bronnan reached for the place her dagger had been, glowering as she remembered the mine guards taking it.

'Glamour.' Wenna said grimly, putting the creature out of its misery by driving her own dagger just below its jawbone. She had to shove the hilt with her other hand to pierce the reptilian hide and she set her lips in a thin, hard line, as she wiped the dark blood on her hip. 'That must be how she got them to carry fire.'

Everyone was terrified. Spriggans ran out of their houses, coughing, carrying screaming children with soot stained skin. Buildings started collapsing and bits of smouldering thatch blew from one roof to the next, clothes pegged on lines dried in seconds and caught light too.

Wenna and Lord Gendal were marshalling everyone towards the gate, where they streamed out onto the wooden walkway, people screaming as they were snatched into the air. Everywhere, spriggans were shooting into gigantic proportions, swiping at the pterydons and managing to knock some of the riders off, their cries cut short as they smashed into the bog.

At that size, they seemed to have no sense or order and some knocked children off the wooden boards into the water. Some were crashing off into the distance in a berserker rage and others tried to fight the fire by beating the disintegrating houses into a flaming mess.

Lord Gendal was handing things out from a leather, water filled bag, his curiously flat eyes eerily calm even amid the chaos of the attack. It was some kind of food, Cora guessed, as the littlest spriggans were hastily shoving it in their mouths. Who would eat at a time like this? To her bewilderment though, after popping in whatever it was, each one jumped into the water and disappeared.

'Hurry!' Bronnon was shouting. 'Over here Cora! Tom! Every faery jump straight into the water, humans and spriggans keep these in your throats!'

The air was thick with smoke and it stung Cora's eyes as she fumbled to take what they were offering. It was a small, live fish, like an anchovy, which twisted and flapped in her palm. The spriggans popped them expertly in their mouths, apparently used to it, though their fingers shook with fear as the spiny shadows of the pterydon continued to glide over their ruined homes. An elderly spriggan was snatched up into the air just as she'd pushed the fish in. It dropped from her lips as her feet jerked violently upwards, making everybody cower in terror.

'Don't chew! It must remain alive, it'll let you breathe!' Wenna was repeating, as was Bronnan, who was handing them out too.

Cora pushed hers into her mouth, gagging a little.

'Hold it in your throat,' Wenna was saying, ducking as a pterydon flew terrifyingly low, 'quickly! Then jump in!'

The smoke was so bad, Cora could hardly breathe the air any more, which made it easier to jump into the water. In the cold, murky dark, she stared up at the broken pieces of light on the surface and the wobbly shapes of those yet to jump in.

The sky was black and orange and she fought to breathe through the peculiar throatfish, trying to force air down into her lungs, even as they burned. The fish twitched and wriggled, making her want to cough it up but she knew it was her only chance, so she forced it to the back of her mouth, trying not to vomit, swallowing without swallowing too hard, until finally, when she feared she'd lose consciousness from lack of oxygen, she managed to breathe.

It was a strange, gurgling sort of breathing. She could feel the freezing marsh water rush in and out of her lungs and the sound of it rattled wetly around her head, but it was keeping her alive and, as arrows whizzed past, streaming bubbles, she followed the others through the greenish gloom, feet slipping in the mush, trying to be grateful for her hammering heart.

It was hard to see more than a few feet ahead and the cold sank deep into her bones.

Cora kept her focus on Wenna, who swam along with her lips slightly parted, with no more need for air than she had above water. Lord Gendal was nowhere to be seen, but a large eel was gliding close by. Cora remembered what she'd seen through the fog when Yestin and Meriwether had first arrived. It hadn't been her imagination then, after all.

They reached deeper water and soon came to a cave, hung with drifting weed. Fish darted away, flashing silver in the brownish murk at their approach. Lord Gendal went first, followed by Wenna, Eseld, Meriwether, Yestin and Bronnan.

Goodwife Jenifry followed along with Tom and Mr Penrose and the elderly spriggan and all the others whose names she didn't know. When it came to Cora's turn, she was unnerved to find it pitch black inside. Fear made her want to gulp but she managed not to, in case it disturbed the throatfish, which wriggled and scratched with its fins.

She couldn't let herself think about anything but the effort of breathing brown water, without swallowing or spitting out the throatfish, as the tunnel grew narrower and narrower, sloping ever more downwards. Terror stiffened her muscles and soon, there wasn't enough room to swim properly and she had to grab the rock where it jutted, in order to pull herself along, desperately trying not to wonder how many had been snatched or killed that day, or how far she was beneath the surface.

Eventually, the tunnel delivered them into open water and Cora's limbs felt oddly loose as she emerged into what seemed like a brightly light space and much clearer, bluer water. It might have been that the water was cleaner there, and so deep it was more like an ocean than a marsh or lake, or it could have been that her eyes, starved of light, were simply dazzled.

Ahead, a vast, translucent dome floated, with shadows moving inside it. It was anchored to the mud by ropes of weed. They swam towards it, gliding between ropes thicker than tree trunks. It was darker under there, in the green shadows, like a submerged forest, and Lord Gendal was wriggling upward into an opening, a sort of tube that must lead, Cora reasoned, to the dwelling's interior. Even though it was so cold, she was anxious about entering. The building, for she couldn't think what else to call it, was almost gelatinous, and seemed far too flimsy for safety as it bobbed and rippled in the current.

When it was her turn, Cora squeezed herself into the squishy tunnel, revolted at its sliminess even though it made it easier to get through. When she emerged, she expected to breathe air, trapped in an underwater bubble, but was dismayed to find that it was still full of water.

'Of course it is,' Wenna spoke directly into her mind. 'We don't fill our homes with water do we? So why would the marshrai fill theirs with air?'

Cora gazed up and around, trying to get used to the darkness. The taste of the water was much worse, reminding her of a receding tide in high summer, when things have been left behind to rot.

Large eels slithered through the gloom and she lost track of Lord Gendal. He could have been any one of them. It was utterly silent. The echoing, underwater sounds, which she'd barely noticed before, had gone, leaving a silence so thick it pressed inside her ears.

All of a sudden the place gave a great shudder, the walls heaving and knocking everyone against each other as the space compressed. She hated this place, Cora realised, truly hated it. The marshrai may be the kindest folk in the world for all she knew, but their home held every sensation that she despised. There was no furniture, no evidence of living even, apart from a few putrefying fish bones that floated past her face, trailing rags of flesh. She hadn't expected a fire of course, but something domestic, something homely at least. Why would anybody want to live like this?

With a jolt, she suddenly feared they might be telepathic, like the faerie. She looked around for Wenna, to ask her, but Wenna was deep in a signing conversation with various marshrai who'd taken on a partial human form. The lower halves of their bodies twitched, still eel, while their heads, torso and arms were much closer to the form Lord Gendal had taken on land. The frills around their necks appeared to be part of the language, though whether in signs for words or inflection or expression, or just for breath, Cora couldn't tell. All she knew was that she felt horribly claustrophobic, even when the bizarre, gelatinous walls expanded again, becoming thinner and transparent enough for her to make out gliding shadows of fish outside.

Why did they all need to come? she thought angrily, if Wenna and Bronnan were the only ones who could communicate? Although she answered the question almost as soon as it formed. Because the pterydons' attack had made them refugees once again, even as they were trying to turn themselves into an army. They were simply following in Wenna's wake, a train behind a bride. A rippling wash behind a ship. They had nowhere else to go.

The marshrai stiffened, their frills standing out like starched collars and quivering aggressively. They pushed Wenna and everyone else towards the repulsive hole in the floor of the chamber, where they were forced downward, fighting their natural buoyancy, until each was expelled into the murky forest of ropes.

Wenna looked pale, but refused to hang her head, even in defeat. She pointed upwards with her index finger, causing everyone, bewildered and exhausted as they were, to kick their legs and propel themselves up, eventually breaking the surface of a lagoon that looked like a darker, wilder part of Broadpuddle.

They swam towards an island of matted weeds and black mud, spitting out their throatfish and coughing water. Nobody wanted to look at the distant column of smoke, which marked the place that had once been Pendlestow.

'What happened?' Cora managed to ask, dreading the reply. 'What did they say?'

Wenna pulled slimy, green weeds out of her hair, which seemed even more insubstantial now that it lay wet and flat; her grey scalp showing through it more than usual. She looked small and frail but determined to hide her dejection as much as she could. 'Raegh wasn't convinced of the threat. He insisted that he'd keep the marshrai safe, as he had for generations, while Morgelyn and others like her came and went.'

'How could you tell which one was Raegh?' Cora asked. They all looked the same.'

'Only because you've never see them before. And Raegh isn't one of them, not exactly. He's their host.'

Cora was confused.

'He was the dome, the creature they all live inside.'

Cora felt sick. Before she could express her astonishment, a shape bulged in the surface of the water and Bronnan's head snapped round.

'Lord Gendal?' Wenna's face broke into a smile, but it was one of sad resignation, not joy.

He emerged fully, pulling on his water-filled helmet before gesturing with his hands, his frill rippling back and forth.

'Really?' Wenna forgot herself and spoke aloud, signing rapidly again as Meriwether and Cora exchanged frustrated glances, wishing they could understand. Eventually, she turned to Cora, Eseld and the others, hoarse with excitement. 'He's going to help. He's thought of a way to warn her without alerting the palace security at all.

Chapter Eighteen

Greenacre

The spriggans began to teach the others how to weave rough stalks together, for mats and shelters, but they soon discovered it was quicker just to do it themselves. Cora tried to make a flame in her palm, but she felt too bleak and couldn't conjure the heat. Eseld created one and the two of them hunted in vain for twigs dry enough to burn. The shelters kept the worst of the wind and rain off, but they dripped all night and by morning, everyone was still damp and shivering.

Wenna insisted on setting off early. Although everyone was exhausted, having slept badly, if at all, they were relieved to get the chance to warm up, brushing the frost from their coats and stamping in the early mist.

The sunless sky was tinged with gold. Ice cracked in the ground beneath every step. The earth was yielding, oddly springy beneath its frozen carapace. Goodwife Jenifry explained, as they crunched and squelched along, that it wasn't earth at all. 'It were knitted by ancient folks, long ago, out of living reeds that're still growing to this day, tangling theirselves ever more tightly. It's a skill we've lost along the way. We can build on stilts and weave anything you like, but nobody knows how to knit an island any more.'

Cora didn't know what to say except, 'what a shame.' She wanted to say something consoling about Pendlestow, but there weren't words big enough to hold such loss.

Wenna, Bronnan and Meriwether kept up a punishing pace and many of the spriggans, particularly the small and infirm amongst them, complained that they needed a rest.

The skin on Cora's arms was sore, as if it had been burnt. The pain spread from her shoulder blades, down over her elbows to the outside of her wrists. It wasn't acute enough for her to mention, yet it unnerved her, and it made the fabric of her single sleeve feel uncomfortably rough against her skin. She didn't remove it though. It was too cold. The sleeve she'd wrapped around Tom's head must have fallen off in the escape from Pendlestow and floated down through the water, for his wound was exposed, the blood having congealed to form a scab.

Wenna turned and put her fingers to her throat, stretching her neck to try and make herself more visible, to address everybody, for there were no natural hillocks on the floating island. 'We'll rest soon. I promise. But if you don't want to spend another night out in the open, then we must reach Greenacre before dark. Anybody who can carry a child, please do. Take turns, help each other.' She shifted the sleeping toddler on her shoulder as she spoke.

Spriggans, faeries and humans turned to each other, passing sleeping spriggan children the size of human newborns from exhausted arms into those more rested. Tom had an elderly spriggan lady on his back and he held the hands of two faery children who kept slipping on the squashy, unfamiliar terrain. Cora carried a child who had looked a lot lighter when she'd offered, and who wriggled and squirmed constantly, while his pregnant mother kept telling her she wasn't holding him right.

More than once, Cora tried to catch Wenna's eye to ask her, with her mind, what Greenacre would be like. The night before, Wenna had been so deep in discussion with Lord Gendal, Bronnan, Eseld and Meriwether that, although she'd tried to hover on the edge and listen while they'd used pebbles and bits of moss to make maps, she wasn't able to contribute, knowing little of the geography above and nothing of it below. So, instead, she'd tried to help entertain the children, who were busy collecting small stones to play a game similar to knucklebones. She'd stolenchew a few sideways glances at Tom, who was jogging around giving piggybacks. Yestin had sat apart from the others, trapped in his own grief. Petrok wasn't mentioned at all.

The journey was long and the landscape flat and unchanging. No landmarks appeared on the horizon for them to pass, so it felt as if they weren't getting anywhere at all. Although they did occasionally stop for breaks, without food or fresh water it didn't restore much energy. Eventually, as the yellow light drained from the sky, leaving it starry and indigo, Cora gazed at the silver disc, which looked as though it had been cut from tissue paper and glued upon the sky. Merlin's moon. The notion that her father could have made it felt, at that moment, as far away as the real one.

Wenna started walking even faster, the grizzling child on her hip surprised into a moment's silence by the jolting motion, before he started up again. Everybody took her cue and did their best to match her pace.

'So, who lives there?' Cora insinuated herself

between Bronnan, who grudgingly made room, and Wenna, who blinked, deep in thought. 'In Greenacre?' Cora persisted. 'Are they spriggans or, um...' She trailed off, struggling to remember any of the other people Wenna had described back at the cottage, 'or something else?'

'Course they're spriggans,' Bronnan replied, briskly. 'We're still in Broadpuddle aren't we?'

Wenna smiled briefly at Cora, though her gaze slid past her to alight on Yestin, who was walking with his shoulders slumped, eyes unfocused.

Cora couldn't imagine his sorrow. Was it worse, she wondered, to know for certain that somebody was dead, or not to know whether they were alive? To nurture hope, or to get on with grieving?

She wiped away a tear, knowing it wouldn't help anyone, disgusted to feel new, prickly feather buds with the tip of her fingers. Another tear joined the first, gathering weight where her lashes used to be. The thought of the cottage on the edge of the wood; of little Gwen and Curnow eating bread and honey at the table, legs dangling, made her heart ache. She wanted to go back there, to make the cold, bleak marsh disappear and to sleep by the fire while Wenna read and Eseld fiddled with her peculiar concoctions. She knew it was cowardly and tried to hide her thoughts, expecting a sneering glance from Bronnan, which never came.

As they walked, she realised she could see more and more thoughts crowding around the heads of the weary, straggling band. A small, smoky picture of a little girl with a pronounced hunchback was floating above the head of an elderly woman who bore the same disfigurement. The child was cowering beneath a monstrous figure in silhouette, its fist raised.

An exhausted man who carried a sleeping toddler was imagining a plate piled with steaming meat and dumplings beside a bright fire. A teenage boy was remembering the horror of the mine and on and on and on. Cora blinked, widening her eyes to take it all in. There were pieces of rainy street and sunlit beach, toppling cards and decadent cakes. Tiny smoke figures were carried on shoulders or knocked to the ground. Some were too muddled or far away to see clearly. In places the crowded, fidgety mass was like a swarm of bees, formed from smoke. Everybody's thoughts were visible and it was overwhelming.

A thick arm was suddenly around her shoulders 'Alright my duck?' Eseld asked, appearing as if from nowhere.

'You can't... I mean, read my-'

'Course not. Got to make do with my ordinary human brain, ain't I?' She rolled her eyes and squeezed Cora closer. 'But I do know when somebody looks out o' sorts. It'll be alright, when we get there. Greenacre supposed to be lovely. They say you can smell the bread a-baking and the blossom a-drifting from the orchards for miles, well, maybe not at this time 'o year, but you get the gist. Hope they got some tobacco. My pouch is soaked through. Might as well be full o' mud.'

Cora tried to smile, to reassure Eseld that her attempt to cheer her up had been successful. But however wonderful they said this place would be, she couldn't help fearing another smoking ruin, more blasted homes and tear-streaked faces.

She dropped back a little, away from the others,

to ask Eseld 'something I've been wondering is, well, why didn't Wenna fight back sooner? If Morgelyn's been in power for a while? Why now?'

'Morgelyn didn't just spring from nowhere, telling everyone her intentions. She wormed her way into the Underwood government, putting addles in the elders minds.' Eseld wrinkled her nose, 'keeping up appearances, you know, of being an upstanding member of society, while all the time she was running a secret band of thugs, who'd make anybody who disagreed with her disappear.'

'Why didn't the royal family stop her?'

'It wasn't that kind of monarchy. It was a, what d'you call it? A constitutional monarchy. Like what we've got. They couldn't interfere. Morgleyn became their prime minister. She promised the voters she'd solve problems in Underwood by picking on those everyone already blamed, and the easiest targets were folk who'd come from other places, especially the poorest ones, like the Tylwyth Teg, 'cos they couldn't defend theirselves. So, when they started disappearing, the faeries assumed they'd gone back to Gwillion. Nobody knew about the mines.'

Cora was confused. 'But, when I was there, there weren't anybody in the mine except faeries and humans.'

'Most of them died in there. Those that survived probably keep quiet about being Tylwyth Teg. Wouldn't you?'

'What do the Tylwyth Teg look like? None escaped with us.'

'How could you tell, if you don't know what they look like?'

Cora shut her mouth, then asked 'do you mean

they look the same as the faeries?'

Eseld shook her head. 'Same as us. Anyway, that was how it started. After a while, once she'd had the royal family practically wiped out, Morgelyn stopped pretending to blame any one group and didn't bother hiding the fact that anyone who stood up to her didn't last long.'

'So, the royal family *knew*? They just didn't interfere?'

'They didn't know. Not for sure. Not until it were too late. And what could they do? The people voted her in, just before she banned elections.'

Cora glanced over at Wenna, whose hood obscured most of her head. Only the tip of her nose was showing. Cora watched her thoughts, which were fractured and scattered, crushing each other, as too many crowded in. There were the burned housetrees of Underwood and, every time Wenna glanced up, tiny soaring pterydons, formed from smoke, zipping across the sky. There was a sort of doll's house too. Its roof was collapsing and tiny figures were running, arms flung out in terror. Cora was so busy focusing on trying to untangle the different images, the faces and branches and columns of smoke, that at first she didn't notice the change in the spongy, matted reeds beneath her feet.

It was only when she became out of breath that she realised the ground was sloping uphill. It was firmer, too, more rock and compacted soil than marsh. Soon, it was thick with heather. What they'd taken for an island was more of a peninsular, a knitted extension to natural moorland.

The slope grew steeper, until they had to lean forward a bit, to maintain their balance. Eventually, they came to a sort of cliff edge. Cora's insides contracted. The only cliffs she'd heard of dropped sharply down to the sea. She couldn't bear the thought of more water, not while her clothes were still damp and rimed with ice. But, instead of foaming waves spreading below them, they were met with another view entirely.

A chalky path zig-zagged down the cliff side, leading them onto a vast, manicured lawn. It was so neatly trimmed, it looked like expensive carpet, the wintry film of frost paling the green to almost white. Beyond the perfect grass was a formal garden, with glistening topiary, elegant statues and clipped box hedges. A glorious fountain, frozen mid-spray, stood before the very doll's house that Cora had glimpsed in Wenna's mind. Only it wasn't a doll's house. It was built from thousands of bricks, silver in the moon's cloudy light.

It was too enormous to look real. It was the size of a town. Most of the windows were a normal size, but they must have run into the hundreds, many glowing a soft yellow. At least fifty chimneys were arranged along the top. One window dominated them all. It was the size of a large house in its own right and positioned directly above the surprisingly modest front door. The massive window reached almost to the roof, made up of a multitude of little panes, lit from within. There were no curtains on it at all and, through it, Cora glimpsed an intricate ceiling of moulded plaster and heraldic symbols.

They followed the path down to a massive, wrought-iron gate, which stood open, glittering all over with tiny points of frost. White cobwebs were strung between the curls of metal, bowing slightly beneath the weight of beads of ice, clinging to the threads.

'Is it bad, that it's open?' Cora was fearful. She'd been so relieved, at first, to reach the Riddler's Fiddle, but it might as well have been a mirage; a thing of vapour. She wouldn't be caught out again. This place looked perfect but she didn't trust anything anymore. She glanced up, where the clouds had parted to reveal pinprick stars. The more she looked at them, the more convinced she became that the twinkling was a result of pterydons gliding invisibly through the black.

'It's always open, is Greenacre,' sighed Goodwife Jenifry, with a wobbly smile that looked as though it might give way to tears.

Cora tried to relax, to echo the shouts of joy as they crunched towards the fountain, which was even more magnificent up close, its crystalline drops sparkling, bright as a chandelier, reflecting the cold, pale moonlight on one side and the golden candle glow from the windows on the other.

Lord Gendal's water-filled dome was frosted silvery white too, clouding his face as they moved toward the great house.

There was movement at the smaller windows, shadowy figures parting curtains. Before they reached them, the front door was thrown wide and spriggans flooded out, welcoming and exclaiming at the damp, bedraggled appearance of the crowd and ushering them all inside, wrapping fur cloaks around everyone who'd let them.

A whole boar was roasted in front of the fire in what must have been the great hall, with long rows of tables lined with eager-faced spriggans on wooden benches. Wenna was seated in a place of honour on a dais at the end, at a grander table, beside spriggans in costlier clothes, whom Cora presumed to be dignitaries.

Sliced meat and savoury jellies were dished up generously by servants who, Cora noticed, chatted easily with those seated.

'Everyone takes turns,' Goodwife Jenifry explained, her mouth greasy with fat. 'No hierarchy amongst the spriggans. It's how we've always been.' She took another bite and continued with her mouth full. 'One month we might be a pot scrubber, dairy worker, fish gutter, you name it. The next we'll go trading, running the pub or sitting on the council. In Pendlestow...' she hesitated, swallowing, and whatever she was going to reveal about Pendlestow remained unsaid. In a softer tone she continued 'Greenacre looks different from the outside but, inside, the ways are the same.'

'So, up there, sitting with Wenna, they're just ordinary folk? Even though they're dressed so finely?'

'Yup,' Goodwife Jenifry nodded, accepting another helping of brown, translucent jelly with orange flecks in it, 'for now. Next month they might be scrubbing out the chamber pots.'

'How bizarre,' Cora breathed, biting into the hot, dead pork. It tasted old and rotten in her changed mouth, turning her stomach, but she was so hungry she ate anyway. She didn't fancy trying to dig down through the snow for a frozen worm.

'Not really,' Eseld said. 'No more bizarre than what we do is it? Making sure everyone what's born poor stays poor, an' those with an easy start in life get an easy end too?' She bit into a rib, tearing the meat off and chewing hungrily, then biting again before she'd swallowed the first mouthful.

The fur cloak was soft as butter and Cora luxuriated in it, managing to enjoy the happy chatter and the warmth as her clothes at last began to dry out. A troupe of singers and fiddlers walked up behind the dais and began to play a merry tune, causing spriggans to jump up and dance, pushing the tables back after everyone had finished eating, to make room. Those who'd just arrived hadn't the energy; the grief at what happened at Pendlestow was still etched on their faces. The dancers twisted left and right, swinging their partners in the air, firelight and candles driving the worst of their fears away along with the cold.

The feasting and dancing went on so long, Cora and many of the others were struggling to keep their eyes open, having walked all day. 'Do you think they'll find us somewhere to sleep soon?' Cora asked Goodwife Jenifry.

'I 'spect so.' She turned to ask a spriggan carrying a silver platter, piled with honey cakes. He misunderstood over the noise and offered the cakes around.

'No, thank you, we've had enough to eat. We want to sleep. Who's in charge of housekeeping tonight?'

He directed her to a slim, dark-eyed spriggan with so many bunches of keys attached to his belt, it was a wonder his trousers didn't fall down.

Cora was astonished to see a male housekeeper. 'Goodsir Uther,' he introduced himself with a small bow. 'There are vacant beds,' he explained in a thin, nasal voice, 'but they're spread all over, so we'll need to split you up.'

'Let the little 'uns and the eldest find a bed first,' said Eseld. So, in order of need, the refugees followed the housekeeper in his neat black coat, the keys at his waist clanking like muffled sleigh bells.

Cora woke suddenly from a deep sleep, as if yanked by her armpits up into the air. She gasped at the violence of it, her heart thumping as she gazed around in the dark at the unfamiliar room. She remembered the candle on the mantelpiece and stumbled blindly towards it, groping for a match. The flame flung shapes and shadows up the walls, distorting the furniture into grotesques before they settled into a bed, a low armchair and a table.

Her heart still battered her ribs. What had woken her? She couldn't remember a nightmare and she was utterly alone, but it was as if somebody had deliberately shaken her awake, by shouting in her ear. She wanted nothing more than to topple her back into the warm bed but a nagging fear kept her staring, sore-eyed, into the dark.

'Cora!' Wenna's voice was directly inside her ear. No, inside her mind.

Cora shut her eyes tightly and did her best to answer.

'Cora? Can you hear me?'

'Yes! I can hear you!' she groped for her bracelet, in case it might help. 'What's happened? What's wrong?'

'Cora?'

Panicking, she repeated 'yes, I can hear you!'

'Cora' Wenna's voice was thin, rasping. 'I know you're awake and only hope you can hear me. I need you to go as quietly as you can downstairs. Get as far down as you can and get out. Head for the trees but don't let *anybody* see you. No-one. It's absolutely vital that you aren't followed. When you get to the trees, be on your guard.'

'But why?' Cora tried to ask. 'I thought we were safe here!'

There was nothing more, only the sound of her own, ragged breath.

Shivering, she wrapped the fur cloak around herself, drawing up the hood and picking up the candle. Then she hesitated. The light would draw attention, the very thing Wenna said she mustn't do.

Head for the trees, Wenna had said. Cora hadn't seen any trees on their approach. A memory stirred in the back of her mind. Eseld had mentioned an orchard, hadn't she? Something about drifting blossom. Cora went over to the window and pushed back the heavy velvet, fringed with tassels. The blackness beyond the glass was opaque until she blew out the candle and peered again. She must have been put in a room at the back, for it wasn't the ornamental gardens and fountain below, but more outbuildings and little shadowy things that might have been milk churns and wheelbarrows, in cobbled yards. Beyond the wall, she could just make out a ragged suggestion of trees.

She hurried to the door, only to find it locked.

Trying to still her shaking heart, for what kind of host locks a guest in? She consoled herself with the fact that she wouldn't have found her way through the maze of narrow staircases anyway. All the left and right turns and the vases and portraits on so many polished tables had blurred into one. She'd trudged sleepily up and down after the others, too weary to take much in, past gleaming banisters and doors she'd had to duck through, which all looked the same by the flickering light of the candle held by the housekeeper. She glanced back at the bed.

The idea nudging at the corner of her mind wasn't a simple one. It might even be fatal, but it would get her out quickly.

Fingers clammy, she tugged the eiderdown and the blanket onto the floor, then pulled the two sheets, still warm from her body, away from the mattress. She tried to tear the sheets into strips but, hard as she tugged, they were too new and their weave wouldn't give. She looked inside the little drawer of the table, in case there was any kind of sharp-edged tool she could use. She found a workbox and, beneath a velvet tray with compartments for needles and thimbles, found a tiny pair of silver scissors. She started cutting the thick, doubled cotton of the hem, trying to crush the fear that Wenna's voice was a dream. Because if it was, then she was committing a gross act of vandalism.

Once she was through the hem, she was able to rip through the weave and tear foot-wide strips that she knotted together. She climbed onto the table, making it wobble, and stretched up to unhook the curtains, which tumbled from their moorings with a puff of dust. The little scissors couldn't cut such thick, fleshy cloth. Even with their velvety lengths tied to the rope she'd made of the sheets, she would still be a long way up from the ground. But that was a risk she'd have to take.

She removed the fur cloak and climbed out of the nightgown she'd been lent and back into to her slightly damp, single-sleeved dress, which smelled of muddy river. Her arm wouldn't fit into the sleeve. Irritated, she stabbed it in harder and felt a painful tug where the burning sensation had occurred the day before, on the long walk from the knitted, ice-coated peninsula.

She rubbed the area and felt, just as she'd dreaded, bigger feathers with thicker quills, stubborn as bone. She tried to pluck one out. It was as useless as trying to pull her finger off. So, instead, she took the little scissors up again and snipped the seam that ran down her sleeve, shoving the feathers angrily out of the opening and leaving the cuff whole. She was glad there wasn't a looking glass in the room.

She dragged the mattress towards the window which, upon being opened, let in a gust of freezing air and a few flakes of snow. With difficulty, she shoved the mattress out. It grew alarmingly small before hitting the ground with a soft whump. Then she tied one end of her homemade rope to the stout leg of the bed and staggered with the rest towards the window. After heaving the armchair onto the bed for extra weight and then the table too, which was more solid than it looked and left her quite breathless, Cora held the slippery velvet as tightly as she could and carefully eased herself beneath the sash of the window. The hood of her cloak slipped down and the cold was bracing against her face, neck and shaved scalp, which still hadn't grown used to its exposure.

Afraid it wouldn't take her weight, or that her hands would slip, she hesitated on the ledge, trying in vain to find the courage to jump into the dark and trust the rope. But every sinew refused, until she heard creaks from floorboards above and murmured voices she didn't recognise.

Window-shaped spots of light on the frosted cobbles below told her that people were waking up.

Footsteps in the hall and a key shoved noisily into the lock of her door gave her the push she needed and she vaulted, friction turning the velvet to sandpaper, burning her fingers like a red-hot poker as she rushed down, down, until it ran out and she kicked empty air.

Chapter Nineteen

Look to the Trees

Too late, Cora realised that the mattress had thudded too far to the right. And she'd grossly misjudged the distance from the end of her rope to the ground.

Arms and legs swinging wildly, she fought her fate without time to think about the pointlessness of it. She would surely die, yet the impact never came.

She was hovering ten feet above the cobbles, a curious draught blowing oddly about her arms and it took much longer than she expected to land, on the edge of the mattress, her ankles protesting painfully, but taking her weight. She didn't buckle into a heap. She was standing. Alive. Dumbfounded, she gazed back up at the rope, dangling hopelessly far above, and down at her outstretched arms, where the feathers were cold to the touch, but there wasn't time to think about it. She had to get to the trees.

She ran across the cobbles, the narrow alleys between empty pigsties spun with sparkling cobwebs and wheelbarrows full of rotten apples.

Deep in her mind, she tried again to communicate with Wenna. She could hear nothing but the clump, scrape, clump, clump of her boots on the icy cobbles, the uneven stones threatening to trip her. 'I'm coming!' she shouted silently, 'I'm coming to the trees. Where are you? What should I do?'

She found a gate in the wall at the back, the bolt so rusted she was surprised when it opened so easily. The woods beyond were wild as any she'd seen.

Black trees crowded together, menacing, mob-like, with spiky curves of bramble stretching out towards Cora as though it were they, and not she, who was moving.

She heard things that made her jaw clamp tight, until her teeth ached.

Wails.

Sharp thuds followed by cries of anguish.

And the cracking, hacking noises of digging. Cold metal slicing frozen earth. She forced her legs to keep going, one foot in front of the other, until she could discern shadows moving between the grotesquely twisted branches. She saw spriggan heads, bizarrely low down. After a horrified moment she realised they were moving, animated and not dismembered. Pickaxes and shovels appeared briefly between them, showering mud up out of the hole they were both digging and standing in.

Around the edge of the hole were more spriggans, holding something circular in one hand and a thick stick in the other. There were larger figures too, bigger than faeries, their heads strangely elongated and rectangular, their backs bulky and hunched. In their hands, they carried what looked like shillelaghs.

'Cora! Over here!' Wenna said, in her mind. 'Quickly! We haven't much time!'

Cora whirled around, scanning the dark and trying to avoid treading on twigs that might snap and give her away, though whatever the creatures were doing, they didn't seem to care how much noise they made.

Then she saw it, a tiny, triangular flame, cupped in pink hands that glowed, for just a second, through the trees to her left.

Eseld.

Cora made her way carefully towards the place it had been and soon found Wenna, Eseld, Tom, Meriwether, Bronnan, Yestin, Goodwife Jenifry, Mr Penrose and Lord Gendal, crouching in the hollow behind a vast, upturned tangle of roots where a tree had fallen. Each of their faces was smeared with mud, presumably to keep their skin from catching the moonlight. Eseld lifted a handful, flecked with frosted leaf, and spat into it to make it sticky. Cora shivered as she smeared it onto her cheeks.

'What's going on?' Cora whispered, as quietly as she could. 'What are those things?'

In order to make as little sound as possible, Wenna spoke directly into Cora's mind. 'The spriggans, the ones who welcomed us in and fed us, weren't spriggans. We were duped. They're ghasts of those they'd already killed.'

Cora's mind raced. So the wide welcoming smiles of the spriggans of Greenacre had been a mask, constructed like the perfectly clipped topiary; false as the faces of the statues they'd passed on their arrival. But she'd seen them eat, hadn't she? Or had they pretended? She'd been so tired and hungry, she hadn't thought to wonder.

'Nobody guessed, Cora.' It was Bronnan who spoke now, her silent words stabbing deep into Cora's mind, firing rapidly one after the other. 'We haven't got time to faff about kicking ourselves for not realising sooner. We must act now. Don't you understand what they're forcing them to do? They're digging their own graves.'

Cora felt as though she'd been punched. All breath and strength evaporated. The slicing sounds of the earth and the whoosh of soil from shovels sounded suddenly like the sharpening of blades. 'But why? Why aren't they sending them to the mines?'

Bronnan was impatient. 'Because a spriggan's no use in a mine. As soon as they got angry, they'd overpower the guards in seconds. They must've put something in their food to stop them being able to change. They're weak as children or humans.'

'But what can we do?' Cora felt her lip wobble. 'How can we stop them? They outnumber us by so many!'

'They don't, not exactly.' Wenna said, then she spoke very quietly with her mouth instead, so that Eseld could hear too.

'We must invoke the power of three again. And help will come.'

'Where from?' Cora whispered, louder than she meant to and her eyes bulged in terror, lest she'd given them away, but the digging noises went on as before.

'There ain't time to explain, duck.' Eseld patted her hand. 'You'll see. If it works that is. Just give us a hand and hope for the best.'

Cora nodded.

Eseld gripped her wrist firmly. 'Now, you trust me, don't you love?'

Cora nodded.

'You ain't gonna squirm or nothing are you? Cos this ain't goin' to be very nice. But it's the only way, understand?'

Cora nodded again, alarmed, as Eseld took out a blade, smaller than a pen, and nicked the fleshy pad of each of her own thumbs, squeezing until a dark drop appeared. Then she did the same to Cora, pressing her reddened thumb against Cora's startled, stinging skin. She cut Wenna's thumbs too, which didn't bleed, and pressed thumb to thumb until the three were joined in a triangle, all the while quietly whispering, Cora copying, '*cwic, cwic, cwic.*'

Tom and Yestin kept watch, a grim set to their features.

Bronnan and Meriwether weren't idle. They'd scraped mud from the dark mess of roots of the upturned tree and were now painting them with something that dripped, colourless, in gluey blobs. Then they pulled the thinnest, frailest roots from the disturbed ground, rubbing crumbs of soil away and looping the fragile threads around Wenna, Eseld and Cora's joined thumbs, wrapping more and more around their hands and incorporating bigger ones, still hanging from the fallen tree, weaving and binding them so tightly that Cora couldn't have broken away, even if she'd wanted to.

Somebody called out, with a deep voice quite unlike a spriggan, 'that's deep enough. Let's get this over with.'

And Cora glanced up, the words drying on her tongue as a match flared in the dark, lighting up a cheroot clamped in the mouth of a male, human face. All at once, she saw what the oddly shaped, rectangular headed hunchbacks actually were. They weren't a different species at all, but human soldiers; British infantrymen, their misshapen backs turned, in that tiny flash of light, to military packs, their peculiar heads to tall hats with braids and fat little plumes, their long clubs into rifles.

The one with the cheroot wore no hat, his nose was large and his keen eyes were fixed on the spriggan, as they begged for their lives.

A shout burst from deeper in the wood, behind the grave pit. 'Let them go! You filthy cowards!' And Cora caught a blurred glimpse, tears standing in her eyes, of a huddle of humans and faeries in the kind of cage carts that had taken her to the mine.

'Cora!' Wenna snapped, inside Cora's mind, though her lips still repeated '*cwic, cwic*'. Concentrate! It's the only way we can help!'

Cora forced herself to repeat the word, letting the tears drop off her chin, keeping her trembling thumbs pressed to Wenna's and Eseld's, to trust them even though she would rather die fighting than watch any more killing.

The sticky gunge seemed to be multiplying, and she watched with fear as it travelled over and under, following the tangled weave of the roots, which started twitching.

The roots touching Eseld's and Wenna's skin were shifting, thin and snakish, fidgeting and protesting against their restraint, but the ones around Cora's were exactly as they had been before; a blackish, muddy bundle.

'Concentrate!' Wenna and Bronnan both screeched, silently, in Cora's head and she did, trembling all over with cold and fright, until the roots started to convulse, slithering over each other as if they were trying to get free. A deep, creaking sound came from somewhere deep below them, the noise branches make when rocking in a high wind, though there wasn't a breath of it.

'The glyph!' Wenna hissed.

Bronnan seized Eseld's glyph, thrusting it into the writhing depths of the fallen tree. Blood red light crackled from the metal, shooting along the roots, which bucked and twisted, breaking free of the six aching hands. The creaking built to a roaring crescendo, making the soldiers stare around and above them in alarm, pointing their shaking rifles in every direction. Red veins glowed beneath the frosted mud, running towards tree after tree and racing up every trunk. One after the other, the trees tore enormous roots from the ground, breaking the freezing earth to whip the soldiers, knocking them to the ground and stabbing into their chests, plunging down through their helpless bodies and back into the earth.

Rifles cracked, filling the dark air with smoke and sparks.

Wenna yelled 'Now!' causing Yestin, Meriwether, Lord Gendal, Mr Penrose and Bronnan to run through the chaos to the cages, dodging the huge, snaking roots scattering earth and flailing bodies, dashing them against each other's trunks. They reached the cage carts and ripped the bolts back, letting those inside spill out to snatch up sticks and join the fight. The wild boar were crying out, straining against their harnesses and tipping over as roots bucked violently beneath them.

Cora wanted to fight too, but it was all she could do to get out of the way as the tree they'd been hiding behind struggled upright, with a deafening noise like a ship in a storm, straining and pushing itself up by its branches.

The spriggans in the grave pit were screaming and Cora ran instinctively towards them, falling onto her stomach and reaching down to help them get enough of a foothold to climb out.

A boy-faced soldier was knocked to the ground beside her, a root fired down through his stomach and into the earth, rushing horribly deep through his flesh and bone and ripping back out. The shock of it stopped Cora's breath. She'd done that, she thought. She'd bewitched the trees into monsters and killed a British soldier!

She couldn't leave his violently struggling side without abandoning the spriggans in the pit. She froze, expecting blood to erupt from his mouth and wound at any minute, but none came. He coughed and spat, struggling to sit up before the root came down again. She stared at the bloodless mess of flesh that used to be his belly. And at his mouth, opening and closing. He was a ghast, she reminded herself, not a British soldier at all, but when the root flew up and away, whirling like a muscular, muddy rope and stabbed down again, finishing what it had started by severing his head from his neck, she refused to look.

When it was over, those who remained alive stared down at the mangled bodies of the ghasts, who still looked for all the world as if they really were human or spriggan, strewn across the frosted mud. As the rifle smoke cleared, the milk wash of dawn made shadows of them all.

They helped the last of the spriggans clamber out of the pit, to join those hugging each other with relief and astonishment. Tears ran down their faces, smudging pink through the grave dirt.

The trees were shrinking, their trunks becoming bodies, their branches softening to flesh beneath tattered red cloth. Faces appeared in the ice-crusted bark, just cracks and hollows at first, until dry wooden eyes moistened, to blink, as human lashes and brows began to sprout. Their hands and faces were covered in coarse, bark-like skin, patched with moss. They flexed their limbs, stiffly stretching and rubbing their faces as though waking from a deep slumber.

'What have we done?' Cora stammered. 'We've turned them into... What've we turned them into? Or were they always able to change? Like the spriggans? Are they tree sprites?'

'Just watch, Cora love,' Eseld said gently.

The curious tree folk were looking more human than ever, though their skin remained mossy and rough and their hair a cropped tangle of twigs. All seemed to be male, and many were missing digits or even limbs. They were staring shakily at each other, moving their arms with difficulty, to pat each other on the back. Eseld rummaged for the pouch of dry tobacco she'd been given at the feast and lit a pipe, which she handed to one of them. He nodded his gratitude and took a deep puff before passing it on. Each of them was coughing hard, expanding lungs that had grown unused to breath. They plucked at the rags of their uniforms, trying to straighten their stocks.

One of them, with a nose as distinctive as the leader of the soldier ghasts, bent to tell a short, stocky chap to collect the rifles, which lay scattered amongst the broken bodies, some half buried in mud. Then he ordered the rest to fall in three ranks, which they did.

'Platoon,' the short fellow who Cora took for a sergeant said solemnly, once he'd handed each soldier a rifle, 'atte-ntion!'

Then the big-nosed fellow went along the line,

from man to man, looking each one up and down. And it was when they stood straight, in a row, that their deformities became even more apparent. Many had twisted limbs, bow legs or a mangled eye. It was hard to distinguish old scars from new wounds in the bark-like texture of their skin.

'Platoon. Stand at. Ease!' They obeyed and, once he'd frowned at them all again, he allowed them to fall out. They visibly sagged, loosening their limbs and immediately examining their weapons, pulling the hammers back to check the barrel and firing mechanism.

Wenna walked towards the leader, who turned to greet her with a bow. 'Your majesty.' he said, making Cora's eyes widen.

'Your grace.' Wenna inclined her head politely.

'Nothing,' he said, surveying the scene, 'except a battle lost can be half so melancholy as a battle won.'

'No,' she shook her head in agreement. 'You're right. And they were all born free, before she poured poisoned promises into their ears.'

'Forgive me,' Wenna said to the others, 'Allow me to introduce his Grace, the Duke of Wellington, noble of the murúghach, who, though more closely related to the fey, resemble humans well enough to walk amongst them, until their long life begins to appear unnatural, which is why he agreed to come below and lend his legendary military skill to our cause.'

'Your servant.' The duke bent to hover his lips momentarily above Wenna's hand, causing a frown to flicker briefly between Meriwether's brows.

Cora was stunned. She stared from Wenna to the duke. He was polite but cold, regarding everyone except Wenna with little more than the appraising glance he'd given his troops.

'Did you find him?' Wenna asked him, her voice so low that if Cora hadn't been close, she wouldn't have heard.

'We did.'

Wenna suppressed a gasp. 'And was he..?'

'Dead? I'm not sure. We had just discovered him, when all at once we were set upon and, well, I was going to say we were given some sort of sleeping draught but, evidently,' he rubbed his cracked, brown cheek with a knuckle, 'we were turned into something more arboreal.'

Wenna nodded, masking her impatience, but not from Cora, who pretended not to eavesdrop.

'And where is he now?'

'I'll show you,' the duke replied solemnly.

'Just a few of us,' Wenna said. 'I don't want to make things any worse for Yestin and besides, every move we make, we seem to be surprised. I can't help worrying that, well,' she lowered her voice even more, 'that we are harbouring a spy.'

The duke nodded, as though this was something he'd wondered about too. Cora managed to hide her shock.

As the sky grew paler, Meriwether gazed at a mound of disturbed soil that had been hidden by the soldier trees. 'I was wondering where they were. The real spriggans of Greenacre.' He lowered his head. Those who wore hats tugged them off.

One young spriggan bent to pick up some bits of ivy, which he twisted into a wreath. He leaned forward and dropped it onto the frosted earth, the gesture so small and hopeless that Cora wanted to punch something.

The soldiers started rummaging through the packs of the fallen ghasts, avoiding looking at the copies of their own faces as they searched for rations, hunger staring from their eyes. Wenna explained that they'd be better off going up to the big house, which was empty now, of ghasts, but full of food.

Cora was worried. 'But how do we know there aren't any up there still?'

'I can see there aren't.' Wenna tapped her forehead.

'If you can see ghasts now, why couldn't you before? When we first got here?'

'She wasn't looking for them then, Cora. That's why.' Bronnan cut in. 'And it's not for *you* to question her!'

The soldiers trudged stiffly away towards the enormous house, where more windows were glowing. Goodwife Jenifry led the muddy spriggans, faeries and humans rescued from the cage carts, helped by Mr Penrose. Only the duke, his sergeant, Eseld, Bronnan, Lord Gendal, Meriwether, Tom and Cora remained. Yestin wanted to stay but eventually acquiesced to Wenna's command.

'Why couldn't he stay?' Cora asked.

Bronnan rolled her eyes.

Cora fumed. 'I am the Queen's cousin,' she snapped, straight into Bronnan's mind, cheeks burning, 'and I will speak to her when I damn well choose.'

Bronnan raised her eyebrows but said nothing.

'Did you guess who the duke found?' Wenna asked Cora, silently. Despite the tragedy of the burial mound, whose shadow stretched towards their feet with every inch of the rising sun, Wenna was invigorated. 'Petrok Noon!'

Cora blinked in astonishment, having taken it for granted that he was dead. 'So, if you're not sure if he's dead or alive, you don't want Yestin to... to have to...'

'Precisely.'

Silently, Cora asked 'can't the duke and his men tell the dead from the living? Surely they know more about that than most people?'

'It's not as simple as that, Cora. Remember, since the curse we faeries no longer have a pulse, nor breath or warmth. If Petrok is under some kind of enchantment, something immobilising, it would be difficult to distinguish such a curse from the one affecting us already. Do you see?'

'I see,' Cora said aloud, causing Tom and Eseld to glance at her in confusion as they walked, making her feel like a freak, belonging nowhere.

'This way!' The duke held up his hand.

They squelched and staggered through the ruined mud, over the bodies of the ghasts. Cora felt sick and ashamed at the lack of feeling she had for them. She kept her eyes up, only glancing down in order to check what she was stepping on.

'So, what about those trees?' she asked, pointing, to distract herself. 'Are they normal ones or are they..?'

'Apple trees,' Eseld grinned. 'It's the old orchard. Must've been hidden by all them ugly, twisted ones. Begging their pardon,' she glanced at the duke but he wasn't listening. 'You can tell by how they're all knobbly.'

'And seeing as there's rotten apples in the mud,' Tom pointed towards the remains of brown fruit, speckled with white mould, barely distinguishable from the snowy mud. They stepped carefully around lumpy roots, which Cora couldn't help eyeing with suspicion, just in case.

The orchard fell away and they found themselves on open moorland, ankle deep in heather. Gorse bushes held traces of snow and shone pale gold, as Merlin's sun rose over distant, foggy hills.

'Here.' The duke held up his hand again for them to halt.

Bronnan glared at him until Wenna frowned at her, causing her gaze to drop.

He squatted down, pushing the snowy heather apart. 'Here. That's him, isn't it?'

Wenna blinked in astonishment and stared at the ground, nodding dumbly as the others crowded around, to see a glass panel in the earth, frost flowers and fine heather roots tracking its muddy surface. Beneath the glass was a grey face, covered in cobwebs. Its eyes were closed.

Chapter Twenty

White Glass

'Petrok?' Wenna whispered, her fingers brushing crumbs of soil from the glass as tenderly as if she was touching his skin.

Cora stared, he was obviously dead, wasn't he? He'd been buried. Not properly, like a Christian, but buried nonetheless.

Bronnan shot her a dirty look and Cora quickly hid her thoughts.

Lord Gendal signed something to Wenna.

'We have to get him out first,' she answered. 'Before we'll know.'

'Surely we should determine, first, whether or not he lives?' said the duke. 'Before we go to the considerable trouble of exhuming him?'

'How?' Wenna asked, trying to be patient.

The sergeant peered around the duke's elbow, his mossy eyebrows drawing together, before he shook his head. 'I seen many fings, your Grace, as ye know, but I never seen anyone that colour draw breath again. 'Sides, that thing's sealed shut. If he weren't dead when 'e went in, 'e is now. As a doornail.'

'It's not that simple!' Wenna snapped, startling the sergeant into opening his mouth and shutting it again, his bottom lip appearing briefly, before it vanished beneath a moustache of mud-clotted twigs.

'Get him up! Get him out!' came a cry from behind them.

Yestin, who'd been secretly following them, crashed between Bronnan and Meriwether. They tried to grab his elbows as he sank to the ground and started scratching the heather away, ripping it up by the handful. In a frenzy, he dug his nails in around a newly exposed, metal corner of the glass coffin.

'No, sir, no,' the sergeant protested, trying to pull Yestin upright, 'that ain't the way.'

'You don't understand,' Wenna said, struggling to keep her voice even. 'Petrok Noon was..is... the greatest sorcerer of our age. If anyone can come back from this-'

'I ain't sayin' don't bring 'im up, I'm sayin' don't do it like *that*! Coffin like that, you wanna give it a tap, break open the top,' he brought the butt of his rifle down hard. Crack. On the glass, making Wenna shriek. 'Like a boiled egg.'

'You're mad!' Yestin charged into the sergeant, who stood his ground, rooted as the tree he'd been the night before. 'You could have cut him!'

'I know what I'm doin!'

'He does,' the duke murmured. 'Don't let on, but my sergeant wasn't always in the army. Made his living by rather more nefarious deeds once upon a time didn't you Bagsby? You old devil. It was the military or the old hemp necklace.' He made a gruff sound in his throat which might have been a chuckle, and a crease appeared below one eye, which Cora took for a smile.

'Grave robbing?!' Yestin choked on the words. 'He'll snap his bones!'

'Never,' the sergeant retorted. 'No good to the anatomy students if it's broke is it? An' if he's so rotten 'e falls to bits then, well, least we'll know 'e's dead won't we?'

Cora was shocked. She'd heard of grave robbers,

but she'd thought they were a myth.

Bronnan held Yestin back again as he clawed for the sergeant's face. Sergeant Bagsby regarded him with mild curiosity for a second, then returned to his task.

The glass was cracked in the shape of a cobweb, but not shattered. He bent down to break pieces off with leathery fingers, two of them ending at a splintery knuckle.

'What you gotta do is, you gotta get a bit o' rope an' sling it under 'is arms. Anyone got a bit o' rope?'

Wordless, they shook their heads.

'Alright, necessity's the mother of whatsisname,' he declared.

He slipped his rifle from his shoulder and placed it beside him on the heath, before calmly lifting Petrok's wobbly head. Then he slid the leather strap over Petrok's neck, the rifle behind his head. He tugged one of Petrok's arms through, then the other, so that he was held firmly at the armpits, shoulders hunched up around his jaw. The sergeant pulled, leaning back and digging in his heels as though in a tug o' war, until Petrok slipped fully out, arms flung at awkward right angles, a cross of moon flesh on a rough bed of heather.

Yestin dropped to his side, eyes wide with shock.

'Well,' said the sergeant, wheezing as he bent to retrieve his gun. 'He ain't rotten.' He grinned, exposing missing teeth and Cora realised that, to him, corpses were as much a part of life as bread and beer.

Yestin brushed away the fragile layer of cobweb, to trace the lines of Petrok's waxen cheek.

Wenna knelt too and Cora thought she'd given

up, that she was saying a final prayer or just goodbye, when she pressed her forehead to Petrok's, eyes tightly closed. 'I can't hear him,' Wenna whispered, her voice shaking. 'I can't hear him Yestin, can you?'

Yestin didn't answer. And Cora understood that, for him, everyone else was a ghost. He huddled closer to Petrok in the bleak, early light and their shadows pooled into one.

Wenna forced herself to her feet, to give them room.

A tear dribbled from Yestin's eye and down the side of his nose as he put his lips upon Petrok's. The tear came to a rest where their lips met, reflecting the sunlight in a bright, tiny point.

Everyone was silent, heads lowered. For a moment, the duke and the sergeant were baffled, before frowns cast their eyes into shadow.

A guttural, choking noise ripped the air, making everybody jump.

It took Cora a moment to work out where it had come from, until Petrok's thin chest heaved, drawing in a ragged breath, and he was seized by a fit of coughing, dust and cobweb puffing from his mouth.

Yestin's face was wet and shining, his eyes stretching in wonder as Petrok turned onto his side, the better to clear his chest. But the coughing didn't stop and so, shocked as they were, each crouched to pat Petrok gently, then more firmly, as his whole body crumpled and shuddered as if he was being strangled.

For just a second, he opened his mouth wide, staring hard at Yestin with yellow, bloodshot eyes, and Yestin shouted 'wait! He says there's something in his throat!'

'What is it?'

'Bit o' mud I s'pect,' said the sergeant. 'Needs a bit of this.' He rummaged in a pouch, when the duke shook his head. 'They can't drink, remember?'

For the first time, Cora saw a flash of real emotion in Sergeant Bagsby's eyes. 'Oh yeah. Poor buggers.'

'It's not mud, it's... it looks like glass!' Yestin heaved Petrok's limp, floppy body up into a sitting position and slammed his palm into his back, making his head jolt back and forth like a marionette.

All of a sudden Petrok's convulsions took on a different shape. His ribcage lifted, thrusting him forward, as though an invisible hook was pulling hard at his chest. He was rising up, away from the heather, still coughing hard. Everyone grabbed him, the water inside Lord Gendal's globe sloshing wildly and it took all their strength to stop him flying into the air.

'Do something! Wenna!' Yestin was beside himself. 'Please!'

Wenna seemed to be in some kind of trance. As if what was happening was too strange, too confusing even for a mind as quick as hers to keep up with. But she snapped out of it.

'It's her,' she said, then shouted 'we have to fight her three-fold! Everyone except Eseld and Cora let go!' She moved Eseld's hand. 'Make the triangle!'

Eseld nodded and immediately positioned her hands flat so that her thumbtips and index fingertips were touching, the space between them, a triangle. 'You too Cora!' With difficulty, the three of them managed to move their hands to make the shapes and simultaneously press Petrok's chest, forcing him back down to earth. Instinctively, Tom reached to help again, but Wenna pushed him off with her elbow.

'No, you'll weaken the bond. You too, Yestin, let go.'

'But..!'

'I said let go!'

And Cora could see it cost them to remove their hands. 'What's happening?' she stammered. 'Surely we need everyone we can-'

'No!' Wenna commanded. 'Quiet. Let me think.'

A strong wind whipped across the moor, threatening to overbalance them. Something sharp started pushing up beneath the skin between Petrok's collar bones, making him groan in pain.

'That's what she wants' Wenna winced with pity. 'She's trying to draw it out!'

And for the first time, Petrok spoke, his voice a rasping croak above the gale. 'Don't-let-'

'We won't,' Wenna declared.

'What's this?!' The duke seemed more annoyed than afraid.

The sergeant loaded his rifle.

The misted sun grew dark, as though a shadow had passed across its face and the clouds twisted, contorting themselves into grotesque shapes. Rain fell in sudden torrents.

'Cora, put your hand on it, there!'

Cora's fingers were wet and trembling as Wenna shoved her hand onto the sharp bump, which was getting longer and more pointed, stretching poor Petrok's skin until it tore. The ragged point, somewhere between glass and metal, cut into Cora's fingertip, smudging Petrok's chest with her blood, which blurred and swirled with the tumbling raindrops, so that everything became frustratingly slippery.

Jerking left and right as though manipulated by an unseen hand, it burst out like the point of a spear thrust from the other side, making Petrok gag and splutter, until it wrenched itself violently upward, away from Cora's grasp. And Petrok fell, exhausted, into Yestin's arms.

'Don't let it go!' Wenna screeched. She and Eseld wrapped their bodies around Cora, who grappled with the razor sharp edges, holding on as it struggled, cutting her fingers to the bone.

Everything stopped.

The rain disappeared as suddenly as if a tap had been switched off. The sky was a smooth, wintery grey again and the sun floated, pale as snow, uncluttered by cloud or shadow.

The thing in Cora's hand had at last stopped jerking but she wouldn't loosen her grip. Wenna produced a kerchief and tore it in half, binding Cora's cut fingers with one piece, to stop the bleeding, and using the other to wrap the object, though she was careful not to let it leave Cora's hands.

'Now, listen,' Wenna said, her face still wet, her white hair a bedraggled mess stuck to her ears, 'this cannot leave you. You must *not* give it to anyone else, not even for a second or she'll get it from them. Until the curse is broken and my health restored, you are the only one who has a hope of controlling it.'

'What is it?' Cora was shaken, her legs feeling as though they might buckle beneath her.

'You know what it is.'

'The Merlinshard?'

Wenna nodded, holding Cora's hands and folding her bandaged fingers tenderly over the bundle.

'So it's over?' Cora breathed. 'The curse? Meriwether said that once we got the Merlinshard, this'd all be over, didn't he?' She looked to Meriwether.

'If only,' Wenna grimaced. 'The main thing is that it isn't in her hands.'

She touched Cora's arm. 'It's yours, for now. You must keep it safe until I can return it to its proper place. Nobody else has Merlin's blood mixed with Mab's magic in their veins, except you. But you must swallow it, to keep it hidden. Eseld, do you have-'

'Already got 'em out. No fresh poppy leaves I'm afraid, just witch hazel and elder, dried ones, but they'll do the job. Now, I'm afraid this won't be nice at all, my duck. But it's the only way.'

Cora felt sick at the thought, but she took the bundle and unwrapped the half handkerchief, using it to wipe off the bloody dust. She folded the dry leaves around it instead, feeling its sharp edges through the dark, papery wrapping, and put it in her mouth, just about managing to swallow, though it was dry and cold as flint and the notion that it had been inside that deathly box under the earth in the throat of a stranger made every muscle in her throat rebel.

It occurred to her that her insides were different from Petrok's. He could no longer digest, but she could. What if the Merlinshard worked its way down through her guts until... Wenna caught her eye with a firm smile. 'This is where being part bird will help you,' she said. 'The shard will lodge inside you, without travelling to your stomach, so that you may regurgitate it, as a mother bird does when carrying food home to her chicks.'

Petrok was whiter than ever, his lips horribly blue. He looked as though he might really be dead now, cradled in Yestin's arms, but his mouth was moving, trying to speak.

'Hush,' Yestin was saying, 'tell us when you're rested.' Cora's heart lurched in sympathy because he couldn't rest, he couldn't sleep or eat or gain nourishment from anything. The thought made her stronger and she appreciated the blood drying tight and sticky on her fingers. She was glad of the hunger gnawing at her stomach and the exhausted breaths running in and out of her lungs.

'We will go back to the house and discuss all that's happened here,' said Wenna. 'I'm sure our friend has much to tell us.' She smiled down at Petrok, who managed to open his eyes a crack and smile weakly in return, as Meriwether helped Yestin to carry him, bare feet dangling, back to the enormous house.

In the great hall, a breakfast of thick porridge was being organised by Goodwife Jenifry. Condensation from a great steaming cauldron dribbled down the windows. The spriggans had washed and changed, but traces of mud in their brows and a haunted look in their eyes hinted at the grisly fate they'd come so close to.

The soldiers sniffed the porridge with mild disappointment and asked if there was any meat or ale, to which the answer was no. They returned the curious glances directed at their twig-tangled hair and bark-rough skin with defiant stares. The noise and clatter of the hall was an unhappy, discordant one, but Cora reminded herself of the feast the night before, when all had seemed so buoyant and welcoming, while all the time dark plots had been hatching, bodies of murdered spriggans were cooling in the earth and soldiers stood, bewildered, freezing rain running off their branches.

Wenna, Eseld, the duke and Goodwife Jenifry sat together at a small table. Their discussion, everybody knew, was nothing less than a council of war.

Yestin had wrapped Petrok in furs and placed him in an armchair so close to the fire that he'd protested about being roasted like a goose. He and Lord Gendal were signing to each other across a game of chess. He seemed to be enjoying weakly nudging knights and bishops into place, as though the effects of his ordeal were draining from his body. Cora had noticed his slightly bent wire spectacles before, but it was only then that she realised there wasn't any firelight reflected in them. The lenses had gone.

After an hour or so, Wenna stood up. She walked with unhurried dignity to the end of the hall, standing beneath the minstrels gallery, hands clasped, waiting for everybody to fall silent.

Expectation hung in the air, mingled with the scent of woodsmoke and oats.

She touched her throat to amplify her voice as she had done before. 'As you know, the night has brought revelation, horror and-' she glanced softly at Petrok, 'reunion.' A murmur of sombre agreement rumbled around the hall, the deeper voices echoing like distant thunder.

'Our next move is to get across the water to Osborne House and invite Queen Victoria to aid our cause or, at least, to warn her of the threat Morgelyn poses.'

'Let the duke do it!' called a spriggan, who looked as though might be responsible for the shortage of ale, 'he knows-hic! Knows her doesn't he? Old pals them two!' He grinned as though he'd made a joke. It wasn't returned and his smile slid down into the sad folds of his face.

'I would have risen to the task, and gladly,' said the duke, with no need to magnify his voice by magical means, for it boomed from every stone. 'Might be a trifle awkward though, since she attended my funeral.'

Some laughed at this and a few soldiers banged their tin mugs.

'I intend' Wenna continued firmly, causing the duke to sit down again, 'to travel east, to meet the queen of the human Britons as an equal. The duke, meanwhile, and his men...'

Mugs drummed on tables and feet began to stamp, until the duke held up his hand, quashing it instantly.

Wenna acknowledged their noise with a graceful nod. 'The duke and his men will travel north, to the kingdoms of the redcaps and the bluecaps. While it's unlikely that they'll ever agree to fight together, there is a chance that some of their number might honour the ancient oath and join us. Though Morgelyn's ghasts have already begun to copy minor government officials there, as far as we know they haven't yet managed to infiltrate the elder councils or the royal family.'

Cora tried to listen, but was struggling to keep her sore, heavy eyelids from drooping. Though she wanted to concentrate on what Wenna was saying, her thoughts drifted over to the fireplace, where Petrok was gazing fondly at Wenna, like a doting father.

She knew Wenna's speech about strategy and supplies must be important, or she wouldn't be giving it, but what Cora wanted to know was why Petrok had the Merlinshard embedded in his throat in the first place, and who had buried him, to what end? A ghost would simply have struck his head off and taken it. So it must have been a friend. But where were they now?

Petrok looked straight at Cora, making her jump. She was so tired she hadn't thought to keep her thoughts hidden. He smiled, answering her with a gentle voice, inside her mind, one that hadn't been ruined by his damaged throat. 'I did it myself, Elowen. That wasn't the hardest part. At Queen Wenna's instruction, I stole the Merlinshard from the crown that Morgelyn stole from Wenna's mother. I replaced it with a piece of ordinary glass, then swallowed the real one to keep it safe. I wrapped it in poppy leaves first, to make my body an effective barrier and stopping it cutting my innards to ribbons. The coffin was reinforced with a powerful spell too, protecting what was inside from her sight. You know she can watch us, don't you?'

Cora nodded bleakly, remembering the black table strewn with butterfly ashes.

'The best hiding place for such a thing is the stillest. She senses the travel of magical objects as a spider knows a fly has brushed its web. But we mustn't fear, little one, we are protected,' he smiled.

Instead of feeling patronised, Cora felt comforted, reassured, and she wondered what it might feel like to have a grandfather.

'Wenna has cast a fogging spell over us all to muffle our words and make our movements unclear. The Merlinshard shines searingly bright for Morgelyn, so anxious is she to possess it again. Though she couldn't control it. She used it for the curse, and you know how that went. She was never a patient student. She never listened when I urged caution.' He looked sad, as though this mess was somehow his fault.

'Were you her *teacher*?' Cora asked, astonished.

'Oh yes. Her tutor. Her parents, well, the faeries who adopted her, were prepared to pay anything to help her control her gifts but, alas, it wasn't a problem money could solve. When she murdered them, it was purely in order to practise a particular kind of hex. She didn't intend them to die as quickly as they did. I ended our tuition. Her magic was irrevocably poisoned by then. I no longer believed she could be saved.'

Cora couldn't imagine Morgelyn ever being young, or needing a tutor or adoptive parents. Had she been a foundling then? Like Cora? The revelation should have shrunk her enemy to more bearable proportions, but instead it put shadows on her flesh, making her frighteningly three-dimensional.

'Don't be a-feared, Cora.' Petrok managed to smile. Though his face was emaciated and his neck ripped and ragged, his eyes shone, reflecting the firelight in twin flames behind glassless rims. 'Fear is what she wants. Fear is what makes us scatter and hide, to be picked off one by one. We will not hide. We will stand. Together.'

The hall erupted into applause, presumably for something Wenna had said, but it was Petrok who'd galvanised Cora's heart. She could see why they loved him.

'What I don't understand,' Cora ventured, 'is why the ghasts welcomed us here in the first place. If they'd already,' she swallowed, refusing to think about the pile of frosted earth among the trees, 'already killed the spriggans who lived here, why copy them and feed us and give us a place to sleep? Why not kill us on sight?'

'They were afraid and outnumbered. Bullies are always cowards, remember that, Elowen. And because they weren't really spriggans, just copies, they couldn't transform into giants. And their magic wasn't nearly as strong as Wenna's, Eseld's or yours. They drugged the spriggans from Pendlestow in order to prevent them from transforming. And they forced them to dig by holding knives to their children's throats. As for us, they planned to pick us off as we slept.'

'How did you know we'd find you?'

'I didn't. I hoped you would, but I didn't *know*. I just wanted to stop Morgelyn getting the Merlinshard. Putting it in the ground on its own wouldn't have worked, you saw how she can manipulate it. It needed to be bound first. I could have killed myself but, eventually, my flesh would've turned to dust and been no good. So I put myself into the deepest sleep I could. That way I'd be as hidden as possible, because it's consciousness that lights us up for her. Makes us visible. I'd laid a trail with the kind of subtle magic that I knew some of you would pick up on, whether you knew it or not. I didn't expect those soldiers to chance upon me. I'm quite glad I was unconscious when one of them slipped on the glass. It might've startled me to death!' He smiled again and, despite it all, Cora managed to smile back.

She could see Yestin becoming uncomfortable, so changed the subject. 'Why did they turn the soldiers into trees, instead of just killing them?'

'Difficult for the spriggan ghasts to do much damage to an experienced, armed platoon. I expect they planned to chop the forest down. Or burn it.'

They turned to listen again. Dismayed, Cora realised Wenna was urging them to leave as soon as they'd eaten, with no more sleep. But first, the soldiers were going to teach everyone how to fight.

Snow was falling, alighting delicately, gracefully, in flakes lighter than feathers, as though upon a peaceful scene, as the duke ordered Sergeant Bagsby to line everyone up in ranks. Everyone held a stick. Cora found herself standing between a plump man with pale eyes and a nervous cough and a spriggan with such a fierce expression, Cora dared not look at her for long.

'He'll have his work cut out,' said the man with the pale eyes, glancing around.

She nodded non-commitally. Tom was looking at her strangely. She couldn't read his expression at all. A flicker of hope sparked in her chest. Was he jealous?

'Silence in the ranks!' roared the sergeant, making the pale-eyed man jump and drop his stick.

Meriwether, Bronnan and Yestin stood with Wenna beside the frozen fountain, watching.

When the sergeant told them to fall in too, a

dangerous gleam sprang into Bronnan's eye.

'Even you ladies!' Sergeant Bagsby said, 'though it pains me to say it, should learn how to protect yerself, should it come to that.'

Bronnan removed the liquorice root she'd been chewing to say 'we are the Queen's personal guard. Do you really suppose you can teach us anything about the art of war?'

How strange, Cora thought, that those two words, at the opposite ends of the scale of human innovation, should be put together.

The smile and small shake of Sergeant Bagsby's head was a red rag to a bull.

'Give me the stick,' Bronnan said.

'Come and get it,' he grinned.

'If you insist,' Bronnan replied calmly. Quick as lightning, she poked him in the eye with her liquorice root and kicked his legs out from under him, catching the stick as it flew up in the air.

Meriwether and Mr Penrose chuckled. Even Wenna struggled to keep a straight face as she bent down to peer at him.

'Perhaps, sergeant,' Wenna grinned, 'my personal guard could assist you in your teaching? There are rather a lot of us now.'

Sergeant Bagsby struggled crossly to his feet, refusing help. As he brushed the snow off his bottom, leaving wet patches, Bronnan flashed a rare smile.

They divided into groups, some learning hand to hand combat while others focused on controlling their magic. Cora hesitated, unsure which she needed more help with.

All of a sudden, Yestin burst out of the house.

'Quick! I don't know what's wrong with him!'

'Cora!' Eseld waved her over as she ran up the steps with Yestin, Wenna following close behind.

They dashed into the hall, down a corridor and into a library. Petrok was huddled in an armchair beside a good fire, his knees two bony bumps in a tartan blanket. His face was horribly slack.

Eseld crouched beside him, talking soothingly as though to a child. 'What's wrong my 'ansome?' She was running her hands up his arms, as though she could rub warm life back into them.

Cora felt useless, like an actress who doesn't know her lines. She tried to keep out of their way as Wenna consulted a book and Eseld made a hot compress to put on Petrok's forehead.

Eseld turned to Yestin. 'Quills,' she said. 'And another blanket.'

Wenna's face fell. 'Is it that bad?'

Eseld snapped her fingers at the motionless Yestin. 'Quills! As many as you can. Wenna, come this side. Cora, you hold his feet, lift 'em up and rub 'em.'

Cora obeyed, bewildered as ever but knowing her place. She tugged the slippers off Petrok's bluish grey feet, which were the size of a child's, but nail-less and flecked with white hair.

Yestin rummaged noisily through the drawers of a bureau, producing a fistful of quills and shoving them under Eseld's nose.

She took them, meeting his gaze. 'You might want to leave for this bit.'

'Never.'

'Right you are.' With a short out-breath, Eseld punctured the skin on Petrok's shoulder with the tip of a quill. Yestin shut his eyes. Wenna did the same on his other arm and they looked to Cora, giving her a third. 'Quickly, Cora,' Wenna commanded, 'this is no time for squeamishness.'

'B-but-'

'Do it!' they both said at once, and Cora stabbed it in, fingers shaking, the tip of the quill just visible beneath his translucent skin.

'Right,' Eseld said, 'next, we need to pull all these feathery bits off, but don't let the tip slip out, whatever you do.'

With difficulty, they ripped the vanes off and as they did so, a dark red liquid ran through the hollow length of the central shaft.

Cora felt queasy. 'Is that blood?'

'Concentrate,' said Wenna. 'It's complicated. It's because it's outside his body, so no longer cursed, because we drew it out in a particular way. And it's not real blood. Not exactly. More like the memory of it.'

As usual, Wenna's response created more questions in Cora's mind than it answered. But she focused on her task, on the red beads forming and dripping, falling a few inches towards the rug then turning to powder and vanishing into thin air.

Eseld used another quill to puncture Wenna's arm, whereupon scarlet drips formed and dropped above Petrok's chest, disappearing before they could land.

'Here!' said Yestin, rolling up his sleeve, 'take mine!'

'Safer not to,' Eseld said briskly, keeping her eyes on Petrok's closed lids.

'Why? I should be the one to-'

'Trust us,' Wenna was gentle.

'Yours is most probably tainted,' Eseld was blunt. 'Corrupted with that rot you been rubbin' in yer eyes.'

'I haven't touched a grain! Not since you found me in the pub!'

'That's as maybe,' Eseld replied. 'But it lingers.'

Yestin's face fell, and he found Petrok's hand to squeeze it. He rested his other hand on his husband's forehead. Petrok's mouth was still open, his lips parted to reveal a dark tongue that, without the sheen of saliva, didn't look alive.

'*Cwic, cwic,*' they chanted, for what felt like hours. Cora's knees ached, then grew numb. Eventually, when she'd decided they would give up soon, stop kidding themselves and re-bury him, Petrok wheezed and spluttered, his sparse lashes flickering.

Yestin's eyes, sore and baggy with anxiety, sprouted fresh tears of joy. He threw his arms around Petrok, then loosened his grip, drawing back, in case he hurt him.

Once Petrok was stable, the three women left them, in the library, closing the door quietly behind them. Cora felt strangely detached. Her exhaustion distorted everything around her, lending it a gauzy, hallucinative quality. If she didn't sleep soon, she feared she'd drop where she stood. Perhaps it was this that gave her the courage to ask the other two 'why me? Why is it always me that has to help you with your magic? Can't someone else do it next time? I ain't got no book-learning, no idea how any of it works. I don't even know what language we're talking in. Why do you always ask me?'

Wenna gave her an impatient look, but did her best to explain as they hurried back outside, where everyone was sparring in pairs.

'The language is simply English. Old English. And the power of three is an ancient, potent structure. It's not just any three that can do it. It's a specific combination of gifted women at different stages in their lives, ones who share trust.'

'The crone,' Eseld pointed at herself, 'that's me. Then you need a maid, that is, an unmarried girl, s'you. And...and er...'

'The mother.' Wenna said, the word hitting Cora and breaking over her like a wave.

'You're a *mother*?' Cora whispered, 'but where-' she swallowed the rest of her sentence. 'Oh Wenna. I'm so sorry. Was it, did they... When they came for your...'

Wenna met Cora's gaze, before dropping it again.

'It's alright Cora. It's nothing like that. I carry my child. With me,' Wenna was oddly shy, 'when the curse is lifted it will continue to grow as it used to.' Cora stared in astonishment, as Wenna touched her swollen belly.

Cora had assumed that the plumpness around Wenna's middle was due to the curse, or her natural proportions, but now that she looked properly, it was blindingly obvious.

'You're having a babby?!' Unexpected tears heated her eyes as Cora threw her arms around Wenna. Startled, Wenna gave Cora a brief squeeze, before gently pulling away. 'You're not to say a word,' she said firmly, touching Cora's lip with an icy finger. 'So, the power of three is an ancient-'

'Where's your husband?' Cora discovered a new energy, marvelling at the thought of the tiny, curled faery who'd been with them in secret, all this time.

Until an awful thought struck her 'Was he... when your parents...'

'No,' Wenna smiled briefly, 'no, he lives.'

Cora knew she shouldn't pry, but she desperately wanted to. 'So who-' all of a sudden she was seized with a dizziness so acute, she thought she'd fall.

'What is it?' Eseld pressed her palm to Cora's forehead, supporting her as she began to slide towards the floor.

'I don't know!' Cora crumpled, bumping into a glass cabinet full of stuffed birds, making them wobble on their perches.

'What is it?' Wenna tried to support her.

'Are you going to be sick?' Eseld bent towards her as Cora collapsed.

Their words were fading, muffled, as though she was sliding underwater.

What happened next felt like a nightmare.

Cora thought she was in the cottage, where everything from the beams to the rug, to the pans on their hooks, was formed from smoke. It was empty. No, not empty. There was a figure huddled in the corner, shaking. Meg! Cora tried to speak, but she couldn't remember what words were. She tried to move towards her, but she had no limbs, no muscles, as though she was formed from vapour too.

There were smashed bowls on the worn flags and Meg was holding Gwen's dolly tightly against her chest, her silent mouth in the shape of a scream.

Cora's eyes flew open. 'She's taken them,' Cora stammered. 'Morgelyn's taken Gwen and Curnow!'

318

Chapter Twenty-One

Scab

Steadied by Eseld, Cora couldn't stop shaking.

Eseld had a fiercer look in her eyes than Cora had ever seen, as Wenna ordered everyone to pack what they could for the journey to Osborne.

'Should they all go?' the duke asked, sprinkling snuff onto the back of his hand and drawing it up with a long sniff. 'A party should go on ahead. You'd travel far quicker without the children and the lame.'

'There isn't anywhere safe to leave them,' Wenna replied. 'We must stay together, so we can protect each other.'

The duke regarded her. 'I wouldn't dream, you majesty, of questioning your judgement. But I have several successful campaigns to my name. And there are times when an army must break and reform. And times, too, when difficult decisions must be made.'

Bronnan bristled at his interference, watching him while picking bits of liquorice root from her teeth with her dagger.

'What I propose,' he continued calmly, 'is that you take the strong with you, and the rest go to the place in-between, where they will be safer, for the time being at least.'

Cora remembered Nancarrow and the others who'd been too frail, or too cowardly, to join them, stepping down into the peculiar smoke and disappearing. She could still smell the awful paste.

'You must impress upon her majesty your equality as a monarch, no mean feat. And your power as a military force,' the duke continued, 'not your plight as a refugee for, I fear, any request of sympathy might fall upon deaf ears. The Queen is still in mourning for both her mother and the Prince consort and, though she does of course wield phenomenal power, it is, at the moment, her ministers, with their hands clamped firmly around the nation's purse, who will make the decision as to whether to come to our aid.'

Cora was trying to listen to their discussion, more to blot out the horrible image in her mind of Meg in the empty cottage than anything else. But it was no use. 'What are you going to do about Gwen and Curnow?!' she spluttered angrily. 'We have to find them! We have to go and get them, they're just babies! Surely this changes everything?'

Eseld opened her mouth to answer, but emotion strangled her words.

Cora had never read Eseld's mind before. Now she saw the agony she was in; the way she was trying to force herself to see her own dear grandchildren as another reason to press on to Osborne, even though her instincts was told her to do the opposite.

Nobody said much as they made ready to leave. With heavy hearts, they turned their backs on the glittering disappointment of Greenacre, closing the silvered gates behind them.

The duke and his men marched north while Wenna, Eseld and Cora performed the ritual that would send those who needed to go, to the in-between place. Each face that sank through the smoke was lined with age or round with youth. Some of the mothers volunteered to go as guardians for the babies and children, until Wenna said it wasn't necessary, they were needed as soldiers. 'Time moves differently there. None of those we send will be aware of its passing. They will be suspended. As though asleep.' Cora glimpsed a brief image beside Wenna's head, of a cloudy place with no land or sky, where shadowy figures floated in bubbles connected together, like frogspawn. She shuddered and looked away.

As they stepped into the smoke to disappear, many held hands with loved ones, whose outstretched fingers were suddenly empty.

Yestin was among those letting go, for Petrok refused to be a burden, insisting that he'd slow them down.

They washed the paste off in a stream so cold it hurt, then tramped for hours across snowy moorland and glistening bog. The heather was a ghostly version of itself, coated in frost, which cracked and crunched underfoot. The landscape was bleak and featureless, but for a few scraggly trees, huddled close to the ground to get out of the weather, crooked branches all growing in one direction, like knotted hair in the wind.

The snow was deeper the farther they went and the few trees grew fewer and further between. Lord Gendal stopped to tip the cloudy water out of his globe and refill it with snow, which he shook until it turned to slush, sliced with light.

Cora tried and failed to get rid of the picture in her mind. But Meg remained, sitting on the floor of the cottage, holding the doll with a broken neck, every time Cora blinked.

She could have asked Eseld why she had suddenly gained the ability to see so far, but she didn't really care why. It didn't matter. And besides, Eseld was doing her best to keep step with everyone else, blinking and widening her pink-rimmed eyes to keep the tears inside. Cora didn't want to make things worse by badgering her.

Unable to blot out the image of the cottage, Cora faced it head on, searching the smoky memory for clues as her feet kicked the snow around her sodden hem and her boots crushed the frosted heather, the holes in her stockings letting the wet leather rub her feet raw. It occurred to her that she might have gone mad. Such an insistent vision might be nothing more than a result of recent events turning her mind to mush. But, somehow, she didn't think she had gone mad. She knew herself better than ever. She trusted her mind, her courage and her knowledge more than she'd ever thought possible. Perhaps that was the perfect confirmation, she thought wryly, of have lost her wits entirely.

In the smoky cottage, she tried to find Piran. She didn't see his absence the way she saw the children's, as holes violently ripped. He simply wasn't there. Had he gone after them? Died trying to save them? And why had poor Meg been left behind? However hard she concentrated, Cora couldn't see him. She discovered, with the deep concentration that came from rhythmic trudging, that in her mind she could retreat backwards out of the cottage and glide through the wood, across the moor into Treleddan and onto Fish Row, where thin, shabby girls sold buns from trays and men leaned against blackened walls to smoke. Piran wasn't behind the fogged windows of the Dog and Duck, so she peered into the Giddock's yard.

Staring past the tools, piles of wood shavings and half-finished spokes, she saw something that made her blood run cold. In the far corner behind a broken cart, Nancarrow's ghast was speaking soundlessly to Victor Morningside. Between them, Piran was nodding. His head hung low, as though in shame and his eyes were deader than ever. In his hand was a half empty bottle.

She felt sick. He was the spy. He had betrayed his own children! For what? For gin? Cold flakes rushed at her face even as her forehead prickled with sweat. She reached out to catch something or someone to steady her. The vision of the smoky yard overlay the wide, white moor like two magic lantern plates, one in front of the other, until she couldn't control which one she was seeing. She staggered, head swimming, and stumbled to the ground until heather scratched her cheek.

'Tom!' Eseld shouted, 'catch her! Too late.'

Eseld hurried over, frowning up at Tom as she lifted Cora's head. 'What you starin' like a bobba for?'

Tom smiled strangely at her, as though she was telling him a joke he didn't quite get.

Cora blinked, the faintness beginning to fade.

Wenna peered down at her in concern. 'You mustn't tax yourself unnecessarily, Cora.'

At this, Cora surprised them all by emitted a dry bark of laughter. 'Tax myself?! Isn't that what we're all doing? Wearing ourselves to the marrow?' She was about to add that it didn't matter anyway. That they were doomed, but thought better of it.

Wenna's eyes narrowed. '*Unnecessarily* I said. Now. Come on, up you get. This isn't you. It's wonderful what you can do now. The old folk called it going seeing. But it'll wear you out. Bring you down. Darken your thoughts if you let it. It's what Morgelyn does, to spy on her enemies, but she needs dark magic to do it, whereas you can just...' Wenna smiled, a touch of pride in her voice. 'Anyway, you mustn't overdo it.'

Cora nodded, trying to shake off the gloom that had settled, thick as fog, around her heart, which had nothing to do with going seeing.

Wenna crouched beside Cora. 'We don't know for certain that he betrayed them,' she said, straight into her mind so the others wouldn't hear.

A soft giggle came from Tom. He was staring at one of the low, ragged trees. 'Did you put that there?' he asked Cora. 'The bauble?'

Cora blinked. All that clung to the tree was a brown, crumpled leaf. As they stared, it broke its weak grip and fell softly onto the heather.

Wenna had been speaking, but she stopped abruptly, to look at Tom.

Eseld was peering at him too. Both began to scrutinise him more closely and he shrank away. 'What?' he mumbled, scratching self-consciously at his stubbled neck.

Nobody spoke for a minute.

'How did I miss it?' Eseld whispered. 'Oh my poor boy, how did I miss it? Is it her?' She whispered, switching from sadness to fury in less than a heartbeat, swinging towards Wenna to shout 'it's *her* ain't it? She's put an addle in his brain!'

Wenna was looking carefully at Tom. 'I don't know. I don't think so.'

Very gently, Wenna asked Tom to bend his head

towards her, and he turned pink with embarrassment as she put her hand to his cheek and pushed his face to one side.

Jealousy flushed Cora's cheeks.

Wenna gave her a hard stare, reminding her that he was young enough to be her great-great-grandson at least.

Cora saw what Wenna was looking at. The glancing blow he'd received at the mine had produced only a superficial injury. A small amount of blood had dried in a dark, messy scab behind his ear. Wenna picked at the wound, releasing a faintly sulphurous smell. Tom screwed up his eyes. She pulled her finger away, revealing an unmistakably bluish green smudge on its tip.

Cora was shocked. 'What's that? I ain't never seen a wound corrupted like that!'

'It isn't infection.' Wenna was gentle, 'this is why he's been acting the way he has.'

'It's glamour,' came Yestin's voice. 'Well, arkanite, which, if it goes straight into the blood, has a distorting, hallucinogenic effect but without the high. It's not fresh though, is it?' he wrinkled his nose at the smell, which was getting worse. 'I'd say that's been there a good while.'

'Since the mine,' Cora murmured, feeling as though her voice was coming from somewhere outside her body. Could it really be the arkanite in his wound, and not her transformation into a feathery freak, that had shrivelled his love for her into the miserable husk it had become?

'Is it-' she swallowed. 'Is it permanent? Is there any way... I mean...' She poked a hand out of her fur cloak. What was left of her single sleeve hung in rags either side of long feathers so black they were shot with blue. 'Is he like me?'

Wenna was unreadable. 'Needs a good clean,' was all she said. 'We'll have to stop soon anyway, light a fire, build some shelter for the night. I think I can see a stream up ahead.'

The stream ran through a natural hollow and, while the others were dragging what branches they could to build a shelter, Eseld dipped a rag and dabbed it gently on Tom's head. It came away streaked with red, shot through with a peacock hue. She rinsed it out, squeezed it and applied it again, making Tom shiver as the freezing dribbles ran down the inside of his collar.

Wenna, Bronnan and Meriwether were pacing around in the heather, scrutinising it.

'What you looking for?' Cora asked.

'Something rotten,' Wenna replied, 'we need to find some maggots. For the wound.'

Caught between queasiness at the idea of putting maggots in his head and wondering what they would taste like, Cora helped search. Eventually, it was Bronnan who found a dead toad and squatted to scoop up its mushy remains, which she carried back to Eseld.

'This is why you been acting such a prune,' Eseld said softly, scraping as much of the blue-stained scab away as she could, then pressing a few of the maggots in. Tom blinked, like one beginning to wake.

Cora hardly dared breathe.

Tom was looking around, a crease appearing and disappearing between his eyebrows every time he shifted his gaze. When it alighted on Cora, she almost cried out, because his eyes were his own again.

'Cora, what happened? You're all birdy.' He took her hand and lifted it, so that the long feathers underneath fanned out. He stared at her beaky nose, but pretended not to. 'But you'd got better, gone back the way you were.'

Cora shook her head. She wanted to say it must have been the wound, its effect had made him see what he wanted to, but the disappointment in his face choked the words back into her stomach.

He hesitated before touching her cheek. 'It don't matter.' He drew her close, folding his arms around her as tears melted into the feathers of her face. Startled joy kept her arms stiff at her sides, until she reached up, hope driving fear from her mind. She knew his kiss might break her heart into even smaller pieces, but she couldn't miss the chance.

'I didn't see it.' Eseld mumbled, dabbing her eye with a rough forefinger. She struggled to keep her voice steady as she added 'an I promised your mum I'd look after you.'

'Oh shush.' Tom shook his head. 'So I got a scratch an' a bit of dirt got in it. Worse things happen at sea. You done a great job looking after me and the nippers.' His easy smile at the mention of his younger siblings caused the faces around him to fall.

'But they're...' Eseld coughed to stop a sob. 'Tom, my love, they've gone. She...'

'Yeah,' he interrupted, 'Meg took 'em to the seaside. You told me.'

Wenna stepped in. 'That's not what she said, Tom. It was the arkanite, distorting things. I'm so sorry, I'm afraid Morgelyn's got them. But it may not be too late...'

'What?!' Tom roared. 'Why didn't anyone tell me?'

'We did, everybody knows, Cora saw it-'

Tom thrust Cora away from him, holding her shoulders. He stared so deep into her eyes it made her draw her head back, squashing her chin into her neck. 'Tom, you're hurting me.'

Instantly, he released her, rubbing her shoulders by way of an apology. 'I'm sorry, I just- I can't believe it. And I knew?' He shook his head. 'I suppose I sort of did, I just... I dunno. I ain't been myself.'

'No,' Cora said gently, the words catching in her throat. 'But you're back now and I ain't letting you go again.'

As they hunted rabbits to roast for supper, Cora didn't know if they were moving faster, or if there really was more blue in the sky, but everything felt different. Brighter.

'Were they magical,' Cora asked Meriwether, around a fire he'd made by rubbing sticks together, 'them maggots?'

'Whose to say where science ends and magic begins?' he replied. 'It's like electricity isn't it? It was considered magical, once, before we understood it.' He smiled and, though she tried to return it, he saw she was unsure. She'd heard of electricity. She was pretty sure it had something to do with steam, but she'd never actually seen any.

'The seasons, then,' he said, twisting a stick that held a rabbit, to cook the sides evenly. A drip of fatty juice fell into the fire with a hiss. 'They're a better example aren't they? Of how science can explain something, without making it any less incredible.'

'But that's God, isn't it?' Cora felt foolish and tried

to find Tom's hand in the dark, but when she turned she saw him staring at the feathers on her arm. She covered them with her cloak.

'Perhaps,' Meriwether smiled. The look in his eyes was tender, fatherly even.

Cora was relieved when Wenna changed the subject.

The clouds gave way to starlight and Yestin and Meriwether went off to hunt bats, which they skinned and cooked over a fire. The humans and the spriggans slept huddled together around the ashy embers, each burying their heads under their fur cloaks, too cold to sleep properly, too exhausted to stay awake. The faeries crouched in the snowy heather, Bronnan sharpening her dagger as Wenna gazed into her blackstone.

The next morning, Eseld found a cluster of orange, velvet shank mushrooms. Cora rubbed her eyes, blinking in the misted dawn, the few bites not having done much to restore her.

'If we get going now,' Wenna said, 'we should reach the coast before dark.'

Having spent so much of their journey on moorland and marsh, beneath a realistic sky, Cora had almost forgotten that they were deep underground, so it came as a faint surprise when Wenna added 'we've a long climb ahead of us, before we get to the thin place.'

'Can't we get there by magic?' she asked.

'Now, Cora, you know by now that magic can only do so much.' Eseld rubbed her hands together and blew on them. 'We ain't got a flying carpet. Though Lord knows I could do wi' one. We got to get to the right spot afore we can cast the spell to get us that last bit.'

The moor sloped upwards and the sky above became translucent, like gauzy fabric, with rock showing through it, fading everything to a bizarre, midday dusk.

All Cora could hear was breath and trudging feet as they plodded on. Snow fell again in earnest, catching in their eyelashes and making it impossible to see further than ten yards ahead. Then she stopped, her heart squeezing tight as a fist. Something was wrong. Something was coming.

People slowed to turn their heads towards a strange, distant sound, a note beginning low and soaring upward, joined by others. Cora tried to believe it was the wind. But there wasn't any. Eyes strained in anxious faces. Fingers flew to lips. When they realised what it was, terror stopped their feet.

The mournful howling was getting closer and they turned to scan the spreading moorland behind them, where greyish forms were moving fast, sending up sprays of white.

'Run! Everyone! Run!' they shouted, their cries growing more hysterical as they scrambled through snow so deep it hindered their speed, making their bodies lurch in exaggerated shapes.

The wolves were quickly closing the gap between themselves and the terrified band. Their pelts shuddered as they moved, thick with winter heft, rippling silver-grey tipped with black.

'We can't outrun them!' Meriwether shouted, moving in front of Wenna, shielding her.

Mr Penrose spread out his arms, as though he could protect everyone. 'Fire! They hate it! We need fire!'

Everybody froze. As the wolves drew closer, their breath forming steamy clouds, Cora couldn't inflate her lungs. She glimpsed bright blue glints in their fur, where hungry eyes gleamed. They slowed to a trot, knowing they could surround their prey at their leisure.

'Quick!' Bronnan fixed the closest wolf with a ferocious stare, dagger drawn, teeth bared. 'Eseld! Get on with it!'

Eseld's hood had slipped and hanks of grey hair had blown free from her bun as she made frantic shapes with her hands.

'What is it?' Cora panicked. 'Can't you do it?'

'I need hope,' Eseld looked angry enough to weep. 'I can't, I can't believe enough. She's got us.'

Yestin shoved a stout stick into Eseld's cupped palms. 'Course you can, you're Eseld bloody Liddicoat! Feel the anger! Light it!'

With horrifying speed, a wolf sprang towards Yestin, seizing his arm in its jaws. Screaming, he brought the stick crashing down on the wolf's head, making it stumble away, shaking its muzzle and scattering drool.

'You have to do it Cora!' Eseld implored her, her hands white and bare. 'You did it before, summon up your blood heat, think about what matters!'

'But-!'

'Do it!' Yestin and Bronnan shouted together.

Cora focused all her energy into her feathery hands. She'd made fire at the mine, so she could do it again. Only she couldn't.

A wolf leapt, flattening a spriggan, jaws stretched wide. With a horrible crunch of bone, the snow was showered with scarlet.

She clenched her fists and smelled burning feathers.

Wisps of smoke curled up from between her fingers.

A wolf stopped growling, snapped its jaws shut and started sniffing instead.

With a spit and a crackle, both Cora's hand were ablaze, black smoke pouring up into the frosty air. The wolves licked their lips in fear and began to back away. Cora thrust her burning hands towards them, sending fat, streaming flames amongst them, making them scamper about, unsure. She saw the spriggan lying white as the snow, blood all around him in looping, scar shapes and anger sent a searing pain whizzing down her arm. A ball of flame shot out from her palm, streaming black and blasting a hole in the snow, leaving a patch of scorched heather.

Too angry to be astonished, Cora hurled another ball of fire at the biggest wolf, setting his fur alight. As he jumped away, whining like an injured dog and running in anguished circles, he seemed to be eaten up by the flames, coming away from the ground like a piece of thin, burning paper, lifted oddly by the heat consuming it.

At their leader's demise, the other wolves collapsed too, becoming nothing but heaps of fur, then powder, which disintegrated into nothing.

'She cannot create,' Wenna said. 'How quickly we forgot. They were just ghosts. Projections, sent to scare us. Show me your arm Yestin.'

'It's nothing.'

'Show me!'

Cora knelt beside the body of the murdered spriggan, her skirts soaked in bloody snow. 'Could a *ghost* have done this?'

'Quiet, Cora!' Wenna snapped, her usual composure deserting her, stunning everybody into silence as she touched Yestin's ripped sleeve, where a bone deep, bloodless wound gaped. She didn't seem able to look at the dead spriggan at all.

Wenna turned to Cora. 'I'm sorry, I'm sorry. I'm angry with myself, nobody else. I should have seen them for what they were. It wasn't the fire that destroyed them, it was our fear departing. Truth flooding in. Fear is like oxygen to them. And you, Cora, Elowen, you mighty girl, you banished our fear by exposing the wolves for the shadows they were.'

Shaken, everyone looked to Cora with naked gratitude. She flushed, despite the freezing air.

'But what about him?' Cora asked Wenna, staring miserably down at the body. 'What happened to him, if he wasn't torn apart?'

'The jaws we saw were merely illusions,' Wenna said slowly, as though struggling to believe it herself. 'They couldn't actually bite, but the terror of it, the belief in the biting was enough, I fear, to stop his poor heart.'

Cora gazed down, wiping a tear away before it could fall. He was more boy than man, with a fine fuzz upon his cheeks and upper lip, where a beard might one day have grown. The reddened snow gradually paled, as she gazed through the false blood. The gashes on his body began to heal, dark innards folding themselves back in, as if pressed by invisible hands.

'Does anyone know his name?' Wenna asked quietly.

'Goodsir Arthek,' Goodwife Jenifry murmured.

'His father was snatched by the pterydons before you came to Pendlestow.'

'Did he have any other family?'

Goodwife Jenifry shook her head. 'His ma died the day she brought him into the world. There was just him and his Pa.' She began to recite a simple funeral prayer and the other spriggans joined in, as the humans and faeries lowered their heads.

> *Earth enfold you,*
> *Sky receive you,*
> *Water embrace your every bone.*
> *Tongues will tell*
> *And stories dwell*
> *Memories linger, though you have flown.*

They burned Goodsir Arthek's body. Cora didn't know whether that was their tradition or if it was because the ground was too frozen to bury him. She choked back tears of guilt as the snow around the pyre melted in a charred pool, greasy smoke slithering up through the windless air and stinging their eyes. If she could have conjured the fire more quickly, he'd never have died.

'We must learn from this. We must see it for what it was.' Wenna held up Yestin's tattered arm. 'It isn't real. There's no wound'

'It hurts like a real wound,' Yestin winced.

'The pain feels genuine,' Wenna said, 'but it *isn't*. You experienced fear, we all did, we still do, that's real enough, but what happened, those wolves, it was an illusion. We mustn't believe our eyes.'

Cora stared in amazement at Yestin's arm, belief

filtering slowly though her brain. The rags of grey muscle were knitting together, just as Goodsir Arthek's horrible wounds had healed before her eyes, the skin reforming without a scratch on it. The bits of hanging cloth lifted, weaving with invisible threads until it looked as though it had never been torn at all.

Miserable and shaken, they trudged through snow that became thinner and wetter, the heather becoming more sparse, the earth hardening with every step. Soon they were walking upon dark granite, patched with lichen, which became a narrow gorge enclosed on either side by forbidding rocks.

A curious starlight, without any stars, replaced the dusk. Black sand filled the clefts and hollows between the stones and the way grew more challenging, the ground sloping ever more steeply until they had to climb, finding footholds where they could. Darkness closed in on all sides, making everyone nervous. They made torches, which flickered, revealing uncanny shapes in the crags, where shadows leapt and slithered.

'Get there afore dark eh?' someone was grumbling. 'What's all this then eh? What's this?'

'It ain't dark like night-dark,' Mr Penrose said.

'It's just the cave.' Tom added in his old, reassuring way, over his shoulder. 'The Cave of Fallen Bones. That's right innit Mamm-wynn?'

Eseld shrugged.

'Why is it called that?' Cora asked. 'Fallen Bones? Sounds horrible.'

'You'll see,' he said. 'It's not real bones in there, its thcm stallythings.'

'Stalactites,' Wenna put in.

'Yeah, them.'

Tom began telling a story about the Cave of Fallen Bones, one Eseld had told him as a boy, which lifted Cora spirits a little and those around them too, although it made her feel very strange when he came to the part where Merlin came to Underwood and his terrible guilt when he fell in love with Mab, Arthur's wife.

'So Arthur was married to my- to Mab.' Cora said. 'I thought he made it illegal for humans and faeries to marry'

'He did, but only because she left him for Merlin.'

'Oh.' The whole thing was very odd. She wanted to know more about her parents, except she didn't, because the more she learned, the sadder she felt, that she'd never meet them. She thought of the mother she'd always imagined, slipping down through the murky river water, sad hair trailing like weeds. And, although she knew that mother was an illusion, created by Selina, Cora wasn't ready to let go of her. Not yet. It was less difficult to accept Merlin as a father, because he wasn't replacing anyone. Mab needed to remain a stranger for a while yet.

When Tom paused in his story, Cora took the opportunity to change the subject, hoping he'd understand. 'She weren't exaggerating,' she puffed, 'Wenna I mean, when she said it'd be hard-going.'

Tom shook his head. 'No, she weren't. But we can do it. 'Specially you.' He gave her a gentle nudge. 'Elowen.'

'Eh?' She managed to smile.

'Elowen Ambrosius,' he put on a haughty accent, 'daughter of Merlin and Mab.'

'Give over.'

'No, I didn't get it before,' he warmed to his subject. 'Not prop'ly. How much it matters. What it means. I only found out just before that damned rock got me.'

'Language, Tom,' Eseld called from further up, making him grin.

'Sorry Mam-wynn.' Then he turned back to Cora. 'Didn't know I were a-courting such quality.'

Cora didn't answer. She didn't want to think about what it meant or how much it mattered. It made her feel as though a ton-weight was pressing down on her. She wished he could see her thoughts and just stop.

'Elowen-'

'Don't call me that. I know Cora's just the name they gave me at the orphanage. Or maybe it were Aunt... Maybe it were Selina. But it's the only thing in the world that's mine, especially after... Anyway. It's my name for good or ill.'

'Especially after what?'

'You know. Since I turned into this. Not that I were any great prize before, but now I got all these dratted feathers and my nose is all... And my feet, don't get me started on my feet.'

'What's wrong wi' 'em? An' I like your nose just fine.' He twisted round and bent to kiss the smooth, bone-hard skin, swelling her heart like a balloon. And she tried to ignore the way his smile was just a little too wide.

'Careful, you two!' Yestin managed to say, struggling to climb as though the pain was lingering, even though he knew the injury to be a fraud.

Cora tried to feel sympathy, but managed only irritation, and wondered what everyone, especially

Tom, would say if they knew that her five toes had fused into three scaly ones, and that a fourth stuck out of her heel. Each had a curved claw instead of a nail. She'd left her boots on since leaving Greenacre, for warmth and because she couldn't face crushing them in every day, when they wanted to spring apart like the toes of a bird, though it meant her boots were oddly stretched and misshapen, the laces straining, threatening to snap.

The climb became more difficult as the boulders grew bigger. Soon it was more like a cliff face than a steep scramble, the dark rock streaked with rusty green stains of copper ore. They trailed to a halt, possessing neither the skill nor the equipment to scale such a sheer wall, until Meriwether found hundreds of carved, narrow steps, which they followed carefully in a snaking line, for there was only room to go in single file, with nothing to hold onto but rock on one side and a sharp drop on the other. Cora was glad of the darkness because, in the eerie glow of the torches, she could kid herself that they weren't so high.

As they climbed, the rock above met and parted over their heads, forming vast archways, barely visible in the smoky light, as if they were climbing through the ribs of a ruined cathedral, though by their raggedness, Cora guessed they were formed from wind or water. She could hear a rushing noise, which might have been either. It grew louder, until waterfalls appeared, just trickles at first, then wider ones, still thin enough to see through. A few of the falls crossed the steps in a rushing sheet, so they had to walk through icy cold, briefly wetting their hair and furs. Some of their torches were put out and, with difficulty, lit again.

The last cracks of false, starry sky disappeared and the violent crashing of the bigger waterfalls soon made it impossible to hear each other. Cora had to summon all her courage when the steps veered away from the cliff to follow a thin archway of rock, curving out into blind darkness like a too-thin footbridge. Torrents of deafening water thundered either side of them, and they held their hands out for balance as they walked carefully across, hearts hammering, licking water from lips coated with spray.

'Salt!' Tom turned to Cora in excitement, once they'd reached the other side and the loudest falls were far enough behind them to hear each other again. He licked his lips again. 'That means we're getting near the sea!'

'Don't tell me you're enjoying this?'

'Course. Every step gets me closer to Gwen and Curnow. I'd run if I could. And anyway, we're *inside* the Cave of Falling Bones! And there, look, they're what gives it its name!' He flashed the grin of a boy who'd found himself in a childhood fairy tale, which, Cora remembered, was exactly what he was. And she followed his pointing finger towards some curious rock formations. They were nothing like the boulders littering the moor, or the square blocks used for building. These pale, eerie, icicle-like forms looked like something between liquid and solid, as though they were dribbling from the unseen roof of the cave and could pool on the rock below at any moment. Some were thin as candles, others thick as trees and Cora shuddered, walking beneath them as they dangled threateningly overhead. She reached up to touch one as they passed and was surprised to find it cold and hard, like any other stone.

The rocky floor of the cave began to descend and dense, cold water clamped around Cora's feet. She looked down to see orange-gold light from the torches reflected in ripples. But their glow wasn't the only source of light down there. Far beneath the water's surface was a cooler, sea green dappling, as though from a distant, underwater sun.

'Stop! Everybody stop here,' Wenna called out, squatting down and feeling her way along the cave wall, holding a torch to the rock until she found what she was looking for. In the dim glow, Cora could just make out the familiar shape. The sign of the Spindleberry Guild.

'Cora,' Wenna was saying, 'and Eseld, join me. Lord Gendal will give you a throatfish each.'

She moved her hands into fleeting shapes.

Lord Gendal signed back, causing Wenna's face to fall.

'There are only a few left alive,' she explained.

She hesitated, but only for a moment. 'We three will remain under, you two use these to breathe,' she held up the water-filled leather bag, where a few throatfish darted. 'Everybody will have to take turns to step down into the water, hold their breath, then swim up through our arms. You'll have to hold it for a while, so take a really good lungful. Everybody stared at her. They knew she wasn't mad, but it was hard to understand what she could be talking about. The water was only ankle deep.

'We'll join hands like this, see?' She took Eseld's hand, then went to grab Cora's, but Cora snatched hers away, hiding them both deep in her fur cloak and almost dropping the slippery throatfish.

'What is it?' Wenna tried to be patient.

Cora knew she was being childish, and drew out her hands, which had grown even longer and more deformed in the last few hours, every bone inside her fingers ached as if tiny saws were being drawn across them. Her fingers were as thin as pencils and four times as long. Her arms were so stretched and wiry she had to fold them into thirds, having formed a sort of second elbow where her wrists had been. It had become more and more of a struggle to pull her cloak around her, partly because her feathers were so smooth and slippery and partly because she seemed to have lost all dexterity.

'Come,' Wenna said gently. And Cora let her take what used to be her hand.

Everybody was looking at her, so Cora gazed down instead at the shallow water, which wasn't much more than a large puddle.

There was something strange about the water. She knew it was shallow, but it appeared oddly bottomless, with that curious light coming from the depths.

'Trust me.' Wenna said. And because she wasn't looking at her when she spoke, Cora didn't know whether she'd said it with her mouth or her mind.

'I do,' she replied.

The three of them held hands in what had become a familiar, almost reassuring, position, though the grip was ever-changing. Eseld and Wenna began '*bufan ufernan,*' and Cora joined in. '*Bufan ufernan, bufan ufernan.*' The solid rock beneath them began to soften, sucking them down like quicksand, inching over their knees, then their hips;

the cold closing, shocking in its intensity, around their muscles, stiffening them to ice.

Alarmed, but managing to keep the throatfish in place and her words steady, Cora sank lower, glancing nervously up at Tom, who gave her an anxious nod, before water engulfed the three of them, closing over Cora's bristled scalp and lifting the pale hair of the other two, to drift in bleached rags around their faces.

The rush of water into Cora's lungs was different this time. It was still deeply unpleasant, but it tasted of minerals and salt instead of the brackish, stagnant tang of the marsh around Pendlestow. Once the pool had closed over their heads, Cora glanced up, water stinging her eyes and blurring her sight, and it was just as well she had a throatfish in place, for she gasped at the acres of empty blue, releasing a few bubbles of astonishment, which drifted up towards the tiny huddle of torchlit people, as distant as a boat would be to an octopus on the seabed.

Just as Wenna had instructed, every member of the group appeared, stepping impossibly from a tiny, blurred figure to their normal size, one after the other, to duck beneath their linked arms and stand between the three. When they kicked their legs to swim up through what seemed now to be miles of sea, they became filmy and translucent, then disappeared entirely.

Chapter Twenty-Two

Osborne

Once everybody had swum up through their arms, Wenna told Cora it was their turn. She leaned forward, the others copying until their three foreheads were pressing firmly together. 'Now,' Wenna said, 'kick. We can't speak to Eseld down here. She'll get it, but we'll have to guide her at first.' Their skulls ground together, skin slipping slightly on the bone to the left and right.

It was the closest that Cora had ever been to anybody. Their skirts and furs tangled in the water. The white and grey hair of the others, pushed down by their upward thrust, slithered over her face and she felt as though they were beginning to merge, as if they were becoming one creature and yet, at the same time, their very closeness made Cora acutely aware of their separateness. In the painful cold, Eseld's skin was as chill as Wenna's and in the watery, close-up blur, their craggy faces looked almost identical, while her own was like nobody else's in the world.

They burst into violent waves that sent them lurching up and down. It was difficult to keep hold of each other's hands, slick as they were with seawater. The moon was high and the water glittered black and silver. Cora struggled and the rushing spray-filled air felt like an assault on cheeks grown used to the windless world below.

Petrified she'd drown, Cora held the throatfish firmly in place between her tonsils. But when she tried breathing air through it made her choke, so she tried to keep the lower half of her face below the surface, with her eyes above.

Light flared, so bright Cora was momentarily blinded.

'That way!' Wenna called. As the wave lowered, Cora saw a lighthouse, by chilly moonlight, perching on rocks that shone bone white when swept by the beam. Little stick figures were waving madly all around the base of the tower, disappearing and reappearing with every swell of the ocean. The three of them kicked and fought until they got close enough for a wet, bedraggled Tom and Mr Penrose to heave them onto the steps.

Cora coughed up the wriggling throatfish, spitting it into her palm and dropping it into Lord Gendal's outstretched hand. He placed it in the leather bag, not seeming to mind the trail of saliva at all, as she gasped for air. Exhausted, they wanted to collapse in a heap, but there was barely room to stand and the waves lapped greedily around their feet, ready to drink them down if they slipped.

'What the bloody-?' came a gruff shout from above.

They stared up to the top of the lighthouse, where a bearded man stood behind a rail holding a lantern, its feeble glow colouring his face for a moment, before the massive lamp behind him cast him into silhouette, then he was illuminated again, pink above a brown beard, then printed black again, the glare making them squint.

'Where'd you all spring from?' He sounded more bewildered than angry. The next time the huge lamp flashed, he'd disappeared, light flooding the place he'd been standing. The glow of his lantern spilled from a window near the top of the lighthouse, then from one halfway up, before he appeared at the bottom, peering at them in amazement, unable to exit the lighthouse because so many shivering, dripping bodies were crammed onto the small scrap of rock.

They stared at each other, without speaking. Cora could hear her ragged breath echoing the wind and the shushing rise and fall of the sea, until Eseld asked 'may we come in?'

Dumb with astonishment, the lighthouse keeper merely nodded, standing back to allow them to come inside, where the briny air was replaced by smells of burning whale oil, pipe smoke and fried onions.

Steps ran up the inside wall, spiralling round and they filed gratefully past the open-mouthed lighthouse keeper, wiping the water from their faces and leaving wet prints, which gleamed in the glow of the lantern.

Cora kept her hood up, head dipped to hide her beakish, feathered face. She lifted her eyes just enough to glimpse a circular room, with a small fire and an inviting rocking chair.

'Hold it!' The lighthouse keeper managed to find his voice again. Only now it was a shriek, as he lifted his quivering lamp towards Meriwether's grey face, yellow eyes shining, the wound in his cheek still hanging in bloodless rags, revealing teeth.

The lighthouse keeper screamed, almost dropping the light in his terror. 'G-get out!'

He shoved Meriwether away from him.

'But they need rest,' Meriwether protested, 'shelter, please, just for a night- we'll wait outside, but at least let the humans-'

'The *humans*?! Get away! Be off with you! Devils, goblins, mermen, whatever you are! Get back down to Davy Jones!' It was then that he caught sight of Lord Gendal. If he was frightened before, he was terrified now. He pushed and thumped and whirled his lantern, which smashed against the wall, plunging them all into blackness.

'We're going, we're going!' Eseld shouted, barely audible over the lighthouse keeper's cries and the waves that had grown angrier. Rocks glinted in the moonlight, sharp and foaming as the teeth of a rabid dog, as they stumbled miserably back out onto the precipitous ledge. The sea rose in great, black peaks, the spray flashing white in the glare of the lighthouse beam. Wenna commanded everyone to swim for the island and she bravely stepped out, plunging through the black air into seething water.

Her head bobbed up, visible only for a moment, arms flailing as she tried desperately to propel herself forward, but she was thrown like flotsam in every direction and the others could do nothing but stare, in shock.

With a monstrous roar, the lighthouse keeper charged the crowd with all his strength, shoving them off the edge and they crashed into the roiling surf, thrown helplessly against the rocks, barnacles ripping their skin until it ran with blood.

Cora was above the water, always about to hit it, to tumble headlong into the furious surf with all the rest. Only she didn't. She slapped her arms instinctively against the air, holding back her fate, except they weren't arms any more, they were wings, beating wings, thumping forwards against wind that had turned into something solid, something she could push against.

She tried to reach down to catch the flailing hands of the desperate crowd but she couldn't. Her fingers wouldn't grip, they remained stubbornly splayed as though they'd never been human at all.

Her boots grazed the frothy peaks, which leapt and sank and leapt again, showering her with cold spray as she tried to get people to grab her ankles.

The moonlit face of the lighthouse keeper was white as death. He fell to his knees, shaking all over, 'banshee!' he cried. 'Hag! I ain't a-feared!' then he stared past her and scrabbled to his feet in some kind of fresh horror.

'Help them! Throw a rope!' Cora screamed in return, the wind whipping her words away. 'I'll- I'll curse you all your days if you don't!', but he'd stumbled inside and slammed the narrow door.

Thrashing wildly, she tried again to guide her feet towards the grasping hands, but they were snatched away by the current as soon as they got a hold. Her awkwardly laced boots and stockings were torn off as people tried to grab on, her black-clawed toes snatching hopelessly at their fragile fingers, but it was no use. The storm grew worse and the din of the waves sounded more like screeching as she was flung in a helpless spiral, her back crashing against the cliff-face, knocking the breath out of her.

But the screeching noise wasn't the wind.

Hundreds, no, thousands of birds were flying towards them. Even in the chaos of the storm, Cora could clearly see that they came not from the sky, but from the sea. By flashes of lighting, gulls, puffins, razorbills and even peregrine falcons were shooting up like arrows from the crests of waves and wheeling around in great clouds, diving down towards the drowning people. They grabbed cuffs, fingers, hair, ears, anything they could, before rising in great flapping mass, taking the spluttering cargo up with them. Flabbergasted, the battered and half-drowned were yanked from the jaws of the sea and dragged through the air, water falling from their bodies as they were carried higher and higher.

Scrabbling desperately for a hold on the rocks, Cora watched with no breath at all as everybody was carried away, a hundred frantic wings clustered around each exhausted figure. What about me? She would have screamed, but she knew why they'd left her. They assumed she could control her freakish dimensions, but she couldn't, could she? She might have hovered a bit before, but she couldn't actually *fly*, surely?

A wave snatched her in a giant fist, plunging her down, down into the black water, turning her over until she didn't know which way was up. Her legs were tangled in cloth and fur, binding as weeds. Saltwater flooded her mouth and nose until, with a massive effort, she unfolded her wings to their full extent, beating the cruel water around her, forcing it down, crushing it beneath her and breaking the surface at last, gasping air and raining diamonds as she shot straight up into the starry night.

She caught up with the others easily, but it was a struggle to slow her pace to match theirs, without dropping alarmingly low. She was shivering violently, even as her lungs and chest muscles strained with effort, but deep down a warmth was kindled, her heart was a single, glowing coal, and the shaking calmed to a tremble, then a thrilling hum. She could fly!

The birds didn't look magical, their eyes were as cold and unfocused as any she'd seen pecking for scraps after market day, as they soared through the moonlit sky towards the spreading bulk of the Isle of Wight. Somehow, though, she knew they'd come because she'd called them; not with her conscious mind, but with her heart. She'd conjured them from their hiding places with a connection she'd had, without knowing it until then, ever since Eseld had regrown her from the bones of one of their own. For the first time, Cora started to wonder if she might be powerful. As if Wenna might have been right to believe in her. As if, perhaps, she could make a difference after all. And the thrill of such a notion was as glorious as the wind rushing over her feathers.

The waves looked almost harmless from a distance, the terrifying surf delicate as lace, sliding over the rocks as if they were caressing them. They flew beneath the real, glowing moon which seemed fuller and brighter than it ever had, after the replica below. They soared over cliffs and sandy bays, isolated farms and snowy fields, barred with dark hedgerows. The few towns were scattered with lit windows and thin streams of chimney smoke, telling them the hour must be late. Dawn would soon come and people were getting up.

Cora was almost disappointed when the birds began to descend towards a little beach, for she'd found she could glide and slip between pockets of air that had a texture and a landscape all of their own. For a moment, she longed to fly back up into the glorious, swooping weightlessness. On the ground, she felt ungainly and bent again, her legs too short, her feet the wrong shape, but everybody else was overwhelmed with relief, gratitude knocking them to their knees to grip handfuls of muddy sand, like shipwrecked mariners, as the waves grasped the shore and fell away, over and over again, as if it didn't want to let them go. They crawled and staggered away, over the shingle, out if its reach.

The birds left as swiftly as they'd arrived, and the bedraggled company watched them go, slipping back down into the water as mist spread across the shifting surface, touched with grey dawn.

Everyone was scratched and battered, some retched and coughed water, but no bones seemed to be broken. Wenna had grazed her forehead, hands and both elbows, but she resolutely led them, small and shaken as she was, to the huddle of trees, so that they could collapse, undetected.

'Where did they come from?' Cora asked nobody in particular, staring at the silky waves.

Yestin was looking at her strangely. 'What do you mean 'where did they come from?' If you didn't call them, who did?'

'I can't even speak to birds,' Cora replied, caught between fear and wonder, 'let alone call them.'

'They weren't ordinary birds,' Wenna was firm. 'Among them, guiding them, were the keepers.'

Cora looked to Tom and Eseld, who were wiping water from their faces and wringing out their hems. 'Keepers?' she said. 'Aren't they the ones what kept Morgelyn in prison? Just looked like ordinary birds to me. Why don't they just catch her again? If they did it before?'

'It wasn't them that caught her,' Eseld squeezed

her bun, making water bulge and run between her fingers. 'They guarded her. Bird magic is complicated, much too old for Morgelyn, or any of us, to understand. They never come into the world, not down below and especially not up here.'

'We'll talk about it later,' Wenna closed the subject, 'when there's time. Those of you who can sleep, do so while you can. And stick close together for warmth. I know you're freezing and soaking wet but we can't risk a fire.'

A few were gathering sticks and they stared, miserable and momentarily defiant, before dropping them again.

'If we are successful, you'll be fed and warmed soon enough.' Wenna pulled her blackstone from her sodden pack, wiping droplets off its surface.

'Morgelyn sent that storm,' she said, to Eseld and Cora. 'The illusion of it anyway. While I was in the water I could feel her grip tightening, my fogging spell growing weaker as she scraped away at it...' she trailed off, looking young and out of her depth. 'You called those birds Cora, the keepers heard you and they brought them,' she said, earnestly. 'but we mustn't waste a second. We have to take our chance and get to Victoria before Morgelyn sends something else, or we all catch pneumonia. First I must concentrate. I need to re-seal the rifts she's made.'

Cora nodded, peering through the trees to try and spot the famous Osborne House, but it wasn't light enough and the mist had thickened. The royal family was vast, Cora had heard. At least twenty children, each surrounded by twenty servants who fed them sweets coated in gold leaf, cinnamon and ground sugar.

'Don't believe everything you hear,' Wenna said, fondness softening her agitation for a moment. 'Now, we've arrived at a difficult time for her majesty, she lost her mother and her husband less than eighteen months ago and the grief is said to be keen.'

'After all this time?' Cora raised her eyebrows.

'It ain't long, Cora,' Eseld remarked, taking up fistfuls of her skirt to wring it out.

'The house is still in deep mourning' Wenna continued. 'Our request, our explanations, even our existence is probably going to be met with hostility.' In Wenna's mind, Cora saw shadows of the lonely rocks and the terrified fury of the lighthouse keeper. 'The main thing is that we get to her majesty herself. I have heard she is open-minded and intelligent. With a generous heart.'

Cora couldn't help recalling Wenna's advice against believing everything you hear.

'Anyone we encounter is bound to overreact, but there's nothing we can do about that. We must hope they see us as a court in exile and accord us the appropriate respect.'

After an awkward silence, Eseld suggested that she could pretend to be a servant, pointing out that there must be dozens she could hide amongst, especially if she stole a uniform from the laundry.

'That might get you inside, but why would they listen to a servant?' Bronnan murmured. 'You'd be thrown out without getting anywhere near her.'

'It's a good idea in theory,' Wenna added. 'But if any subterfuge was uncovered, they mightn't trust us when we told them the truth. Our appearance must be our advantage. It backs up what we say about the parts of Britain she doesn't know about.'

'Our appearance didn't help before,' Cora pointed out. 'At the lighthouse, he thought we were devils. Called me a banshee.'

'They're bound to be more educated than that idiot,' Tom said.

Meriwether raised his eyebrows. 'Let's hope so.'

'So, that's what we'll do. Approach calmly, visibly, in an honest and unthreatening manner, by the front entrance.' Cora could tell Wenna was trying to sound more certain than she felt. 'We'll wait until the sun's fully risen.'

'Why?'

'Because everybody's a little less reasonable when dragged from their bed.'

After another hour or so, the sun had dried their hair a little, matting it with dried salt. It had warmed the colours too, but not the air and thick, gold-tinged snow muffled everything, crunching steadily under their feet. The only other sound was the sighing hush of the sea, as the seven shivering figures walked from the little bay up towards the house. The cold bit deep into Cora's damp flesh, as a yellow building rose ahead of them, out of the mist, like a castle in the clouds. Its design was so unusual, so un-English, with square towers and row upon row of narrow, arched windows that Cora was worried they'd got the wrong place. 'Are you sure this is it?' she asked.

Wenna patted her blackstone in her bag. 'Positive.'

It was enormous, with balconies, balustrades and fountains. Cora had never seen a bigger house, except for Greenacre. The main entrance and many of the windows, all shuttered, were hung with black swags of fabric, rimed with frost. Beneath the portico, on the front door, black crepe was tied with white ribbons in a wilted rosette, a macabre cousin to a Christmas wreath.

The first fountain they passed held a statue of a boy, leaning against a huge swan with outstretched wings. It must look beautiful in summer, Cora thought, but that morning the boy's hand, meant to shield him from a sunlit shower, held only snow and shadow.

A shot cracked the sky, jarring their bones.

Terrified, they looked up and around to see who'd fired. A bearded man in a thick jacket and swinging kilt sprung from behind a tree, a rifle at his shoulder, pointing straight at Wenna's head.

Bronnan reached for her missing dagger, Meriwether shoved himself in front of Wenna and Eseld scrabbled for her glyph.

'Oot the way!' the gruff man barked, shoving Meriwether with the butt if his rifle and snatching Eseld's glyph, breaking the string.

'We mean no harm!' Wenna's voice came from behind Meriwether's sodden greatcoat.

'We wish only to speak to her majesty on a matter of grave national importance!'

'You'll speak to nobody,' he hissed, and it was then that Cora realised he wasn't afraid.

He didn't stare at them in horror or accuse them of being monsters or devils. Which could mean only one thing.

'Aye,' he growled, no breath to form a cloud as he read Cora's mind. 'A've replaced a fella by the name o' John Brown. Foolish old woman made a pet o' him. She's no idea he's a-rotting under the yews.' With a nasty grin, he pushed the rifle towards

Meriwether's face. 'Now, ah dunnae want tae have to clean up this pretty path, nor carry your bodies, so you'll oblige me by walking over here, under the trees, so I can tidy you away nicely, once it's all over.'

Afterwards, Cora was unable to explain why they obeyed. It might have been the shock at encountering a ghost in such a place, or their exhausting journey or the raw cold clawing through their sodden clothes or simply the stark fear that this was it, *this* was how it ended. She couldn't have explained why they walked, meek as lambs, before his rifle, without even putting up a fight. Even Bronnan, whose fiery nature never dampened, seemed to have sagged.

All at once, the tramp of boots on snowy gravel heralded a group of soldiers, running towards them. Instantly, the ghost of John Brown scuttled around the group to change the direction, as if he'd always been herding them towards the house.

Their leader called 'halt!' before muttering 'what the-'

'What are they then?' murmured one of the men.

'Foreign. That's what,' replied another.

'Silence in the ranks!' called the one in charge.

'Ah've got it all under control, lieutenant,' said the ghost of John Brown. 'Ye've no need to bother yerself. I'm after sending a boy for the local constabulary.'

'Nonsense, Brown,' came the clipped reply from within a bushy black moustache. 'This is entirely out of your jurisdiction.'

As the two men started to argue more vehemently, and words such as Sassanach gobshite and skirt-wearing monkey were bandied about, Cora noticed Lord Gendal slipping away.

Just as John Brown's ghost shouted at the captain to 'away and boil yer head!' she saw Lord Gendal disappear, slipping to the ground in the form of an eel, his glassy globe lying upside-down, rocking gently, half full of seawater, on the grass.

Cora took a careful step backwards and slowly, slowly managed to hide behind the fat trunk of a nearby yew tree. Knowing he wouldn't be able to breathe without it, she reached over the roots to grab Lord Gendal's orb, pushing it into her bag with difficulty, her long, feathery fingers refusing to co-operate.

'Good girl!' Wenna said, directly into Cora's mind, as the tramp-tramp of feet died away, as everyone else was taken into some kind of custody. 'Follow him!' Wenna added. 'Help him get in!'

Cora waited until they'd gone, then scanned the snow for the slithering trail. She spotted it quickly, despite the fog, and followed it as it diverged from the scuffed prints of the soldiers. Lord Gendal had sliced a narrow, curving stripe in the snow, frosted grass in the cut. Keeping low, Cora followed the track, which looked as though someone had tried to ride a boneshaker and struggled to keep their balance, until she heard a deep, rattling cough. She froze, ducking as quickly as she could behind the low balustrade.

Between the posts, she saw a boy and an old man in rough, gardeners aprons, each wearing black bands of mourning cloth around their upper arm. They were wheeling barrows along the path. The hoarse voice of the old man was frequently interrupted by fits of coughing and, occasionally, a high, clear question from the boy. The rumble of the wooden wheels grew louder and louder. There was nowhere to hide. The thin trail carved by Lord Gendal disappeared around the right side of the house, but there wasn't time to follow it.

Cora made a swift decision. After a brief run up, she whacked her wings towards the earth. Her feet lifted, then fell, wing tips grazing the snow and scattering it in puffs.

She flapped harder, running faster, until her feet lifted again, just before the boy and the old man appeared round the corner. She zig-zagged clumsily up into the air, the weight of the orb sloshing in her bag and throwing her off balance, but she managed it, and soon landed awkwardly on the roof.

Both the boy and the old man kept their noses buried deep in their scarves, snow-flecked caps pulled low over steaming breath. They didn't notice the scars and ripples in the whiteness at their feet, just trundled their barrows through it, their minds on their tasks.

Up on the roof, the wind was stronger. Cora scanned the ground, trying to find the trail again. She stretched out her wings to dry them, making an 'M' shaped shadow on the snow, and the wind blew her softer feathers back on themselves, making her shiver. She was grateful for the warmth lent by the downy fluff that had sprouted around the roots of the sleek, shinier feathers, which looked as though they'd been stitched from mourning silk.

Much of Lord Gendal's trail had disappeared and the freshest part was rapidly blurring, as new flakes fell. She saw a blackish green streak in the snow, clear as paint on paper. Sparing no thought for being seen, she dived like an arrow toward the snakish form, which was beginning to fleck all over with white. He was frighteningly still as she grappled in her bag for his globe, almost spilling its precious contents as she lifted his bony head, fighting the urge to recoil at the sliminess of his skin, and poked it into the glassy ball.

She gazed through the wobbly surface of the greenish water, where his eyes remained firmly shut.

Her breath formed ragged clouds and the seconds stretched, until his liquid black eyes suddenly grew wide, as though in astonishment. He blinked rapidly, his dried lids translucent once more, the colour and texture of seaweed. Tiny needles of teeth appeared on the edges of his long, narrow jaw. His eyes were just as cold and unreadable as they'd been in his other form, and Cora wished she'd been more observant; that she'd bothered to learn the gestures Wenna and Bronnan had used to communicate with him.

But she needn't have worried. As soon as he'd regained enough strength from breathing inside the globe, Lord Gendal slithered out. Glancing quickly at her to check she was watching, he slipped straight up a drainpipe.

Cora marvelled at his cleverness, wishing she could follow, and his bravery too, for he could easily die from lack of water and if he encountered anyone, he wouldn't be able to tell them that he wasn't a threat. If a housemaid spotted him while she was lighting the fires, she'd take him for a snake and batter him with her poker or behead him with her shovel. She imagined that his plan was to transform once inside and to open a window for her. But which one? She flew up and managed to hover. It started snowing, the air filling with so many rushing flakes that anyone glancing out would struggle to see her. But somebody would; somebody was bound to.

All of a sudden, a dark rectangle appeared in the blizzard. Lord Gendal had pulled up the sash of a frosted window and thrown out his arms. He nodded to her and, for a second, despite the driving white, she glimpsed something like encouragement in those black, liquid eyes before, starved of oxygen, he slumped and tumbled out onto the balcony.

Cora rushed towards him. He'd started to transform, but only in part. His whole body had narrowed and shrunk; his legs were fused and his features elongated, but he'd lost consciousness before he'd finished. Sweaty with panic, she grabbed him, but he was heavier than he looked and the fabric of his clothes had become smooth as eel skin, so there was nothing to hold onto.

Using all her strength, she managed to flap her wings against the weight, to lower him as gently as she could to the ground, where his orb was half buried, and pushed it onto his head. She flew up to the window, heart hammering, and clambered inside with no idea which room it would be. She hoped for a coal store or a boot room; somewhere she could gather herself before she set out to find the queen.

She'd never thought of herself as particularly poor, but the scale of everything, the hushed quality and richness of each detail made her feel grimy and ragged. The size of the room and the arrangement of chairs and chaise longue suggested some kind of parlour, but a grander one than Cora had ever seen.

With a sinking, thrilling sort of shock, she realised

that behind the chaise longue stood an enormous bed, with an opulent, fringed canopy.

Beneath the coverlet, a lump moved.

Cora didn't dare breathe.

Beside the bed was a chair holding an oil portrait of a man, who looked very similar to the picture of Prince Albert on a cup back at Fish Row. Across the pillow was a gauzy ribbon and a few wisps of fine, brown hair. Cora started shaking. She didn't think it would feel like this. She didn't think she'd be the one to actually do this. There was no way she *could* do it. She'd be hauled off and hanged for treason before she could say a word.

She caught the eye of a cherubic child in a small painting and felt as though he was accusing her of being a coward. She thought of Gwen, Curnow and all the others who'd fallen victim to Morgelyn's cruelty, and she stiffened her resolve, physically pushing her shoulders down and pressing her lips together to stop them quivering.

She pulled the window closed and, once the wind had been silenced, heard the gentle snores of Queen Victoria, the woman who most of the world called 'majesty'.

She folded her wings as well as she could, to hide them beneath her tattered sleeve and cloak, both of which glittered with frost. It began to melt and drip on the thick carpet as she tiptoed past a sumptuous fire, to see an astonishingly ordinary face upon the pillow, surrounded by a frilly nightcap, with lace and ribbons and hair escaping a sleep-fuzzed plait to spill over the pristine linen.

What should she do? Wake her? Wake the queen of most of the world and send her shrieking for her maids? A soft voice in the back of her mind was trying to guide her. She closed her eyes to blot out the extraordinary sight, so that she could listen, despite the blood thundering in her ears.

'I've sent her a dream, Cora,' Wenna was saying. 'I've shown her what will happen if she doesn't act. You were in her dream, as was I and the others. Go ahead, wake her gently, she will be startled, alarmed even. But she should recognise you.'

'I can't.' Cora's plea was silent, ashamed.

'You must,' was the firm reply.

Cora reached out a wing, her spidery fingers at its tip like the angel of death, as they alighted on the queen's shoulder and, very gently, rocked it.

This was probably a gross breach of etiquette, but she had no choice. Any speech might wake whatever servants slept nearby.

'Your majesty?' Cora whispered, leaning close. Her nerves were wound tight, liable to snap. She was more aware of her strange, feathery face than she'd ever been, when the queen opened wide, drowsy blue eyes to blink.

'Your majesty,' Cora dipped into a wobbly curtsey.

When she rose again, Cora saw the grief descend as clearly as if a veil had been drawn over Victoria's face. Sleep had smoothed the lines that sorrow had carved, but those few precious seconds of forgetfulness, the only comfort of the bereaved, quickly evaporated. She bore the weight of loss once more, as her gaze slid to the portrait perched on the chair. Cora understood that her own presence, unexpected and bizarre as it was, took up far less space in the queen's consciousness than the absence of her husband.

This wasn't what she'd expected at all. She'd anticipated shock, revulsion, alarm, but not this.

'Your majesty,' Cora said quietly, 'Please, do not be afraid. I mean you no harm.' She swallowed. The queen remained silent. 'I'm afraid I bring grave news.'

The queen's eyes remained locked, painfully, upon Albert's portrait, as if she wanted to look away, but couldn't bear to; the way someone might stare at the burning of their childhood home. For a second, Cora wondered if the lady had grown disordered in her mind. Cora had come across similarly stricken faces during her days as a medium, but rarely anything as extreme as this. Most of the mourners she saw expressed their grief with contorted faces, sliding tears and angry gestures. Sorrow leaked from their eyes, paining them as they spoke, and spoke and spoke of their loss, but this was a face that'd had all the life wrung from it, all the hope drained, so that even the appearance of a monstrous creature like Cora wasn't enough to vivify it.

'Your majesty,' Cora tried again, 'did you...' It sounded too absurd. 'Did you have a dream last night?'

The queen blinked again, more slowly, as though she wasn't keen to open her eyes. When she did, she shifted her focus to Cora, and for the first time she seemed to notice her feathers, the beaky curves of her face and the curious, lashless violet of her eyes. Something like recognition flickered within the forget-me-not blue.

When she opened her mouth it seemed to take great effort. 'I did. I dreamed about you. And others too, but-' her brow creased, 'they didn't look like you. I recall a threat...' she trailed off into a sigh. 'But what does it matter?' she said, so quietly that Cora had to strain to hear her. 'Nothing matters now.'

'Forgive me,' Cora said, her skin prickling, 'my friends matter. Many have died already. We are at war.'

Cora heard distant movements in the house. Steps, a door opening and closing. Urgently, she tried again. 'Your majesty-'

'Stop calling me that.'

'Oh... er, Victo-'

'Ma'am.' The word was crisp as cracking ice. The queen wriggled upright, so pretty and petite that Cora had to shove thoughts of china dolls out of her mind, as Victoria reached for a silk bed jacket with pagoda sleeves and put it on, smoothing her plait and flipping it over her shoulder.

'This is *not* the way to do things,' she said sternly, looking older than her years. Around her head, Cora saw kings, marching armies, tattered banners and glorious parades, as though the queen was calling on her ancestors for the strength to steady her. Perhaps, Cora thought, she must appeal to the warrior in her.

'I heard, Ma'am, of an attempt on your life. I heard that a crazy fellow fired at you with pistols and you got away. You stayed calm and you got away.'

'My Albert,' her gaze slid to the portrait again, 'he steadied me. He held me and reassured me. But now I'm all alone.'

Cora was flooded with sympathy as, in the queen's thoughts, the ghostly image of a tall man appeared, sitting beside her, far more handsome than he was in his portrait. He folded his arms around her little shoulders and she leaned for a moment, eyes closed, into the filmy nothingness of his chest.

Cora felt more like an intruder than ever.

'Your majesty...'

Victoria held up a stubby finger.

'Ma'am,' Cora corrected herself, 'if I could explain,'

'There is no need.' Victoria gathered herself and Albert's ghostly form receded into mist, replaced with a hard, glittering crown. 'The dream was sent to me, was it not? Using some sort of voodoo? It felt wholly unnatural.'

'Well, not voodoo-' Cora stammered, 'not that but, I mean-'

'I am not intimidated by superstition or magic,' Victoria stated. 'There are more things in heaven and earth, Horatio, than are dreamt of in your philosophy.'

Cora was worried. Either she called anyone whose name she didn't know Horatio, or the queen really had lost her marbles.

'My Empire extends,' Victoria said coolly, 'from Samoa in the east to Canada in the west, Heligoland in the north to Antarctica in the south. I have been given extraordinary gifts from those vast tracts filled with primitive natives we are yet to fully civilise. Masks from the dark continent and shrunken human heads from the Amazonian aborigine. Weapons and amulets, trinkets and exotic powders from all four corners of the earth. So please, do not think you can shock me.'

Cora swallowed, trying to think of a way to phrase what she must say, which didn't sound insane. There wasn't one. 'Your m...-Ma'am, I fell down a hole and there was another... Another country down there. I know it sounds ridiculous...'

'No more ridiculous than sailing over the sea and finding new worlds there, I'm sure,' Victoria replied calmly. 'The voodoo dream was clear about one thing. You need my help, yes? An army?'

'Yes,' Cora nodded, so relieved she could cry. 'Yes an army, that's what we need, so we can fight Morgelyn and free the slaves.'

'Slaves? How barbaric. How American. But you must understand, Clara, that the British army is fully occupied already. They put down minor rebellions and uprisings every day. The expansion of the British Empire is a slow process, hard won. People don't know what's good for them, you see.' She shook her head. 'Where did this Morgelyn person get her slaves? Jamaica? The Ivory Coast?'

Cora blinked. 'I don't know where them places are, Ma'am. I never been up north, or Wales or anywhere like that, but she's been getting them from all over. Broadpuddle, Underwood, Redhill, Cornwall-'

Victoria's mouth fell open and pools of pink appeared on her cheeks. '*Cornwall?* Do you mean to say she has been taking *English* subjects and forcing them into-' she ran out of breath and emitted a very un-queenly sort of gurgle. 'I don't believe it! I shall summon Viscount Palmerston immediately, and Augusta, that is, Lady Bruce, too.' She snatched up a bell with her little fist and rang it with a surprising violence.

A maid appeared, dressed in mourning black bombazine, gliding soundlessly towards the royal bed, head lowered, until she spotted Cora and staggered backwards in horror, tripping over a potted aspidistra with an undignified display of stockings and petticoats.

'Pull yourself together girl,' Victoria rolled her eyes. 'And fetch us our breakfast. Now, I would be dressed. Clara, you may wait for me through there.'

Cora sank into a half-bow, half-curtsey, shooting the maid an apologetic look for alarming her, which only made it worse. The maid scuttled away as Cora went through the door Victoria had pointed at, and found herself in a neat little dining room. It was still larger than the whole ground floor at Fish Row, but, compared to the opulent bedroom, it seemed small.

The snow outside the window was falling more gently now, like dust motes floating, weightless, in sunlight. Cora sat on one of the chairs, unable to think about where she was or what she was there for, without sweating and setting every feather trembling, while servants brought silver tureens to place upon the table, trying not to stare at her. Her smiles weren't returned, but one of the younger ones bobbed a curtsey, to which Cora had no idea how to respond.

She guessed that they were used to seeing foreign dignitaries, or at least pictures of them, with unusual features and clothes, so had probably decided she was from a distant land where everybody had a feathered face.

After what felt like a dreadfully long time, a middle-aged gentleman appeared. He had a prominent lower lip and, behind his balding pate, possessed a great mop of curly grey hair, all sticking forwards as though he'd been standing with his back to the wind. He gave her a good stare, thumbs in his waistcoat pockets, then studied her from different angles, as though she was behind glass in a museum.

A tall, dark haired lady glided in, bringing the scents of bergamot and neroli oil. Everything about her breathed wealth and breeding, from her perfectly clean skin to her thick, glossy hair in its complicated arrangement, to her black silk gown trimmed with glittering jet and, most tellingly, the way she glanced about the room, giving the servants, who stood around the edges, still and silent as waxworks, the same assessing gaze as the food and the weather at the window.

The lady and the gentleman discussed current affairs, as if Cora wasn't there.

After what felt like an age, the door opened and Cora's heart jiggled uncomfortably beneath her ribs, not knowing what or who was coming next. A small figure appeared, wearing a black dress and a garibaldi jacket with military frogging. Her face was obscured by a black, crêpe veil, which was lifted by small, gloved hands. Cora let out a small gasp of joy to see Wenna's face appear, framed by sparse, white ringlets escaping a lace cap. Mourning, Cora realised; the perfect disguise.

Cora leapt from her seat to throw her arms around her cousin. With a soft pat on her back, Wenna managed to pull away and told her, silently, to be patient.

Victoria soon appeared, resplendent in inky silk, trimmed with little waterfalls of lace. Jet trembled at her ears, throat and wrists. She wore more jewellery, in fact, than Cora had ever seen on one person and the effect completely washed the little colour she had from her cheeks.

A footman appeared behind her with a strapped leather box, its buckles were large and looked very old. He placed it carefully on the table, beside Victoria's plate.

'First, we shall eat,' Victoria said.

Spiced kedgeree and devilled kidneys were served, along with thin, white toast, roasted chicken, bacon and pressed ox tongue.

The minister made a show of listening when the ladies spoke, Cora noticed, without actually doing so. He merely paused, flicking crumbs off his knee or cutting into a kidney as they addressed him, then continued with whatever dreary thing he was saying as though they hadn't spoken, hiding his rudeness with a liberal sprinkling of 'Ma'am's' and 'dear ladies'. It was a common enough trait of human nature, but Cora found herself disappointed, realising she'd expected more from such a high-born creatures as a prime minister.

Her thoughts kept straying to the box, wondering what could be inside, but hunger soon overtook her, making her stomach ache, so she ate as much as she could manage, though the rich, dead food tasted of grease and she knew it wouldn't stay inside for long. Her teeth, too, were becoming very tender, as though they were wearing away or shrinking back into her gums, which felt different. Harder, more bone and less flesh.

'What's in the box?' Cora asked Wenna, silently.

'A wonderful thing. You'll see, soon enough,' Wenna replied. And Cora saw the prime minister's wrinkled eyelid flicker.

Had she imagined it?

'Minister,' Cora said, directly into his mind, 'your breath could kill a badger.'

He glared at her, astonished, but just for a second.

A second was all it took. 'He's a ghast!' Cora shouted.

He sprang immediately to his feet, hand whipping inside his jacket. A footman jumped gallantly between the ghast of the prime minister and Queen Victoria, eyes round with fright. The ghast drew out a pistol and pointed it at the footman's breast. One of the maids sauntered to his side, all meekness evaporated, leaving nothing but cold hate.

'What do we do?' Cora asked Wenna, in silent horror.

'As you so *cleverly* deduced,' said the prime minister out loud, 'we can hear everything.'

He waggled the pistol with a dull rattle. 'We know everything. *She* knows everything. She's been watching your pathetic little adventure as an amusement. A diversion. A penny dreadful. Now we come to the final act.' The ghast of the maid walked over to the door to wedge a chair beneath the knob.

Victoria let out a short, strangled scream and Augusta sprang to the hearth, snatching up an ash-smeared poker. 'I don't know what's going on but, between us, her majesty and I have faced the horror of the birthing chamber thirteen times and lived through it! Forgive my vulgarity, Ma'am. So don't you *dare* take us for weak, feeble creatures.' She wielded the poker as if she was fencing, her eyes the colour of steel.

Wenna shot Cora a meaningful look, dropping her gaze to Cora's chest and quickly bringing it up again.

'What?' Cora said aloud, without thinking. Then she understood and she started to cough, blood spraying into her palm. She bent over, unbuttoning her collar and forcing her gagging reaction to the greasy breakfast to push the bundle of dried leaves upward, slimy with spittle and gastric juices, until it plopped out into her hand. She picked up a napkin and wiped her mouth. She hadn't a clue how to use it, but the ghasts weren't to know that, as long as she refused to think it.

'In my hand,' she told herself, and therefore the ghasts, 'I have the most powerful magical object in the world. I can use it. It's mine.'

She unwrapped the sharp, glassy object and held it up. Light slid across it in strange colours, as it does upon the surface of a bubble. Both the maid and the minister lunged towards her, their eyes bulging with greed.

The Merlinshard leapt up and twisted against her fingers, cutting fresh red lines among the healing scabs. Morgelyn's violent, invisible tugging grew stronger, until Cora was lifted clean off the carpet. Warm blood ran down over her feathers, but she held on firmly, telling it that it belonged to her, purely for the effect of those listening, to make it seem as if she knew how to use it, but it had a curious, marvellous effect.

The glass grew calmer. It was as if it had decided to trust her, to stay with her. She felt it fighting back against Morgelyn, becoming heavy in her hands and allowing itself to be held, no longer resisting as she closed her fist.

The ghasts' sneering expressions faltered.

Cora opened her sticky fingers to look at the blood smeared glass, which rose gently to balance on her palm, on its tip. It seemed to be beckoning her, reassuring her, giving her a strange new confidence as she held it up, to look through it.

Through the glass, everything was slightly distorted and tinged greenish red.

Impulsively, Cora lifted her other hand to look at her finger, hoping it would show her the pink skin she used to have. Instead, her feathered digit, which seemed bigger because it was closer to her eye, pushed the ghast of the prime minister over, without being near enough to touch him at all.

It swung into him like a battering ram and he smashed face first into the remains of his breakfast, breaking the plate and revealing the food hidden beneath it.

Cora was so astonished, she almost dropped the Merlinshard.

The ghast maid stared at him in alarm. Augusta took the opportunity to grab her by the throat.

Queen Victoria seemed to recover from her initial daze. 'Hold her firm, Augusta. William, go immediately to fetch John Brown. In dear Albert's absence, we must look to him.'

Cora and Wenna exchanged glances. But this wasn't the time to reveal John Brown's fate.

'You,' said Augusta, 'get those.'

It took Cora a moment to realise Augusta was addressing her. 'Me?'

'Those curtain ropes, girl, pull them off the wall and bring them to me.'

Cora hesitated, telling herself that this one couldn't be a ghast as well. But, just in case, she said directly into Augusta's mind 'your eyes are like currants in a suet pudding head.'

Augusta showed no sign of being insulted, so Cora yanked the silky tasselled ropes from their moorings and helped tie up the maid and the semi-conscious Prime Minister, whose nose looked badly broken.

'Why isn't he bleeding?' Victoria asked.

'It's a bit of a long story your majesty,' Wenna answered. 'All will become clear, I assure you.'

Chapter Twenty-three

Overland

A pink-cheeked ensign was despatched with his orders for Portsmouth. Cora watched his shining bay gallop into the snow, kicking white. The three ghasts were carted off in a Black Maria, its forbidding bulk sending a shiver down Cora's spine as it lurched in the wake of two mud-splashed cobs to the nearby prison.

The ghast pretending to be John Brown had upset Victoria terribly, spitting foul personal insults even as a soldier struck him repeatedly with the hilt of his sword, fuming at the lack of blood.

Victoria stared down at them from her bedroom window, a small woman, bowed with grief, but not broken by it. She let the curtain fall and was gone.

A fleet of coaches and carriages were assembled, many of which were bright and so new that the leather squeaked, others so old they had pale mould on the seats and woodworm in the chassis. They were soon trundling away from Osborne House, with an escort of foot soldiers, following a major on his glossy stallion.

Augusta had wanted to come, much to Victoria's angry bewilderment, but she obeyed her monarch and stayed behind.

Bronnan, Tom, Eseld, Meriwether, Wenna and Cora were squeezed into a closed coach that smelled of new paint. On Meriwether's lap, Lord Gendal was curled in eel form inside his water filled globe, eyes closed, resting after his ordeal.

The major rode ahead, the troops marching smartly behind. For the first time, Cora felt a surge of hope. They'd all been given dry clothes; castoffs put aside for the poor, which were far newer than what they'd all been wearing for years. Cora and the faeries were given mourning clothes, replete with veils for the women, so that they could hide their unusual features. Yestin, Meriwether and the other male faeries wore their scarves high and their hats low.

Cora hadn't wanted to part with the remains of the dress Meg had lent her. Stained, torn and wet as it was, with only one ragged sleeve, she didn't like to leave it behind, to be made into rags, until she imagined Meg's face when she discovered that bits of her old dress were polishing beeswax into royal banisters, or wiping dust from a princess's windowsill. She closed the door on the thought of the cottage, with its aching absences.

Once they were settled in the coach, with straw packed around their legs and travelling rugs on their laps, Cora concentrated on the warmth, that rare luxury, inching through her skin beneath a thick, quilted petticoat, woollen stockings and a dress and matching cloak of fine, black wool, trimmed with violet velvet. It had worn slightly thin at the elbows and the hem was frayed, but she'd never worn anything of such quality in her life. Eseld had helped her unpick some of the stitches at the sides of the bodice and, because the sleeves were of the full, draping kind, like a short cape from each shoulder, they just about accommodated her wings. Her bracelet had become so tight and uncomfortable she feared it might snap, so Eseld had untied it, threading it over and under Cora's feathers, instead of trying to fit on a wrist that wasn't really there anymore.

Because of their size, the spriggans agreed to dress as human children, in order to avoid attention. Some managed to find their fat petticoats and little sailor hats rather funny, but most found it humiliating and took no joy in it at all.

They bumped along winding lanes to the steady clop of hooves, Lord Gendal's orb water sloshing to the gentle rhythm between dark-thatched cottages and sprawling hedgerows. Eseld and Tom soon fell asleep, his head resting on top of hers. Steaming suffolk punches pulled ploughs across frosted fields, as though nothing was amiss in England, while Wenna consulted her blackstone.

'What happened?' Cora asked. 'How did you convince her? What was in that old, buckled box and where are we going?'

'So many questions,' Wenna smiled, but it didn't reach her eyes. 'We must be careful. It's impossible to know how much she's able to see or hear.' She spoke so quietly that Cora strained to listen, hairs prickling on the back of her neck, as if Morgelyn was just outside.

'The box,' Cora said, directly into Wenna's mind. 'On the table, in the queen's dining room. Did it have anything to do with us?' She noticed Bronnan glowering, 'Queen Victoria I mean, I know you're a queen too...'

'It doesn't matter, Cora,' Wenna answered. 'For one thing, you're my cousin and for another, you aren't from Underwood, so you're not my subject anyway.' Wenna gave Bronnan a meaningful look, until Bronnan turned to glare outside at the morning sky, where the trees parted to reveal drifting seagulls.

'In answer to your question,' Wenna said, still silent in case Morgelyn was listening, 'the box on the table was a curious object. It contained a very old book, one I never knew existed. It was handed down to Victoria upon the death of her uncle, when she acceded the throne. She told me it had passed from monarch to monarch, ever since the time of Edward the Confessor who, incidentally, knew your father.'

'I asked to look at it,' Wenna went on, 'but she said no-one ever set eyes upon it unless they wore an English crown. I did try to point out that I do have an English crown, it's just on the wrong head. But she had enough of a job believing our story, without accepting me as a fellow monarch. Her thoughts told me she tends to judge royal families by wealth and fame. In which case, in her eyes, I'm small fry.' She swallowed. 'Anyway, I glimpsed the corner of a page. It had a beautiful, coloured border, with gold leaf in the pattern, but she made sure I couldn't see the text. All she said was that it was a codex. She said that Underwood was in there, so she believed our tale. I don't know if she'd have put up more of an argument if it wasn't for her grief. She's like a sleepwalker. I don't think anything could penetrate her melancholy enough to shock her. Except when you told her about the kidnapping of white English people. That made her care.'

'But she won't face Morgelyn in battle,' Cora clarified.

'She's far too fragile. Hopefully, it won't last much longer, but the grief she finds herself in at the moment is quite debilitating. You saw that. And she isn't a battlefield queen. She promised a company of men, almost a hundred footsoldiers, under the command of Major Hawker, who's riding up front. We'll meet them at Portsmouth. I believe we have all the military support we are going to get now. The mission to Redhill seems to have met with success. A regiment of mounted bluecaps, along with a few mercenaries who'll fight anyone as long as they're paid, is returning south, under the command of the duke. And the king of the Murúghach, the duke's own folk, have pledged two hundred fighting men, who sailed yesterday morning from Rosslare. If the weather was on their side, they will have landed at Tintagel and set up camp by now.'

'Where are we going to challenge her?' Cora tried to sound braver than she felt. 'Is that the right word?'

'She moves around a great deal. I plan to strike at the very heart of the empire she's attempting to build around herself, which means taking the Great Oak back. If she isn't there at the time, then all the better.'

'Can't we just use magic to go there?' Cora asked. 'Do we really need to travel overland like this?'

Wenna nodded. 'Treleddan is the nearest thin place. Even if we could get below now, we'd still have to fight our way back through Greenacre and Broadpuddle to get to Underwood.'

'But there's a thin place in Broadpuddle. When we sent Nancarrow and the others,' she swallowed, remembering the eerie bubbles, 'to the in-between place, we must have used one.'

'Each allows travel in only one direction.'

'Why? That doesn't make sense. What's the point of a door that-'

'It's a law of nature,' Wenna explained. 'Gravity

only works one way doesn't it? It's like... I don't know, baking bread. You can't turn it back into flour and yeast can you? Or the ashes of a fire back into coals? If there was a way to travel more quickly, don't you think we would?'

Cora couldn't argue with that.

Wenna glanced down at her blackstone, which had begun to shimmer. She looked up to stare to the shuddering fringe of the curtain, making Cora frown, following her eyeline, in case an unseasonal wasp was crawling there.

She was about to ask Wenna if everything was alright, when Bronnan said 'shh. she's getting a message,' and Cora realised that a wraith-like image must be hovering before Wenna, just as Wenna had accidentally appeared before her in the attic.

After a few minutes, Wenna nodded and turned with a grave expression to those in the carriage who were still awake. 'I've received both good and bad news,' she said silently. 'Word of your escape has spread. There have been uprisings throughout Underwood and Broadpuddle and revolts in the mines, a few of which have been successful.

'Well,' Cora ventured, 'that's good isn't it?'

Wenna lifted heavy eyes. 'It is, yes. But war is always soaked in blood and every drop is a tragedy. Few have the scientific knowledge of Professor Polperro, no faery has been able to make fire since the curse and no living humans can do it as far as we know, except you and Eseld.' She swallowed, a shadow passing over her face. 'Morgelyn has reacted with curfews and public executions, trying to extinguish the spark. But this only fuels the fire. They've heard that we're coming. I've sent messages to those I trust to join us at the Great Oak.'

In the quiet that followed, they heard only the croaking of rooks and the gentle moos of cows herding together to be milked, over the steady clop of hooves and the rumbling of wheels. It began to rain and drops blew in thought the glassless windows. Cora tried to pull the curtain across, but she couldn't co-ordinate her long fingers properly, so Meriwether reached over and did it instead.

'How did you get away from John Brown's ghast and the guards?' Cora asked, hoping a change of subject would make Wenna feel a little less bleak.

'Morgelyn wasn't the only one who managed to sneak a spy into Osborne House,' she replied, with the ghost of a smile. 'Sir Gryffyn Flowerdew, one of my most loyal knights, managed to infiltrate Morgelyn's court and become a ghast of a guard at Osborne. Morgelyn expected him to work for her. But all the while, he was working for me.'

Cora was shocked. 'What happened to the real guard?'

'He took a bribe,' she replied. 'Gryffyn pinched enough gold from Morgelyn's, by which I mean *my*, vault beneath the Great Oak, for the real guard to buy a farm in Norfolk, where he moved with his family. Gryffyn told Morgelyn's court he'd gone to the mines. Nobody checked.'

'So, is he travelling with us?' Cora asked. 'Among the soldiers?'

'No, he slipped away on other business.'

Cora waited for her to explain, but Wenna simply reached out to move the curtain, letting in a slice of icy air. She gazed outside at the sky, which had turned from bone to slate and threatened more snow.

Eseld and Tom were still asleep, heads bobbing slightly with the movement of the coach, making Cora yawn. She was exhausted too, but had so many questions, she didn't want to waste the chance to ask them. 'How did I call the birds?'

Wenna smiled. 'Bird magic has been studied by far cleverer minds than mine and much remains a mystery. But one thing I do know is that they're descended from the enormous lizards that roamed the earth long before our ancestors. Dragons, some called them. That reptilian ferocity is still there, beneath the softness of feathers and gliding silence. Inside a bird's heart beats magic more ancient than anything we can understand. Eseld knew she needed a powerful creature to regrow you. A bird is the most powerful of all.'

Cora swallowed.

After a moment, Wenna opened her leather bag, which had mostly dried out, the leather stiff and marked with salt. She pulled out a small, bluish-grey book, wrapped in oilskin. One corner was swollen where a little seawater had got in and another was burnt black. She gave it to Cora, who stared at the text, which jolted with every pothole. It took her a while to sound out the words, running a feathery finger that looked more like a giant spider's leg beneath each letter. *Tricks with Glasse. A Discourse on what Might be Done with Mirrours by Merlin Ambrosius.*

'But, didn't he live hundreds of years ago? This book can't be more than fifty years old.' She checked the publication date inside and read *Barnicoat and Trelawny, Underwood 1804.*

'It's not the original. It's a reprint of a reprint of how who knows how many? The original was written by hand on vellum, but it's the words that matter. This is the last copy we know of. We managed to rescue it from the fires at the university. I wanted you to have it, Cora. I went back to the safe house in the sewer to get it while you were in the mine, hoping I'd get the chance to give it to you. It should tell you everything you need to know about the Merlinshard. It's a piece of an incredibly powerful mirror that your father made. It spoke the truth, whether people liked it or not. It was smashed by a vain duchess when it told her she wasn't as beautiful as her step-daughter, so she had her murdered.'

'That's horrible!' Cora blanched.

'It's a story,' Wenna added. 'Might not even be true.'

'Thank you,' Cora said, turning the pages. The print was dense and there weren't any pictures. It made her queasy when she tried to read it, rattling along. Self-conscious, she wished she could tease the meaning from the words, without having to whisper each sound under her breath.

*A note on the importance of **Truste Bonds**, or **Binds**, in the working of **Brittanick Magickal Glasse**. The method is not, as is oft suggested, a purely chymical one (See also **Bludde Bonds**, pp134). Like mead, stepony or good beer, a **Truste Bond** depends on regular exchanges of truste, to be taken over many monthes or, far better, yeers, so that the sowls are steeped together,* *as anisedes or elder flowers when they are set to damson wine. The flavour is suckd up by each to make the wine tayste all the better.*

Stopper welle with the swapping of truths, without the mouldey creep of judgment, as an ale-wife will carefully stopper her jar when concocting her brew, to keepe out the foul air. Do this and be always thrice and the truste will steep all the better.

Cora felt Bronnan's scorn and she pushed the book very carefully into her pocket, to study later. 'It's because of the jerking,' she muttered.

Bronnan shrugged.

'I'll read it when I can keep it still.'

Eseld let out a loud, guttural snore, which Cora found oddly reassuring. The sky flashed intermittent white between dark branches.

'Wenna, I wanted to ask you...' Cora began, when all at once they were thrown violently from their seats.

The horses screamed and a deafening crash came from somewhere ahead.

'What the hell was that?' Bronnan whipped her dagger from her hip.

They shoved the door open and jumped down into the mud to stare, horrified.

A chasm, deep and wide as a river, had opened up the earth, tearing the road in two. A tree on the opposite bank hung at a drunken angle, half its roots ripped out, those still embedded in the earth all that stopped it falling into the abyss. Behind the tree, Major Hawker had regained control of his frightened steed and glared, open mouthed, at the freak of nature yawning behind him, separating him from the coaches and his men.

Wordless, Cora and the others edged forwards. When they dared to look into the chasm, accidentally tipping small rocks that bounced and skittered down the newly ripped cliff, they saw the awful remains of the coach, horses and passengers in a broken mess at the bottom.

Not a single voice cried out from the wreckage, though they called down, cupping their mouths and shouting frantically for rope, until Eseld said 'it ain't there. It ain't there! It's one of her tricks!'

'It can't be,' Cora breathed, trying to think rationally. 'She killed the butterfly, so she must've killed the wolves too, to send their images. But even Morgelyn couldn't kill a chasm. She's done it for real! She's split the earth!' Cora gazed at the sky in dread, as though giant, clawed fingers might rip through the clouds at any minute.

'No, Cora. Eseld's right,' Wenna said, struggling to keep her voice steady. 'The more she kills, the more poisonous and powerful her magic becomes. It must be so toxic now, it's a wonder it hasn't killed her. This is an illusion, we must see through it.'

And, as they watched, forcing their hearts to understand what their brains knew, the coach began to rise, along with the muddy, icy ground, which rushed into the gorge like a flood after a drought, lifting the smashed detritus of the coach, horses and the passengers until they came to rest, no longer at the bottom of a chasm but on an ordinary, curving lane on the Isle of Wight, the tree planted firmly upright again as though it hadn't moved an inch.

Those who could see the reality swarmed around the coach, hoping for a survivor to groan, but there was no sound at all, save the wind. Terror must have made them expire, because their limbs cracked back into place just like the splintered pieces of wood, joining together again as though they'd never been broken.

The soldiers were completely bewildered. From their point of view, with no understanding of Morgelyn's illusions, Cora, Wenna, Eseld and the others had hurried out into thin air, feet running on nothing at all. The soldier's faces bleached white, greasy with sweat. One of them fainted. Another fired his rifle, to swift admonishment.

Eventually, after a lot of demonstration, persuasion and expletives on both sides, Wenna and the others managed to convince the soldiers and coach drivers that it was quite safe, solid earth. Some proceeded slowly, staring around and down with eyes that were wobbly at the edges, unable to comprehend, but managing to trust. Others struggled to control their anxious horses, which crabbed and snorted, refusing to trust the sensation of earth beneath their hooves, because it didn't match what they could see with their eyes. An aggressive whipping eventually made them gallop at breakneck speed towards the false image of the other side, making the coaches bounce and rattle, terrifying their occupants.

Exhausted by events that remained inexplicable for most, they proceeded toward the coast in a sober mood. The loss of those who'd perished weighed heavily and a few who'd known them remained to oversee the clearing of the road and the funeral arrangements. Cora felt guilty about abandoning the awful scene with such haste. But the unfortunate dead cannot be revived, she and Wenna silently agreed, while those in peril could still be saved.

They crossed the Solent by paddle steamer to Lymington, lodged overnight at a coaching inn and took the earliest train the next morning to Bristol, the soldiers commandeering two coaches while the civilians found places where they could. The mourning garb had its desired effect; nobody approached them and the veils allowed those without human faces to pass unnoticed.

Bristol was the biggest city Cora had ever seen and she hated it. Her anxiety about travelling by train for the first time was lessened only by the notion that at least she'd escape the crowded, towering buildings that seemed on the point of collapse, the stinking factories, butcher's stalls and animal dung and the grinding din of the carts and omnibuses clogging the streets and the clamouring hawkers who shoved pocket watches, meat pies and whelks under her nose at every turn.

Stepping onto the platform, she felt as though she could be alighting on a strange planet. It was very wide and far too big, surely, to have a roof? She felt dizzy. Sick with nerves and the sour smells of coal and engine oil, she gazed unhappily up at the monstrous engine, its chimney pouring smoke. The whole contraption was balanced precariously on narrow, metal wheels, and she jumped as the air was pierced by startling whoops from some kind of horn. Without any horses to pull it, it struck Cora as bizarre in the extreme. The engine had a train of metal boxes attached to it, enclosed on all sides with tiny windows. As she climbed in, Cora had to swallow her fear and trust Mr Penrose, who'd explained that hurtling at an ungodly speed in a great smoking, rattling snake, was actually reasonably safe. He'd been on one before and come to no harm.

Eseld wasn't keen either. She and Cora held hands, sitting as close together as possible as flags waved, whistles shrieked and the monster huffed, grunting fire and scraping metal against metal as it shuddered along the track.

Cora tried not to picture the drawings of derailed locomotives and explosions she'd seen in the newspapers, and she held on tight as they lurched westward, doing her best to blot out the noise and swallow her nausea.

Tom, however, was fascinated by the whole thing, as was Bronnan, and they stood at the window, side by side, watching the world flash dizzily by.

The tension was exhausting and Cora tried her best to relax, or to sleep, but when she finally managed to doze off, her dreams were crowded with unnatural grins and smoking ruins. When the heads she'd taken for busts started screaming she woke in terror, their voices becoming nothing more than the ghostly wail of the train.

When they finally arrived at Liskeard station, the light was fading and they walked the last few miles to Treleddan in the gathering dusk. Because the lanes were deserted, Cora tugged off her boots and stockings to allow her strange new feet to spread the way they wanted, with a long, clawed toe at the back and three at the front. The ground was an icy mix of mud and slush, which squished unpleasantly, making her shiver, but it was better than the hobbling crush of the boots. Rainwater shone in the channels carved by carts and in scattered, hoof-shaped puddles. Snow briefly filled the sky, driving at them at an angle, the wind catching in their capes and cloaks, making them billow even as they held them fast.

Once they reached the shelter of the woods, a starless night had fallen and the moon was fuzzy with cloud. They were surprised at the change in weather. It wasn't nearly as cold there and, at first, they were relieved, lowering their hoods and lifting their veils, until they smelled smoke.

It wasn't the bitter, coal waft of the town they could smell. It was sour, like burning paper. Instead of pressing on toward the waterfall and the thin place behind it, they peered through the lattice of oak and hawthorn that cut the snowy sky into jagged shapes.

The Treleddan factories weren't smoking.

From the ancient cottages, slumped against each other in the oldest part of the town, to the terraces of Fish Row, Paternoster Street and Brook Street, none of the chimneys exhaled so much as a wisp. Yet a stain hovered above the buildings, pouring from something other than the usual square brick throats. An odd, orange glow lit the smoky bellies of the clouds, as if the sun, which had set hours ago, was trying to rise at an unnatural hour. They sniffed the air, brows drawing together, and saw a flickering light in the marketplace, casting the church spire into silhouette. As they focused, their eyes and brains struggling to make sense of it, they glimpsed the source of the uncanny warmth; the flaming tip of an enormous bonfire.

'It's the books,' Wenna's eyes widened, her voice quavering. 'That's what she does first. She's taking the town.'

'What are we waiting for?' Tom was impatient.

'You want to run down into the middle of that, do you?' Yestin rubbed his nose with his knuckle. 'Think we'd last two minutes?'

'I say, what's the delay?' asked the major, his soldiers standing uncertainly in the dark of the trees. 'Thought we were going down to this underplace, what?'

'There's a fire,' Wenna replied.

'So?'

'She's burning the town's books.'

'Good God,' he murmured. 'Anyone who kills a man kills a reasonable creature. But he who destroys a book destroys reason itself.' He stroked his thin moustache.

'Milton's Areopagitica.' Wenna nodded, distractedly and, for a second, Cora saw a hazy image of the university near her head, the way it must once have looked.

The major stared at her in surprise.

She pulled out her blackstone. 'I'll send word to the others to meet us here. Merlin's cave at Tintagel is a thin place, so the Murúghach will try to get to Underwood through that, rather than come further inland.'

'Do the Murúghach have blackstones too then?' Cora asked, but Wenna was busily moving her hands around in the blue mist that rose from its surface, her eyes closed in concentration.

Cora could hardly bear to look at the town that had been her home. It's eerily smokeless chimneys made it seem abandoned, but the wind was blowing towards the wood and they heard occasional cries and savage laughter.

'We can't just stand here and *watch!*' Tom stuck his hand into his hair. 'I'd rather die.'

'What we need,' murmured Yestin, 'is a way of getting in, which nobody would expect. Something that'd catch them off guard.'

'You mean like a disguise?' Cora warmed to the idea. 'Put winter cloaks over the soldiers' uniforms and pass them off as ordinary men? Then-'

'Heavens woman!' squawked the major. 'Have you taken leave of ya senses? A British soldier doesn't *hide!* You'll suggest we carry branches over our heads like those Birnam woods chaps next. Damn foreign rot. Redcoat wouldn't be seen dead.'

Eseld and Cora exchanged glances.

'I don't know how much you've been told,' Wenna said quietly, 'but I'm afraid many of your soldiers will certainly be seen dead if you underestimate Morgelyn.'

'Who is he anyway? Doesn't sound like a turk name. Frenchie? '

Cora watched Wenna's heart sink. He didn't know anything. Wenna explained who Morgelyn was and his eyes darted towards the town and back to her face as he listened. 'So you see,' she finished, 'we cannot know what she might do. She possesses extraordinary magic.'

The major was silent for a while and Cora saw, in his thoughts, how little he thought of being instructed by women and how, like poor muddled Nancarrow, only for very different reasons, he saw their faces as human, twisted only by poverty and low birth.

'I've an idea,' Meriwether ventured. 'But it isn't going to be... pleasant.'

Chapter Twenty-Four

Treleddan

Everyone turned to Meriwether, to listen.

'What if we get in through the sewers?'

The major's face puckered in disgust. 'The *sewers?*'

'Go on, Meriwether,' Wenna ignored him.

'Well, it's as simple as that really. I was thinking if we found a manhole near the edge of town, we could climb down the ladder and pop up in the middle, take them by surprise.'

'And what then?' Eseld was unsure. 'I mean, how'd we overpower 'em? We won't even know who's a ghast and who ain't.'

'We will,' Cora put in, 'cause we'll hear their thoughts. What's that?' She squinted into the gloom, toward the road that approached the town from the other direction.

'What?' The others strained but couldn't see anything.

'Can't you see that straggly line? Looks like a few dozen ponies laden with some kind of cargo, with at least fifty soldiers!'

'Soldiers?' The major frowned, his features hardening.

Yestin and the others craned to see, but they all shrugged and shook their heads. Cora noticed Lord Gendal regarding her and, like so many times before, she wished she could communicate with him.

'Your eyes,' Wenna said. 'It's your eyes Cora, you're seeing as a bird does, better than any human or faery can. What are the ponies carrying?'

Cora squinted, struggling to believe that she was the only one who could see it. 'I dunno. Just side panniers, you know, big 'uns. There's sort of sacking over the top.

'Now, Cora, look hard at their faces, at their leader's face if you can. Watch it and think about it. I'll see your thoughts, and everyone else who can must do so too, in case we recognise the face.'

Cora obeyed and focused her newly clear gaze upon the stubbled face of the faery at the front of the procession, who wore a breastplate over a dark tunic and a helmet with a broken plume. Then she looked closer. He wasn't a faery. He was a man, leading faeries in the same uniform.

'Gryffyn!' Wenna gasped. 'Gryffyn Flowerdew! You remember he got into Morgelyn's court and became a ghast of an Osborne guard? He *did* it!'

'Did what?' Cora asked.

'We must move,' Wenna said. 'Now! We find a sewer, as Meriwether suggested, and-'

'Never!' snapped the major, turning away and striding towards his men, then vaulting neatly onto his horse. 'Company! Atten-shun!' They snapped upright. 'Company. Fix bayonets!'

'No! If we split up, my fogging spell won't reach you anymore! She'll know you're coming!' Wenna pushed the branches back and stepped out between the trees, staring after them in shock as they marched down the hill.

'Poppycock!' Major Hawker called, lightly.

Nobody else could speak, their throats were swollen with dread as they watched the soldiers march, a bugle spraying a staccato tune.

Cora scanned the sky for the awful crosses of the pterydons, but what floated up out of the town and drifted towards them was nothing of the sort.

They were like balls of fluffy cotton blossom, only grey instead of white. Each was roughly the size of a cauliflower, or a man's head. They looked as if they were blown by the wind but with a trajectory too precise for that. They stopped to hover, one suspended directly above every soldier. The steady, tramping rhythm of their feet began to break apart, as they looked at each other, uncertain.

'On!' shouted the major. 'Come on you maggots! Charge!' He lifted his sabre high above his head, at which point the ball above him unravelled, the spidery silk of it catching and tangling down his sword and all over his body, even as he slashed, binding his arms and head and horse until they crashed to the ground, the terrified whinny stopping abruptly as the threads bound the poor beast's mouth.

The six-legged, two-armed lump kicked and struggled. The soldiers scattered until each met the same fate and eventually, every single one lay tightly bound. Deathly still.

A cracking of branches overhead made everyone look round.

Goodwife Jenifry was growing, shooting up though the splintering trees into a gigantic version of herself. Her eyes held a terrifyingly vacant look, like the old man at Pendlestow, before he flung his victim across the marsh.

She let out a great, bellowing cry. 'Oo is 'un?!'

One by one, all the other spriggans started rising up, their features distorting, their shiny hair growing matted as old rope. Cora, Wenna and the others scrambled out of the way as massive fists smashed the undergrowth.

'Oo is 'un?' roared Goodwife Jenifry, the depth and volume of her voice making Cora's bones vibrate. 'Oo is 'un killin' Cornalls?!' she boomed. 'Oo is 'un killin' fae?! Is killin' no more spriggans!'

A deafening cry of 'Oo is un?!' went up from the other giants, some jumping and swiping at trees, which fell like wheat before a scythe, showering snow and water. They crashed out of the forest, stamping huge, muddy prints in the snow.

'She'll see you!' Wenna screamed, but they didn't listen.

'No! Wenna!' Meriwether tried to stop her as she burst after them, his hand brushing her curved belly as he begged. Keeping her invisible fogging spell around them, protecting their monstrous, lumbering bodies, she was vulnerable as a lamb among charging elephants.

Without hesitating, Meriwether rushed to her side, dagger drawn, followed by Cora, Eseld, Yestin, Bronnan, Mr Penrose and the rest. There was no time for sewers or cleverness or tactics. Their longer legs meant that the giant spriggans could cover the ground much faster, yet their disorganised zig-zagging and occasional collisions meant, as long as they could avoid getting crushed, the humans and faeries were just about able to keep up.

Blood pounded hot in Cora's ears as she ran, though the air rushed cold as it caught in her hood and blew it flat over her back. She struggled to keep pace on her awkward bird feet, so she beat her wings instead, rising into the air without thinking of anything but staying with the others and getting to the town alive. The grey, bound bodies were strewn across their path, the tangled thing that was Major Hawker and his horse like a lumpen statue, fallen from its plinth. The spriggans kept their gaze on the flames of Treleddan, crushing the limbs and heads of the soldiers under their enormous feet, making the runners shudder.

Cora could feel Wenna's concentration. The effort of keeping them all hidden came off her in waves. The strain was showing on her face as it juddered, appearing and disappearing with every beat of Cora's wings. Wenna looked more haggard and ancient than ever and Cora wished there was something she could do to share her burden, as the town edged closer.

Firelight spilled onto the snow in pools of bloody orange, spiked with black shadow.

Cora cursed herself for failing to read the cramped print of her father's book, which swam in indecipherable clumps before her as she tried to recall a fraction of it. She was a pretender. A fool about to die. The Merlinshard felt sharper, clogging the flesh inside her chest, as though someone was trying to yank it away and, as she flapped, it scraped violently upward, into the back of her throat. It must be Morgelyn, Cora fumed, sweat beading amongst her feathers. 'It's *mine,*' she thought, hard, heart swelling with venom at Morgelyn's greed. 'It's *mine,*' she swallowed the Merlinshard back down, pain slicing the inside of her neck. 'God damn you!'

At once, her throat felt full of heat. At first she feared a tide of blood had risen to spill from her mouth but it was a different kind of heat, a flood of energy, which spread from the Merlinshard up into her head, down through her body, out into her wings and beyond, into the night wind. It quivered, growing into a vast cloak over them all. She couldn't see it, but she could feel it as if it was her own skin, pulled taut.

Through it, the dark bricks of the town were ever so slightly distorted, as though she was seeing it through old, wrinkled glass.

Wenna glanced up, gaze narrowed. 'It's too much' she said, silently. 'This is my burden.'

'Let me,' Cora replied, astonished at the power coursing through her.

Conflicted, Wenna lowered her fogging spell, inferior as it was to the protection cast by the Merlinshard. Cora felt the air shudder and buck like reins as Wenna handed over control, but she managed to hold it steady. It took a colossal amount of focus, but she could do it. With a thrill of absolute clarity, she knew that Morgelyn couldn't see them. They were, to her, made of nothing but air and light. Without scent or sound. And it was with fierce glee that Cora flew on, no longer in defence, but in attack.

They thundered into the streets of Treleddan, crashing past the shuttered lamp-black factory, abattoir, tannery and dye works. The bakery flashed past and the chandler's shop, the grocer's and the silent pubs. Bun trays were abandoned, crumbs and currants ground flat into the cobbles. A cart had been overturned, its horse lying dead in its harness, the bluebottle crawling on its eyeball didn't fly up. It was oblivious to their approach. Cabbages, spilled from their sacks, were crushed by the spriggans, who smashed chimneys in their rage, filling the air with soot and brick dust as they caught strings of washing across their middles.

Doors and windows stood wide open. Net curtains flopped out over sills, soaked with rain. The hallways were a riot of opened drawers and trampled plants. A sampler embroidered with an alphabet lay muddied in a broken frame, covered in splintered glass.

With every sickening thud of her heart, Cora strained to hear pterydon wings and spot cottony spheres in the smoke. Determined as she was, fear made her eyes round as buttons.

The din the spriggans made was tremendous but, as they exploded into the square, they remained unseen. Unheard. The townspeople who hadn't managed to flee stood shivering and mute, a picture of misery. They'd been herded together like sheep on market day, coats and shawls flung haphazard over their nightgowns, feet bare on the icy cobbles. Some had managed to grab boots but not stockings and babies grumbled sleepily on shoulders.

Cora spotted Killigrew, her features crumpled with fear as she comforted a little girl. Selina was there too, fright and fury vying for control of her face. The grey-bundled bodies of those who'd tried to fight back lay around their feet in warning. Rows of faery soldiers with menacing expressions and drawn swords stood sentinel.

Cora hovered a little higher, to see further, and that's when she saw Morgelyn, as she truly was, for the first time.

A throne made of bones and stretched skin had been constructed in front of the town hall. Seated upon it was a hunchbacked figure, printed in silhouette against the raging flames. There wasn't a trace of the gentleness or prettiness that the glamour had cast back at the Great Oak. She was surrounded by faery courtiers and cronies, as she had been before, still dressed in their finery, but their plump beauty was gone too. This time the makeup was caked on withered, sunken faces, marked by the curse. Not one of them was smiling. They wore a look of grim, hollowed out exhaustion. Every time another book was thrown upon the fire, a joyless cheer went up.

The ghasts were easy to distinguish from the humans now. Their eyes had sunk and their lips seem to be disintegrating. They were huddled, discarded, sitting on the worn steps of the town hall, having served their purpose and been abandoned. Every now and then, one of them coughed a spray of grey and Cora remembered Wenna saying they couldn't live very long. She saw the deteriorating, stolen face of Nancarrow amongst them, and, though she didn't want to look, the ghast of herself too.

Victor Morningside sat upon a stool beside the throne, his face haggard in the firelight, his usually immaculate hair unkempt and thinning. A man, then, Cora thought. One who'd betrayed his kind. Was it guilt, Cora wondered, that was eating away at him, or had he simply been used and rejected too?

The throne creaked as the figure turned its head.

Cold sluiced through Cora's body. Dozens of snakes coiled where Morgelyn's hair should have been. They were all different sizes, some thick as an arm, others thinner than a pencil. A few hung, slack, as though dead down to her waist, but most were writhing, flickering forked tongues. The fire burned brighter. Colour slithered over poisonous patterns, glittering upon a circlet that she wore across her forehead, where a piece of glass, the same shape as the Merlinshard, caught light the colour of flame. Her throat was cluttered with necklaces, the beads of which Cora took, at first, for pearls until she realised that they were teeth of different sizes. Ivory, yellow, brown and black. She wore a long cloak and gown, which captured and dissolved the light in a way Cora had never seen fabric do, as it rippled over the skulls and shinbones of the throne to hang in an uneven hem. It was woven hair, she realised, appalled. Brown, black and red, with grey and blonde plaits down the centre of the bodice, looped around withered fingers for buttons. One of her hands was long, bony and pale, the other stubby fingered, purplish black and rotten-looking, with recent stitches attaching it to her arm.

The little band stood, transfixed, and even the spriggans ceased their chaotic vandalism and began to shrink.

A wheelbarrow of papers was tipped into the blaze by the faery soldiers, catching in great tongues of yellow. They had the thin, official look of birth and marriage certificates, deeds and bonds and contracts. Ledgers and boxes had their innards torn out and flung, high on the hot wind. So it wasn't just science and stories going up in smoke, Cora realised. Morgelyn wanted to destroy every trace of bureaucracy, banking, family histories, ownership of property and merchandise, dissolving the glue of information that holds society together.

As the fire consumed its latest meal, it burned brighter, revealing Morgelyn's face. Her eyes were high, small and black in a pale face. Her mouth was cracked and bluish white.

If she had any lips, they were too thin to see. Cora thought she might speak and for a moment she recalled that soft voice in the mirrored ballroom and the distant, mournful bell. And the way her muscles had felt like cushions against her bones. And a little of her old craving for glamour began to flutter.

A hard, rasping chuckle shot from Morgelyn's throne.

With a jolt, Cora gathered the fogging spell more tightly around them, just in time. Morgelyn turned. Cora realised she had no eyes at all. Just shadowy, shrunken spaces where they might have been. The snakes did her seeing.

'Pa!' came a cry from beneath her. Tom was elbowing his way between the shrinking spriggans.

Cora followed his gaze and saw a man huddled on all fours, his forehead on the ground. He was filthy, his feet bare and bloody.

'Why have you stopped?' asked Morgelyn in a cold, clear voice, with a hiss running underneath it. 'Do you not love her after all? Are you a liar, Piran Currigan? Do you love your wife?'

'I do,' came the croaked reply from beneath a sweaty mess of hair, as he lifted his head from the ground.

'Who told you to rise?' Morgelyn snapped. The snakes reared toward him, eyes glinting. And Piran hovered, beyond tears, lowering his face to the cobbles again, until her laughter cracked the air. 'A joke! Rise, Currigan, rise and dance some more, so we may know your love is true.'

With ragged clothes and haggard eyes, Piran

shuffled upright, broken glass catching the light around his feet as he danced a mournful jig, to the steady beat of drums and eerie flutes that hung in the air, playing themselves.

'Faster!' Morgelyn screeched and her cronies joined in, cackling gleefully as they threw bottles to smash around his toes.

Tom rushed forward, but Meriwether held him back. 'Wait!' Wenna was firm. 'We'll get him out of there, but with our heads, not our hearts.'

'This bores me.' Morgelyn's grin dropped. 'Time for another entertainment.'

'B-but-' Piran's lip wobbled like a child's, 'but you promised!'

'Patience, Currigan. Don't you trust me? The fulfilment of that promise is to be our next entertainment.'

He looked stricken. 'Entertainment?'

They watched, hardly daring to breathe, as a mouldy, muddy coffin was carried into the square by four faery guards. The nails were rusted brown and they carried it as if it weighed very little.

Tom rubbed his head, struggling to understand what he was seeing.

'She can't do it, Tom,' Wenna was firm, gripping his arm. 'It cannot be done, not even by the greatest sorcerers. Life, once fully gone, can never return.'

'What's she playing at then?' he hissed.

What happened next brought vomit to the back of Cora's throat. Sweat prickled hot and cold all over her body as Morgelyn stepped down from her throne, her cloak dragging across the cobbles, towards the wooden box. Piran had been frozen to the spot, but he lunged forward, collapsing beside the coffin, his arms flung over it.

'Careful,' Morgelyn said, quietly. 'That coffin is cheap. It's been in the ground three years. You don't want it collapsing in on her, do you?'

She spread her arms, muttering in the language Wenna and Eseld used for magic, but in her hissing voice it sounded very different, each consonant spiky with malice.

The sickly sweet, burned sugar smell filled the air, catching like smoke in Cora's nostrils. The snakes lifted their heads, coiling and striking at each other. The night clouds turned an ugly red and curled in on themselves, spiralling over the moon's face. The street lamps guttered and went out.

Nobody spoke. Nobody breathed. The only sound was Morgelyn's voice and the crackling blaze. The smell grew worse, growing more acrid until a thump came from inside the coffin.

Cora's scalp drew tight, lifting her feathery stubble. A scratching sound came from the underside of the lid. Piran started clawing at the nails that held it down. His voice quavered, hoarse and broken as a teenager's as he whispered 'Rosie? Rosie! It's me! I'm getting you out!' His head whipped around. 'Help me get her out!'

Tom's nostrils flared, his eyes filling with tears. Yestin and Mr Penrose moved to hold his arms, partly in comfort, partly in restraint as Piran dug at the nails and the scratching grew louder. A female sob escaped though the wood and Piran's nails bled smudges of red into the grain as he tried and failed to prise off the lid. 'Won't anyone help me? Get me a hammer! Or a crowbar!'

The townsfolk were horrified, yet moved. Was

this a miracle? Cora could see them thinking, didn't Christ rise from death? Or was it as unnatural and demonic an act as it was possible to behold? Would something horrible fly out and sink long teeth into them, sucking their blood from their flesh? Over the noise of their thoughts Cora heard a man in dusty builder's clothes call out 'I've a crowbar at home.'

'Nobody move.' Morgelyn flung up a hand and the builder, who was standing more than ten feet from her, smashed to the ground as though she'd punched him.

'Nobody interfere,' she said slowly. 'It will spoil the show.' She walked back to her throne, the longer snakes curling around her armpits and waist. A breeze stirred one of the skins hanging from the throne and Cora glimpsed something moving underneath, before Morgelyn sat upon it once more, hiding whatever it was.

The sobbing inside the coffin built into a wailing scream and Piran was pouring sweat as he fought and struggled with the wood, eventually splitting it open.

'Aha!' Morgelyn cried out, licking her lips with a forked tongue.

A sulphurous smell spread from the broken coffin and a figure, badly discoloured, clambered out. She wasn't quite a skeleton, but her flesh was so withered it had shrunk to the bone. Her arms were spindly as twigs, sticking out of a dress rotten with so many holes it was like mouldy lace. Her cheekbones were sharply defined, the skin stretched too tight and the ridges around her eye sockets protruded, making her look at once terrified and terrifying.

Piran tried to wrap his arms around her but she struggled and fought him, still screaming.

'It's me!' he wept, 'it's me!' But she staggered away from him towards an alleyway, as though he wasn't her husband at all, but an assailant.

Piran stumbled after her, distraught and bewildered. Morgelyn laughed harder, slapping her knee.

Cora glanced at Eseld, whose cheeks were wet with tears. 'It ain't her,' she heard Eseld repeating in her mind, 'nothing but clockwork. Not my girl at all.'

Rosenwyn didn't seem to know where to go. There was something childlike about her fear, as though she was lost in the dark. She hurried into the alley and out again, pushing past Piran's open arms and knocking over a dustbin, which made her jump in fright as its contents spilled, the lid rolling and clattering. All the while she moaned and cried, as a sleeping child does in the grip of a nightmare.

She passed close to Cora, bringing a waft of icy air that smelled of decay. Her eyes were filmy white, with something moving inside them, like deep water running under ice.

'It ain't her!' Eseld shouted, spittle flying. 'Piran, don't fall for it!'

'He can't hear you,' Wenna put her arm around her friend, tears welling. 'We're hidden, remember?'

'Look,' Cora whispered, hoarse with dread, 'over there.'

A gallows stood on the other side of the square, its macabre wares displayed for all to see. As they watched, the dangling figures started to twitch.

Chapter Twenty-Five

The Fall

The beams of the gallows began to creak as the dead kicked and fought, taut ropes jerking as everyone beneath scattered in terror. The faery guards seemed startled and even Morgelyn looked uncertain, as the snakes reared to stare.

'She never could be bothered to get the hang of things,' Yestin muttered. 'She's spilled the awakening spell all over the place.'

'Cut 'em down!' somebody yelled, and the people in their nightgowns started clambering onto the scaffold, the faery guards too stunned to do anything. More and more people pushed hard against the timbers until, with a terrible groan, the whole thing was askew and the recently dead landed on the wooden platform, many toppling onto their knees as they struggled to loosen the ropes around their necks. Cora expected them to stumble, weak and clumsy as if they'd just woken, but they were like the spriggans in the grip of their giantish rage, and they pushed the fluttering hands of frantic loved ones away, fighting to get to Morgelyn.

Morgelyn responded by commanding the guards to draw their swords.

She scratched the air with a single fingernail of her bizarre, transplanted hand, as if cutting it into neat pieces, muttering all the while, to whip cottony balls of web into the throng, but it had no effect on the dead, who continued to press towards Morgelyn, making them look like ghouls from a nightmare, trailing grey and catching red moonlight.

From the black gates of the workhouse infirmary came a bewildered, unhappy procession of the recently deceased poor, in rags and shrouds, having been laid out but not yet buried. Most of them were bent and wrinkled with age but a few were whey-faced, swollen-bellied women, some clutching tiny, red newborns who screamed as if their lungs would burst. And from the wealthier part of town came those freshly woken from gleaming, lace-filled coffins in quiet parlours, smart in their Sunday best. Each wore the same savage, fearful expression and none spoke in any comprehensible way, but roared and wept, all heading straight for Morgelyn.

Cora could sense the anguish of hundreds more, buried deep in the snowy earth, stirring and thumping in wet, icy graves. Those with enough flesh to wail did so and those who were bare bone lay helpless, bewildered and afraid.

From the alley that led to Fish Row came a bizarre procession of animals. Some were exotic, some freakish, all stumbled with the same furious glare, whether two-eyed or four. Each emitted rasping screeches, bleats and miaows and a deeper voice came from behind them exclaiming 'it's a miracle! A miracle! Everybody look! Come my darlings, come back, this way, no, not over there!' And Granville appeared, unmarked by smoke or blood, pipe in hand, his astonished grin fading and his white fluffy hair beginning to wilt, as he took in the scene. 'Good gracious. What's going on?'

Morgelyn continued to laugh, though it sounded forced and hollow, and she knocked the crush of bodies backwards with casual flicks of her hands. But they kept getting up. One even got close enough to swipe at her throne and a faery guard struck him with his sword. Despite the wound, the dead man kept going. The faery courtiers flapped their silk handkerchiefs in nervous encouragement as the guards cut off his arm, then his head, but he kept on pulling and rattling the throne until Morgelyn, who was too busy striking at the surging crowd of both dead and living, toppled to the ground. She sprang up immediately and her guards surrounded her, fighting with all their might against the mob.

Cora could barely watch as the unarmed were slain and the dead dismembered, one after another, until blood-spattered cotton-clad limbs littered the cobbles. 'We can't just stand here!' she fumed. 'There must be something we can do!'

'Don't you think I've been wracking my brains?' Wenna snapped. 'She's too powerful. We mustn't draw attention to ourselves. We must await reinforcements. The duke...'

Cora stopped listening. The Merlinshard jerked violently again, chafing back and forth in her throat. She imagined herself looking through it and as she did do, a dark, rainbow hue spread across her vision, turning the red blood black as she tried to do what she'd done before, when she'd pushed Lord Palmerston's ghast into his breakfast. She saw her own fingers, greyish blue in her new, eerie sight, and they shook as she began to push Morgelyn towards the fire.

Morgelyn's laughter became a howl of fury as she whipped around to see who was pushing her. The courtiers and the guards were knocked over into the crowd, jumping up in fright and scrambling after their queen, who was being pushed by invisible hands towards the flames. The dead still pressed towards her, though the fire was spreading through them, felling them one by one, as the guards continued slashing.

The snakes reared and opened their mouths wide, even as Morgelyn's feet skidded sideways into the embers. Snakish eyes with black slits for pupils focused, in their dozens, on Cora.

Cora's heart lurched and stopped beating.

In her anger she'd dropped the fogging spell. She hadn't even noticed it unravelling and now Morgelyn could see them all.

'You!' Morgelyn screamed. 'You little *brat!* I should have killed you when I first laid eyes on you!'

'Only you couldn't, could you?' Cora roared, fury making her brave. She advanced with the others, pushing Morgelyn further into the fire with the force of the Merlinshard.

Morgelyn flung her hand out towards Cora, who shielded her face with her wing as she staggered back, temporarily blinded by the flash. The threads of her bracelet must have absorbed the impact, for they fell to the ground in sooty tatters.

For a second, Morgelyn was stunned into silence. Her lipless mouth opened just a little, like a cut too fresh to bleed. 'How dare you?' she spluttered. 'You think you've won? You really think a little kindling can harm me?' She spat a blob of saliva into the flames, turning the fire into great ropes of black smoke that writhed like an injured animal, then died, leaving her standing in a heap of ashy books and the lingering stink of singed hair. Without its light, the only glow came from the red moon.

'You really are more stupid than you look,' Morgelyn sneered, walking slowly towards Cora.

'Get away!' Eseld pushed in front of her and Tom darted forward too.

Morgelyn parted them with a flick of her wrists, knocking both to the ground.

'Of course I could have killed you, but why didn't I? That's what you'd have asked yourself, if you'd anything bigger than a birdbrain. When I first called you into Underwood, you'd have splintered every bone upon landing in that pool, falling from such a height. I saved you from that. Why didn't I send a hundred wolves to tear you and your ridiculous friends to shreds? Why didn't I drown you in the storm at the lighthouse? Because I want you *alive*.

'You're a curious halfbreed, Elowen Ambrosius. A rare specimen, even without this avian malformation. I'll enjoy dissecting you.'

'That's a lie!' Cora couldn't stop her voice shaking. 'You tried to kill me, but Eseld got me out!'

'I did nothing of the sort,' she said, crushing ashy spines underfoot. 'This elderly fool dabbles in the magical sciences, but she hasn't a clue. I was merely attempting to preserve you, via a process of embalming that I've developed, which isn't hindered by the subject being alive. I didn't want you to die too quickly, you see. Or to rot before I'd finished.'

Cora was numb.

'You are familiar, are you not? With the process? *Taxis*, meaning to arrange, and *derma*.' She paused, annunciating slowly. 'Skin. From the Greek.'

Morgelyn stretched the smoke-stained fingers of her horrible, rotting hand and, with a sickening wrench, Cora rose into the air, above the heads of those who were trying to shield her. She felt like a puppet on strings, as Morgelyn twitched her fingers, grinning and flipping her upside down. All the blood rushed to Cora's head, making it ache.

Eseld started muttering an incantation but, with a wolfish leer, Morgelyn kept the rotten hand in the air, controlling Cora, and at the same time made a claw with her other hand, which she thrust at Eseld, who spluttered, reaching up to her mouth as it shrank, her lips melting together and disappearing, until there was nothing left but a scar.

Eseld's eyes widened in horror as she touched the place where her mouth had been.

The Merlinshard was writhing in Cora's throat, churning her flesh until she coughed blood and bits of dried leaf.

Morgelyn's face, upside down, spread into a wide grin.

She reached out her hand and wiped a bit of bloody leaf from Cora's lip, her skin cold as metal, and lifted it to her one of her snake eyes. 'Wormwood? No, elder. How primitive.'

Desperate, Cora kept trying to swallow the Merlinshard back down, but she could feel the wrapping coming loose and she gagged, coughing more blood, before it flew from her mouth, fast as an arrow, into Morgelyn's outstretched hand.

'Mine, I think,' Morgelyn crowed.

'*Mine*!' Cora cried, the word scraping painfully. 'My father meant me to have it!'

'Is that what you thought? No, if he'd wanted you to have it he'd have sent it to the orphanage with you, wouldn't he? It was always intended for me. It was foolish of me to break it, I admit that. And over such a trifling matter, easily resolved. Before he eloped with your harlot of a mother, he only had eyes for me.' She sighed theatrically. 'All ancient history now, of course. You know, if it hadn't been for her, you'd have been mine.'

'You're lying!' Cora croaked, 'he died hundreds of years ago!' But a dim memory was surfacing. Didn't Wenna say that nobody knew where and when they had died?

'Time isn't a constraint for everyone,' Morgelyn retorted. 'You only think it is, because your backward little race hasn't even begun to grasp it.' Her voice was hard as stone grinding stone.

'Guards, I tire of this entertainment,' she nudged a mangled body with her foot, 'I shall return to my palace.'

For the first time, Morgelyn noticed Wenna, virtually hidden behind Bronnan and Meriwether.

She shot her a nasty smile. 'Why, if it isn't Wenna the pretender? The clay queen! I can smell the sewer stink from here!' She cackled and, after a moment's astonishment, the courtiers joined in, stopping abruptly as soon as Morgelyn did.

'I've turned your family's old ballroom into a perfect place for my trophy collection. Your parent's heads are in there. I shall place yours in between them.' She made a frame with her hands. 'The three of you will make a very pretty ornament.'

'You *harpy*!' Bronnan spat. Quick as lightning she stooped to snatch up a piece of flint. She threw it like a dart. Morgelyn dodged and it thudded deep into a snake, inches from Morgelyn's throat. The creature's mouth opened wide, long fangs squirting venom before it fell.

Furious, Morgelyn slid the sharp little rock out of the snake's muscular flesh and lifted it to her mouth, touching the blood with her own forked, flickering tongue.

'*Asælan, Wenna Skyburiow, asælan, asælan drycræft,*' Morgelyn whispered, repeating the words, becoming louder as Wenna staggered, clutching her heart. '*Asælan, Wenna Skyburiow, asælan, asælan drycræft,*' the snakes reared, hissing and twisting, every pair of eyes fixed on Wenna. The sickly sweet smell of poisoned magic was overlaid with one of decay and it clogged Cora's eyes, mouth and nostrils. She tried to twist towards Wenna, to aid her somehow, but it was no use.

With a flick of her fingers, Morgelyn lifted Wenna into the air too. Wenna bore the humiliation with all the dignity she could muster, even as the courtiers laughed their nasty laughs. Meriwether, Bronnan and Yestin all reached up to snatch her back down, but it was too late. Cora could feel something terrible happening inside Wenna's mind. It was as though Morgelyn was pouring acid into her thoughts, burning and corroding them so that they bubbled, distorting and turning black.

'Why don't you do something?' Cora cried. 'Fight back?'

'I'm- trying! She's hexing- me!' Wenna said, with difficulty, her jaw tightly clenched. 'She's- binding- my magic.'

'What should we do with the others?' asked a guard, glancing casually around.

Morgelyn turned to glare at him, every snake hissing.

He panicked, stammering 'I mean, ah, permission

to speak your majesty, what shall we do with them, your majesty?'

She knocked him to the ground and indicated that another guard should finish him off, which he did.

'Stupid question anyway' Morgelyn shrugged. 'We'll send them to the mines of course.'

Horrible, winged shadows began to glide over the square, dark in the bloody moonlight. Cora braced herself for the impact of claws, the wound in her shoulder aching in anticipation but, to everybody's utter astonishment, when they swooped it was the faery soldiers the pterydons snatched, kicking and swearing, high above the rooftops.

Morgelyn's features fell slack. She obviously hadn't been expected this. 'What? No, no you clumsy great-' her words were cut off as a pterydon swooped alarmingly close and her snakes recoiled at the lashing wings. She glared at the sky, firing balls of cottony web and, in her distraction, she let Cora and Wenna crash painfully onto the cobbles.

'Gryffyn!' Wenna cried, her voice her own again, her thoughts visibly uncurling and blooming around her face. 'He did it!'

'Did what?' Cora couldn't believe what she was seeing as she staggered dizzily to her feet, helped by Tom, while Bronnan and Meriwether assisted Wenna.

'The eggs!' Wenna's grin was fierce. 'He must've found the eggs and got them to safety! She's losing her grip!'

The deep, clear sound of a horn cut through the reddish gloom.

Morgelyn's head whipped around, even as her

soldiers and scattering courtiers were being snatched high, higher into the air and dropped, with horrible cracking noises.

Morgelyn thundered to her throne and reached underneath, to snatch her onyx table, but before it was out, Cora saw again what she'd glimpsed before. Two little figures, huddled together.

'Gwen! Curnow!' Cora rushed towards them, taking their hands.

'No!' Morgelyn pushed them apart. 'I have a plan for them, and you can't-' but the rest of her sentence was snipped off, because a pterydon had clamped one of her snakes in its powerful jaws. Morgelyn screamed in pain, kicking hard as she was lifted off the ground. She sent a ball of web slithering over the pterydon's head, which made it drop her twenty feet onto the cobbles with a crack. She tumbled awkwardly, her leg bent the wrong way.

The horn sounded again and there was a shifting, shushing noise too, like falling water.

A stream of the most beautiful creatures Cora had ever seen appeared from every alleyway. Each rode upon a white, armoured stag and carried a sword. Without needing to be told, Cora knew that they were the Murúghach, with long, aquiline noses and high foreheads. Over golden armour they wore cloaks of pearly, fishlike scales, which caught the light and sent shivering pieces of it all over the smoke-stained, body-strewn scene.

The faery guards lowered their quaking spears, glancing from the Murúghach to the furious, hobbled Morgelyn, as more and more appeared. From the high street, the Duke of Wellington galloped in, astride a great, shining horse. Behind him marched his men, their twig hair poking from beneath their hats, limbs stiff as though their muscles were still encased in bark. Behind them rode a company of stout, stocky men in moss speckled armour, who looked as though they'd been hewn from rock. They wore blue caps at an angle, carried an enormous axe apiece and rode upon large, fierce-looking badgers.

'Fools!' Morgelyn crowed. And with that she thrust her hands forward, the Merlinshard glowing in her fingers. Veins stood out on her forehead and throat, as though it was extremely heavy. She twisted her hand and used it to cut down through the air. The moon grew darker, its surface mottled.

A sudden wind, hot with ash, caused everyone but Morgelyn to stumble and shield their eyes from flying debris. The ancient cobbles of the market place began to tremble and sink, making people fall to their knees. The noise was deafening as a crack ran across the square, opening into a great chasm, which tore a milliner's shop apart on one side and a coffee house on the other, sending twin avalanches into the void. Bonnets, feathers, ribbons and splintered wood rained to the left, while copper kettles, tin mugs, benches and newspapers poured from the right in a collapsing tide of bricks and lumps of plaster.

'It's fake!' Cora cried out, 'remember she can't create, she can only destroy! It ain't real!' They tried to see through it, to see the illusion for what it was, but dozens of people were tumbling into the pit.

'Cora's right! See through it!' Wenna forced her shoulders back and, while everyone else was fleeing in the opposite direction, she stepped out.

Instead of appearing to hover, as she had on the

Isle of Wight, Wenna disappeared, falling like a stone into the flaming gorge.

The last Cora saw of her was a terrified face.

Without thinking, Cora flapped her wings as hard as she could, swerving between the pterydons and the falling bodies towards Wenna's shrinking form. The heat was fierce and it singed her feathers as she flapped harder, faster, deeper into the earth, every muscle burning as she caught Wenna with her feet, gripping as hard as she could and driving her claws into her flesh.

It took a massive effort to flap back up towards the narrow fissure above, where the crack of smoky red sky was dull compared to the sizzling orange beneath. Past mud and stone and broken pipework Cora struggled, beating her wings as hard as she could. She landed on the cobbles in the middle of the fighting, to see Eseld huddled around her screaming grandchildren. Tom was protecting them by swinging a bluecap axe in great, thundering circles.

He swung the axe just as Morgelyn staggered past, dragging her broken leg. He struck her black, withered hand clean off.

It thudded a few feet from Cora, still clutching the Merlinshard in its horrid fingers. She thrust her hand out to snatch the foul thing, wrestling to open it.

In the corner of her eye, she saw a faery guard throw his sword at Tom. The blade narrowly missed him and slipped noiselessly into the huddled form of Eseld, who fell sideways, fingers slipping from the shoulders of the children.

Fury welled inside Cora, frantic as a thousand battering wings. She crashed to Eseld's side, ripping the Merlinshard free from the dead hand and holding it to Eseld's temple, as though its magic could penetrate her skin. But Eseld remained pale, her folded lids still and closed.

'Wenna!' Cora screamed, 'help me!'

Wenna was at Cora's side, taking the black, rotten hand as though it might explode and tossing it into the chasm. Tears of shock appeared on her cheeks as she let herself look at Eseld, the fighting all around them knocking their backs and elbows as Wenna gathered the children to her. Tom was fighting hard, too busy staying alive to see further than his axe.

'Hold on Eseld,' Wenna managed, 'just hold on.' Eseld's lipless scar that once was a mouth turned grey, her life pooling between the cobbles as Wenna spoke the ancient words, Cora joining as best she could.

'*Cwic, Eseld Liddicoat, cwic*' and for the first time, Cora knew what she was saying. Life, Eseld Liddicoat, life. She didn't know what the language was, just that she could understand it and that it was running out of her, as unstoppable as the blood from Eseld's belly. Fractured images of her father's book floated before her, trust bonds and steeped suffering became real as flesh. The raging battle became muffled, as if she was hearing the clashes and shouts from underwater. The Merlinshard burned in her fingers and she knew that all it wanted was truth and she told it that Eseld was truth, that Eseld must live, and it told her that Morgelyn must die.

And she felt the Threads, between herself and all faeries. Between herself and all humanity. Between herself and all birds. She saw clearly, as if from above, the power of three in clover-shaped clusters.

Three threes. Herself, Eseld and Wenna formed one. Morgelyn had forced Gwen and Curnow to form another. And there was another. Herself. Her identity was a trinity. Human. Faery. Bird. And she knew a stronger, darker magic than she had ever known. She reached up and lightning cracked the sky, as the red moon was blotted out.

The air turned black with birds of all sizes, which poured over the chimneys, out from the alleys and up from the fiery chasm.

Claws bared, birds of every size and colour landed on Morgelyn, making her snakes rear in alarm. They gaped and struck as hundreds of razor-sharp beaks dug in, ripping and gouging, and Cora was suddenly amongst them, plunging her beak into Morgelyn's rank, dead skin, biting and tearing the flesh beneath. Morgelyn thrashed and cursed, covered in wings, fighting and cursing and screaming until there was nothing left but a slimy skeleton with a hunched spine and a rocking skull with no eye sockets, surrounded by feathery snake bones.

The birds disappeared as suddenly as they'd arrived, flapping up over the houses and vanishing into the night.

The roar and clash of battle gradually died away, as everybody realised what had happened. The faery guards and the courtiers dropped their weapons in surrender, the ghasts gazing on in miserable defeat. Victor stared at the ruined mess of bones as if it was his own heart lying there.

Cora staggered away from Morgelyn's remains and hurried, half-scuttling, half-flying, towards Eseld's motionless form.

Everything was distorted, towering above her as

she reached for Eseld's shoulder, which was higher and bigger than it should have been.

'Eseld?!' Cora tried to say, but only a rasping cough came out. 'Eseld?' she tried again, managing nothing but a scratchy, wheezing croak.

Tom was on his knees, eyes full, holding Gwen and Curnow so tightly that only their filthy, matted curls were visible, a little sobbing face buried in each shoulder.

The moon became white again, free of cloud, and it shone into the dark blood spilling from Eseld's belly. Her lips were parted, her mouth returned to its natural shape. Reflected in the pool was a strange bird, the only one that remained. When she looked around, Cora couldn't see it.

The truth only dawned on her when Tom released Gwen for a second. He tried to shoo Cora away, as if she was a vulture on carrion and she fluttered up, no bigger than a raven, heart clattering, tears dropping into the blood.

'It's me!' she croaked, but the words were no longer human.

She cried out for Wenna, silently, desperately, beating her wings in mid-air as she rose up to see further, but she couldn't find her anywhere. A woman who hadn't been there before, with thick, white hair and pinkish-gold skin was reaching for her, nodding, but Cora was too shocked at how small and lifeless Eseld seemed, to understand, until Wenna bent and tugged the shining circlet from Morgelyn's skull, making it rock among the feathery snake bones.

She rubbed it clean with her sleeve. The circlet was made of twisted silver leaves and set with fire opals. Wenna lifted the Merlinshard that lay motionless beside Eseld's fingers. She tugged the piece of glass from the crown and set the Merlinshard in its place, smudged with soot and blood as it was, before fixing it upon her own head.

Everybody stopped. Nobody moved. Meriwether dropped to one knee, followed by Yestin, Goodwife Jenifry, Lord Gendal and all the rest, including the fearful guards and courtiers who'd turned a sickly shade. Soon, Wenna was the only one standing.

Cora descended, wings burning with exhaustion, to alight miserably upon Wenna's smooth, newly plump hand. She stroked Cora's wing, very gently, and knelt beside Eseld where, together, they allowed themselves to cry.

The duke's horse clopped sombrely towards the sorry huddle, cracking and trampling Morgelyn's bones beneath its hooves. He alighted with the grace of a much younger man and knelt beside Eseld's body. 'She will be buried with honours,' he murmured. 'May I?' he asked Tom, who nodded dumbly. The duke picked her up, as though she weighed little more than a bundle of sticks. Blood dripped from her middle and the sole of one of her worn-out boots fell off. Cora flew to retrieve it, picking up the scrap of leather in her beak and dropping it shakily onto Eseld's chest, cursing the futility of the gesture.

Smoke.

'Wait!' Cora tried to shout, emitting only a shrill peep, as the smoke took shape beside Eseld's head. It was fuzzy, unformed, but it was definitely there. 'Wenna!' She shouted silently, 'Quick!'

Wenna's unhappy features creased in hope.

The duke lowered Eseld enough for Wenna to run her fingers beneath her friend's nostrils, feeling for heat. Eseld's eyelids fluttered.

'She's alive!' the duke declared. 'A physician! Bring me a physician!'

Encouraged by the crowd, the duke strode towards a crouching man, who was stitching a wound in a child's scalp, a trembling mother parting his bloody hair and trying to keep him still.

Cora flew higher, and as she did so, Eseld joined the groaning mass of bloody figures awaiting aid. Everybody who could help did so. Wenna and the other faeries, who were barely recognisable with their gleaming skin and thick white hair, used what magic they could to curb bleeding and alleviate pain, assisted by the bewildered pharmacist. The haberdasher fetched new thread and needles. Mr Penrose used his powerful blacksmith's arms to realign broken limbs under the surgeon's instruction and those who could do nothing else made hot beef tea to comfort the weeping and the frail.

The woken dead fell once more, with a final look of peace. Neither Piran nor Rosenwyn returned and Cora imagined him mad, staggering on the snowy moor, hopelessly searching for the wife he'd lost long ago.

At last, after she'd been bandaged around the middle, Eseld regained consciousness. She was too weak to hold them, but as Curnow and Gwen buried their faces in her neck, she managed to lift a hand to cradle each little head.

Tom was gazing at the motionless figure of Cora's ghast. Her skin was beaded with damp and her hair was sticking to her forehead. Her cheeks and lips were a feverish pink. The skin beneath each eye was falling a little, like unravelling stitches.

Cora alighted on the water pump, watching him, feeling like a sawn off limb.

A hand appeared, golden-rose as sunset. Cora hopped onto it, blinking hot tears back. Wenna lifted her to her shoulder and Cora hung on, trying to grip the shabby fabric without digging her claws in. 'Where will you go now, Cora?' Wenna asked.

Miserably, Cora imagined herself building a nest, gagging at the taste of twigs as she tried to weave them together, nothing to shelter her but dripping branches as she nudged her head beneath her wing.

'Cora! Do you think I'd leave you? To fend for yourself in the wild after all you've done? If you feel you have no place here, then you'll come back with me, to the Great Oak. And we'll set everything as it was.'

'There's nothing to be done for me, is there?' Cora managed to say, without a sound, her throat too tight to form human words even if she could. 'I feel it.'

Wenna was silent for a moment, her thoughts hidden. She walked towards the alley that led to Fish Row.

'How long do birds live?' Cora asked.

'How long do any of us?' Wenna answered, glancing back at the carnage.

A fishy smell wafted from her old street. Cora had never noticed before how the weekly market of herring and pilchards staring up from their slabs had spoiled the air. The house she'd lived in all her life was smaller and shabbier than she remembered it. The brass knocker was stained, the paint lifted and cracked.

'We're free, Cora.' Wenna whispered, turning her head so that her warm breath tickled Cora's feathers. 'We can go home.'

24476692R00256

Printed in Poland
by Amazon Fulfillment
Poland Sp. z o.o., Wrocław